The Apocalypse War
The Undead World Novel 7
By Peter Meredith

Fictional works by Peter Meredith:

Chapter1
Neil Martin

There were only fourteen steps for him to overcome and they were no steeper than any other set of steps in the valley and yet Neil found himself winded and his head spun just a touch as he made his way to the second floor of the house. He gripped the rail and took a moment to compose himself. It wouldn't look good for him to go into the interview sweating and gasping from a single flight of steps.

It wasn't as though he was out of shape, it was the altitude. Estes Park sat at over 7500 feet above sea level and the air was gossamer thin. Breathing in the pure mountain air was nearly as effective as breathing in the used air from last year's birthday balloons. Until they adjusted to the altitude, only people in top physical condition managed to operate at peak strength. Neil was at about seventy percent, at least physically. Mentally, it felt as though he was bopping along at around forty percent of brain capacity and this was simply because he didn't feel that any more was really needed.

You could say that he was on a mental vacation.

Ever since the renegades had made it to the safety of the valley, he had happily turned over all responsibility to the military governor, General Johnston. Since then he had slept ten hours a night, eaten voraciously at each meal, read when he felt like it, napped every afternoon and generally tried not to think if at all possible.

He felt like a hollowed-out pumpkin and that was just fine. Letting go like this was a form of healing that was desperately needed. He had a lot to let go of and, when he wasn't actively trying to let go, his thoughts turned to Eve or Ram or Sarah, or Jillybean. He thought of the little hell-child most of all. She had been his biggest failure. Ram and Sarah had been adults and had been driven to their deaths by their own ghosts, while Eve had been murdered through no fault or lack of supervision on Neil's part. Eve had been perfect and Neil took a lot of credit for that; he had been a great dad to her.

He could not say the same thing about Jillybean. He had never officially adopted her as he had Eve and Sadie, which, in hindsight had been a mistake. Jillybean had needed him, badly. She had needed a father, not only to guide her but also to protect her. She needed someone to protect her from herself.

Standing there on the edge of the second-floor hall, his mind turned to the little girl once more. *Where was she?* he wondered. Was she dead? Had the grenade that destroyed the truck killed her? Or was she in captivity, held by the Duke for sale to some horrible pedophile? Or had she escaped and was even then struggling over the last seven hundred miles, fighting her way to Colorado?

This last was Neil's hope and it was the reason he was there that afternoon, appealing the ruling that had placed him in the position of farmer.

With a last deep breath, he went to the furthest door on the right and gave it a light knock. "Come," a curt voice said.

Neil stepped into the converted bedroom. The entire house had been repurposed and was now known as the CAB to the military government. In human speak it was the *Civilian Administration Building*. There were twenty-four hundred non-military personnel in the valley and they were treated, in the nicest possible way, as little more than serfs. Their lives were ordered almost as if they were prisoners and the minutes of their day were regimented and accounted for, down to the second.

It wasn't an arduous life, just a controlled one. No one complained since they were as safe as could be and the soldiers weren't anything but polite. The civilians were free to leave the valley at any time; no one did unless they were one of the hunting teams that left in packs of ten or more and brought back game of all sorts: deer, elk, mountain sheep, and sometimes bear. The only other people who left the valley were the salvage crews that dared to creep down out of the mountains under the cover of night to scavenge among the ruins of Denver or Boulder or far off Colorado Springs.

"I'm Neil Martin," Neil said as soon as he stepped into the room. The walls were purple and the carpet white shag. He guessed a now-dead teenager had once lived there. The room was spare; it held a heavy desk and seven tall filing cabinets. On the purple walls, instead of posters of teen pop stars, there were fifteen clipboards nailed into the drywall.

Behind the desk was a man in BDUs. He was balding and bespectacled—his glasses being what the soldiers called 'birth-controls' since they were so hideously ugly, they would automatically turn off any woman who happened to see them. On the shirt of his camouflaged blouse was stitched the name: *Willoughby*.

Willoughby sighed. "Yes, hello Mr. Martin. I received your note. Thanks for being punctual." He didn't offer Neil a seat, mainly because there wasn't another chair in the room other than the one beneath his buttocks. He simply gave Neil a once over, his face registering a slight curdling of displeasure.

Neil pretended not to notice. He knew what he looked like. The swelling and bruising, though faded in the last week, gave his skin a strange yellow tint which was made all the more unsettling by arcing pink scars that ran along both sides of his jaw line and on his right cheek. He was missing most of his left eyebrow and the top third of his left ear. He wasn't pretty by any measure, in fact, most people tended to look away when they were in his presence.

"You received my note, and?" Neil asked, letting the word hang.

"And…" said Willoughby, busy shuffling papers on his desk. "You aren't really salvage crew material. Sorry, but it takes a certain, I don't know, toughness to make it out there. It's my recommendation that you accept the position as farmer. It may not be a glorious job, but it is a necessary one. You've read over the handout, yes? You will be able to keep a full forty percent of what you grow. And look at the acreage you've been given."

Willoughby pulled out a map of Estes that had been stashed in a drawer and pointed at a strip of green along one of the smaller, finger-like valleys that branched off the main one. "Here. Look, it's barely a three mile walk and…and see this?" He pointed at a tiny line of blue. "That is a runoff stream. Half the year you'll have access to that water and will be able to retain a twentieth of it. And, look at all this on the side of the hill. It's forested now, but you can clear that and add to your tillable land. Really, this is a primo spot. You can thank your friend the captain for that."

"You don't understand," Neil said. "I want to be a farmer, really, it sounds perfect for me. I just can't at the moment. I…I left someone back out there and she may be trying to get here. But she'll…"

Movement outside the window caught his eye; men were running in all directions. They ran with a purpose and there was no panic to them.

"You'd risk the outside world over a woman?" Willoughby asked with a snort of skepticism.

More men running and Neil began to have a familiar sinking sensation in his gut. "No," he said, vaguely, going to the window and looking down. It appeared that half the base was on the move. "It's a girl. A little girl, I mean. Someone I should have taken better care of. Tell me, do you know what's going on out there? Do you have drills here?"

Willoughby glanced out the window but for only a second. "Yes, frequently. Back to the issue at hand. I'm going to deny your request. I'm sorry, but you aren't cut out for salvage work. Look at your hand for goodness sakes. How do you even fire a rifle with missing fingers like that?"

Neil took his eyes from the soldiers and glanced at his left hand. His pinky had been bitten down to the nub and his ring finger was half gone. "It's not so bad. Using the axe is a bit of a challenge, however."

"You use an axe to kill them?" Willoughby asked. Again, the skepticism was obvious in his voice and manner. Neil understood. Few of the remaining people left in the world liked getting that close to a zombie. Any mistake, any unnoticed scratch, any minor mishap could spell doom.

"Yes," Neil said. He pointed at one of the scars on his face. "You see this? And the missing fingers? All from zombie bites. I am immune. I was inoculated in New York, which makes me the perfect candidate for a salvage team, wouldn't you agree?"

Willoughby gave Neil a closer look, squinting despite the thickness of his 'birth-controls.' "Immune? Really? We didn't think that was legit. We thought it was a scam. Well, that would change things if it weren't for the fact that salvage teams do not go into the field in order to find lost children. It is an admirable goal; however, we won't be able..."

A sharp knock interrupted him. Willoughby had only time enough to cast down his thick brows behind his even thicker glasses before a soldier stuck his head into the room and spat: "We're going to Alert 1. Formation in five minutes." The soldier was gone before Neil could blink once.

"Alert 1?" Willoughby asked, glancing out the window. "How could we be at..." He was interrupted again, this time by rifle fire. It was distant and metronomic in its cadence: pop...pop...pop. Whoever was shooting was doing so in a deliberate manner. "I have to go," Willoughby said, coming around the desk and shooing Neil to the door. "We'll reschedule in the next week or two."

Neil was back in the hallway before he knew it.

The house, which had been sleepy with the quiet drone of people working, now was bursting with energy as soldiers with stern faces rushed about. Neil was nervous and curious—the single gun was no longer a solo act; a dozen more had been added to the first—and so he joined the throng of soldiers racing for the outdoors. They barely gave him a second glance as he was practically carried along by the momentum and urgency of the men. Down the stairs they went, and the next thing Neil knew he was jostled right out the front door.

Along a steeply sloping street from the house, nearly half a mile away, stood the famous Stanley Hotel. It was three stories of pure white elegance. Two wings boasted seventy rooms a piece and the views were amazing. It was here that General Johnston and his senior officers lived and worked, and in the wide open area in front was where the soldiers held their daily formations.

The soldiers jogged for the hotel at a rapid clip, leaving Neil quickly winded and unable to keep up. "Go...on," he said, his chest, heaving like bellows. "I'll...catch...up." A few men gave him odd looks as if he were somebody's unwanted kid-brother tagging along. The rest simply ran around him as though he were a rock in the middle of a stream.

Panting, Neil straggled up to the stately hotel. He wasn't the only civilian who had come down to see what all the fuss and shooting was about. Hovering behind the solidifying formations, were hundreds of people standing and chatting in little knots. The renegades, who Neil had shepherded across the country, were the largest of these groups and the most noticeable. They wore their fear openly. One week wasn't long enough to make them complacent and as always they were waiting for the other shoe to drop.

They all looked to Neil for answers. Before he could catch his breath or get his quivering muscles under control, they had surrounded him and were whispering urgent questions.

"All I know is that they are on a *Priority 1* alert," he told them.

Since no one knew what that meant, the information only caused a new muttering to erupt. Neil left them to their mutterings and their fear. He went searching through the group of renegades, looking for Sadie. She was his one remaining responsibility and the last thing in this life that he truly cared for. Even his own life was a distant second to hers.

She wasn't in the crowd. Her black clothes always stood out from the civilians in their blue jeans and bright dresses and even more so against the backdrop of the uniformity of the soldiers in their camo.

"Damn it," Neil said, looking to the east, past the stables where the two dozen horses were kept, and beyond the wheat fields, where the firing had picked up; any semblance of regularity in the shooting was gone. It sounded like a battle was fully underway—Sadie could only be there in the thick of it, Neil would bet his life on it. He started toward the sound of the shooting only to be turned around by a strong arm.

Captain Grey had come out of nowhere and had Neil by the bicep. "Don't go down there, Neil," he said. His voice was stern, commanding and yet there was still a note of friendship in it. The two had barely seen each other over the course of the last week. Grey had been busy acclimating himself to his new command while Neil had been busy trying to heal both mentally and emotionally.

"Sadie's down there," Neil answered. "She's going to need me."

"No," Grey told him. "The situation, at least for the moment, is in hand. I need you up here. I'm pretty sure General Johnston will want to talk to you after formation."

"But..."

A stern look from Grey shut him up. "You don't say 'but' to an officer, and especially not General Johnston, remember that. Secondly, if Sadie is down there, she's fine. The wall will hold. You've seen it. Stay here and await your orders."

Grey was gone before Neil could say 'but' again. Really, he was on the verge of throwing out the fanciful version of but, the 'however,' only before he could, Deanna was at his side and was turning him back to the others, again by his arm. He felt like he was at a hoedown.

"Neil," she said, with a note of warning.

"Neil, what?" he asked, showing a flash of anger that had been rare in the last week.

She pulled him in close and, wearing a bright and cheery false smile, said in a low voice: "Don't make it worse for him. He's new to his command and there have been whisperings. Mostly jealousy on the part of those who were passed over, but still it wouldn't help him for you to be seen back-talking him."

"I wasn't back-talking," Neil shot back, testily. "And so, what if I was? He may have been promoted, but I'm not his to order about and…and what would the general want with me? I have nothing to do with any of this…probably."

In the pit of his stomach, Neil feared that he was up to his neck in what was going on. A part of him knew that Duke Menis or his brother King Augustus was behind the shooting. If that was the case, there was a good chance they would demand his head on a platter.

"We both know what's going on," Deanna said, gesturing with her chin toward the sound of the shooting. "It doesn't take a genius to see what precipitated this, it's the duke's doing. I know it. He wants revenge or some sort of outlandish payment. I suspect he'll want me and you as part of some sort of diplomatic blackmail." She suddenly bit her lip and looked to where Captain Grey was standing at the head of three solid blocks of men. "I hope they don't blame him as well. He didn't do anything wrong."

Neil raised his remaining intact eyebrow. "And I did? I guess I don't remember things the same way you have. I was only trying to…" Just then someone called the formations to attention and Deanna shushed Neil. There had to be three thousand people in an area the size of a football field and yet, other than the crackle of distant rifle fire, the thin air was altogether silent.

General Johnston, a tall black man with an aura of intense self-assurance that was palpable from fifty yards, came to stand before the formation. There was a quick ceremony of salutes and counter salutes, the gist of which was lost on Neil, and then the general stepped forward and said in a voice that could carry to the least soldier in the hottest battle: "Men! What you are hearing are the opening shots of a battle. I have just received a message from the Azael. It seems that we are now at war!"

When the general said this, his eyes flicked in Neil's direction and even with the distance between them, the two found themselves locked in their own strange battle of wills. On one side was accusation, on the other a bitter, angry defense.

Chapter 2

Sadie Walcott

The apple-cheeked soldier who had run down from the wall had a name tag which read: *Morganstern*. He stood tall and lean as a birch-sapling, looking down on the mega-herd of zombies, gulping down oxygen, waiting, with his radio half-cocked toward his ear. When nothing came from it, he practically yelled into it: "Red Leader! Come in Red Leader! We have a major event down the hill from Red Gate. Can anyone read me? I'm looking at five-thousand stiffs. Say again five-thousand stiffs advancing toward Red Gate."

"I hear you, Morganstern," a hissing, static-filled voice replied. "Get your ass back here on the double."

Morganstern glanced once at the radio in annoyance, then looked down at the horde filling the roadway and his expression changed to resemble curdled fear.

For Sadie the sight of the multitude was just as frightening; however, it also represented an ugly status quo that had taken the last week off for vacation and now was back, refreshed and ready to go with its usual deadly repercussions. "Let's get out of here," she said in a low voice. "There's no use hanging around. If they see us, they'll only come on faster."

The pair slunk away keeping low until the edge of one of the sheer hills cut them off from sight, then they jogged upward against the pull of gravity. Even Sadie found the uphill run trying, though she did her best to keep her breathing from getting ragged. The soldier was damn handsome, after all, and she could feel his eyes on her.

They huffed up the hill, each doing their best to hold back whatever fear was escalating in them as the moans of the undead began to build louder and louder the closer they came. Breathless, the pair came to the first barrier that represented the Red Gate: three stacked bundles of concertina wire where a pair of soldiers were waiting with the coils parted for them to pass. "How bad is it?" one asked.

"Bad," was all Morganstern had the breath to say.

"Worse than bad," Sadie added, recovering from the run more quickly that the young man. "We haven't seen a fraction of them yet." After another huge gulp of the thin air, she added: "I would guess there are a hundred thousand or more coming this way."

A staff sergeant was in charge of the men guarding the barricade. His chest rig, filled with spare magazines, hid his nametag, making him an unknown authority figure in her eyes. He gave Sadie an uncertain look. "A hundred thousand? No way! We've never seen that many up here in the mountains. The most we've seen is a thousand tops."

Sadie nodded to his stated wisdom, but she had her own wisdom and her own experience. "Ask PFC Morganstern. The stiffs filled a half mile of road from end to end and there were more pushing them on, a lot more." Although Morganstern nodded emphatically, the sergeant looked unconvinced. Sadie huffed, angrily at not being believed. "If you don't believe me, go down and look for yourself."

"We can wait until they get here," the staff sergeant replied.

"We can't," Morganstern said through gritted teeth. "You may not know her, but you know me. I haven't seen so many stiffs since our last days in Castle Rock, and I'm sure I didn't see the entire horde."

"More than Castle Rock? Shit," the other soldier at the wire said.

The sergeant tried to peer through the foliage as he considered what had been said. After a moment, he shrugged slightly, still uncertain. "I believe you, Morganstern but a hundred thousand? Sorry ma'am, but that's just...that's just crazy. What makes you say a hundred thousand? It sounds like you're just pulling a fanciful number out of your butt."

Sadie smirked, a dangerous look that should have been a warning for the staff sergeant. "Listen," she said with her head cocked to the side. Everyone around them took a second to tilt their chins slightly to listen. The God-awful moans were preceding the horde; it was enough to send a chill up the spines of a number of the soldiers. "Does that sound like something fanciful coming from my butt?" she asked. The moans were of such a scale that no one made a single obligatory butt-joke.

Even the sergeant was stirred to action by the sound. "Let's get this concertina wire buttoned up and then I want everyone behind the wall and out of sight. And Winston, call this in as a *Priority 1* situation."

They slipped past the wire, crossed the three-foot wide wood plank that bridged a fifteen-foot deep, waterless moat, and then ascended a metal ladder that was affixed to the wall of cement that represented the main defense of the Red Gate.

The men, a platoon of eighteen, didn't need to be told to keep quiet and out of sight. The only one who made any noise was Corporal Winston, who was hissing in a high voice: "Yes, I mean it. We have a *Priority 1* situation. I can fucking hear them, Lloyd. It sounds like a fucking million of them coming right at us. Damn it, shut up and just alert HQ."

The staff sergeant, along with a dozen others, hushed Winston as the first movement could be seen through the trees. "We shouldn't be just sitting here," Sadie said. To her, waiting made no sense. The wire would be flattened in seconds, the moat would be filled in half a minute and then the walls would be tested—and they would fail. That was a given, and it wasn't even her experienced powered pessimism talking. It was straight up fact.

"We are following the plans laid down by our superiors," the staff sergeant said in a whisper. "These plans have worked quite well for the last year and they'll work now if you'll just shut the fuck up."

Sadie raised an eyebrow, suggesting by the tiny movement: *We'll see.*

A minute later the staff sergeant did indeed see that Sadie was correct. The roadway below them was three lanes wide with an extra fifteen-foot break-down lane on either side. The first row of zombies walked shoulder to shoulder, filling the area all the way across; Sadie counted fifty-three of them in the first line. Behind them came rank upon rank, filling every inch of the black-top, fifty deep, seventy deep, a hundred deep, three hundred deep…

"Holy fuck," the staff sergeant swore.

"Yes, holy fuck," Sadie said. "Now do something."

The staff sergeant swallowed once, raised his head to risk another peek and then shrugged. "I've called it in and we have our orders." He shrugged a second time, suggesting that was all he was required to do.

"They're not going to just sit there," Sadie hissed. "You have to know that. They are being driven from behind. They're going to fill this entire defile and then overflow it."

"Yeah, and when they do, we'll kill them," the staff sergeant replied. "I don't know what more you expect. It's too soon for artillery. I mean, so far all we got are a few thousand stiffs. The men we have here is enough to handle the situation."

He was soon eating his words.

The zombies came on like a tremendous grey flood. When they hit the concertina wire, the first line fell into it, bending it down. They were caught in it like fish in a net and, although they struggled, they could not free themselves. The succeeding waves crushed them underfoot, using their bodies to bridge the entanglement—the first barrier had been breached in twenty seconds.

The moat took fifteen minutes to prove its inadequacy against such a monstrous horde. The first zombies fell straight into it as did the next line and then the line after that. Its dimensions: ten feet wide, fifteen deep and seventy-five long was filled by nearly two thousand eager bodies.

At the bottom of it, the pressure was so great that skulls shattered, bones splintered and zombie meat was turned into a foul brown jelly. Those along the middle suffocated and their bodies were pressed into an even strata. Those at the top struggled despite most of their bones having been broken from the trampling feet of those that came later. Viewed from above, the entire trench wriggled horribly as though it had been filled with hideous grey worms with human heads.

Finally, they came to the wall behind which the eighteen soldiers and Sadie crouched. The wall itself was a marvel of engineering and yet Sadie didn't have the same trust in it that the men around her did. "Try to relax," Morganstern said, seeing her distress. He slapped the five feet wide wall that he was kneeling on. "This stands twenty-five feet high." He then elbowed the parapet. "This adds another four feet for a total of twenty-nine feet. The rolling gate below us is solid iron, four inches thick. We should be safe."

"And reinforcements should be coming, soon," added the private with the radio on his back. "That's what Lloyd over at the HQ said. They're forming up now at the hotel, but not because of us…" He paused, dramatically until the staff sergeant was within a breath of yelling at him. "It's because we're now at war with the Azael. Can you believe that? They fucking declared war on us. It's what all this is about."

The others began to curse the Azael up and down, while Morganstern gave Sadie a sharp look. "How did you know?" he asked. "You said down there that war had come. How did you know?"

Before she could answer, the first zombie made it across the now jam-packed moat. It went right to the iron door and began attacking it, making a sad echoey *gong* with every heedless strike of its fists.

"I just did," Sadie said, moodily, remembering the tremendous hordes flowing across the plains. There was only one reason why they would've made the trek through the mountain roads and that was because they'd been herded up them by someone, and the only someones who could do that were the Azael.

She let out a shaky sigh as the first zombie was followed quickly by another and another. Soon the ground beneath the walls was filled with the dead and their stink and their dread moan was enough to shiver the soul. One with a gimpy leg fell and was trod upon by the others. Another tripped over its skull and he, too, was crushed.

With so many thousands pushing forward, it wasn't long before more fell and were trampled. As each did the ones on top were that much closer to the rim of the parapet. It was a danger, but one that would be slow to develop just as long as the soldiers and Sadie stayed out of sight. Being quiet was no longer an issue. The moans drowned out any normal conversation.

They started to relax behind the parapet when Morganstern's blue eyes suddenly went to squints. He was looking past Sadie, down the length of the wall. Sadie turned and her young eyes picked out the movement in a blink. There were zombies swarming on the southern hill where the wall was built into it.

"What the hell?" Morganstern cried. "How in God's name did they get over there? That hill is way too steep for them to walk along."

"Who cares," a soldier further along the wall said. "Shoot them!"

Before bringing his M4 to his shoulder, Morganstern glanced to the staff sergeant who nodded and ordered: "Do it."

The young PFC was well practiced with his rifle. With calm deliberation he started firing at the slow moving beasts. He didn't miss.

There was no use hiding anymore and so Sadie stood and started stretching. When the sergeant gave her a questioning look, she explained: "Someone has to go and find out the extent of the problem. There could be another ten thousand of those things flanking us."

"I want to say that would be impossible because of how steep the hills are but," he paused and shook his head, "but if those ones got up here, others could as well. Ok, Dallas, take your squad and recon that hill. Go around the base so you don't get them crazed."

"What about me?" Sadie asked, as the six men moved out.

"You are a civilian," the sergeant said. "What I need from you is to go back to the valley and report to the CAB. They'll have jobs for you to do."

Sadie knew what sort of job she'd be relegated to: water carrier or cook or seamstress stuck making mittens for the men. That wasn't going to be her lot. "How 'bout I check out that hill?" she said, pointing north where the wall ran up against another steep hill. So far there weren't zombies on it, but who knew what was behind the crest?

She expected more of an argument, but the sergeant only shrugged and said: "Sure, knock yourself out and when you're done, report to the CAB." He was letting her go? Alone? Unarmed? For the first time in a week, she had left her Glock back at the apartment that she shared with Neil; at the time she had felt that leaving it had been a triumph over her paranoia, now she felt naked without it.

The fact that he was letting her go recon the hill so easily meant there was likely nothing over the hill but cliff walls or something similar. He saw the realization come over her and smirked. "The river is over there. The hills are too steep for most people and there's no way the stiffs can get by that way."

On the south hill, the squad was already running into zombies and the shooting was picking up. Below them, the zombies had been stirred past the simple drive to plow forward. There were humans on the wall and now they were doing everything possible to get up at them, including climbing on top each other.

"They're pyramiding," Morganstern said in awe. Sadie leaned out over the parapet and saw that the zombies were going crazy, pulling down their brethren and mindlessly using them as stairs.

"I need you to follow orders, miss," the staff sergeant. "Go to the CAB and if you happen to see Alpha Company, tell them to double time it up here."

Sadie began backing away from the soldiers, heading to the northern hill. "I'll check out this hill first." She tilted her head so she could see Morganstern around the sergeant. "See you later," she said to him and then turned and jogged along the wall.

It wasn't a long jog and she didn't have near enough time to wonder why she had said that to Morganstern. What happened to her feelings for Nico? Where had they gone that she could so blithely flirt with some strange man? Ashamed of herself, she didn't look back, though a part of her wanted to.

She ran to where the wall hit the hill and started to climb. It was a steep hill, too steep for zombies. Sadie went from tree trunk to tree trunk, pulling herself up until she reached the ridge of the hill. Somewhere below her, obscured by the trees was the river—the sound was the only thing pleasant on the air just then. Besides the moans and the crackle of rifle fire, a pair of machine guns had added their angry chatter to the din.

With the river unseen below her somewhere, Sadie turned her eyes to the valley three miles west of her. The air was perfect, making everything distinct, down to the last detail. She could see the crystal blue of Lake Estes and she could see the red roof of the Stanley Hotel and on the front lawn, where a thousand weddings had been performed, the land was strangely uniform in shape. What looked like large green rectangles stood one right next to the other.

These were the formations of men being briefed by General Johnston. Had she the eyes of an eagle, she would have counted eighteen hundred soldiers and surrounding them in an irregular crescent were another thousand civilians. In that group was Neil Martin; he'd be worrying about her. More than likely he was even then turning from the general as he spoke to look up at the very hill she was on.

"I'll be down in a minute," she said.

First, she wanted a peek at the river. It was the Big Thompson River below her; its waters, coming straight from the surrounding mountains, were icy cold. It ran fast but wasn't very deep, and was usually only as wide as a two-lane road. In the last week, Neil had tried his hand at fly fishing on it only to draw secret smiles from the other fisherman and jeers from the fish which would splash nearby as though to tease him.

That afternoon the only splashing came from the thousands of zombies trudging slowly against the current. They were so thick that the silver glinted water could hardly be seen. Sadie was halfway down the steep hill when she heard the moans over the sound of the rushing water. A couple of steps further and she smelled the beasts; a raw, mean odor that assaulted her nose. And then she saw the second prong of the Azael's attack.

"Oh my God!" she cried, turning on the spot and fighting her way back up the hill. She had to get to the radio. She had to warn Neil—there were no walls or barricades across the Big Thompson. The river was a straight shot into the valley.

Chapter 3

Captain Grey

The formation lasted all of three minutes. General Johnston was not one to waste everyone's time with a bunch of nonsense and blather. He placed the 1st and 3rd Battalions on immediate alert. They were to gear up and prepare to move out when called. As the designated "Ready" force, the 2nd Battalion was simply waiting on orders to go. With the firing escalating in the east, there wasn't any doubt in Captain Grey's mind that this would not be a "hurry up and wait" situation.

The second Johnston snapped the soldiers to attention and marched away, Grey barked to his men: "Company, at ease! Let me have the platoon leaders up here on the double."

Since it wasn't proper military form, this raised more than a few eyebrows and caused a number of smirks. Grey didn't care. He had hated the pomp and circumstance of military drill since his days at West Point where everything with the least hint of metal had to shine as though there was fire within waiting to burst out, and where creases, be they either in a dress uniform or a bunk, had to be sharp enough to cut cheese.

He hated that sort of busy-work. He was a fighting soldier and it showed in his men—they weren't the prettiest, but they had quickly gained the reputation of being the toughest.

The four lieutenants jogged up and the relaxed manner in which Grey ran things was apparent as not one of them locked up at attention. They huddled close to their commander, resembling a group of men playing backyard football. Like a quarterback calling plays, Grey touched two of them on the shoulder. "Gannon, Adams, I need your platoons to get their asses down to the Red Gate on the double. We're part of the ready force; let's show them how ready we are. Take what the men are carrying and go."

Gannon and Adams nodded and then Grey turned to the other two officers. "Seaver, I want you to load up 3rd Platoon with all the ammo they can carry and hump it down there, ASAP. I want them to look like God-forsaken pack mules, you understand?"

Lieutenant Seaver, a skinny ginger with a fine eye for terrain and a quiet way of leading his men, nodded at the request since there was no sense arguing. Yes, there were trucks available; however, the fuel reserves were finite while the strength of the men's backs was infinite, at least as far as Captain Grey was concerned.

The last man standing there was a lieutenant named Dent. Having been recently transferred from 3rd Battalion, Grey knew the least about him and his fighting qualities. "Dent, I want to hold 4th Platoon in reserve. Keep them ready and rested but have them set to go at a moment's notice until the situation firms up. They'll likely have a long night ahead of them." Grey nodded, his casual signal that his officers had their orders and, unless there were any questions, they were to carry them out as quickly and efficiently as possible. He even left the dismissal of the men in their hands.

He turned and began jogging up to the Stanley Hotel, his mind completely focused on the distant rifle fire, the fact that they were at war, and a thousand possible scenarios centered around an attack from the Azael. He was on the broad stairs leading up to the lower floor ballrooms when he heard from behind him: "Hey, Grey, wait up."

Deanna, looking golden and fresh-faced was running up the stairs toward him. She was breathless from the thin air and her bosom heaved appreciably. He wished he had time to appreciate it more; however, the firing in the east was picking up and the scent of war was strong in his nostrils; he had the business of battle to contend with.

Behind her, and looking as though he was on the verge of passing out from the short run, was Neil Martin. Had it been only Deanna there, Grey would have clasped her hand, told her not to worry and then said good bye to her with a kiss, but for some reason, the sight of Neil with his no longer innocent blue eyes, triggered something.

"Come with me," he ordered the two. "Don't speak unless spoken to. Stay near the back and try to keep out of the way. I get the feeling that the general is going to want to talk to you, Neil."

"But not me?" Deanna asked. "Then why am I going?"

Neil grinned his lopsided grin and answered for Grey: "Probably because Johnston is less likely to curse me out with you there."

Grey could only shrug since that was exactly the reason he wanted Deanna in attendance. Johnston was unfailing polite around civilians, especially women and extra-especially polite around women who held themselves with the poise and grace that Deanna possessed. "He's right," Grey said, turning from them and speaking over his shoulder as he advanced up the stairs. "I know it's a bit chauvinistic, but your presence may keep hackles from being raised. We both know how prickly Neil can get."

"Me?" Neil said. He clearly meant for it to be an exclamation of faux-outrage; however, after the twelfth stair, he could only husk the word out.

"Yeah, you," Grey answered. "Now concentrate on not fainting. Johnston frowns on grown men fainting in his presence." Neil could barely gather the breath necessary to heave out a quick: *Ha!*

Deanna looked less than pleased with her role, but she kept a stiff upper lip over it and said nothing.

The three of them passed through the lower ballroom and into a large, stately room, what once had been a sitting room for the rich and pampered crowd of the 1920's. Now it was the general's office and was wallpapered with maps of the valley and furnished with a single economical desk that seemed lost in the large room.

Johnston sat on the edge of the desk facing one of the maps. On either side of him were Colonels Aramo, Carny and Meade of the first, second and third Battalions. The General's adjunct, Major Sayer, stood off to one side next to Major Reynolds who headed up the reinforced heavy weapons company. Standing among the various company commanders and looking as though he was trying hide was the last of the senior officers. Major Gilbert Wyatt, who was the commanding officer of the headquarters "battalion," which was comprised of little besides a tiny logistics section, the Civilian Admin platoon and the twenty-person medical corps. Wyatt stood in the back, almost forgotten; he was a fine administrator, but not so much of a warrior.

The general opened his full-lipped mouth in what Grey knew was going to be a hard rebuke for his being a minute late for the meeting, but then he saw the general's attention slide over to Deanna and his hard eyes softened. The glare crept back when he noticed Neil. He brought a hand up to his clean-shaven chin and rubbed it, taking the small man's measure.

There was a flash of something between the two men and then it was gone. "Thanks for joining us, Mr. Martin and Ms Russell," the general said with his usual gracious manner. "I was going to call upon you and now you've saved me the trouble. I'll be with you in just a minute. First I have other matters to attend to." He glanced back at the map, his dark eyes pouring over its details, seeing nuances that few noticed.

"What do we know of the Azael?" he asked rhetorically. "They can corral the stiffs, that we've known for some time, but what else? They have declared war on us? Why? They claim we're harboring fugitives, but to attack with such a force for a few lost pilgrims? I hardly think so."

Neil surprised Grey by answering before anyone else could: "We pilgrims, as you call us, are simply the excuse for war." Grey shot him a look to which the smaller man gave only a tiny shrug before continuing: "Yes, we are the excuse, not the cause. But the answer is obvious to me. Why do any strong men resort to war on their neighbors?"

When General Johnston turned his dark eyes on subordinates, they usually quailed under the fierce gaze. Neil, who had stood up to men and women of purest evil, didn't blink an eye. Grey couldn't help but smile. Johnston had an altogether different response: at first, he tried to wither Neil with a hard look and, when that didn't work, he turned to Grey and, upon seeing his open smile, said: "Answer his question, please."

"Yes, Sir," Grey said. "History suggests that there's only one reason for unprovoked offensive warfare: the one nation perceives the other as weak."

"Exactly!" Johnston exclaimed. "And yet weakness is relative. From every perspective we can hardly be considered weak. We have a strong force of experienced and trained soldiers. And we are very nicely situated within a valley that is easily defended. So what does that suggest? That the Azael are either fools or they possess a force far stronger than we know."

"It could be both," Neil said. Grey gave him a little nudge that he hoped conveyed: *Time to zip your lip!*

Johnston pretended not to have heard. He looked over the room full of officers and asked: "What makes the Azael so confident?"

Colonel Aramo gave a shrug and answered: "For starters, we know the Azael have a large force of zombies."

"And?" Johnston asked, his annoyance at the obvious answer clear on his face.

Grey knew the answer as he was the one who had been debriefed under the razor-sharp eyes of the general himself. Addressing the room, Grey said: "One of the Azael we were with let slip that: quote-*We have some cool toys, too*, unquote. I saw a few hundred canisters of Napalm, a few fifty cals and some mortars, but that was at a small depot. If I had to guess, I'd say they could also have some artillery, maybe a few gunships. Possibly some TOWs or worse, some MLRs."

Napalm was enough to shiver the guts of the toughest veteran, but it was only slightly more terrifying than a normal artillery round. The M270 Multiple Launch Rocket System, on the other hand, was on a totally higher scale of fright. It could drop 2500 grenades over the size of a football field with pinpoint accuracy from thirty miles away. It could literally wipe out every living thing around any of the barricades in seconds.

"My fears exactly." Johnston glanced over at Major Reynolds and said. "Activate the radar systems. I want our anti-air up and running…"

Just then the door of the office shot opened. Grey, Neil and Deanna spun, reaching for weapons, each still subject to reflexes honed by the constant danger of the last year. The other officers, though all tough men, had grown complacent in the last seven months. Their walls and out of the way location had made the zombie menace a nuisance only and their reflexes weren't as finely honed as they had been.

The person barging in on the staff meeting was one of the general's admin people; a woman without rank on the faded and baggy ACUs she wore; she was a civilian.

"I'm so sorry for interrupting but we just got a call from the Red Gate," she said, breathlessly. "There are stiffs coming up the Big Thompson." She held out the brick-sized radio she was carrying to the general.

Before taking it, Johnston glanced at the map; everyone did. They saw the winding river as it curved in and out along Highway 34, sometimes running next to it, sometimes looping around this or that range of hills. The area of the river adjacent to the Red Gate was two miles from the leading edge of Estes. It was perilously close.

"Red Gate, this is Temple. How far down the river are they?" Johnston asked into the radio. "And what sort of numbers are we looking at?"

The radio crackled static for a few seconds before it spat out: "The leading edge is just even with our position." In the background, there was a chatter of small arms fire, lending urgency to his words. "As for the numbers, well...that I don't know. The recon was carried out by a civilian. She claims a number that is not feasible."

"And what is that number?" Johnston asked.

Again, the radio crackled. "We believe that there may be some overflow from the highway. Possibly a few thousand."

Johnston squinted again at the map. He was just opening his mouth to make a reply when the radio crackled louder than before and there was a strange ruffling noise and a cry of: "Give me that!"

This was followed by a voice Grey knew well. "Temple, this is Sadie Walcott. I saw a few thousand, yes but there are more, I guarantee it."

"And you base this on what?" Johnston asked.

"On common sense." Sadie's tone was just as snotty as a teenager could manage. "What else but a butt-load more zombies could get the ones I saw moving upstream against the tide of the river? Is Captain Grey there? I should speak to him."

Grey felt suddenly lonely as his fellow officers drew away from him and cast cutting looks his way. Johnston let out a sigh, but didn't offer the radio to Grey. "How about I talk to the soldier in charge there?" he asked.

A second later: "Temple this is Red Gate Leader, over."

"Red Gate, do you have the manpower to do a proper recon?"

"Negative Temple. We have stiffs on the hills to the south of us. There is a deer trail that they are using to flank us. We have a few thousand crawling like ants all over the place, but we are holding our own for the moment. Can I get an ETA on reinforcements?"

Before the General could answer, Grey said: "Five minutes, sir. I have released two of my platoons to the area, and the third is following with munitions."

Grey's commanding officer, Colonel Carney, glared with his eyes, but forced a smile and a nod as if the idea was his. As usual, Johnston saw the truth. "Without orders? Bold and dangerous, Grey. You can't make such assumptions."

"I can when I don't have orders to the contrary," Grey replied. "I felt that the situation warranted a quick response and I knew that I could recall my men if I was given orders that contradicted…well, common sense, sir."

Johnston grinned, saying: "Had I been a young and daring captain of men, I would have done the same thing. It's a wonder that more of you didn't do something along the same line."

The assembled officers shifted from foot to foot at the suggestion that they weren't also daring and bold—no soldier worth his salt wanted to be cast in a cowardly light and yet each knew the danger of overstepping their bounds. A false move could doom their men and sink their careers. And yet the rewards were in proportion as well.

"Go, Captain Grey. Lead your men. Give me a proper recon on the situation at the river and stop those stiffs, if you can."

Grey paused only to grab Deanna's hand and look into her beautiful blue eyes. She was afraid for him; he could see it in her face. The sound of the gunfire over the radio had been frightful and Sadie's words had been taken as utter fact by her, Neil and Grey. He was going to pit his hundred or so men against tens of thousands of zombies and there wasn't going to be a wall between him and their endlessly hungry teeth.

"I'll be careful," he said, knowing that being careful wasn't part of his orders. He was to lead his men and stop the horde with his handful of men, pitting their living flesh and blood against their eternal evil.

Chapter 4

Jillybean

If facts were discarded and reality ignored, Jillybean was doing just dandy. Eve was under control. King Augustus and Duke Menis had not called on her in a few days and she had a friendly adult companion who looked out for her.

Jillybean went around with these lies carefully overlooked and unexplored. She smiled at the Azael when they looked in her direction, and she pressed her lips tight when Eve laughed something horribly inappropriate into her mind, and she acted as though Kay Gallagher wasn't always walking about on the verge of hysterics with her hair hanging lank and untended and a tic working nonstop next to her right eye.

The truth would have made her life unbearable. The truth was that the Azael spat on her and blamed her for the deaths of their friends. The truth was that Eve was like a time bomb…a nonstop, talking time bomb that was only waiting for Jillybean to show the smallest crack before she would pounce. The truth was that Kay was a quivering, blubbering bruised–up manikin that went about huffing under the weight of a twenty-five pound dumbbell.

The dumbbell, as well as the handcuffs, was the Azael's way of keeping Jillybean and Kay from running away. Jillybean was handcuffed to Kay's right hand and the dumbbell was handcuffed to Kay's left. Kay was a thin woman with arms like sticks. When she was forced to walk with the weight, she could only move at a shuffle with her back bowed and her body quivering. She couldn't haul it very far and she thumped it down every forty feet or so.

On top of all of this, the pair was stuck, riding in the same bus as the traveling whorehouse. The sex slaves were so utterly cowed by the constant abuse that any attempt at escape was screamed from the rooftops. Kay was beaten only once for a supposed escape before Jillybean learned her lesson. She had been tired of the cuffs, which were in truth very simple devices, and decided to take them off for a spell. The little girl had the cuffs off the dumbbell in half a minute using a little flick of metal she had broken off a pen. A woman sitting in the next seat saw and raised an alarm.

After an ugly brute of a woman, who doubled as both the driver and the guard, beat Kay with a stick, Jillybean gave up the little fleck of metal. From then on, Jillybean kept her secrets just that, secret. Still, she longed for escape. She knew that she could, she just needed to get Kay alone in order to do it; this was a tall order now that they were winding with painful slowness up into the mountains.

Jillybean had never been on a real mountain before. Sometimes the views were spectacular and sometimes they were altogether terrifying, but mostly they were imprisoning. The walls of the surrounding cliffs were almost always unassailable and even when they weren't sheer, they led only upward to scraggy, desolate peaks, all of which were freezing even though it was still early July.

This was a fact she had trouble wrapping her head around. Since the women on the bus were of little help and wouldn't talk to her, Jillybean could only conclude that Colorado was in Australia, the land down under, where it was a well established fact that everything was a bit topsy-turvy.

She knew only a handful of "facts" concerning Australia: toilets ran backwards down there and they had Christmas in the summer and went to the beach in January. It was all quite exciting and she looked forward to seeing her first kangaroo and her first Tasmanian devil, which she understood to spin like a tornado instead of running on its four legs.

So far, she hadn't seen any animals except for birds and these stayed high up in the air and followed them as if they were lookouts for the invading army. The Azael army was very big, bigger than anything Jillybean had ever seen. Two days before, the king had pulled his fleet of trucks and army vehicles over at a town called Lyons. It wasn't much of a town and there weren't any lions in view, much to Jillybean's disappointment.

The only things to see that were of any interest were the two "tanks" that the Azael had and the gobs of monsters being herded along. The tanks had very sharp angular noses, machine guns instead of big cannons and wheels instead of tracks. The Azael called them Strykers. More impressive than the tanks were the gazillions of monsters. A hundred Azael on their horses prodded the monsters forward, following a road that crept up through the foothills going north-west. The monsters marched past them for hours and hours. The afternoon wore away and still they slogged by in an endless parade.

The king had summoned Jillybean to watch with him for part of the time. Kay was an afterthought who knelt down next to the dumbbell and did her best not to be noticed. The little girl was very nervous to be around the giant of a man, but she fought against the feeling—Eve grew stronger when she was afraid and there was no telling what she would do if she ever got free again.

With difficulty, Jillybean swallowed her fear, and spoke first: "How many of them are there?"

A shrug from Augustus was followed by: "This herd? Maybe a quarter of a million. It's hard to tell, but hey, you're the genius, you should be the one telling me."

Jillybean wrinkled her nose. "How would I know that?"

"Some sort of math-shit, I suppose," the king had said with a grunting laugh. The men around him laughed as well. Jillybean didn't understand vulgarity as humor and only raised a dismissive brow and looked out over the marching zombies. She didn't like the laughter of the men; it was creepy and made Kay shake all the harder.

"It'll be ok," Jillybean said to the woman. How it would be, she didn't know and she was glad that Kay didn't ask. If she had, Jillybean would have been forced to confront the very real possibility that it wouldn't be ok. Then she would be afraid and, slowly, Eve would take over, which would be horrible.

Just then, Eve was thinking that slitting Kay's throat with the jagged piece of metal she had stashed under the seat on the bus, was a good idea. An image of blood spraying in a greasy red geyser played on the dark screen in Jillybean's mind and sent a shiver down her back. To combat the hateful thoughts bubbling up from the blackness inside of her, Jillybean turned her mind to the problem of figuring out the sort of math needed to count so many monsters without actually touching each on their rotted heads and saying: one, two, three...

Her formal education with math only went so far as adding and subtracting simple terms and yet she knew there were greater and more complicated maths yet to be discovered. She had heard of multiplication and division but didn't quite understand their meaning beyond the facts that multiplication meant to make more of a number and the division meant to cut a number up into pieces.

But why would anyone want to do that?

She shrugged and watched the monsters. The road up into the mountains was narrow and only so many could go side by side. Sometimes it was twenty, sometimes it was twenty-two, and sometimes it was twenty-three. In a blink, she bridged five years of mathematics and hit upon the concept of *averages*. Next, she noticed that the rows would pass a skinny pine, which had grown up out of a fissure of rock, at intervals of about one every three seconds.

The idea of *rate over time* was playing on her conscious when one of the king's brothers said: "I still don't see why we need her. She's done nothing at all so far."

"Except try to escape," another put in. There were twelve men comprising the king's inner circle; eight relatives of which six were brothers. They all wore their beards thick and long. Some kept them under control with heavy rubber bands, while some let them run wild and loose.

Menis had his forked, which, along with the nasty look in his eyes, gave him the air of a demon. Even though Jillybean had risked her life to save his, she kept well away from him when she could. He acted as though she was a reminder of Neil, whom Menis hated with a passion. She was also a reminder of Deanna, whom Menis acted crazy over whenever she was mentioned.

"She's done as much as you, Baldwin," the king said to the first complainer. "So far all you've done is brown your nose with my ass. I need more than yes men around me. It's one of the reasons that I want her. *She* is not a yes man. Isn't that right, Jillybean?"

Tell him to fuck off, Eve said. *Tell him that you'll stick a knife in his eye if he doesn't let us go.*

Jillybean didn't react to the voice that sounded as though it was being spoken just over her right shoulder. The voice meant she was 'crazy.' She knew that now and she didn't like how the king's men would make fun of her when she allowed the crazy to show.

"I don't know what a yes-man is," Jillybean admitted. "But if I had to guess, judging from your friends, it's people who copy you and agree with you even if you say dumb stuff."

For the most part, the men of the Azael glowered. The king, on the other hand, laughed loud enough to turn the heads of the distant monsters.

Tell him to stop his fucking laughing, Eve hissed. *He sounds like a mule.*

Jillybean hated the cursing nearly as much as the voice itself. She hated the idea that such talk could come from somewhere inside of her and she wondered if it meant that there was a cancer in her. When she pictured cancer, it was as an evil green blob that sprouted tentacles that had suckers on them. Each of the suckers ate you, slowly.

She sure felt thin, thinner than she ought to be as if she were indeed being eaten.

"I haven't copied shit," Paulus, the king's youngest brother said. "The rest of you brought a few lousy stiffs and a few hundred horsemen and Menis brought a little, fucking girl. I brought God's thunder." He lifted his chin to the line of trucks at the very back of the fleet. Each was towing a 155mm howitzer behind it. "Nothing they have will be able stand up those beauties."

"Wrong," Duke Menis said. "They have artillery, too and they'll be manned by real soldiers."

Paulus waved a hand. "Bah! They have 105s. They don't have nearly the range. We'll be able to stand off and shred them up and they won't be able to hit back. And once their artillery is gone, we'll be able destroy their walls and their buildings and everything else we want."

Menis glared at his younger brother and when Jillybean was dismissed, he grabbed her and hissed in her ear: "You had better come through when the shit hits the fan."

Jillybean had no clue what 'coming through' entailed, especially as the force of monsters, and artillery, and the thousands of soldiers, looked fully capable of destroying anyone. No group she had ever seen would've been able to stand up against such power. Not the people of New Eden, not Yuri and his hodge-podge of boats, not the River King and not any of the different groups in Philadelphia, either.

She was altogether superfluous. Everyone thought so. All except Kay, who constantly nagged her to come up with a 'plan' to 'win.' But that was not how Jillybean's mind operated. She needed to see the barriers impeding them in order to overcome them and so far the only thing in their way were the steep mountains.

For two days, the horsemen of the Azael drove the monsters ahead of them. They went at it day and night, working in shifts, constantly pressing forward. The army of men followed after, trudging along in uneven lines with sweat pouring down their faces despite the slowly cooling air. They stopped frequently and took long smoke breaks and even longer naps.

They weren't in a hurry. In fact, they were amazingly relaxed for an army marching to war. They didn't think that they would do much hard fighting, figuring that the monsters would do their dirty work for them. The beasts would go first; they'd tear down the walls and overrun the valley. The king's enemies would be stuck with the options of fleeing for their lives or seeking refuge in this building or that.

If anyone was still alive once the monsters were rounded up, they'd be easily crushed. And this left Jillybean in a dilemma. She was being pressured to be helpful, but the Azael already seemed irresistible.

The next day, the human half of the army came to a stop as the noise of gunshots, sounding like the crackling of far off fireworks came to them. Everyone but Jillybean grew excited. They let out cheers and when Paulus unlimbered his big guns they danced and threw their hats in the air. Some even shot their pistols at the surrounding mountains.

Even Kay started grinning. She turned to Jillybean and hissed: "You can do it, Jillybean. You can save us."

"How?" Jillybean wondered. She tried to back away from the woman as well as the very idea, but the handcuffs wouldn't let her. "They don't even need my help."

With manic strength, Kay pulled her in close and loomed over her, leering down in a strange and scary manner. "Of course, they need your help. Those are just zombies. Zombies, Jillybean. Do you think fucking zombies will be enough? Think about it. You're supposed to be smart. So use that fat brain and think about Captain Grey. Could a zombie kill him? No! And how many men just like Captain Grey do they have over there? A thousand or more, right?"

She dragged Jillybean forward and stood staring at the Azael, who were still whooping it up. "Those morons can't win without us, Jillybean. I mean that. Because, think about it, if they do, what will happen to me…to us? They won't need us, Jillybean, and if they don't need us…"

Kay lifted her and Jillybean's arm to point at the bus where the women who were virtual sex-slaves stared out of the squares of dirty glass with their blank eyes in their blank faces. "You know what they'll do to us, Jillybean. They'll turn us into one of them."

Jillybean didn't want to think about; however, she couldn't help it and her fear over the idea was so great that she found herself smiling...smiling Eve's wicked smile.

Chapter 5

Sadie Walcott

She handed over the radio to the hard-eyed staff sergeant and gave him a sweet grin that she hoped would convey some sort of apology.

"Son of a bitch," he said, snatching the radio from her hands. "Don't do that again. Now, get your ass back to the valley and turn yourself over to the CAB. I'm sure they will have a use for you."

"You have a use for me here, I bet," Sadie replied. "Give me your extra gun. I can shoot as good as the next person." This wasn't close to being true; she had gotten better; however, the soldiers were clearing the south face of the hill with an accuracy that was amazing. Calmly, they stood in a line and fired their rifles. They didn't flinch from the masses of zombies and their aim was deadly.

The soldiers on the wall were just as good, though it wasn't easy to tell. They were able to shoot from a position of safety and the number of stiffs packed shoulder-to-shoulder, was so great that even a poor shot couldn't miss. Sadie held out her hand for the staff sergeant's pistol.

"Not on your life," he said, covering it with a hand. "Now, go. I won't ask again. We have work to do here."

She saw that she wasn't going to be able to beg a weapon out of him and with the ugly moans filling the air, she didn't think he was going to fall for a cute smile even if she could manage one. "Fine, I don't need a gun," she said feeling distinctly teenager-ish. With a little wave to the apple-cheeked Morganstern, she turned and began heading along the wall to the string of hills to the north.

"What the hell do you think you're going to do?" the staff sergeant yelled after her.

"I'm smart. I'll think of something." She liked the uncertain look that spread over his features at this. Of course, as soon as she turned away, her own face twisted into a matching one. "What am I going to do?" she asked herself. The declaration of being "smart" hadn't been true. She didn't think of herself as stupid, but smart? No, she didn't think she was close to smart. "Something will come to me, I'm sure."

As she climbed the hill, nothing did.

Her breath came sharp in her chest as she struggled from tree to tree. Behind her the shooting went on without let up and, other than feeding the growing fear blooming in her chest, the gunfire became nothing save a backdrop to what felt like an endless climb.

Winded, she crested the hill and, where before she had paused to catch her breath and look around, now she plunged down, again going from tree to tree, each catching her as gravity sucked her downward toward where the moans grew in volume.

Two hundred feet down the slope, she saw what had been the silver-tipped waters of the Big Thompson River. It was no longer silver-tipped; it was choked grey with zombies. The numbers of horrid, diseased bodies was staggering and seemingly endless. Her stomach rolled unpleasantly and she began to feel the butterflies in her chest start to swirl.

She stood over ten thousand zombies, weaponless and a little witless. She had no idea what to do.

Running away was her best plan and she felt the strongest urge to fly from there. Yet, she couldn't. The zombies had to be stopped before they poured out into the valley...and besides, she'd feel awfully foolish going back to the staff sergeant having done nothing.

"If only Jillybean were here," Sadie whispered. "She'd figure out...she'd figure out...what?" Sadie was trying to goad her mind into a Jillybean-esque plan, only she didn't know what Jillybean would do and she lacked the imagination to come up with a cool idea to stop the beasts. "An avalanche would stop them," she said. Unfortunately, the hill was heavily wooded and altogether stable. "A flash flood might do it." She looked up and saw the pretty blue sky was just as empty as her head.

She ground her teeth in frustration. "The only thing I can do is drop some rocks on them." It was pitiful as far as plans went.

Feeling somewhat useless and with her fear growing, she went further down the steep hill, collecting the largest stones she could carry until the sloping hill cut away into a sharp drop of about fifteen feet.

She was standing high above the rotting beasts and tried to tell herself that other than losing her footing and falling and being eaten alive, there wasn't much for her to fear. "It's too steep for the zombies," she said with a nervous laugh. She was sure it was; the riverbank was carved out of granite; it was practically a straight vertical wall, and covered in damp moss—it was unclimbable, her rational side knew it, but there was just so many of them. It was hard to think past all those thousands of zombies.

Sixty feet to her left, the lead wave of beasts was already past her, slowly chugging up-river toward Estes Park, to her right they were dense as flies and seemed to go on infinitely.

It wasn't long before she was spotted and a great moan almost like a collective bellow erupted. As though they were sharing one rather dull mind, every zombie in sight turned and splashed through the thigh-high water, angling their way toward her. She stepped back and grabbed a tree, both to keep her legs from buckling and to keep her feet from flying.

"Ok, I guess I should've expected that," she said, as the beasts began piling over themselves to get at her. It was a second before she realized that by standing there, she was in fact keeping them from progressing on to the valley. "This is good. This is like a plan without the thinking." It was her kind of plan...except for the fact that she was basically bait, like a worm on a hook dangling over countless piranha.

The only thing missing from this "plan of opportunity" was that the lead elements hadn't seen her and were still slogging on toward the valley. "Hey!" she screamed at the top of her lungs. "Hey, you morons! Dinner is this way." This got their attention and most turned back, but not all.

The zombies liked her yelling. They grew excited at being so close to an easy meal and were moaning with a sickening animation that drowned her out.

She tried clapping two stones together but it did almost nothing to attract any more of them to her and a vanguard of a thousand or so zombies kept going upriver. "But at least I have you, my loyal fans," she said. The main body, probably ten thousand strong was now pressing in at the base of Sadie's hill.

Those directly below her scraped at the rocky cliff and stared hungrily up at her. The ones behind, mindlessly clawed at the ones in front, first dragging down one, then another, and so on. Those that fell were crushed by the mass of bodies and drowned.

At first, Sadie grinned at this since they were killing each other, in essence doing her job for her. Her grin faded when she realized that with each body pulled down, the grasping claws came closer to her. "Pyramiding," she said, remembering the word used by one of the soldiers at the wall. She was watching the word as it was put into action, once more. Already a mound of the dead was building below her as the zombies began using the corpses of their brothers to get at her.

The cliff, steep and slick as it was, wasn't a place of safety.

"It'll be just a few more minutes," she told herself. "The army will get here really, really soon." The zombies were halfway up the wall when she remembered the rocks in her hands. Feeling stupid, she threw them down at the mass of rotting bodies struggling to get at her. She used all her strength and when they struck, they made a very satisfying sound; sort of a cross between a *squish* and a *splat*.

"Huh," she said, reaching for more rocks, her grin returning. The hill was full of rocks, it was practically composed of little more than rock and root and trunk. Right away she went for the bigger rocks and, hefting them as high as she could, she flung them down.

It was fun, at least for the first twenty stones or so. When she managed to crush a skull, which occurred with at least half her throws, she would cry: "Score!" Or she would say: "Down goes Charlie." She didn't know where in her young mind that saying had sprung from; she just thought it was appropriate.

The fun started wearing off some time after that twentieth stone. Her cries of *Score* and *Down goes Charlie* were replaced by the sound of her breath, ragged in her throat. Bending, hefting and chucking fifteen pound rocks became a chore. But at least it wasn't an endless one. With each crushed head, the pyramid below her grew and the zombies came closer and closer.

Further downstream, the backlog of zombies was causing them to overflow the lower banks and now hundreds were on "her" hill, fighting the sharp slant to get at her. Still, she was relatively safe and as long as she was, she decided she would continue to pull up the heavy rocks and throw them down.

37

Closer they came. Closer. Long minutes went by and still the beasts did everything they could to get at her. They were soon piled as high as the cliff and were crawling up the steep hill. She threw rock after rock, slowly backing away and she kept telling herself she wasn't afraid; however, she breathed a sigh of relief when she heard the sound of gunfire from the west. The reinforcements had finally come! All she had to do was hold on for a few more minutes and she would be safe and everything would be just peachy.

It took twelve minutes before the vanguard of zombies was destroyed and she could see the first of Captain Grey's men creeping downriver in a long line. By then the mound of bodies had grown to overflow a hundred feet of the bank and Sadie had backed well up the hill and was surrounded on three sides.

She was hurling the stones desperately now, as fast as she could. Her arms had grown too weak to pick up the bigger rocks and her legs shook from the strain of holding her upright on the slope. Sweat lathered her face and she was gasping and reeling, and she wanted to run so badly. Every natural part of her wanted to bunny right out of there before any of the creatures got behind her and cut off her escape.

Then came the snap and crackle of rifle fire. It was close. A squad of soldiers suddenly appeared out of the brush and laid down a withering barrage of lead, exploding heads and sending blood flying. Sadie let the last stone fall and staggered eagerly toward them. But then one turned a gun in her direction, she put up her hands. "Wait, I'm…human."

He fired anyway and she had only the strength to cringe. The bullet singed a path through the air, passing unsettlingly close to her left ear. "What the..."

"You're welcome," he said as something thudded into the dirt behind her. When she turned she saw a grey body, lying on its back on the face of the hill. It had somehow come up from the high side of the hill.

"Oh, thanks," she said, breathlessly. She probably should have felt foolish over thinking the soldier was going to kill her; however, she was just too spent.

"You're welcome," the soldier answered without casting a single eye at her; he had his cheek pressed against his assault rifle. When he fired, she lacked the strength to follow the line of the bullet. Assuming the sixty or so men were good shots, she let her legs collapse. She lay down on the hill, closed her eyes and rested until her muscles stopped their quivering and it was no longer a strain to suck in air.

After some time, she rolled onto her side, and propped her head in her hand, looking as though she were at the beach having a picnic. She watched as the men cut down the zombies with grim efficiency. They would fire, pause, fire and pause. As they had been going at it for some minutes, they would sometimes take short breaks, letting their weapons hang from their straps while they shook out their hands, or rolled their shoulders.

"Don't want to get stiff," the soldier closest to her said.

Before she could reply, a lieutenant yelled: "Gorman, stop your flirting and get down here." The hill was carpeted in dead bodies and now the rest of the company was standing knee deep in the river, forming a single line stretching from one end to the other.

"I wasn't flirting," Gorman groused. "I just didn't think it was right to leave her up there all alone like that." There wasn't much justification in this statement. Zombies, being drawn to the closest or easiest to get at prey, were no longer fighting to get up the hill. They were going after the soldiers in the water.

"You weren't protecting the girl," another soldier joked. "You were just trying to keep your nuts from turning to ice cubes."

It was only after that comment that Sadie remember the water was practically at freezing temperature. "Poor guys," she said, under her breath. They were stoic about the cold and no one complained, but their lips began to turn pale and their hands shook, making their aim an uncertain thing.

Guessing that Captain Grey would be sending reinforcements soon, Sadie went upstream to where the hill wasn't nearly as steep. She kicked at the floor of the forest until she had a patch of barren dirt. She then gathered twigs and leaves, arranged them into what resembled a foot-tall teepee, and lit the leaves at the base with the lighter she'd been carrying around for weeks.

When Captain Grey arrived with his remaining two platoons, he gave the fire a quizzical look and she explained: "The water is icy. They'll need to warm up."

"Right," he said. "Good thinking." Terse as always, he didn't add anything or ask about how she was doing or wonder how she had managed to stall an army of ten thousand zombies, single handedly. He had his dark eyes downstream where his men were firing into the horde, killing dozens with every volley, turning the water an ugly dark maroon. There were nauseating chunks of flesh floating as well; the river was fast becoming a foul, running soup.

Thankfully, it was, for the most part, flowing downhill, away from the men. For the most part, but not entirely.

The soldiers were firing with such efficiency that the zombie corpses were falling in heaps and mounds that gradually rose up out of the water, damming the river in more ways than one. Slowly, the water level began to rise, forming an evil pool that was soon waist deep and where before, the men had been stoic, now they began to grumble as they were slowly coated in the tainted, maroon slime.

"Shut your cake-holes!" a sergeant roared over the firing. "You're doing the Lord's work here."

It looked like hell to Sadie. The wall of torsos, stray arms and grey, rotted heads grew with every volley. It had to be crawled over by the other zombies coming up, slowing their advance even more. The horde was being checked by the firepower and accuracy of Grey's men; however, the pressure from behind was even greater—again the steep hills were being covered by the dead as they came on inexhaustibly.

Grey took all of this in with a long sweeping glance. He turned to one of his lieutenants. "I want 4th Platoon here on the double to take over in the water. Send two squads of 2nd Platoon to the hill on the north side of the river and two to the south. Have 1st Platoon rotate back here to warm up. We'll switch them out in a round robin every twenty minutes."

The captain then turned to Sadie and said: "I'm going to need more and bigger fires. Probably three going constantly until this is all over."

"And when will that be?" Sadie asked. She was already tired and flagging.

"Not long," he answered. "I'd say we'll be close to finishing when we've killed a quarter million zombies." There was no smile on his face or laughter in his eye when he said this.

Chapter 6

Neil Martin

The remainder of the meeting did not last long. More companies of soldiers were sent to shore up the defenses at the Red Gate and the Big Thompson River, while others marched to bolster the handful of men at the Blue Gate. Three more companies were broken up and sent out to throw up hasty barricades along the less likely avenues of attack.

The remaining three companies were held in reserve. The company commanders of these grumbled about not being able to join in the fight, but they were quiet grumbles—General Johnston clearly wasn't a man who would allow much in the way of insubordination.

And yet Neil was feeling very insubordinate. Johnston had flicked his dark eyes Neil's way time and again during the briefing and each time there had been judgment in those eyes. Neil had thought that he was long past caring what others thought of him; however, the looks bothered him.

When the soldiers had been dismissed and there was only Neil and Deanna left, General Johnston came to stand so close to Neil that the toes of their boots nearly touched. Johnston loomed over Neil. He was a barrel-chested man with large, python-sized arms. His entire aspect was one of command; he was perfectly in control.

Where Neil sweated under the dark eyes, the general was cool and dry. He smelled pleasantly of talc and his uniform sat on his muscular frame, completely unwrinkled. Where his officers had been edgy or angry at the attack, he had been calm. Where they were bristling and ready to charge into battle, he was a rock. All in all, he was one of the most physically intimidating men Neil had ever seen.

And yet Neil wasn't intimidated. He was tired of the very idea of intimidation. "Yes?" Neil asked, pleasantly.

Next to him, Deanna, looking uncomfortable with the general being so close, made an excuse to move away. She stepped back even as she held out her hand to him. The general didn't shake it; he kissed it before switching off the scrutiny and giving them both a genuine smile that was equal parts weariness and worry. "First off, I don't blame either you or your group, Mr. Martin, for the attack today."

"Thanks," Neil replied. "And we don't blame you, either."

The smile faltered. "Yes," the general said, dryly. "Captain Grey told me to expect you to be a bit prickly. He told me about your troubles. I want you to realize that you are among friends."

"Then why the looks?" Neil asked. "Every time I see you, I get the feeling that I'm being appraised like a pig in a county fair."

"That's because you are. This world rarely allows for second chances or mistakes, and I can't afford to make any, especially at a delicate time such as this. War does things to people. It tends to bring out the crazy in them. It can make them dangerous. This craziness is precisely the reason I wanted you and Deanna to talk to me."

The two renegades shared a look of confusion. "About what?" Deanna asked.

"About…well, it's a delicate situation we have here in Estes. When we first founded this community eight months ago, I had an idealized society in mind. A republic guided by Christian morals ruled by laws. Power was supposed to be transferred from the military to this government gradually in preplanned stages, so that in the end, the people would be able to rule themselves."

"Sounds great," Neil said. "Great, except for the big 'but' you're about to drop on us. Let me guess, you want to hand over power but really keep it on the sly? Are you looking for one of us to be your puppet?"

Johnston shook his head. "No. You are completely wrong. I don't want a puppet, because I really don't want to deal with any of that crap. I'm a soldier, not a politician. That's the truth. I'm a warrior. I like to kill monsters and break things, preferably with very large explosions. I don't want…what is it, Neil?"

Neil caught himself staring off over the general's shoulder and he jerked back into reality. The words the man had used had reminded him of Jillybean and that had triggered a guilt response. "It's nothing. You just sounded like someone…one of my old friends that I lost. Sorry, please go on; you were saying you don't want to be a politician?"

The general looked ill at the very idea. "No, I don't, it's abysmal. The paperwork and the dull minutia and the whining. I simply hate the whining. That's something I should warn you about going in, all you're going to get is complaints."

43

"Hold on," Neil said. "All *I'm* going to get? You want me to run things around here? That's...that's...really, that doesn't make any sense. Aren't there other people here better qualified? I mean, I just got here. No one is going to vote for me and they probably won't listen to me, either."

"First off, I'll appoint you, so there won't be a vote. It's an emergency situation and I'll say there's no time for an election. Secondly, they will listen to you if you take charge. That's very important. If you act the part of the leader, they will follow. People are like that. And you will have the backing of the military. That's key. That alone will give you the status needed to be seen as the leader in their eyes."

This was all going too fast. Only an hour before he'd been contemplating life as a farmer. "But...but why me? Really, there has to be others who are qualified for the job and others who actually want the job, which I don't know if I do. And I'm a stranger here. Wouldn't you rather have a leader that you know?"

"I know enough about you to make this decision. I see how you comport yourself. I hear how others talk about you. Captain Grey, for one, speaks very highly of you. As for the others who may want the job..." He looked pained, as though speaking badly about someone was against his nature. "Yes, there are others who would want the job. Some aren't qualified, some are vindictive, some are quarrelsome a few of them are simply too nice. Also, if I give the position to the leader of group A, then group B will be mad, you see? In my opinion, there are three serious contenders in the valley; however, they're populists. They parrot the people instead of putting forth bold ideas. They remind me of the old politicians that got us into this mess in the first place. They feed into the complainers."

Most of the people in the valley were exceptionally sweet, but there were some hardcore complainers: *the soldiers were lazy; the general was a slave master; there was never enough of this or that.*

Every one of the renegades had shaken their heads in disbelief over this. The valley wasn't perfect by any stretch; however, it was ordered, neat, protected, and best of all, relatively well stocked with goods. The people owed a certain percentage of what they produced or scrounged to the community, and the rest was theirs to do with as they wished.

The soldiers could hardly be called lazy as they stood guard over the valley around the clock and when they weren't on guard, they were training or working in some capacity. They were never drunken, rarely disrespectful and would be punished severely for anything that even smacked of bullying. Over all, Neil had been exceedingly happy with the arrangement—and now the general wanted to change it? And worse, he wanted Neil to be the agent of that change?

Deanna spoke up for the first time: "Don't you think that now is the wrong time for all of this? We were just attacked for goodness sakes." For emphasis, she pointed to the window where the day was bright and sunny and the world seemed utterly peaceful…if one could ignore the quiet crackling of the distant gunfire.

"I don't think the timing could be any better," Johnston answered. He also pointed out the window. "I need to be out there. I need to be in the fight. What I don't need is regulating farm sizes or overseeing fights between neighbors. I took the position of governing out of necessity and I kept at it because there wasn't a good candidate to take my place. I never wanted the job."

"And I do?" Neil asked. "It sounds like a thankless task and quite frankly, I don't think I want it."

General Johnston's face clouded at this and he continued to stare out of the window and was quiet for a long time. Eventually, he reached out and pressed the tips of his long brown fingers to the glass. "What would you say if I told you that I need you? What would you say if I told you," he poked the glass now, "that they need you?"

He turned towards Neil. "Here's the truth: I am a fair man and an honest man, but I'm also a military man and have been practically my entire life. I'm also a student of history. I know how a militarily controlled government will end."

Neil knew enough history to have an idea that it wouldn't end well. "Fire, war, rebellion, torture, general unhappiness?" he asked.

Johnston nodded. "Maybe not this year or the next, but I will die eventually. There might be a squabble over who's next in line. Power does that to people. Even the best of us."

Now it was Neil's turn to gaze out the window. His eyes were drawn to the grey peaks that hemmed them in. They formed walls fourteen thousand feet high and yet they were still too small to keep evil out of the valley.

"We bring the evil with us," Neil whispered. Johnston raised an eyebrow at this and Neil tried to smile away the comment. "I won't be a puppet," he announced. "And I don't want to be president for life or anything like it, and there should be a separate court system that can hold *everyone* accountable; that includes me and the soldiers."

A nod from Johnston was followed by: "Sounds proper. Go on."

Deanna, who had been somewhat ignored, said: "Hold on a second. I don't understand what I'm here for. Was it just in case Neil said no?"

A rueful grin broke across the general's face. "Something like that. I think you're equally qualified and you were my second choice. I also wanted to use you as a sounding board. You wear your emotions on your sleeve in an honest and open manner. I wanted to judge your reaction to my proposal to Neil. From what I could tell, you were surprised but certainly not repelled by the idea. I could see you weighing the pros and cons, and I could see that the pros overwhelmingly won out."

"Easily so," Deanna said. "Neil is a strong, resourceful leader. He is smart and far wiser than he gives himself credit for. He knows his limitations and yet surpasses them time and again. The truth is, I would vote for him over anyone here. Sorry to say, but the civilians in the valley are soft. They have been more than just protected, they've been shielded from some of the hardest realities of this new life and it has made them dependent."

"I agree," Johnston said. "It was another reason I wanted an outsider and another issue Neil will have to face if he accepts the position. Can I assume you want the job?"

Out of habit, Neil pinched the bridge of his nose and closed his eyes. He had thought he was done with all of this. He thought that he would scavenge for a few weeks in the hope of finding Jillybean on the off chance that she had managed to escape from the Azael. Then he figured he would become a farmer.

In his mind's eye, he saw himself mopping sweat from his brow with a red kerchief and leaning on a pitchfork, though he wasn't sure exactly what a pitchfork was used for. Poking things, he assumed, perhaps like a pig's butt. They didn't seem likely to move if you didn't poke them. He was just wondering why he would want to move a pig in the first place when the general frowned. "I have things to do, Neil. Every minute counts in battle, so if you need some time to think about it, I can give you a day or two, but then I'm going to have move on to my second choice." He indicated Deanna.

"She would be a great leader," Neil replied, but at the same time he wondered: *Would she be better than me?* He was an honest person and that honesty included his assessment of himself. He knew full well the mistakes he had made leading the renegades; for the most part they had been mistakes of trust. He had trusted the River King and Ernest when he shouldn't have. He had trusted the words coming from Sarah's mouth and not the pain in her eyes. He had trusted Jillybean's resiliency when he should've been sheltering her.

His biggest mistake of trust was that he hadn't trusted himself until it was almost too late. That lesson had been hard bought and the sole reason he didn't want Deanna as leader. There had been a sharp learning curve as leader, with each mistake marked by death. Errors in judgment now with battle raging on their frontier and a new government to establish could spawn rebellion among the people or mass enslavement by the Azael.

There was too much on the line for Neil to trust anyone but himself.

"I'll do it, but there will be conditions," he said. "We'll talk about them as they come up, but the first and foremost one is that the military will be mine to command." At this Johnston's mouth set like a wedge of stone and, when Neil added, "Completely," his eyes blazed.

It was for a moment only. Johnston let out a long breath saying: "It can be the only way."

"Yes," agreed Neil. "We'll start right now. I want you to spend the next five minutes filling me in on the military situation. I need to know the number of men we have, the type of equipment they use and their overall state of readiness."

The general extended his hand in a dramatic sweep toward the window where the guns were going nonstop and where, in the distance there was a worrisome trail of smoke in the sky. "What the hell, Neil? You see that, right? You can hear the guns, can't you? This isn't the time to try to grind me under your heel, because I can take back my offer in a snap."

Neil raised an eyebrow. "So, you're saying I'm in charge right up until you decide different? If so why did you bother with all this? If I'm in charge, then stop your whining and spend the five minutes filling me in. Do you not trust your men to do their jobs? Are they poorly trained, is that it?"

Johnston glared furiously; looking as though he was about to tear Neil's arms off. "You're testing me? You're testing me right this second?"

"Yes," Neil replied simply and calmly. "It's the only way to know if the offer is sincere."

Slowly the general forced an angry, tight-lipped grin onto his dark, handsome face. "Ok, fine. I understand. I will give you your five minutes, but if men die, needlessly, it will be on your shoulders."

"Establishing civilian control of the military is far from needless," Neil countered. "Now, begin, please."

Johnston checked his watch, took a steadying breath and then spoke slowly: "We have approximately eighteen hundred officers and enlisted men in the valley. They are broken up into three infantry battalions, a heavy weapons company and auxiliary units. Each battalion is comprised of five companies, each of approximately one hundred and ten men. These are again broken down into platoons and then squads. It's all very standard."

Neil nodded politely, not knowing what was standard and what wasn't.

The general went on: "In order to reduce our logistical strain, the infantry companies use only two types of weapons: the M4 and the crew-served M240 heavy machine gun. If anything more substantial is needed then we bring in the heavy weapons company, which has a variety of tactical systems: a Javelin anti-tank missile launcher, 120 mm mortars, 105mm howitzers and lastly a Patriot anti-aircraft platform. The men are all cross-trained on at least one of these."

The general paused for a breath; however, before he could go on, Deanna stepped between them with her hands out. "Ok, Neil, that's enough. You've proved your point. There's no need to make him go on or do I have to remind you that your best friend and your daughter are out there fighting while you're in here wasting time."

"I don't need to be reminded," Neil said, looking again to the window. "I know what I'm risking but…but you are right, Deanna. The point is made. There's no reason to belabor it."

"Good," Johnston said, quickly. "Now that you're in charge, here's what I need from you and the other civilians…"

Chapter 7

Captain Grey

Miles to the south of the Red Gate was the Blue Gate. It stood guarding the other main entrance to the Estes Valley. In exactly the same configuration: wire emplacement, fifteen-foot deep moat, thick concrete wall, it sat across Highway 36, which also had a river that ran next to it for many looping miles until the land flattened out on the Eastern Slope of the Rockies. Some long-dead pioneer, displaying his limited imagination, had christened the river: The Little Thompson. The soldiers, in their endless pursuit to reduce confusion, had not tested their imagination either when they had renamed the little river: The Little River.

There were zombies here as well.

A great, grey wave plowed ever forward, and just like the Red Gate, the Blue Gate was in danger of being swallowed as if by a snake of infinite size. Because of the width of the road and the gentleness of the slope, two companies of men were needed to hold the Blue Gate.

The Little River, on the other hand was barely a foot and a half deep and only as wide as a two-lane road. Other than the frigid waters, the company who fought there had little to complain about; compared to what was happening at the Red Gate, it was a cake-walk.

At the Red Gate the machine guns had been running hot for an hour and now there was a tremendous mound of corpses before the soldiers. The dimensions of the mound were frightful: it began a hundred and fifty feet from the wall, rose thirty feet in height, and ran a hundred feet from one side of the gorge to the other. It was so vast that there was no sight of either the moat or the barbed wire barricade; both were buried, deep.

This huge, stinking hill, more than anything else, slowed the endless horde in their attack. Painstakingly they'd climb to the top only to be "popped" by one of the soldiers; their dead bodies adding to the mass. It was considered a good kill if the body fell back on the far side of the hill. Anything else only made the hill that much bigger and many of the men began to wonder how big the hill would get before it broke like an ocean wave and collapsed on the wall and drowned them in corpses.

Although it was a nightmare vision, it was an unlikely possibility. The greatest numbers of the undead were already overflowing the smaller hills hemming in the road and of course they were surging up the Big Thompson.

The big river was Grey's sole responsibility. His command: the 7th Company, 2nd Battalion, comprised of a hundred and eight men, had one of the most dangerous zones. The mountain river with its frigid waters sapped the strength of the men. Their hands grew quickly numb, causing their aim to suffer. They lost feeling in their feet and they stumbled frequently among the slippery rocks that lined the bottom. To Grey, it felt as though someone had cobbled the riverbed with skulls, and there wasn't one among them who wasn't soaked up to their necks.

The fires that Sadie kept going helped to a degree. It wouldn't be true to say that she worked tirelessly, it was the opposite, really. The girl's breath huffed in and out as she dragged her feet up and down the hills, searching for branches and sticks. Her face and hands were scratched and her black shirt torn, but she still went at it nonstop. She needed help, but no one had come, despite Grey's demands.

His own soldiers were in no shape to help. Every hour, they'd come slogging out of the river to throw themselves down in front of the fires. They thrust their frozen limbs toward the flames and could do nothing but shake for their fifteen minute rest. They would then rotate to the south hill where the last of the sun's rays would add a final touch of warmth before they crossed over to take their turn at the north hill where, in true Colorado fashion, it was twenty degrees colder in the shade.

It was a taste of things to come. More than anything, Grey feared the sun setting. With the surrounding peaks so tall, evening came early in the valley. When it did, the sudden temperature drop would only add to the misery of the men. Of course, worse than that would be the dark itself; he knew that the monsters would be ten times harder to kill when they appeared to be nothing but moaning shadows against a black background. Fires just behind the lines would have to be kept going all night long and one girl, no matter how tough wouldn't be enough.

For two straight hours, Grey kept moving, going from platoon to platoon, sometimes encouraging the men, sometimes fighting alongside them and, infrequently, stopping at the radio. When it was answered, which was only about half the time, he would scream demands at whoever was on the other end of it. His company was getting desperate for ammunition. It was flying downrange at a ridiculous rate.

When two thousand rounds had been expended, Grey turned from the fight to stare back in the direction of the valley, hoping to see someone, anyone, coming, but the pine-studded hills were barren of life all save for the storm crows who watched the fight in a moody silence, waiting for their chance to feed. They had been eating well, these crows. They were plump as partridges and struggled to gain altitude when they bothered to fly.

"Son of a bitch," Grey swore as the sound of an explosion jerked his head to the north. A grenade, he hoped. It would be a bad sign if a mortar crew was working already. When no further explosions were added to the first, and there was only the ongoing tat-tat-tat of distant gunfire, he relaxed the tiniest bit. There were a total of five gun battles going on. Three were large affairs like at the Big Thompson, and two were smaller brush-ups where rarely a dozen guns would get into the mix.

There would be more battles, he knew. The longer the soldiers fought the undead to a standstill in the larger valleys, the more the smaller, finger-like gullies branching off of them would fill up. Each would have to be held, each defended, each a drain on their supplies.

If Sadie was correct and the numbers of zombies exceeded a quarter-million, then there was going to be a simple problem of math that the people of the valley were going to run into: according to the quartermaster, they had just above 80,000 rounds of 5.56mm ammunition, 6,000 of the fast flowing 7.62mm ammo used by the heavy machine guns, and another 10,000 or so rounds of various calibers for the very wide assortment of civilian weapons.

The deficit was worrisome.

Every bullet had to count. His men simply could not afford to miss. With this on his mind, Grey waded into the rising river. When the fight had begun, the waters had been an inch or two above his knee, now, after they had built a veritable damn of bodies stretching all the way across the river, the water was at his diaphragm. "Men!" he bellowed over the sound of the guns. "Move up! Move up! Get as close as you can get."

They had been shooting at a distance of about fifty yards, and had it not been for the icy water and their numb hands, and the fact that their targets were the size of melons and were constantly in motion, the men could hardly miss, but given these factors, only half their shots were striking home. It was unacceptable.

Grey led the way, pushing deeper and deeper until the freezing water was just below his nipples. The water was so cold that it physically hurt. He moved right up to the mound of dead bodies that the stiffs were struggling over and shot the first one from point blank range. "Keep them on the other side! Make this our line, men! Do not let any get by!"

His men, their teeth chattering and holding their guns up out of the water, drew up in a new line stretching across the water and began firing. They were, as always, very thorough and professional, not wasting a bullet, and just as important, they didn't waste any energy bitching about the cold or their crap assignment. They called a target, fired, pressed the warm stock of their weapons to their face for a moment, called another target and fired again.

When he saw that his men were well in hand, he splashed ashore to find that help had finally arrived in the form of Neil Martin. For some strange reason, Neil had changed out of the ill-fitting BDUs he had been wearing and was back to jeans, a denim shirt and a bright yellow sweater vest. The only nod that he gave to the fact that they were at war was that he still had on his jungle boots and had not gone back to wearing the fruity crocs. He waved at Grey, as if this was a chance meeting during a nature walk.

Thankfully, he wasn't alone. Behind him in a long line were forty civilians: an equal mix of men and women, each weighed down with boxes or bags. Grey was happy to see that the majority of it was ammo. The rest was food and water.

Neil nodded judiciously at the four platoon rotation set up and then pointed at the brisk battle going on and said: "Very good. Looks like you have the situation in hand."

Grey found himself frowning. Something was different about Neil. It was in the way he was looking at Grey as though he expected some sort of explanation or report. The strangeness was also in the way the other civilians were looking at Neil like he was something new and not the same quiet man who had been all over the valley during the last week walking with Sadie or just picking flowers. They were looking at him with a mixture of confusion and awe.

"I suppose we're doing ok," Grey answered.

Jauntily, Neil said: "Good! I've brought you some volunteers. What do you need of them?"

The captain shot a puzzled glance at the civilians before he asked: "*You* brought volunteers?" Neil had been one of the quietest people in the valley. It seemed unlikely that he could round up anyone besides a few of the renegades they had come in with. There were only two in the group: Connie Markson, a brave and steadfast woman, and William Gates, who was giving Grey a hard look.

William's sister-in-law, Marybeth Gates had been going downhill steadily since their arrival. There were no actual doctors in the valley. The closest thing they had was an ex-emergency room nurse, who was in way over her head when it came to Marybeth's case. Grey could offer little advice except to pump her full of fluids, morphine, and antibiotics, and then pray for all they were worth. One thing Grey knew was that another surgery would mean her death.

In the last week, Grey had little time to visit Marybeth, which was a sore spot with the family. He gave William a curt nod before turning back to Neil. "We need these people to…" he started to say, however Neil interrupted him.

"My people, you mean."

"Is there something going on that I should know about?" Grey asked.

"You haven't heard? I've been appointed the interim acting Governor of Estes Valley. General Johnston stepped down this afternoon. He'll still be in charge of the military but he answers to me and, before you ask, yes, it's weird."

This brought a chuckle from Grey. "I'd say it was more than weird, it's downright strange. But I guess it is what it is and it doesn't affect our current situation or our current needs. We need wood, lots of it. It'll be dark soon and we'll need light to fight. If we can't keep fires going, this position will be untenable. And we'll need more food and ammo."

Neil nodded and clapped his hands together like an eager basketball coach. "Ok, you heard the Captain. Divide yourself into four squads of ten people each. We're going to need one group to go back to the valley and get a bunch of chainsaws and axes. The other three squads will start scrounging for dead wood. Let's get moving."

They moved out smartly without the least grumbling. William looked as though he wanted to say something to Grey, but thankfully Neil pulled the soldier aside.

"You know about the ammo issue, correct?" Neil only allowed Grey to dip his head once before he went on: "If Sadie's right about the numbers, we're going to be in serious trouble."

"She is right," Grey replied. "If I had to guess on how this will play out, the Azael will sap our strength using the horde. It will be three or four days of endless zombie attacks followed by a military strike. Though my biggest fear is what they have in surprise for us. Remember what Brad said about their military having 'toys' too. I'm praying that they're pinning their hopes on tanks; they would be practically useless in this mountain terrain. Gunships would be bad. A good helicopter pilot would be able to use the hills to devastating effect. Artillery would also..."

"We can't worry about that just yet," Neil said, interrupting. "The truth is if we run out of ammunition none of that will matter." There was indeed truth in that, a deadly truth. "I need your advice, Grey. Do we just keep going as we are and hope there are fewer zombies than we have bullets?"

"I think we can't stake our existence on hope. We are going to have to deal with this old school. Have some of your people scrounge up baseball bats, hammers, sledgehammers, spears, swords, tire irons, and machetes. Basically, anything that can be swung to deadly effect. We're going to have to go toe-to-toe."

Neil leaned in close and asked: "What about our artillery? Shouldn't we use it?"

The soldier shook his head. "Only in an emergency. We only have so many rounds and it's best to save them."

"Then it will be hand-to-hand combat," Neil said and then clapped Grey on the shoulder. "Good luck, here."

Grey punched Neil in the arm as though they were brothers. "You keep your luck. You're going to need it as governor." Neil started to leave, but Grey grabbed him by the back of the sweater vest. "And do me a favor; take Sadie back to the valley. She's run herself into the ground." Neil started to turn away and Grey spun him back a second time. "How's Deanna," Grey asked, his voice pitched low. "Tell me she's somewhere safe."

"She is. I've appointed her to my one-person staff. I thought about bringing Sadie on board, but I know that she would just get frustrated at how people are and then she'd start threatening them with her pistol. That's a bad precedent to set."

With a grin, Grey asked: "What about Fred Trigg? You know that if he's not on your staff…in other words if he's not safe and warm, he's going to make life hell for you."

"I should send him here," Neil said looking out at the soldiers who were shooting zombies at point blank range. Neil went a touch green at the sight of the blood spraying and the rotting brains splattering, and the ugly waterlogged mound of corpses where arms and legs stuck out at odd angles, and the pooled river water which was dark red; even the shoreline where the soldiers crawled out onto dry land was stained maroon with old blood.

"Please don't, for our sakes," Grey said. "This is the River Styx already. No sense making it worse."

The name: The River Styx had been overheard and it stuck. The water was hell, but it got worse when the first delivery of melee weapons arrived. There were three basic weapon types at hand: the bludgeoners, your baseball bats, your tire irons, your basic cudgels; these crushed skulls, turning them to pulp. Then there were the bladed weapons: axes, machetes and in one case, an actual saber. It was a terrible weapon. The blade of the saber started dull and it only became more so every time a skull was struck.

The last type Grey labeled as *miscellaneous*. An African spear with a metaled tip was found, four stout table legs with long screws were provided, three poles with metal tips were stripped of their flags and hauled down to the river and lastly, a number of lengths of copper pipes were in use. These were odd weapons in that they "clanged" with a disjointed musical sound every time they struck a skull just right.

Eventually, as night fell and each man had his gun traded for a melee weapon, the battle became surreal. Grey figured it had to be the quietest battle in the history of war. On one side, the enemy came on in an eternal moan—a long, soulless, haunting sound that was enough to shiver the heart of the hardest warrior. On the other side of the fight came the grunt of men too tired to speak.

Their work went on hour after weary hour. As a plus, wielding melee weapons the way they were was hard exercise and they were able to bear the near freezing temperatures better than they had. As a negative, death was so, so close; at best it was just over an arm's length away; sometimes it was inches away.

Grey shared the fate of his men. Wherever the fighting was thickest, he would charge into battle wielding the saber that had been passed from man to man, each quickly discovering that the blade was too dull for the job of killing in a quick strike. Whenever he took a break, Grey honed the blade endlessly.

The fight was deadly to friend and foe alike. Even on the sloping hills above the river it wasn't easy. Each man had to rely on the man higher up on the hill as they soon grew too tired to strike at any angle other than downwards. It took nerves of steel to ignore a creature coming at them with their mouth agape and their teeth slashing in.

Still, nothing beat the river for outright terror. No fire could be built behind the line of men, and with the dark, the creatures were horrifying shadows that suddenly morphed into real terrors, always just within arm's reach. Grey fought here, exclusively.

Hours went by and every stroke of the saber was a torture for him. His soaking wet uniform clung to his body, pulling tight to his arms and shoulders, restricting his swings and adding what felt like fifty pounds to his body. He slogged back and forth through the river, fighting until his muscles ached. By the time the moon finally peeked over the mountain, he was thinking he wouldn't be able to go on much longer.

And then a scream erupted. So far, there had been a few angry shouts and some curses at near misses mixed with the moans of the undead, but they were infrequent. The scream was blood curdling. It snapped Grey's head around. He was standing where he had thought the line was the weakest, where the men needed him most—he was wrong.

57

Chapter 8

Private First Class Paul Wesley

The battle at the River Styx became a test of human endurance, both physically and mentally. It was beyond medieval. It was an endless slaughter punctuated by what felt like the briefest respite spent in front of a fire. These respites weren't long enough to make a dint in the exhaustion of the men. All the men were feeling the strain except, of course, for Captain Grey, who was in the thick of every battle.

He seemed to spend half his time in the river, swinging the saber until it went as dull as a butter knife and began to bounce off the skulls of the undead. He would then look at his weapon as if it were an old friend who had betrayed him by not keeping up with his inhuman pace.

PFC Wesley could commiserate with the sword. He was sure he wasn't going to keep up the frantic pace of the fight. He had seen nothing like it. The stiffs slithered and crawled over the mound in a relentless wave of grey bodies and always they came at the soldiers mouth first, showing their cracked and fissured teeth; it was the stuff nightmares were made of.

Things had been bad when they had first started banging away with their M4s. The killing was ugly, and the red-brown water they stood thigh-deep in had been worse. Then the captain had ordered them forward so that the killing was up close in 'living' color.

That had been much worse.

What was much, much worse was when they had been told to switch out their guns for sticks and hunks of metal. "What the hell?" Wesley whispered to the man next to him, a tall ginger with a drooping nose like the beak of a parakeet. "They don't expect us to fight with this stuff?"

The ginger's name was Kaslowski; he stood a head taller over Wesley, who was built along the lines of a fire hydrant. Kaslowski, who went by the abbreviation: Kas, bent low to speak into Wesley's ear: "Trust the captain. He knows what he's doing. He's probably conserving ammo."

That was a scary thought; in Wesley's mind, conserving ammo equated to a shortage of ammo. When it was his turn to pick from the remaining weapons, he jumped at the opportunity to take one of the table legs. It seemed to be the sturdiest of the rather pathetic weapons arrayed before them. His friend Kas grabbed an aluminum bat that seemed to have been made for a little leaguer and had asked in a beggy sort of whisper to trade. Wesley wished he had.

The table leg had been the better weapon…at first. It was so heavy that it could cave in a skull with ease. Unfortunately, the weight of it had a serious drawback—after an hour Wesley was gasping for breath and his arms felt like they were weighed down by lead. The five-inch screws jutting out of the head of the weapon had a bad habit of snagging either in the remnants of clothing or in the loose skin of the zombies, causing Wesley to have to expend as much energy pulling the weapon free as he did in the initial strike. On top of that, each time he hit home with his weapon, it bit into his frozen hands until he had blisters growing on top of his blisters.

His grip on the table leg grew weaker and weaker and he was forced, time and again to step back and ask his friend Kas to cover him as he readjusted his hands on the awkward hunk of wood. With its beveled edge and its gentle curve it was just not designed to be wielded as a weapon.

Kas didn't understand. He would step up because they were friends, but he would do so with a look. It was a look that nagged at Wesley as much as his running blisters. They were *Soldiers of the Valley* and that was supposed to mean something. It was why Wesley went at it long after he should've asked to be pulled from the line. His pride was greater than his pain and weariness. It was so great that it ended up killing him.

"How much…longer…till…we switch?" he asked Kas through chattering teeth. Whenever they were in the river, it felt like time slowed to a crawl.

"Eight minutes," Kas gasped before pounding a zombie in the head. The first blow stunned the creature and dented its skull. It took a second blow to send shards of bone into the thing's near useless brain.

Wesley took his own swing at yet another zombie; the impact nearly jarring the table leg out of his frozen fingers. When he looked down at his hands, they seemed welded into the clawed position needed to hold the wood. He tried straightening the right one out but it wouldn't bend. "Fuck," he said as he waited on the next stiff. With the mound being so large now, they came every five seconds or so.

The next one; however, was fast and it was there in two. It was also a particularly virile looking zombie and yet Wesley felt no fear. Part of his lack of fear was exhaustion, which deadened his emotions and part was the knowledge that no matter how big it was it was just a stiff. It was nothing to fear as long as Wesley stuck to his training and his natural skills.

It crawled over the pile of bodies, crabbing eternally on, pushed forward by the relentless force of those behind and drawn by its greedy hunger. Wesley took aim and swung the table leg. The swing bore little resemblance to his first swing, which had been a Babe Ruth-like homerun swing. This swing was halting and because of the ache in his hands and his exhaustion, it lacked the finishing power. Worse, it was ill-aimed. The pile of corpses was uneven and a three inch drop was all the difference between a perfect hit square on the top of the cranium and a miss with deadly repercussions.

The leg glanced off the temple of the beast, tore its ear half off before the screws jutting from the varnished wood bit good and hard into the zombie's shoulder. The strike hurt Wesley far more than it did the zombie. Pain zinged up his wrists, loosening his grip even more, and thus it took only a spasming buck from the beast to wrest the table leg from his hands.

For the moment he was weaponless; this didn't cause the scream that had Grey lunging through the water as fast as he could push his exhausted body.

Unlike so many cowards outside the valley who wore the uniform but who owed their continued existence to running and hiding, Wesley was a real soldier, a veteran of countless battles against what felt like infinite numbers of undead. His main weapon might have been wrested from his grip, but he wasn't close to being panicked. Quick as a wink, his right hand went for his Ka-bar. It was out, flashing silver in the weak light of the fires that the civilians were keeping alight just behind the lines.

With confidence borne of skill and experience, he sunk the seven-inch blade up to the hilt right into the temple of the zombie. It struck home with a solid thunking sound as bone gave way to the sharpest metal.

"Cover me, Kas," he said with an almost casual air, to his friend, because why wouldn't he be casual? Hadn't he fought this fight in one of its many permutations a hundred times before? The icy river was different, but his exhaustion was familiar and the zombie with its grey skin and the foul, evil hunger in its eyes was ever unchanging. He had been here before and he expected to be here ten years hence, doing the same thing: killing so that others could live free.

Yet, this time was different and he was the last to realize it. Again, there was a casualness to him as his left hand went to the forehead of the zombie to pull the blade free, only as he extended his hand, he saw that he had, for the first time, missed his mark. By some quirk, or by some slight movement of the beast, or some unforeseen shift in the pile of dead or some evil intrigue brought upon him by the constantly moving water of the river, the blade had not pierced the thin bone of its temple. Instead it had traversed through the thing's ear at a downward angle to come out below its jaw line.

What would have been debilitating to any human, barely fazed the zombie. For all intents and purposes, the blade had all the effect on the zombie as if Wesley had stuck a feather in its ear.

Where Wesley was slowed by confusion and the drag of many hours of fighting in the line, the zombie was just as full of its vile vigor as when it first woke in its undead state. It grabbed Wesley's left hand with both of its hands and before Wesley knew it, three of his fingers were in the thing's mouth, and ragged, diseased teeth were crushing down with unstoppable power. The pain was sharp, unbelievably sharp; however, the realization that he was now a dead man was what caused him to come unglued. He pulled his hand away, saw the raw stumps and simply lost it.

His mind blanked and he *reacted*.

Reacting was one of those things his captain had long preached against. A soldier reacting to his environment was a soldier one step behind, a soldier one second too late. Captain Grey preached making the enemy react to you.

61

Wesley was too far gone down the roads of panic and exhaustion. He pulled his hand away, inadvertently yanking the zombie toward him. It came down off the mound with a splash and promptly disappeared. The waters, once clear and clean, were now a murky soup of blood, chunks of zombie, and half submerged corpses.

"It's in there!" Wesley screamed at the top of his lungs. "It's in there somewhere!"

He tried to run but his foot slipped on the round, slimed-over rocks and he sunk up to his chin which only had his spazzing worse. He could think of nothing except getting away. The soldiers around him were also backing away from the thrashing man and the turbulent waters. A zombie under the water was a dangerous thing. It was likely turned around or upside down and would bite the first thing it came in contact with.

Four men backing from the line would doom their position if things weren't fixed quickly. Just at that moment, Wesley didn't care about the line. There was a zombie in the water and it was worse than any shark that had ever lived. As he struggled to get away, he ran into Captain Grey who picked him up out of the water with one hand.

"What the hell's going on?" he growled.

"There's a z-zombie in the w-water," Wesley said. He went to point but the stumps of his fingers drew all of his attention and he could only gape at his hand, his mind tipping over. The other soldiers were pointing in the general direction of where Wesley had been standing.

Grey barked: "There's going to be a dozen of them in the water if you don't do your jobs." Dropping Wesley, he stabbed his saber into the riverbed, pulled the M4 off his back and shot it six times at the slithering undead crawling over the mound. Six more corpses were added to the mound. He then reslung the weapon and rearmed himself with the saber.

Boldly he stepped forward, running the sword through the water until it struck something meaty. "Here it is," he said, lifting the zombie out of the water. He had speared it under the armpit and now it wiggled at the end of the metal as it tried to thrust itself further onto the sword to get at Grey. It was a hideous sight.

Wesley found himself unable to look away, unable to think past the terrible fact that the zombie had his fingers in its belly. He had the irrational thought that they were still good and that all it would take to reattach them was to snap them back in place.

"Kas!" Grey snapped. "What are you waiting for? Kill this thing."

"Careful of its stomach," Wesley hissed. Its stomach; that's where his fingers were, of course. Kas stepped forward and brought the dented-up aluminum bat down with one vicious stroke and stove in the thing's head.

Without regard to the fingers that were likely still wriggling inside of it, Grey flung the now dead zombie into the river. "Get back in line, men. And let's try to keep our heads on straight. We don't want to frighten the civilians with..." He stopped in midsentence as he saw Wesley's bleeding hand. Grey's hard look softened at once and he whispered: "Oh, holy hell."

"I'm so sorry," Wesley said, suddenly realizing that not only had he lost his fingers, he had let his captain down. "I didn't mean it, sir. I-I missed. The table leg got caught and...and then the knife..."

"Hey, don't worry about that stuff now," Grey said, gently taking Wesley's arm.

He began to lead Wesley out of the water, but Wesley stopped and pointed at the corpse. "It still has my fingers. We should get them back."

"Let's get you to the fire, first and then I'll go back and get them."

"But it's not yet time for the fire, sir," Wesley replied, stopping again. Now that the finger-eating zombie was dead, Wesley was beginning to feel like himself again, all except for the shakes that had entered his chest and limbs. It was adrenaline at having such a close call, he told himself and not the virus. "I need to get back in the line. It's not fair to everyone else that I get to go warm up early. In fact, I should be pulling a double for messing up. That's what I'll do."

He started to pull back from Grey's grip, but his captain was far too strong. "No, let's get you to the fire."

Wesley was propelled to one of the fires further back where the civilians rested when they had a moment. There was only a single girl at the fire and she seemed dressed in shadows. Only her pale face stood out from her dark clothes. She had been looking sleepy; however, when she saw it was Captain Grey coming, she perked up. "We're going to be pulled out of the line in two hours and given a six-hour rest. 12th Company is going to take our place."

"Our place?" Grey asked. "Since when did you join the Army?"

As he spoke, he helped Wesley down. Out of habit, Wesley stuck his hands out to the fire. The left, with its three little stumps dripping blood, fascinated him to such a degree that he could barely follow what was going on around him. The two spoke for a bit, then there was a long quiet and then the girl seemed concerned with Wesley, and his captain asked if he was in pain.

"I don't feel anything, sir," Wesley answered, hiding his hand close to his body. "It's the cold water. I just need a couple of minutes to warm up, then I'll be good to go."

"Get him some food and water," the captain said to the girl.

Wesley shook his head. "No food. I-I don't want any food. And just a sip or two of water. I don't need any more than that. It should last me until..." Wesley stopped speaking, abruptly. He was having the darnedest time coming to grips with what was happening to him. His mind was swirling with images of the zombie and its grinning mouth and the blood...his blood in its teeth. The image kept coming, over and over again. Then he would lift up his hand and wiggle the little stumps.

"How am I going to fight?" he asked his hand at one point. He felt like he was cracking up. Time was getting away from him as well. At one point he looked up from his hand and found himself alone at the fire, at another point the girl was suddenly there with a water bottle filled with brown liquid.

"Hot cocoa," she said.

He tried to push it away. "I have to go," he told her. "I'm needed in the line."

She shoved the bottle at him and there was an edge to her voice when she said: "Drink it. Those are your orders."

It was good and the heat of it went right to his heart. He hid his mangled hand from himself by stuffing it into his BDU blouse. He thought he was ready to go and he looked around for Captain Grey in order to demand to be sent back to the line. There was a constant motion all around him. Civilians, long lines of them came and went. They carried heavy burdens: wood and wiring, boxes and crates. They were everywhere but, for what seemed like ages, there was no sign of Captain Grey.

He finally came back, carrying a man across his shoulders. When he laid the man down, Wesley leaned back away from him with a gasp. The soldier's face was half-eaten away: his nose was nothing but a bloody hole, he was missing an eye, and his right cheek had been torn off so that an entire row of teeth was visible.

"Who is this?" Grey was demanding. At first Wesley thought his captain was asking him and so he tried to make out the mauled soldier's features, but found it impossible. But Grey wasn't talking to him. The captain was on the radio. "Horner? This is Red River Leader. Where's the Goat Man? I need to talk to him."

There was a pause in which the chewed-up soldier breathed out bubbles of blood and then Grey was speaking again. "This is Red River Leader. I need eyes on my position ASAP."

The radio crackled: "Four minutes."

In those four minutes, two more men were brought to the fire. Although neither seemed bloodied in any way, they both looked like they were at death's door. They were uniformly white, had listless, glazed-over eyes, and both shook from head to toe. One was Wesley's friend Kas and the other was a sergeant from 3rd Platoon named Renfro.

"Hypothermia," Kas said. "I'll be good as new in a few minutes. I just need something for this headache."

Renfro shook his head. "Ain't no hypothermia. We're as fucked as this guy." He gestured at the man who was missing most of his face. Wesley's eyes lasered in on Renfro's hand; in the webbing between the thumb and index finger there was blood and ragged, loose skin where a number of blisters had formed one over the other, each bursting and then tearing away until there was no more skin to tear. Renfro was bleeding.

Kas looked at his own hands—he was bleeding as well.

"It doesn't mean anything," Wesley said. "You may not be infected. I'm not and I'm worse off than any of you." Renfro and Kas looked away and said nothing. "I'm not infected!" Wesley insisted. The poor guy stretched out on the ground was certainly infected, and Renfro sure looked like he was turning a shade of grey beneath his pallor, but Kas was always very white and Wesley felt fine.

Yes, his hand had begun to thrum and sharp pains had started to shoot up in his temples, and he was beginning to sweat, but none of that meant he was infected.

"I'm fine," he said when the silence around the fire had carried on for too long. He held up his left hand, which still trickled blood. He thought that was a good sign. It was washing away the germs. "I'm a righty anyway, and I don't need a left hand to kill the stiffs. Kas, can I borrow your bat?"

Kas stared around with his washed-out eyes until he saw the bat sitting in a bush a few feet away. He reached for it as Renfro buried his head in his hands and groaned in pain. Before Kas could hand it over, there was a blare of lights that had the three lucid soldiers cringing. The light seemed to carry with it needles of fire that burned right into the stem of their eyes.

"Turn that shit off!" Renfro screamed.

A dark figure, like a ten-foot tall demon, stalked toward them, its face filled with rage. Wesley grabbed the bat and brought it back, only before he could swing it a hand caught his arm.

It was the captain. "Careful, Wesley." He nodded at the demon, and now Wesley saw that it wasn't a demon at all. It was General Johnston and his face was far from angry. He looked sad.

"Let's move these men back to the valley," the general said in a tone so low it was hard to pick out over the crackling fire.

The captain agreed with a nod. "For their sake and for the morale of the others. It's the river, sir. The water is not just as cold as ice, it's also diseased. It has become a pool of filth. And perhaps worse, it's rising. Every stiff we kill adds to the dam, which then adds to the height of the water. I have men trying to fight with the water up to their armpits. It's treacherous."

"And your suggestion?" Johnston asked.

"M240s," Grey said. "We can set them up at head-height on the riverbanks."

Johnston drew in a sharp breath at the suggestion. "I can't authorize that. I'm sorry. We have less than four thousand rounds left. It has to be preserved in case of a general attack by the Azael. Is there any way we can continue a defense with hand weapons?"

Grey shrugged. "Of course, but we can expect a very heavy casualty rate. The men aren't accustomed to these sorts of weapons. Kaslowski, hold up your hands. You see, it's just blisters. Any cut or scratch is a death sentence. We have to change tactics."

"Then we use the big guns," Johnston concluded. Now it was Grey's turn to look skeptical to which Johnston said: "We're out of choices. Mortars won't cut it in the river. The water will absorb too much of the force of the explosions. They'd be a waste. And we don't have a large enough stockpile of 7.62 rounds to make a difference. It wouldn't last an hour. It has to be artillery. A few rounds will decimate them and buy us some time."

Wesley watched the exchange with little comprehension. He understood the deadly nature of the virus as well as anyone; however, he just couldn't wrap his mind around the idea that the deadly germs could have possibly entered *his* system. After all, he had fought the beasts for so many long months. There had been a dozen times he had gone into battle with cuts or scratches and he had always been fine.

"We don't need artillery!" he declared to both of the officers. His headache was making him cranky and the way they were both tap-dancing around the real issue was annoying. "What we need is for men to step up." He snatched up Kas's bat and brandished it. "We need to keep fighting like we were trained to do."

He started marching off toward the river when Captain Grey magically appeared at his side. "Wesley, no. We have plenty of men for the job. You need to rest."

Wesley could not admit to himself what everyone else knew, at least not on a conscious level. It was his subconscious that was the cause of the tears that ran down his face, unnoticed. "I'm fine. I really am," he said. "Fine enough to crack a few skulls." The laugh that accompanied this was burdened by a sob which he couldn't explain. He pulled his arm from Grey's strong grip and pleaded: "Let me do my job."

Grey stared for a moment and then put a hand on Wesley's shoulder. "Ok, soldier. Do your duty."

"Thanks," Wesley gushed. "You can count on me."

"I know I can," his captain said. The officer watched him for a second and then turned to General Johnston and practically ordered: "Spin up the artillery."

For reasons Wesley could not understand, he felt an urgent need to get back into the line before the artillery struck home. He went straight away for the river though he had no idea if this was where his platoon was. He simply knew that was where the fighting was the hardest and he was a warrior in his heart.

With the bat cocked, he waded in with a battle cry that screamed out of his soul. It was filled with anger and sorrow and the pain that had built up inside of him. The bat was so easy compared to the table leg. It clanged off of skull after skull sending strange vibrations up his arm. It was so easy to kill with it that Wesley understood how Kas had formed blisters so quickly.

The bat was light enough to wield without tiring. He had clubbed down a dozen stiffs and all around him the unknown soldiers had backed away in awe of the one-handed soldier.

When the first of the 105mm shells ripped through the night sky with what sounded to Wesley like a rebel yell, he joined in.

A hundred yards downstream, the shell exploded fifty feet above the surface of the river in a tremendous fireball. The soldiers in the river hunkered low in the foul soup of blood and fleshy chunks. Wesley did not. His battle cry rang out in the gaping silence that followed. There were still zombies to kill and there was still time to kill them, not much time it felt, but enough.

Shell after shell screamed overhead, landing with pinpoint accuracy in the river, changing forever its course and composition. Great hollows and deep pools were dug in seconds and for years afterwards they were lined with the shards of millions of pale bones.

Wesley gloried in the destruction. He felt as though he had reached some sort of peak in his life and he strove with all of his dwindling strength to retain the feeling because on some level he knew the feeling would be fleeting.

And it was.

He was witness to twenty explosions of epic proportions and in that time, he killed thirty of the beasts. He was standing on the dam of the dead, exhausted, breathing out great gasps and wondering why his head was splitting and his arms were as heavy as downed tree trunks when he saw streaks in the sky. They were lines of fire, but they were heading the wrong way! They were heading towards the valley.

His eyes tracked the progress of the streaks until they disappeared behind the far hill and then there was a pause, followed by a flash of light and a distant rumble. "Shit," he whispered. Even with his head pounding like the worst hangover he had ever experienced, he knew what the lights had been: counter-battery fire. The Azael had waited with unexpected patience to unleash their own artillery and now they were filling the Estes Valley with deadly shrapnel.

Wesley waited for the answering shots coming from his side, but there were none. The Azael fired round after round without a single shot in response. "They're all dead," he whispered. He could picture the burned-out wreckage of the valley's four guns. He could almost smell the charred flesh. Unbelievably he felt a sudden pang of hunger.

"Fuck that!" he raged.

Although the artillery had practically vaporized the entire horde of zombies flowing up the Big Thompson, there were still a few hundred to take care of. Private First Class Paul Wesley planted his feet on the dam of corpses. At that time, it was horribly impressive in its dimensions; it ran the length of the gorge cut out by the river and was as wide as a four-lane highway. He stood in its direct center and swung his bat one-handed, cursing in a screeching voice. His head felt like it was about to split wide open, but at least he was warm.

The zombie fever baked the chill of the river right out of him. It made him numb to everything except the desire to do his duty. He wasn't going to let his fellow soldiers down again no matter what. No matter that there were zombies all around his legs feasting on his flesh. That didn't matter. The only thing that mattered to him was making sure no one else would die that night.

Chapter 9
Jillybean

As night fell, the Azael grew as eager as children on Christmas Eve. They sensed that victory was only hours away and they went about grinning or rubbing their hands, greedily. Their tremendous zombie hordes had been whipped and kicked and pushed up the twin highways leading to Estes. This undead army was unstoppable, invincible. Their numbers were beyond count...though Jillybean had a fair estimation.

The seven-year-old had found her stomach aching at the sight of the seemingly endless march of the monsters and her nerves jangled and tears were close as Eve hissed in her ear about killing and blood and what baked brains would taste like. *She* was trying to break Jillybean's mind. As a refuge, the little girl threw herself into the intricate dance that numbers unexpectedly revealed.

Jillybean scrounged up paper and pens and began to explore math in a manner similar to how a person might take on the Rocky Mountains. She trudged her way uphill against the incomprehensible numbers through sheer will, her progress aided on some occasions by sudden intuitive leaps and on other occasions by Kay, who would explain various things such as the multiplication tables or long division.

Then the way before her would suddenly open up and there would be vistas of understanding as majestic as any mountain and as beautiful as any lush valley.

It wasn't long before she could solve the simplest algebraic equations with barely a pause and she was well down the path to learning the principles of Superposition, though she had no idea of its official name, when the shooting from the west began to taper off.

Everyone agreed that it was a portentous sign and that the end couldn't be long in coming. Everyone included Eve, who pushed her way past the math and to the forefront of Jillybean's mind.

Stupid Neil is dying, Eve said in a hissing whisper. *He's being eaten right now. Same with dumb 'ol Sadie and all of them. They're being eaten alive. Aren't you glad we killed that ugly baby?*

"Oh, shut up!" Jillybean snapped.

Why? You should be happy we killed her. If we hadn't, she would be being eaten alive along with the rest of them right now, and wouldn't that be sad?

"I said zip it! I didn't kill her at all. It was you. And besides, you don't know what's going on up there."

Kay, who was sitting as far from Jillybean as possible, which because of the handcuffs, was the seat next to her on the bus, gave her arm a jerk, yanking Jillybean halfway around. "You're doing it again."

The woman got the heebie-jeebies whenever Jillybean spoke to Eve; it was a visible reaction. Her lip would curl, her eyebrows would drop into a line across the lower ridge of her forehead, and sometimes she would do a weird shimmy as if a giant spider were walking up her spine.

"Sorry. I can't really help it," Jillybean said, not looking up. That wasn't exactly the truth. She could control Eve as long as she could control her fear. Just then she was afraid for her friends. The gradual decrease in the amount of gunfire from across the tips of the mountains most likely meant that the people of Colorado were being overwhelmed. She could picture them trapped in dark caves with mobs of the hateful monsters struggling to get in.

This fear made Eve strong.

Jillybean decided to refocus on the work she was doing. Eve hated math, it sent her sulking in some dark crevice of Jillybean's mind. Unfortunately, the evening was turning into a chill night and there wasn't any light on the bus. She tried squinting at her papers, but couldn't make out anything besides a few scratchings on a white background.

Yep, they're all getting eaten now. Chomp! Chomp! Chomp! Eve cackled.

Now it was Jillybean's turn to get a shiver up her spine. She tried to force her mind away from the awful visions that were filling it and was successful for a few hours. She was happily trying to calculate the number of monsters that had been drawn together in the Azael army when the bus door came open with a long, metal, creaking sound.

All of the women on the bus sat up straight as they had been trained to do, though not a one lifted their eyes from their laps.

Only Jillybean, who considered herself way too young to be a part of the adult things that were going on with the sad-looking women, dared to look up. It was a repetitive sight for her. Very tall men of the Azael were let onto the bus by the grizzled woman who was not only the bus driver but also the guard. The men would go down the aisle looking at the women, sometimes lifting their chins, sometimes opening their blouses.

The women never seemed to breathe during these times. The bus would be stone-quiet until one was picked and led away to the small pup-tents that were set up on the ground next to the bus. Only then would there be a collective breath let out by the remaining women.

This time was no different. It was one of the king's brothers who came in this time. Not many men were allowed to frequent the bus. Generally, only the royals with high ranks got to choose a woman. This big, bearded duke went by the name of Baldwin; he had a vile reputation and a voracious sexual appetite. A number of the women began to shake as he strutted onto the bus.

"It's fun time," he said, in a growly sort of voice. He stood at the front of the bus, behind the white line, gazing up the rows with an ugly grin on his face. When he started advancing, Kay grabbed Jillybean's hands, their handcuffs making a merry clinking sound as they shook.

Baldwin stopped a step from them and it was Jillybean he was looking at with perverse lust in his eyes. This smote her well down into her soul and there was an ensuing echo that caused her chest to hurt. What was he going to do with her? She had read, in the vague manner that dictionaries provided, what prostitutes did: they were 'sex workers' who engaged in sexual relations in exchange for payment.

She supposed being a prostitute was bad in some way, but she had never thought that it was dangerous. And yet, by the way the women were acting, Jillybean had every right to feel the fear blooming inside her.

"Has anyone gotten at you yet?" the duke asked her. Jillybean could only shake her head, not knowing exactly what was being asked of her.

Next to her, Kay slid away to the far side of the little padded bench they shared. Jillybean looked over at her but the woman was studiously staring forward. When the seven-year-old glanced back she found the duke leaning over her, one of his beefy paws on her skinny thigh.

"I'm n-not a prostitute," she stammered. She didn't even know what sex was beyond the little the dictionary had told her: a means of procreation. It was how babies were made, but she was too young. And she wasn't married. Only mommies and daddies made babies, not little girls. Everyone knew that.

"Well, you got to do something around here and it doesn't seem like we're going to need that big brain of yours." He seemed to be correct in this. The gunfire coming from the Estes Valley had petered into nothing two hours before. Any logical reading of that sign pointed to the complete destruction of the Colorado Army. "You're going to have to earn your keep another way."

The hand on her thigh tightened until it hurt. "I'm only seven," she gasped, unable to think of anything else.

Tell him, if he touches us, I'll cut off his balls, Eve said. The evil girl inside of her wasn't actually angry. She was looking forward to what was going to happen. She knew it would be her ticket to control of their shared body.

"Seven? Sounds like a perfect time to start training you." Baldwin put out his hand and Jillybean was forced to put her tiny one in it as though he were her daddy.

He is not daddy! Eve raged, growing stronger. *I'll kill him. I'll cut off...* Her rant was cut off as Jillybean was caught up suddenly. Baldwin had tugged her along so quickly that Kay hadn't had time to pick up the twenty-five pound dumbbell to which she was handcuffed.

"What the fuck?" the duke growled.

"I'm sorry, I don't have the key," Kay whined, as she struggled with the weight.

Baldwin's lip curled at Kay's battered face and then he muttered a curse as he saw the handcuffs. Jillybean thought he was going to explode in anger, but after a moment he shrugged and his features relaxed slightly. He said to Kay: "If you're going to come along, you might as well give the girl some pointers."

Kay blanched, unable to hide her look of disgust. "You want me to come with you? You want me to..." She seemed unable to go on.

"Yeah, and don't piss me off or you won't have any teeth left after I get through with you."

73

"Yes, sir," Kay said and then hefted her dumbbell. She pushed Jillybean ahead of her in a rush and was only slowed by the stairs of the bus which were difficult to manage, handcuffed as they were and with the fact that Jillybean found her legs practically giving out on her.

Duke Baldwin was going to do something to her; something bad judging by the reaction of the other women on the bus. She feared that he was going to put a baby inside of her. She was too small for a baby. She would be split wide open by it and her guts would pour out onto the dirt.

The thought had her going limp and, as Kay was in an awkward position with the heavy weight, they both toppled off the last step to land on the shoulder of the road where gravel bit into their hands.

Kay cried out since the handcuffs on the dumbbell had already chaffed away a good deal of skin and the remainder split and began to bleed. This infuriated Baldwin, who raised a hand to strike the woman, yet the blow did not fall. Just then there came a loud rumble from out of the west.

With his hand still raised, Baldwin turned to stare in the direction of the sound. Seconds later there came a flash of light from over the mountain. It lit up the darkness and was followed seconds later by the roar of an explosion that bounced along the rock walls of the highway.

"That can't be," Baldwin said.

"What is it?" Jillybean whispered.

Reluctantly and with a fading voice, Eve answered: *Artillery.*

The explosions continued, lighting up the sky and dimming the stars. The sex slaves on the bus were much encouraged by it. They crowded to one side of the bus and stared out, wearing broad grins as if they were kids watching a fireworks show.

Even Baldwin was caught staring. His brother Menis came hobbling out of the dark. "What the fuck is this?" he demanded.

Baldwin jerked in surprise. "Huh? Menis is that you? I was just...I was just..." He turned and pointed at Kay and Jillybean, his mouth opening and closing like a landed trout as he tried to think of something to say. Eventually, he came up with: "I was bringing them to see you. I figured you'd want to see the girl."

Menis looked into the frightened eyes of Jillybean. What he saw there, she didn't know. He was slow in answering. "I do. I knew we were celebrating a bit prematurely. Help them up. We should be with Augustus."

Jillybean was lifted to her feet by Baldwin; his grip on her arm was hard as iron. There was a warning look in his eyes—he didn't want her to say anything about what had almost happened. With a final, harder pinch, he let go and repeated the same process with Kay.

"Keep her quiet," Duke Baldwin whispered to Kay.

She nodded back. "She'll be quiet, I promise." Jillybean didn't know what she was supposed to be quiet about. She could be as quiet as anyone except for maybe Captain Grey who could walk through broken glass without making a sound. But was she supposed to be quiet about nearly being forced into being a sex worker? There was no way she would...except, who was she going to tell? Menis didn't seem to care about her at all; he only wanted to use her. That was true for the king as well. Kay was supposed to be her friend, but she was so very chicken that it was hard to tell.

Don't trust any of them, Eve said. Before Jillybean could whisper a 'No duh', the voice in her head went on: *Find a way to kill them*.

The thought rattled her because there wasn't any good reason why she shouldn't kill them. For once she had to agree with Eve, and Jillybean thought it a very bad sign.

Despite his wounded ankle, Duke Menis could get along very quickly on his crutches. The king had set up his tent fifty yards away and Menis beat Baldwin, Kay and Jillybean there by ten yards.

The king's tent was a long and tall, white affair, something like a tent to host outdoor parties in. Before it, roared a bonfire. With the monsters all pushed up the valley, the king and his brothers and a number of beautiful women sat around it, completely safe.

"Just in time to see the show, my brothers," Duke Paulus said. He was smiling but he was the only one. Everyone else had been hoping that the zombies had done the hard work for them.

The king had brought his grand damask-covered chair with him to the battlefield and now it was close enough to the fire for him to roast meat over the flames. Everyone else sat on folding chairs and seemed so much smaller and insignificant than the king. He coughed up something, chewed it for a second and then spat it into the fire where it hissed.

Augustus waited for the hissing to die away before saying: "Just get on with it."

"Of course," Paulus said. "We just have to wait on the computer to do its thing. This isn't easy you know. There is a lot of high-tech gadgetry involved. For instance there are two radars set up on those two peaks." He pointed up at two tall hills. "They feed data into the tracking computer and that allows us to triangulate the position of the enemy artillery."

"Will it work?" Augustus demanded. "That's all I want to know."

Paulus' smile dimmed slightly. "Yes. My man and I tested it a month ago. It was...wait! I have a green light!" He turned to look down the road where the 155mm howitzers were parked. With the dark and the distance, they were only strange needle-nosed machines to Jillybean. "On my mark," Paulus said into a radio, speaking with much importance. "Three, two, one—fire!"

A great orange blast of flame erupted from the muzzles of the howitzers. It was a blinding strobe light that had Jillybean trying to blink away bright blobs from her vision. Everyone around the fire sat quietly with their heads cocked as they listened for the distant explosions. When the rumble came to them, they broke into grins.

"Reload!" Paulus ordered into the radio. He looked at his watch and when thirty seconds had passed, he said: "On my mark. Three, two, one—fire!" Again, the dark was interrupted by a flash and a blast of sound. Again, everyone listened and when the sound came this time, they cheered.

"You better give them one more round," Augustus told his brother, "just to be on the safe side."

Paulus was only too happy to obey. When he had gone through the sequence and the air shook and more people died in the valley, and there was only silence from the west, the Azael clapped their hands. Paulus bowed to his brother, the king, and said: "Now that I have destroyed their artillery, they will be helpless against us. Whatever walls they have left, I can blow to smithereens. They will be at our mercy."

"*My* mercy, I think you mean," Augustus said.

Again, Paulus bowed. "Of course, my brother and my king. It is your mercy that they will have to rely on because I will rain fire down on their heads. By noon tomorrow, my artillery will wipe away all opposition and the stiffs will flood that valley. The soldiers will have no choice but to run or hide."

"Noon?" Menis asked with an air of innocence. "Why not blast them away now?"

A twitch turned part of Paulus' smile down, but only for a second. "Because my spotters need to be able to see their targets. I guess they didn't teach you this in school, Menis, but radar works on the principle of line of sight. It can't see through mountains."

There was general laughter at this to which Menis smiled dangerously. When Paulus started going on about what a stroke of genius it had been of his to bring the artillery and how he was even then ready to send his spotters out so that they would be in position at first light, Menis bent down and whispered in Jillybean's ear: "Why won't this work?"

Surprised at the question, Jillybean could only shrug her slim shoulders. "It will work. I know what 'splosions are and what bombs are. If there are walls, a bomb will blow them up."

"That's all you have for me?" Menis asked, icily. "You are here only because of your brains. You had better use them or I will find another use for you, one you won't care for."

The threat proved valuable. Jillybean's mind clicked into overdrive as she examined the variables before her: artillery, targets, spotters, 'splosions, and walls. The most obvious reason why Paulus' plan wouldn't work was that his artillery could miss their targets.

That's what spotters are for, stupid head, Eve said in her usual unhelpful manner.

No other answer came to mind. Experience had taught her that no wall was strong enough to stop bombs. Paulus' plan would work unless... Jillybean had simply thrown the 'unless' in there since her future rested on finding one.

There had to be an 'unless.' She stepped around Duke Menis so that the fire was behind her and she could see down the road a bit. The king had halted his human army well back; there were thousands of them, some in the bright armor that Brad Crane wore, but most were dressed in the mad swirl of the multi-hued scarves.

Strangely, none wore the camouflage that Captain Grey was always uniformed in. Right away, she saw that was an enormous mistake on their part. The scarf outfits were 'good enough' to fool the monsters, but against the soldiers of the valley the Azael would be ideal targets.

"Excuse me, Mister Duke Paulus, sir," Jillybean said, breaking in on the king's brother as he spoke at length.

At first he glared; however, there was still enough of the old mores left in the group that it seemed impolite to be harsh to a little girl when she was as cute as Jillybean was. Displaying a faux fatherly air, he asked: "Yes?"

"Can I ask where your spotters are?"

Now Paulus let his sneer show. "What's that to you?"

"Because..." She paused to glance up at Menis. "I think I see a mistake in your plan."

Menis stepped up next to her, quickly. "A mistake?" he asked with surprise. "Are you sure?"

"Uh...yeah," she answered, uncertainly. Hadn't the duke asked her to find a problem? "I think so, Mister Duke, sir. If the spotters are you Azael guys, they'll be dressed in the scarves and the army guys will be dressed as bushes, you see? The army guys from the valley are super-good shots. Captain Grey, he was this real brave man who helped us out sometimes, was a real good shooter. He could kill a monster from, like, a mile away. And he's real smart, too. He knows all about bombs and artillery. He's going to guess right where your spotters are gonna be and then..." She mimicked being shot in the heart.

Duke Menis clapped Jillybean on the shoulder and gave her a warm squeeze. The rest of people around the fire checked the enthusiasm they'd been displaying and turned to Paulus with questioning eyes.

"We have camo, too," Paulus declared. "We'll have them decked out. It'll be no problem."

The king spat again into the fire, sending up a wisp of smoke and another fresh sizzle. "Camo won't cut it with these guys." He gazed up at the peaks for a moment before adding: "If I was them, I'd be sending men up there right now. They aren't stupid, Paulus."

"Maybe it's a chance we have to take," countered Paulus. "Casualties of war and all that."

The king ground his teeth at this and his stare was as hot as the fire. "I expect casualties but we don't throw away men uselessly. We either send a thousand men up there or we don't send any at all, and it's way too early in the game for something like that."

"I can send a company up to each..." Paulus began, but the king stomped his foot in the dirt, quieting him.

"This fight isn't going to be about who controls the peaks. A fight like that plays right into their hands. It's where they excel. They'll see your men coming a mile away. Son of a bitch! We need to fight our fight, and part of that means using our zombie army to its utmost, which means we need to break down their walls. Any suggestions?"

His dark eyes went right to Jillybean and her soft, downy brows lifted slightly. Was he expecting her to dictate the direction of his battle for him? When no one else said or did anything besides examine the tops of their shoes or follow the licking flames jumping off the bonfire, she said: "You can still use the guns. You just have to..."

She stopped suddenly as she realized what she was doing. She was giving her enemies the means to kill her friends. That wasn't right. It was far from right.

Having started the sentence, she couldn't exactly leave it unfinished. She wanted to say something really smart-allecky to cover her slip, however nothing came to mind. *You can tell them to shove the guns up their asses and pull the triggers*, Eve suggested.

Jillybean blushed at the suggestion.

The king glowered as he waited for an answer. "Well? What do we have to do?"

Ideas failed her, but not her courage. "You can shove those guns up you're a-asses and uh, pull the triggers." The sentence had started loud enough but had finished only slightly louder than a whisper. The king's glare had turned ferocious.

"Maybe it's time we remind her who's in charge here," the king said. He snapped his fingers and pointed at Kay. The woman folded at the knees and immediately began begging. She was wasting her breath. The Azael understood pain and screams. Begging only egged them on.

As Brad rushed forward with murder in his eyes, Jillybean steeled herself for what was to come. They would test her by hurting Kay and maybe herself. None of that should matter, she told herself. There were more lives at stake than theirs.

Just as she expected, Brad, almost gleefully, began to beat Kay. He swung his fists without mercy and soon blood was flying.

"I'm s-so sorry," Jillybean said to Kay. She wanted more than anything to run away, but they were handcuffed together. The best she could do was to turn her head away and she was in a perfect position to see the king roll his eyes.

"Give the girl a whack," he said. "Just don't ruin her sales value."

Jillybean turned to Brad just as he swung his hand. He wasn't gentle. The open-handed blow struck her flush on the cheek. Her head rocked back and her eyes were pinned to the dark sky above. Another blow struck her, but she could barely feel it. She was falling into the black and then a voice was speaking.

It was a high, child's voice. "Is that all you got? You hit like a pussy." It was Eve. *She* was back in charge.

Chapter 10
Jillybean

Brad Crane smacked her again, but Eve only grinned through the blood. "Pussy," she hissed, daring him on. He struck her again, harder and Jillybean's body reeled along a short curve defined by the length of her and Kay's arms. She toppled onto the highway and again she found herself staring up at the black.

Eve's mind spun in a vast circle with the dust of the Milky Way in its center. For a moment no one was in control of their shared body and Jillybean was able to jump back in—though why she wanted to, was beyond her. Her mind was a see-saw and her soul held all the rhythm and music of a cowbell. Her head ached and her face felt raw. Next to her, Kay was nothing but a ball of quivering flesh and a mat of black hair covered in blood and tears.

"Now the other one," Augustus said.

Jillybean felt instant relief that she wasn't going to be hit again, which gave way to the pain of guilt. Brad punched Kay for all he was worth. She begged in the shrill cry of a dying hog, not for Brad to stop, but for Jillybean to tell them what they wanted to know.

"No," Jillybean said in a whisper. She was able to get to her knees, but that was all. Her muscles were jittery and the tears on her red cheeks were like diamonds in the firelight. "I-I can't. T-Two lives are meaningless. You c-can kill us both," she dared the king.

"Don't listen to her!" screeched Kay at the top of her lungs.

This seemed almost a catalyst for Brad's volcanic anger; he started stomping on Kay. His knees would piston up and then shoot down; on his feet were cowboy boots with two-inch heels. They came down with such force that Kay could no longer scream, she could only grunt from the blows.

Jillybean, though attached to the woman by handcuffs, stoically looked away. She wished with all her might that she was far away; miles away. Jillybean felt every blow the woman suffered as if she was being the one tortured and still she did not relent.

Finally, the king put up a hand. Brad stopped at once. "Empty the bus. Tie up the girls and bring them here. We'll see how many lives it will take for this girl to agree to talk."

In a flash, Jillybean calculated the number of women on the bus: an average of two per row, times sixteen rows. She didn't know enough math to carry numbers. She could only break it down into sets: two tens were twenty; added to this was two sixes which she knew to be twelve. A sum of thirty-two.

The number staggered the little girl.

You might as well give up, Eve said. *There is no way you can watch thirty-two women beaten to death in front of you. You'll give in. You'll talk. You'll betray your friends and you'll never see them alive again, and I'll take over. You'll be mine. You should give in now and let me have the body. I know what to do with it.*

A sudden image of Jillybean gleefully slitting the king's throat came to her. It made her want to puke. It made her want to faint and, again, the night spun. Her head dropped and her fly-away brown hair hung before her face so that no one saw the look of victory in Eve's blue eyes as a smile suddenly broke across her face

Jillybean had weakened and now Eve was back!

"Stop," Eve said, as she stood. The word carried all the force of a royal order. Brad turned back to stare at her, expectantly; everyone around the fire had the same look. She loved how they looked to her, how they needed her. She wanted to prolong the moment but she could already feel Jillybean fighting back. "You can't dress in scarves," she said, looking pointedly at Paulus. "They'll kill you, easily. And you can't go up to the peaks. They'll expect it and then they'll kill you."

"Right," Paulus insisted. "You said that, already."

Eve's eyes flared up at the interruption. She had a sudden desire to throw him into the fire and watch him burn. The picture in her mind almost distracted her enough for Jillybean to take over again. Quickly, she said: "Your only chance is to have your spotter mix in with the monsters. You can get in close but only if you dress like them and act like them and be them."

This wild statement caused a muttering to spring up around the fire. It included everyone except Kay, who lay on the ground a foot from Jillybean, crying softly, and Brad, who was staring at the little girl with cold calculations in his eyes, and of course Duke Menis. Menis had seen Jillybean the night the renegades had made their escape—the little girl had been dressed in the mud and rags of her monster outfit.

"It is the only way to get close," Menis acknowledged.

Paulus threw his hands in the air, crying: "Are you crazy? What she's saying is suicide and it's stupid. Weren't we just talking about not wasting men, unnecessarily?"

"Not so fast, Paulus," Augustus said. He was eyeing his brother, and Brad Crane; these two were wearing nearly the same calculating expressions. "Is this possible? Does this fool the stiffs?"

"I have seen it for myself," Menis said.

Brad raised a hand that was wet with Kay's blood. "And I'll bet my life that it'll work. I'll go amongst the dead with the radio and direct the artillery." This raised eyebrows all around in what was a comical display, almost as if they were a group of bad actors over-doing a scene.

Eve didn't have an opportunity to laugh at them. The shared mind was teetering against her. Enraged at the treachery, Jillybean fought her way back into control. It was like waking up from a bad dream, except her reality was just as bad.

For the moment, she was an afterthought and no one noticed her chest rising and falling as she panted like a dog, nor did they see the wild, uncertain look in her eyes. She wanted to run away from her guilt. She wanted to run away from her life. Unfortunately, that wasn't an option.

"You won't be able to do it," she said to Brad. "You're not smart enough. You have to be stealthy, that's what means extra sneaky. You're too loud—they'll get you."

"They'll get *us*, you mean," Brad replied. "I plan on taking you with me." This brought on another general stir of surprise from the on-lookers, who were treating what was going on like a soap opera. "You'll come with me; you'll do what I say and you will behave, or else I will set the bus on fire with all those women in it, do you understand?"

The idea appealed to Eve. *She* could picture the flames swamping the vehicle, pouring up its sides as though it was a perverse liquid that could defy the laws of gravity. *She* could hear the roar of the flames and beneath that the utter despair of the women as they burned to death. *She* grinned at the prospect and Jillybean found herself grinning as well. Her mind was coming unbalanced again.

Disgusted, the little girl stuffed Eve away, which was sort of like crushing down on the lid of a garbage that was over-flowing with refuse—the imagined screams kept on echoing until she shook her head.

"Ok," Jillybean said to Brad. "I'll do it, just...just don't hurt anyone."

Brad grinned but made no promises. He unlocked the handcuffs from Kay's wrist and then kicked the woman one last time. "Go back to the bus and don't even think about trying to run away." In the dark, she could have run; however, Brad did not ere in his judgment of the woman. The beatings had cowed her into a sniveling servility and she went to the bus without a glance left or right.

Neither Jillybean nor Eve could understand this. Kay was under no duress. The lives of an entire busload of people weren't yoked on her shoulders. She could have walked away and have been half-way to Denver by the time the sun came up.

Pathetic, Eve whispered and Jillybean had to agree.

As Jillybean was watching Kay walk away, Duke Menis grabbed her by the shoulders and pulled her around to face the king. "Do we have your permission to undertake this mission, your Highness?"

The king glanced once at Paulus before nodding. When the youngest brother began to splutter, Augustus slapped his hand down on the arm of his great chair. "You shouldn't be angry, Paulus. You should be thanking Menis for having the foresight to bring this little girl along. Without her, I think it is safe to say it would have been a waste of time and resources to haul these guns all the way up here."

"What about the counter-battery fire?" Paulus demanded. "They were worth it, right..."

"Enough," Augustus said, cutting him off in mid-sentence. Dismissively, the king turned from his brother to look at Brad. "Why are you still here, Crane? Get your ass in gear."

Brad bowed and then dragged Jillybean away. When they were out of earshot, he began to grumble. "Why are you still here, Crane?" he mimicked in falsetto. "Jeeze, what an asshole."

"That's a bad word," Jillybean reminded him. "But, since you're bad yourself, it doesn't matter."

"Shut your mouth," Brad said after a quick look down at her. "Or I'll tape it shut."

She was quiet as they marched down the road to where the big guns were erected. In the dark, they resembled towering insects from an alien world. Jillybean looked upon them with some trepidation. They had belched so much fire when they had gone off that she was sure that if they went off again with her so close her hair would get burned right off.

As Brad got instructions on how to work the radio and what was to be expected of him as a spotter, Jillybean stood nearby, touching her face where Brad had hit her. Something didn't feel right. Her head felt lumpy and swollen and her nose was way bigger than it was supposed to be. She remembered what Kay looked like after her beating and Jillybean was afraid she looked the same way.

That's why we need to kill him, Eve said.

Jillybean glanced over at Brad who was talking to the Captain of the Guns. The captain was a tall, rangy man with hair as long as a woman's and tattoos like some sort of green-tinted skin disease that seemed to grow up from his chest to strangle his neck. Neither he nor Brad seemed to have heard Eve's remark.

The little girl turned away and whispered: "We can't kill him. Think about what will happen to all those ladies on the bus."

Who cares about a bunch of whores? Eve demanded. *You should be thinking about the greater good. What about Neil and Captain Grey and all of them?*

"But you hate them!" Jillybean cried. "You're the one who keeps stabbing them in the back over and over. It was your fault that..."

Brad suddenly appeared at her side. He gave her a shove that sent her to her knees. "Shut up!" he snapped. "While you're with me you need to keep your crazy yapping in check, do you hear me?"

Jillybean nodded sullenly; the idea of killing Brad was now quite appealing. She guessed that the disgusting desire to hurt him stemmed from Eve, but there was no way to know for sure and she didn't question it, either way. Brad was a very bad person and she thought that he needed to come to a bad end.

But not yet, she thought. She still had to worry about the poor ladies on the bus. She also worried about Captain Grey and Mister Neil and her sister Sadie, but just not as much. They were strong and smart and fast. They could take care of themselves, even with a big monster attack going on.

Brad thanked the Gun Captain and, carrying a heavy brick-sized radio in his hand, he directed Jillybean back the way they had come. All along the road, they passed groups of strange men. In the dark, they were scary shadows to Jillybean. Shadows that talked in low voices and laughed in whispers. Many had the glowing embers of cigarettes dangling from their lips, which only added to the aura of wickedness that hung in the air around them.

A few watched Jillybean as she passed, their eyes filled with the same perverse desire that she had seen in Baldwin's eyes. As odious as Brad was, she stayed very close to him and would've reached out to take his hand if she dared. His mood kept her from making the attempt.

He was no longer the amiable liar who had steered them in circles around the state of Kansas. He was curt of speech, coldly determined, and quick to anger. He marched them to another tent that was pitched up next to an army deuce and a half, and swept inside. The light blinded Jillybean for a few seconds; however, she didn't need her eyes to know who was in the tent.

"If it isn't his Royal Highness," a man said. Jillybean knew instantly that it was Duke Menis' quartermaster. She knew him only as Jim. On the day that the renegades had escaped from the duke, she had followed him and Brad into the theater where all of the duke's ordinance had been housed. She could have blown it all sky high, but she had opted to buy the renegades time to get away, instead.

"Shut it," Brad said, his anger right on the edge of getting out of his control. With the escape of the renegades coupled with the loss of a dozen men at McConnell Air Force Base, Duke Menis had been in no mood to bestow titles on anyone; Brad Crane was not yet *Baron Crane* as he had expected.

Jim bent into a mocking bow before waving his hand at the tent which was crowded with supplies of all sorts—the majority of it being ammunition, but there was also a crate of C4 and, much to Jillybean's chagrin, radio-controlled detonators. She hadn't been able to find any the last time she had searched the munitions storage facility back in the theater.

"What can I do for you at this late hour?" Jim glanced briefly at Jillybean before adding: "Do you need a crib?"

"I'm not a baby, Mister Jim," Jillybean said. Jim's face registered surprise at hearing his name.

He glanced at Brad. "How the hell does she know my name?"

Brad also looked at Jillybean with an odd eye, but then he shrugged, saying: "I really don't care how she knows. I need some supplies for a trip. That length of chain for one." Among the boxes of clothing and the crates of ammo and the stacks of MREs there were many oddities, including rope, tools, tarps and ten feet of half-inch chain.

Jim gave Brad an odd look, but handed it over. The odd look deepened when Brad wrapped one end of it around Jillybean's neck, attaching it snugly using a pair of handcuffs as a locking mechanism.

"I won't run away," Jillybean told him, as she tugged on the chain. For the little girl, the chain was uncomfortably heavy, plus she knew that where they were going, being chained in any manner could be deadly. "I promise I won't."

"Come on, Brad, she promised," Jim said with a smirk.

Brad glared at the quartermaster and muttered: "Shut the fuck up. Now, Jillybean, what are we going to need?"

"To fool the monsters? Not much of this stuff, unless we can have some of those shirty things."

Jim looked behind him at where she was pointing. "The ponchos? Sure you can have some ponchos, but I'm afraid they aren't very good at monster-fooling. But they are good if it rains, which it probably won't. But who knows, I ain't no weather forecaster or nothing. It could rain."

"It's not for the rain," Jillybean said, grinning at how silly Jim was being. "They're for camel-uhk…"

Brad, who had hold of the other end of the chain, gave it a yank. "He doesn't need to know what they're for," he snapped. "Now, anything else?"

Normally, she would have made do with mud to turn her pale complexion into something that no longer resembled a little girl's soft skin; however, there were some camo-sticks in a box, the sort Captain Grey had used when they first met him. Meekly, she pointed to them.

Jim followed her finger, saw what she wanted and reached for them, as he did, Jillybean noticed something else that she needed. There was a stack of forms on a box right next to Jim. Within the papers there were a number of paperclips...paperclips that could be used to unlock the unnecessary collar around her neck.

As Jim reached for the camo-sticks and Brad went to the unkempt pile of ponchos, Jillybean reached out and slapped the paperwork off the box. As she expected, the papers went everywhere. She followed them with a sharper eye than any adult would've given her credit for.

She knew exactly where the paperclips landed.

"I'm so sorry," she said, going to her knees and grabbing handfuls of paper. Right next to her hand gleamed a clip. She slid her hand over it and, just as she did, Jim was suddenly there. He saw what her hand landed on. She had been caught right off the bat.

"I... uh." Nothing else made it out of her throat. She was not good at lying, especially when it seemed useless. There was no denying what she was doing; she had been caught as red-handed as she could be.

Jim glanced up at the sour look on Brad's face; when he looked back at the little girl, he said nothing, he only shrugged and acted as though he hadn't seen anything.

This miniscule touch of kindness deep in the camp of her enemies was almost enough to overcome her. Before she knew it, tears were in her eyes threatening to come splashing out, threatening to alert Brad that something was afoot. Jim widened his eyes, giving her a warning not to over-react.

"Stupid girl," Jim growled, making a big show of gathering up the papers. When he had them stacked well enough, he tossed Brad the camo-sticks and then went to the ponchos and held two of them up for Brad to see. "All I have is large and extra-large. Are you expecting a monsoon?"

"Give me one of each," Brad snarled.

The second they were handed over, Brad hustled Jillybean out of the tent before she could say a proper goodbye. He kept one hand on the chain and the other on her back as he guided her down the road to a spot where they were somewhat alone. He made a show of looking all around so as not to be overheard.

"So how does this work? You can't just fool the stiffs by dressing weird, can you?"

"I don't know about dressing weird, but I know that if you don't look human exactly, they'll leave you alone. Oh, and you can't talk, neither. Really, the more you look and act like a monster the better. And you have to moan, too. There aren't any quiet monsters. They all say stuff. You know, *uuhhh*, or *muhh*h. Stuff like that."

"*Uhhhh*? That works?" His question made no sense to Jillybean.

"Not just *uhhhh*. You have to do it all. You know, the walk and the arms and the look. The monsters are real dumb, but they're not that dumb. They'll sniff you out if you don't do it all at once. Really there's only one way to get it right."

"And that is?"

Jillybean wanted to laugh at the silly question, but Brad still had the dangerous look about him. "You have to practice, of course." He seemed as though he was going to balk at the suggestion, but, abruptly, he shrugged and allowed her to teach him everything she knew about how to be a monster.

There really wasn't all that much to it beyond the big three: having the right costume, staying in character, and being brave. This last was what tripped up most people; any display of nerves was generally a dead giveaway to the monsters.

Brad displayed a talent for mimicry and his costume, a mudded-up face and a shredded poncho was weak, but good enough. The only thing left was to practice with real zombies, only Brad argued that they didn't have time. He explained they had four hours to cover ten miles of mountainous and zombie-filled land.

The first two miles zipped by as Brad commandeered a 4x4 truck; they drove it up the winding highway until they came to a group of men sitting around a fire. Off to the side of the road, hitched to the guardrail, was a row of twenty horses, each chomping oats out of nose-bags.

Jillybean wanted more than anything to go pet the horses; however, she knew better than to try. Brad was completely mission oriented. "Who's in charge?" Brad asked.

One of the men held up a hand. "I am Baron Graves. What do you want?" Like all of them, he wore armor like a knight; it caught the orange glow of the fire and seemed to burn from within.

"I need a horse," Brad answered. "A fresh one, preferably one with a good nimble step." When Graves opened his mouth, Brad answered his question before he asked it: "King's orders. How much further until things jam up?"

Graves pulled a stick from the fire and pointed up the highway with the lit end. "A mile or so."

The answer caught Brad by surprise. "That's it? One mile? We've had contact for six hours, why aren't they further along?"

"Who knows?" Graves said with a shrug. "Our job is to herd the stiffs up the highway. Who knows what's stopping them? My guess is that the soldier-boys don't want to get eaten and are putting up a fight. Big surprise, right? So what're you going to do with one of my horses?"

"Take it to Estes," was the simple answer. "Someone has to spot for the artillery."

This caused heads to shake and a few chuckles. "You're going on a horse?" Graves asked. "That's suicide. They'll see you from a mile away and put a hole in your head like that." He snapped his fingers. It was a dry sound, like a twig cracking.

"That's a chance I have to take," Brad replied. "Now, let's have that horse."

No one asked about Jillybean. They gave her and the chain she wore around her neck questioning looks, but as Brad was in a sour mood and in a hurry to go, no one said anything. In no time the pair was mounted on a great black beast of a horse. Jillybean felt as if she were ten feet in the air.

She sat in front of Brad and was able to run her fingers through the horse's mane and she was able to touch the surprisingly hard muscles of its neck. She was even able to talk to it, at least at first.

When they had trekked upwards for the mile that separated the drover's camp from the main host of zombies, she was forced to say, "What a good boy," one last time and then she threw the hood of the poncho over her head and became just a silent green blob.

In front of them, stretching as far as the eye could see were approximately two hundred and fifty thousand zombies. It was a mindboggling display. They filled the highway from end to end and then overlapped it and filled both shoulders of the road. Behind them in a single line were twenty more of the drovers on horseback.

They were tired men; they sat in their saddles with their backs bent and their long spears carried listlessly. Normally they used the spears to drive the zombies on, but it was clear, even to Jillybean, that the zombies weren't going anywhere. They were pressed into the gorge cut through the mountains with little room to even breathe.

Brad wanted to take them right into the stinking mass. It seemed utterly impossible.

He gave a low whistle to the drovers, who parted for him and then clopped his way right past. One of them cursed in amazement: "Mother-fucker!" Another whispered: "Don't do it, man."

Undeterred, Brad aimed the horse square into the middle of the pack and, at the same plodding rate, they plunged into the horde. The zombies were thrust aside by the massive beast and in seconds they were in the thick of things. Even though she was so high up, Jillybean pulled her legs in towards her. She had never been in the midst of such an ungodly host. Ugly, rotting heads turned in their direction, teeth champed in hunger, and evil eyes watched them, looking for any sign of humanity.

Even her brave heart was unnerved by being so utterly surrounded by the walking dead.

Brad gave no indication that he was in the least bit nervous. He steered the horse expertly through the throng and it plowed ahead like a battleship cutting up a small river. It was hard going for the animal and many times it staggered as one hoof or another came down awkwardly on one of the zombies. When this happened, Jillybean's heart would leap into her throat; however, the horse was indeed sure-footed.

It was a long uphill journey for both man and beast. They trudged through the mob for three hours, until the horse began to stumble in weariness and Jillybean was just about to faint from the sickening stench rising from the corpses. Brad steered them to one of the softer hills shooting up all around them. It rose gradually and bristled with a young pine forest.

A few zombies were on its slope; perhaps a hundred, not many in Jillybean's opinion and yet there were enough to cause Brad's courage to falter. "Aw, shit," he whispered. The horse had gone thirty feet up the hill and just plain stopped. Its legs shook and it breathed in a wheeze; it was finished as a mount, which meant they had to dismount under the watchful eyes of the zombies.

"Do exactly what I do," Jillybean whispered.

She began to moan: "*Uuughuhhh...*" Ever so slowly, so as not to betray her humanity, she brought one foot around, twisted in the saddle and then slid down the horse's withers to plop down in the wet leaves. "*Uuughuhhh...*" she went on moaning and only gradually did she try to stand.

With the dark and the shredded poncho and the hood it was hard to tell what she was and the zombies barely gave her much of a glance. Now, it was Brad's turn.

"*Uhhgh!*" he said in what was practically a bellow. It was too loud and too short of a sound and the way he swung his leg over the pommel was far too human!

Jillybean had stepped away from the side of the horse until the chain at her throat had stopped her. Now, she took a willing step back, saying: "Uughuhhh..." the way a zombie was supposed to sound. Brad gave her a quick and altogether human look.

"*Uughuhhh...*" she said again and let her head hang and her eyes loll listlessly in their sockets so that nothing was exactly in focus.

He seemed to catch her meaning. "Uughuhhh..." he said, more accurately this time. He then came down off the horse and landed in a crouched ball. The zombies all around stared at him as if waiting for him to jump up and betray himself as human.

"*Uughuhhh...*" Jillybean encouraged. None of the zombies batted an eye at her. Even the chain around her neck was strange enough not to be considered human. Brad waited in his crouch and Jillybean guessed he was waiting for the monsters to turn away, but she knew that they wouldn't unless acted upon by an outside force. "*Uughuhhh...*" she tried again.

Finally, Brad got the idea. "*Uughuhhh...*" he said. From then on things went a little more smoothly. After surreptitiously looping the horse's bridal around a branch that Brad pretended to stumble against, the two humans slowly made their way up the hill. There were zombies all the way to the top though there were fewer with each step up. When they reached the peak, they found a crag of rock to hide behind. Each leaned against the rock, huffing thin air into their lungs for well over a minute before Brad slid a pair of binoculars out from beneath his poncho.

"Damn," he whispered. Far away and far below them the land opened up and in the dim starlight they could barely make out the Estes Valley. "I can't see the highway from here. Come on, we have to get closer." He gave the chain a tug and started pulling her down the hill. For a time they went quickly. There were only a few zombies to worry about on this side of the hill and the slope was easy.

It didn't stay easy. At the bottom of the hill was a ravine where water ran when it rained or when the snow melted. Now it was a thin river of zombies going single file to who knew where. Going into their routine, the two joined the stream for a time until Brad took a sudden lunge to his left, dragging Jillybean up another hill.

This one had only a partial view of the highway because of a much taller ridgeline that crowded in from the north. Down again they plunged, Brad going at a pace that wasn't safe at all. He was trying to beat the sunrise. Already in the east, the sky was no longer pure black, it was a dark, velvety purple.

They struggled up toward where the ridge crested at about nine thousand feet. Far below them were trees and dark hills and between them was the highway that had looped around a mountain and was back, heading straight for Estes.

"We need to get closer before the sun rises," he whispered, dragging the bone-tired Jillybean on. Brad went slower now, acting like a zombie who had lost his way. He was afraid of military snipers. His head flicked around at any sound. It wasn't a good zombie performance; however, it got them practically to the level of the highway without getting killed.

They found a little hollow in the side of yet another tree-covered hill and hunkered down just as the sun broke the horizon—they had a perfect view of the Red Gate and the sea of zombies in front of it.

Jillybean wanted a better view; however, Brad brought her up short by the chain. She turned to see him wrapping it around a branch high out of her reach. "Can't have you running away," he said with a grin.

93

Chapter 11
Sadie Walcott

Sunrise was the slow reveal of nature. As the sky in the east went from indigo to navy to a pretty cobalt, the forest and the hills gradually came into focus. The colors weren't right, not at first. Everything had a strange orange cast, even the green trees were washed out by the diffuse light. It was all very pretty and Sadie didn't enjoy a second of it.

She was sitting in the dew, crouched against the trunk of a pine tree, her legs growing stiff beneath her. She hadn't climbed to nine thousand feet for the view. She was there to kill if she could.

The morning was pretty, but the earth was hard and chill and damp. The morning sung with birds but the earth gave up only sly, furtive noises. She hugged the earth, hiding behind the wormy trunk of a downed tree. Across it and pointing out was an M4 she had snatched from a sleeping soldier.

As things came into focus, she scanned under every tree and bush, but if there was a spotter for the Azael somewhere on the ridgeline across from her, Sadie couldn't see him.

Against her explicit orders, she rose up slightly to get a better view of the land. She had been told by Captain Grey not to move a muscle. She was to remain perfectly motionless because movement drew the eyes, movement gave away her position. Movement made her a target.

That had been four hours before when Grey had reluctantly chosen her to accompany his picked team of men who were there to hunt down and kill any enemy spotters that everyone agreed had to be up in the hills somewhere. "They can't hit what they can't see," General Johnston had said when he asked for volunteers. "They're up there waiting for sunrise to rain hell on us. Your job is to kill them before they can radio in any messages."

The enemy artillery barrage from the night before had been one of the scariest things Sadie had ever seen. With her heart thumping, she had watched as the incoming rounds had landed with pin-point accuracy on the valley's artillery position. The explosions were beyond thunder; the loudest thunder was an itty-bitty firecracker compared to these explosions. They were far more massive than she could have guessed; they had taken her breath away.

She was lucky she had insisted on staying with Captain Grey's company. The brief artillery barrage had ended up killing everyone within a hundred yards of the gun emplacements. Along with thirteen civilians, who had been hauling ammo from a munitions truck, an entire heavy weapons platoon had been wiped out.

Three of the four 105mm howitzers had been destroyed, utterly. They were bent into unrecognizable alien shapes. The one that wasn't destroyed had its carriage assembly damaged. It could no longer elevate its barrel beyond fifteen degrees meaning it was no longer serviceable as a howitzer.

One of the remaining artillerymen, a sergeant named Ortiz, who had chosen a very lucky time to take a leak, said that the gun could still be fired, the one problem: it could be used in direct fire missions, only. Sadie found out that meant they could only shoot the weapon in a straight line; with all the hills and peaks surrounding them, the gun was next to useless. And, sadly, that was the good news.

There was bad news on every other front. Both the Red and Blue Gates were on the verge of being overrun. Neither had been built to take on the numbers being pressed forward. The mounds of corpses in front of the walls were so vast that it was now similar to a tidal wave about to break over the wall. When the undead were struck down, they could fall nowhere else but onto the men on the wall.

It was a horrible thing to experience, and though the men were fighting with courage and strength, everyone knew that neither virtue was limitless. The soldiers were so exhausted that they came off the line and fell asleep, still covered in gore.

Worse than the exhaustion of the men and the fact that they were slowly being overwhelmed was the night's appalling rate of attrition. Grey's company had suffered eight deaths during their six hours in the Big Thompson River. The 3rd Company manning the Red Gate had ten men killed and the Blue Gate saw seven die. The deaths among the various smaller gorges and vales branching from the two main routes of attack were in equal proportion.

All in all, that first night of the siege saw seven percent of the soldiers die—it was a rate that couldn't last. Each death put that much more of a burden on the living. Yet the deaths weren't in vain by any stretch of the imagination

PFC Paul Wesley set a standard of heroics that became the fabric of legend in Estes. Fighting like a hero to the bitter end, inspired the others who were bitten or scratched to make their final hours count in service to their people. Not a man inflicted with the zombie disease asked to be taken out of the line; they remained until they were overwhelmed or they were so far gone that they had to be put down by their fellow soldiers.

During the night, the lines held, barely, and everyone hoped that daylight would bring with it a renewed vigor from the men. They would be able to see what they were swinging their make-shift weapons at for a change, which meant they had a fighting chance—but only if the walls held, something that didn't seem likely now that their enemy had a tremendous advantage in artillery.

Sadie lifted herself higher. There was a fire in her belly, an anger that burned away all caution. So what if the spotters saw her? Let them see. Let them shoot at her if they dared. They would give away their position if they did and she wasn't the only one hidden in the hills. Close to three hundred men had foregone sleep in order to give the rest a fighting chance.

She scanned until her eyes were scratchy tired, and strained her ears to hear anything that might sound like a radio or the whispered words of someone about to direct fire, but there was nothing to hear except the caws of a few corpse-fattened crows.

Ten minutes went by in which the world firmed up before her. Ten wasted minutes.

Suddenly, there was a thump to the east as though part of a mountain had fallen to the earth. This was followed by a tearing sound above her as if the sky had been woven out of blue cloth that was now being ripped down the middle. She knew exactly what the sounds were and her heart was in her throat; she turned to look back toward the Red Gate.

The gate lay far below her. It was a strange sight with the flood of zombies rising higher and higher before it, so that the wall was practically invisible. From that height it appeared to be a damned river and, in truth, that was exactly what it was.

The first of the explosions missed by a good three hundred yards, landing on the side of one of the many surrounding peaks. There was a blast of smoke, but otherwise the damage seemed muted by the distance.

Forgetting her purpose there, she fretted over the next strike and waited for the next shot. She was brought around by the radio hooked to her belt. "This is Sierra Six, does anyone have anything?"

Sadie jerked her head around to scan the hills before her—nothing. Everything was all perfectly natural. She was still staring when the distant thump came once more. Afraid, she spun and watched the wall as above her the sky was ripped again; this time the explosion occurred only a hundred yards further beyond the wall. It was also seventy or so yards north of the wall.

That was far too close.

"Everyone up!" Captain Grey's voice came over the radio. "Get up and charge at anything that even looks like it could hold a spotter." The order was pure desperation. Regardless, every one of the three hundred men and the one teenager, jumped up and charged at every dark place in front of them.

Sadie ran down the short slope in front of her and then labored up to the ridgeline, expecting at any moment that someone would stand up and blast a hole in her. No one did. She huffed up the hill and went to every spot that had seemed evil to her from across the ravine. The only enemy she found was a frightened chipmunk which chattered in terror as it scampered beneath a log.

A few seconds later the sky ripped again and, unable to help herself, she swiveled her head to follow the progress of the sound until there was an explosion somewhere to the north of the hill. Smoke billowed on the far side of the hill where, the day before, a squad had been fighting in a deep gorge.

For a brief moment she pictured the apple-cheeked Private Morganstern and wondered where he was and if he was still alive. "That doesn't matter," she said, with a shake of her head, as again there was the faraway *thump*.

There had to be a spotter! She ran from place to place and not far away others from the valley were dashing everywhere there was the least bit of cover. Once there was a gunshot and Captain Grey asked, eagerly over the radio: "What do we have? Who was that?"

"It was nothing, sorry."

"Who is this?" Grey demanded.

"Private David Alvares. It was a bird, sorry. I was shooting at a bird."

"Everyone, keep looking," Grey growled into the radio. "He's on one of these hills, damn it."

No one considered the possibility that the spotter was lower down, mixed with the zombies. Logic dictated that the spotter was sitting up in the hills overlooking the valley. Eventually, even Grey had to admit defeat. Artillery shells were now landing all around the wall of the Red Gate. The enemy had found their mark.

"Attachment, bring it in," Grey said over the radio in a quieter voice. "Meet at the start point on the double."

Sadie paused to catch her breath, and as she did, she saw an explosion right on the wall of the Red Gate itself. "Shit," she muttered, before taking off at a loping, ground-eating run back to where they had initially started. The further she went, the more she found herself surrounded by the men who had volunteered to hunt down the spotters. They were all despondent and ran with their chins down.

Grey was in the clearing staring down at a map as Sadie arrived. She was one of the first and she was one of the first to catch her breath. Grey counted the men and seemed disappointed that they were all there.

"No one saw anything?" he asked. "Footprints? A glob of spit? A broken branch?"

The men shook their heads and Sadie was right there with them. The land had been barren of any human touch. "Sorry, *Possum*, we got nothing," Grey said into the radio.

"Son of a gun," a voice replied in muted anger. Sadie recognized the voice as Neil's. Even under these circumstances, he couldn't bring himself to curse like a man. "I'll be right there."

Grey glanced at the radio in puzzlement for a moment, before looking around at the press of soldiers crowding around him. When his eye caught Sadie's, his shoulders jerked slightly. It seemed to wake him to his duties. "Alright men, fall in. I don't care about pay-grades just give me four ranks."

All around Sadie the men shuffled about, finding a spot. Each 'dressed right' and then stood at attention. It was an odd mix of officers, buck privates, grizzled sergeants and one Goth teen girl who stood apart from them.

Soon a Humvee came roaring up. Out of it jumped Neil Martin and General Johnston. Neil was first to speak: "You got nothing?" he asked, looking up at the hills. "How is that possible?"

"They could be using a drone to spot with," Grey suggested gesturing with a finger at the sky. "Or they might have someone who knows what they're doing, like a Seal or a Delta. If so we'll never find them. Who knows? They might have a traitor in the valley."

General Johnston grimaced at the suggestion. "Not likely. But however they're spotting for their artillery, they got it dialed in and it's just a matter of time before the Red Gate fails." All eyes swung to look down on wall. Sadie was surprised that it was still standing with all the bombs landing all around it.

The tremendous hill of corpses was, for the moment, protecting the wall by absorbing the greater part of the blasts with their bodies. Fountains of gore and black blood were flying everywhere. The carnage was so great that it finally stopped the assault on the wall. The few zombies that lived through the barrage seemed numbed by the violence; they stood staring vacantly all around and not attacking.

Neil, who looked sickened by the sight, was the first to turn away. "The wall won't last and neither will the second one the civilians built last night out of cars. The only way to stop this is to stop the artillery." Johnston and Neil shared a look, seeming to come to some agreement.

"I need volunteers," Johnston said, heavily. "I need twenty men to go take out the Azael's artillery." Of the three hundred men present, all raised their hands. "That's what I thought," Johnston remarked. "I guess I should have said I need twenty of the fittest men we have. Drop your hands if you did not have a perfect score on your last PT test."

Only twenty-two hands remained up in the air—one of these was Sadie's in spite of the fact that she had never taken a PT test in her life; she had run track in high school and was still in great condition and figured that was close enough.

Johnston nodded at the hands—except Sadie's, which he ignored. "Everyone with their hands in the air remain. The rest of you make one more sweep of these hills and then report to your units."

When the main group of men departed, the remaining twenty-two arrayed themselves in a much smaller formation. Sadie affixed herself to the back row; she felt tiny next to the tall men and couldn't see a thing in front of her as she came only to shoulder height of the smallest of them.

The general walked down the rows, his eyes darting over each man. In the third row he came upon a lieutenant with a bandaged hand. "Sorry Boyd. With that hand you won't be able to cut it." Lieutenant Boyd left and Johnston finished his brief inspection, stopping in front of Sadie. "If you don't mind," he said, "I would appreciate it if you left my formation."

"Let her stay," Neil said in a voice of command. "What we need is endurance and she has plenty of that."

Johnston's jaw clenched, briefly, before he turned away from Sadie as if she wasn't there. He cleared his throat and said in his deep, rumbly voice: "Your mission is simple: you will find where the Azael have made camp, assault it, and destroy their artillery before they can take down the two walls erected across this highway. You have less than two hours to complete this task and that is why I asked for the fittest among you. A third wall is being erected but it won't be completed for two more hours. In the mean time we will be fighting the stiffs man to man on open ground so you can understand why it's imperative that you complete the mission in the time stated. If a man falls out on the way, leave him and go on."

None of the soldiers was so undisciplined as to speak in formation; however, many shifted uneasily, Sadie included. The general consensus was that the Azael were camped on Highway 34 nine miles to their east; nine extremely mountainous miles. The idea of even getting to them in two hours seemed ludicrous and then if they did, they would have to fight at five hundred to one odds.

Though many of the men shifted, General Johnston only appeared to notice Sadie's discomfort at the arduous plan. "It is a difficult task," he said, "But not an impossible one. There is a steep little trail that winds over that ridgeline." He pointed at a run of ten-thousand foot peaks which blocked their view east. "We have scrounged up five ATVs that will transport the twenty of you over it. From there you will have to go on foot."

"It's five miles," Neil said. "But that's five miles as the crow flies. It's double that on foot and that's why we need people who can keep up." Neil pointed to the largest of the soldiers there. He was a hulking man with a back that was as wide as a doorway. "He won't be able to keep up. I'm sure he's in great shape, but this will be an endurance run and he's not built for it."

For a second, Johnston's dark eyes blazed, but then he gave the hulking man a second look. "The Governor is right. Tomes you're out. Miss, you're in." As Tomes stepped away from the formation, swearing under his breath, the general went back to the front. He held up a map and said: "Captain Grey will be leading you. Since we don't have a second to lose, you'll be taking the weapons you have on you. Prepare to move out in one minute."

One minute? Aghast, Sadie glanced down at what she was carrying: her Glock 17 in a hip holster, two magazines of 9mm ammo in her back pocket, the M4 she had 'borrowed', one extra magazine of 5.56mm ammo for the M4 in her right pocket and a bottle of water in her left.

Without hesitation, she undid the hip holster and dropped the Glock to the ground; the two extra mags went into the clump as well. Next, she unzipped her jacket and let it drop but not before she took from her pockets the extra 30-round magazine for the M4 and the water.

She looked at them, knowing she wouldn't be able to carry both. Figuring she wouldn't be able to make it without water, she was ready to drop the mag when a hand grabbed it from her.

"Stop," Grey said. "When we get there, you'll need it. Here, watch." From his chest rig, he pulled out a circle of silver duct tape. Without asking, he took the M4 from her and then, turning the extra magazine upside down, he taped it to the one protruding from the M4. "When the first one runs out of ammo, simply turn it over."

She was about to say thanks, when he abruptly handed the weapon to her, spun her around, ran his hands up and down her sides as if checking her for an unseen weapon, and then spun her back. "You're good to go," he declared, and then went to the next man and did the same thing.

Sadie's head was spinning. Sure she was good to go, but for what? Had she known that she was going to be assaulting the entire Azael army along with just a handful of soldiers she might not have been so quick to put her nose where it didn't belong.

Chapter 12
Sadie Walcott

While the men hurried to get ready, she was still standing there, feeling useless, when suddenly, Neil appeared at her side. "Be careful out there, will you?" he said, his scarred face folding into what he probably meant to be a look of concern.

How was one supposed to be careful on a suicide mission, she didn't know. "Yeah, sure," she whispered. Self-consciously, she brought a shaking hand up to touch her cheek, certain that she was just as white as a ghost, certain that everyone could see how scared she was. The other members of the squad didn't seem nervous in the least. They were quietly checking their gear, their rugged faces set in stone.

Neil patted her on the back, paused for a moment in indecision and then leaned in and kissed her cheek. "Be careful and come back in one piece or you're going to be grounded. And I mean it this time." He tried to laugh but failed as the sound dried up in his throat. Sadie wanted to laugh as well, but she couldn't, nor could she think of anything to say in the two seconds before Grey barked them into motion.

The next thing she knew she was jogging down the hill, trying to keep up with the soldiers. With Captain Grey leading, they practically sprinted down to where a Humvee was parked in front of a row of green ATVs. They looked like miniature dune-buggies to Sadie. "Mount up!" Grey shouted as he reached the first.

There was very little room for any actual mounting. Perching was closer to what occurred. The driver and one passenger had seats; the other two people had to cling as best they could to the back. As Sadie was the last in line, she ran to the furthest ATV and climbed on the back, wondering how she was going to hold on going up and down the steep ridges.

The man in the passenger seat glanced at her, made a face and then started to get out. He was going to do the chivalrous thing and offer up his seat, however the driver grabbed him. "We don't have time for that. Get in." Grey was already gunning his loaded ATV off down a very narrow track.

"D-Don't worry about m-me," Sadie said, her frayed nerves embarrassing her as she stammered.

"No, switch," the man said to Sadie. She did a double take, amazed to see that it was PFC Morganstern offering up his seat. She had been so preoccupied with her escalating fears that she hadn't recognized the apple-cheeked soldier.

With a soft: "Thanks," that was barely heard, she ran to the front and jumped in next to the driver, who barely waited for Morganstern to climb on back to peel out.

"I woulda let her sit on my lap if I was you," the other soldier clinging to the back said. "That's what I would call..." He couldn't go on as their ATV was suddenly engulfed in a cloud of dust and dirt kicked up by the passage of the previous four vehicles. "Don't follow so close," he yelled. "It's not like we're going to get lost."

The driver slowed and for the first twenty minutes they hung back a ways as they climbed the towering ridge. It was a frightful ride for Sadie as the ATV was frequently pitched up at an obscene angle and it was a wonder they didn't fall backwards at times to go rolling down the hill. More than once she silently thanked Morganstern for switching positions with her.

The view from the top of the ridge was utterly fantastic and utterly brief. They were barely in the open for five seconds before they went hurtling down the other side of the ridge. Gravity became their enemy as it pulled them toward steep drop-offs at every turn of the crooked trail. There were times when Sadie was literally staring down at sheer, three hundred foot drops with her heart in her throat and her hands in a death grip on the dash of the ATV.

Faster than they had ascended, the train of ATVs was down in another gorge. They followed it until the land opened up somewhat and they found themselves in a craggy, boulder-strewn valley, a half mile in width. They dashed across it while above them the sky continued to scream as if in pain as the 155mm shells tore through the air.

The sound seemed to send Captain Grey well past the point of prudence. He led them across the valley at break-neck speeds and it was all the men could do to hang on for their lives. In five minutes, they had crossed to the far side and were ranging up and down hills. This part of the ride was smoother, but unfortunately it didn't last.

The trail ran up against another tall ridge and then turned north. The moment it did, Grey leapt out of his ATV and consulted his map. "This is it! Dismount! Take a drink and let's move. Any man who falls out will be left behind. If you fall out, do your best to catch up." His eye caught Sadie's at this; she quickly turned away, fully expecting to be the first to drop out of the run.

It was going to be hell. The Azael were five miles away, on the other side of what looked like a mountain or maybe two.

Sadie swallowed half her water and slung the M4 across her shoulder. In that short time, the others were already moving out. Grey set a blistering pace. She had always been a runner; however she was used to speeding on a flat track with just the wind and an occasional runner to pass as her only obstacles. The mountains of Colorado were the complete opposite of this.

There were fallen logs to leap, streams to splash through, sudden drop-offs to keep from falling off of; and there were small rocky hills and medium treed hills and tall steep hills that caused her legs to burn as if they were on fire.

The pace was so fast that Sadie was absolutely sure she wasn't going to make it. There was no way she could run for so long at such a speed—every part of her was in some sort of agony and yet, after two miles, they hit the first ridge line, she was surprised when she passed one of the soldiers. He had slowly dropped back in the formation and soon she was on his heels.

"On your right," she said as she worked her way around him. He cursed but with his breath gone it came out in a mumbled, hoarse whisper. He continued to drop further and further back and soon, even his panting couldn't be heard.

The ridgeline saw two more men drop back. Grey took it at a diagonal, adding to the length of the run; it was a necessity. The hill was a few degrees short of vertical and even the path they took demanded a fair bit of climbing and a grueling degree of self-discipline.

Any slip of the foot meant a sprained ankle as a minimum penalty, while a broken neck was a very real possibility. They climbed so high, and the way so steep, that there were points where Sadie swung from the spindly trunks of shallow-rooted pines with dreadful drops below. Very soon, her hands were raw and her shoulder ached where the M4 was a constant thump of metal against muscle.

Still, she made the top when two men hadn't. One had literally dropped out of the run when part of the hill crumbled beneath his feet. He fell thirty feet down the slope before crashing against the trunk of a stunted pine growing out of the slope.

Sadie yelled down to him: "Are you ok?" In answer, he waved her on. She left him with her heart full of worry. No one else had even looked back, perhaps because they knew they were all running to a far worse fate than a few broken ribs.

The next man she passed was less of a medical issue—he was simply fetched up against a tree, gasping for breath and looking as white as a ghost. She gave him a crooked smile as she darted around him. He gave her an odd look as if he were about to ask her a question. When she paused and cocked her head, he threw up on the side of the hill. It was a great green mess; it looked as though he had been eating a soup made from crabgrass.

She left him and this time she didn't look back.

Just like with the ATVs, she hit the top of a ridge and wished she had time to stop. The view was magnificent, an oil painting depicting high summer, all green and gold; but it wasn't just the view that made her want call a halt to the insane run. Her lungs burned with a fire she had never known and her legs felt weighted as if liquid cement was running through her veins.

There was another soldier at the top. He was on all fours and, even as she watched, he keeled over and passed out. Though he might have been dying, she didn't stop. No one did. The time it would take to save one life on the torturous run could mean the death of a thousand. They all knew it. They all accepted it.

The man was left behind and so was the next whose foot slipped off the side of a moss-covered log. There was a snap and then he was down among the old pine needles writhing and groaning. Would he be able to crawl back to Estes? No one knew and no one spared an ounce of energy wondering.

Down on the other side of the high ridgeline, another rock-strewn valley greeted Sadie. It was open enough for her to see that the remaining men had broken into two groups. Captain Grey led eight of the hardiest men; they were a hundred yards ahead of the second group that was slowly dropping back, losing momentum. With the land somewhat flat, Sadie made an effort to catch the first group. She put her head down and concentrated only on two things: her breathing and where her next foot was going to land.

Around her, men sounded like broken horses and gradually she left them, gagging or puking or fainting as she caught the first group. She was spent, almost to the point of stumbling. There was no way of knowing how long they had been running or how far they had yet to go. Sadie only knew that she was using the last dregs of her energy but, then again, so too were the men around her.

All except Captain Grey.

They hit the base of another ridgeline and he didn't even pause to look up at the immense wall before them. Everyone else stared up in dread. "Let's move!" Grey demanded. Sadie, who had been bent over, sucking air, looked up at the side of the mountain, turned and saw that Grey was already twenty feet up the slope. She couldn't help wonder if he had flown there.

With all her heart, she wanted to stop and just breathe, only she couldn't. Neil was back in the pretty Estes Valley. He was in danger and every second that she procrastinated meant he was one second closer to death. Whenever her life had been on the line, he hadn't rested; he hadn't stopped until he had done everything possible to save her.

She was the first up the hill after Captain Grey. The climb was easier on her than on any of the men. There were many spots where she was pulling herself up by the strength of her arms alone. It wasn't as if she was stronger than any of them, she was simply feather-light and her burden was a fraction of theirs. They had come prepared to fight while she had brought only enough ammo to be a nuisance to the Azael.

Yet, her presence among the soldiers was worth far more than that. The men saw her, not only keeping up, but also passing others. They forced themselves on far beyond their natural endurance. Of course, it wasn't just Sadie's presence that pushed them, it was their captain. He seemed limitless both in body and spirit.

Where the men could barely find the breath to grunt if their ankle turned and a bone broke, the captain somehow found the air to bellow constant encouragements. He was steadfast where they were weak. He was undaunted in the face of every one of the hundreds of hills they climbed, while they quailed before each. Where they cast aside what they could to lighten their loads, he picked up more. Unlike the others, his chest-rig was full of magazines and around his neck was a string of odd shaped little bombs.

He pulled the soldiers along in his wake and, very quickly, Sadie lost track of everything save for the heels of his boots. With dogged determination, she put her feet where he put his and she breathed in the same rhythm he did. Nothing else seemed to matter. She was going to make this run, even if it killed her. Even if she got to the end and could only fire her weapon once before her heart exploded.

She was going to make it.

Eventually, they broke once more into the sunlight and found themselves at the highest peak within miles. Far down below them to the east was an open expanse of highway where thousands of men, looking like toy soldiers with the distance, stood around waiting for the zombies to finally surge ahead. It was the army of the Azael.

Now, Grey finally paused. He stood with his great chest heaving, running sweat from his brow in rivers, while looking over every one of the little hills and water-filled gullies and small stands of trees that lay between the base of the mountain and the howitzers—those monsters were still belching fire and metal every thirty seconds or so. They fired only twice before Grey said: "Let's go."

Sadie cast a weary glance back at the others—there were only five soldiers left, each looking as though they couldn't take another step. "You heard him," she wheezed and then loped off after the captain. The way was all downhill—the only reason she was able to keep up with Grey. She let gravity suck her on and it was only a matter of luck that she didn't trip and run a stick through her eye or fall off a cliff face.

Exactly ninety minutes after leaving the ATVs, the remaining men, and Sadie, reached the forest just above the open space where the men of the Azael had made their encampment.

Grey didn't waste a second. "Dornier and O'Hannon, take the left flank. Use that stretch of trees to get close. Riley and Morganstern take the right, go up the stream bed. Sadie and Rogers, you're with me. If you see a stockpile of shells, unload everything you have at it. If not, take out the gunners. Any questions?"

Hearing Morganstern's name, Sadie sluggishly turned and saw the handsome private. She smiled but so dead were her muscles that by the time the expression reached its fullest, he had already turned away, following orders. A hand turned her around.

"Sadie? Are you okay?" It was Captain Grey staring into her face, looking worried.

"I can't feel my hands," she said, everything from her elbows down was dead to her. She didn't mention that her head was spinning and that there were strange dark spots in her vision that would flare wide for a second and then shrivel into nothing.

"That's normal," he said kindly. "Give it a few minutes. That was a bit of a rough trek. Here, let me take this." Gently, he pulled the M4 from her hands. He unloaded it and tossed the taped magazines to the soldier named Rogers. Grey also unslung the bandolier of little bombs from around his neck and handed them to the soldier.

Rogers, who was gasping for air and swaying on his feet, grimaced as he slung them across his shoulders. He looked as utterly exhausted as Sadie felt. She was so done in that she was slow to realize that she had been disarmed.

She grabbed Grey's arm as he turned away. "What am I supposed to shoot with? You took all of my bullets."

"It'll be for the best," he said putting a hand on her shoulder. "We only have so many rounds and Rogers is a proven marksman."

"Then what did I come all this way for?" she asked, shaking the hand off. "You didn't think I would make it, did you?"

Grey ran a hand through his short hair, looking tired for the first time. "Honestly? No I didn't, but I didn't want to say no to you. That being said, now that you're here, you'll follow orders without question."

"And what are my orders? Stand around picking my nose while you men do all the fighting?" She knew she was being strangely childish. In truth, she didn't want to fight at all; Grey was right, she was only average in a battle situation such as this. She only excelled when she was close and she had the edge in hand speed.

"You won't be standing around," he said. "Keep low and keep out of sight. If one of us gets shot, you're to move up and take his weapon and continue the fight." She could tell that he had thought up the idea on the spot. Neither of them looked happy with the orders. "If...if you have to move up," he added, "Don't fire from the exact same position. They'll have the spot dialed in. Move first and then shoot. Got it?"

"Got it," she answered.

The Azael are going to kill you, a voice inside her head said when Grey turned away.

"Yes," she whispered to herself. "Yes, they will kill me." The field in front of them was so open and there were so many enemies camped up the road that she knew she had no chance to get out of there alive.

Chapter 13
Deanna Russell

Neil's job was simple yet tremendous in its scope: In the course of one day, he had to win over the twenty-four hundred civilians in the valley, convince them that he was their true and legitimate leader, and then, essentially take away all of their rights and command them in the surprisingly dangerous auxiliary roles that General Johnston was in desperate need of.

Deanna, who was given the title of Lieutenant Governor, had the sole job of organizing these civilian "volunteers," assessing where they were needed the most, and getting them there before the defenses crumbled and they were overrun by the endless hordes.

At first, her role was rather small. The walls were holding and the various off-shoots of the two main hordes were being contained. She basically concentrated on keeping the men supplied with ammo, food and water; a relatively simple job. Then came the double realization that the ammo wouldn't last and that the night would see the zombies breakthrough if something wasn't done about supplying the men with light.

She formed teams to scrounge for makeshift weapons and other teams to gather wood; at that point she had nearly a thousand people working for her. Her head began to spin with how much had to be done. It was simply too much for one person and so she grabbed two of her fellow ex-whores: Joslyn and Veronica, and created the positions of Deputy Governor and had them head up the two projects.

Deanna was still running around like mad when the Azael blew up the valley's artillery in the middle of the night, vaporizing a team of civilians in the process. She didn't have time to mourn. General Johnston found her in the Stanley Hotel and added to her burden.

"I need secondary walls built behind the first ones," he said, his eyes, manic and twitching. "The ones we have aren't going to last, not when they get their artillery zeroed in. We need at least one fallback position, per gate. Wait, make it two, and I need them by sunrise."

He wanted her to build two fallback positions for both the Red and the Blue Gates? By sunrise? Her mind was reeling. "What am I supposed to make them out of?"

"I'll leave it to your discretion," he answered. "I have to go; we have another hot spot to stop up. The stiffs have found their way into the valley by way of Dry Gulch Road. How the hell they managed that, I don't know." He then walked away from her so quickly that she didn't have time for a follow-up question.

Right at that moment, she wanted to give up. What was being asked of her was impossible. She had the equipment and the supplies: cement, mixers, rebar, and the forms all ready to go. There were literally tons and tons of material in a Department of Transportation stockpile just off of Route 36; it was all useless.

The thirty-foot walls that were the main line of defense at the Red and Blue Gates had taken weeks to build, she had hours.

Her eyes strayed to the large map of Estes pinned to the wall. She should've been looking for places to start construction, instead she was looking for ways out of the valley. There were only two, Route 7, which meandered south and then bent back east towards Denver, and Highway 34 which snaked west into the heart of the Rockies.

She was just tracing 34 when Neil came bursting into the room. "Good! I see you're on top of the new walls. Time is of the essence. I have two-hundred new volunteers right outside. I know, I know, it's not enough, but trust me I'll find you more."

After a flash of a smile, he breezed out of there just as quickly as he had come in. "Shit," Deanna said. For the next minute, she felt lost. It felt like the entire weight of their defense had been heaped on her shoulders. It also felt like running away was the thing to do.

Then she went out to look at her volunteers who were massed in the parking lot, standing with their hands stuffed in their pockets and with their faces lined with worry. They were a motley crew, made up of men and women of all ages and sizes. There were even a few of the renegades thrown into the mix. Fred Trigg was right in front and, for once, he wasn't sneering or looking haughty.

He was the first to speak. "How do we defend our home?" he asked.

The simple question sent a jolt through her. She'd been on the run for so long that she barely remembered the concept of home. Home was a place of comfort, of safety, and of love. Since coming to the valley, she had enjoyed all three in abundance and she realized they shouldn't be given up so easily.

"One second," she told him. As they waited, she tried to picture what the valley looked like in the daytime. There were many new farms and many pretty, little houses. There were shabby hotels that had, back before the apocalypse, charged an arm and a leg during the peak tourist season. There were also tall trees, mostly pine and aspen.

Then there was the clutter of the old life: derelict cars, termite-ridden telephone poles, satellite dishes and traffic lights that no longer blinked. She bent her mind upon all of these and an idea formed: the telephone poles could be uprooted and, along with enough hewn-down trees, a new wooden palisade could be built across the narrower portions of the two main highways coming into the valley.

"Ok, here's what I need done right away," she said. "There is some construction equipment out by 36. We need a couple of dump trucks. I'm thinking about using the old telephone poles that are all over town to build a wooden wall like the ones the old settlers used to build to repel Indian attacks. While I find the best locations for the new walls, I want you to dig up the poles and start collecting them in the trucks.

One of the volunteers, a stick thin man with a protruding Adam's apple and bulging eyes raised his hand and asked: "Aren't those, like, cemented into the ground? I think they are."

Deanna didn't have a clue, but if they were, then digging them out wouldn't work at all. The idea of cement triggered a new thought: even if they could get the poles out of the ground, how was she going to plant the poles across a highway? She'd have to dig up the entire stretch, stick the poles into the ground, fill the holes back in and hope that would be proof against a hundred thousand zombies stacking up against it.

She was sure she didn't have the engineering skills to pull it off, especially overnight. In her mind, she could picture the entire thing swaying slowly back as the undead piled up against it...and then falling right over.

"Unless we brace it with something else," she said to herself. Boulders were the first thing that came to mind, the valley was strewn with them, yet they were monstrous and she worried how they would lift them into the back of the dump trucks. They only had one crane and it was the slowest machine Deanna had ever seen.

"It's too bad Jillybean isn't here," Fred said, not realizing that at that moment Jillybean and Brad were even then working their way closer, intent on destroying the walls protecting them from the zombies.

Slightly miffed that Fred didn't think she could come up with a way to build a wall, Deanna spat out: "We don't need her. I have a plan. It just needs shaping." *Or bracing*, she thought. *What else can I use to brace the wall?*

Her eyes fell on the nearest thing in the parking lot: a dead car. Its gas cap was popped and its wheels were sagging; it appeared altogether sad and almost useless. The sight of it clicked something in her mind. Given enough of them stacked one atop the other it could brace the wall better than any number of boulders.

"Hell, it could be the wall," she whispered, realizing suddenly that stacked cars would be simpler and easier to build a wall with. "Change of plans," she said, dropping down the stairs, lightly. She went right to the car, a green Subaru Outback with faux wood panels, and slapped it on the hood. "We'll build the wall out of cars. Break up into teams of ten each. You'll push the cars up to where the new wall is to be built and then we'll use the crane to put them into place."

Fred raised a hand. "Can't we tow the cars up?"

That was a better idea. "Sure, but only if we can find rope or chains very quickly. Send out the smallest of you to find some, the rest of you need to start hauling. We need..." She paused to calculate: how many cars would it take to create a wall a hundred and fifty feet long by thirty feet high? A rough estimate gave her ninety per wall and she would need four walls. "We need three hundred and sixty cars, stacked and ready to go in six hours."

It didn't seem like a lot to that many people and so, in an excited mood, they allowed Deanna to divide them into teams and send them out. It was a much harder job than anticipated. First, there were very few tow ropes or chains to be found in the dead of night. Estes Park had been a tourist town and thus the great majority of cars were expensive and the owners far more likely to call Triple A, than to attempt to tow the cars themselves.

Another problem that presented itself was that unless keys were found to the many cars lying about, their steering wheels would remain locked and their transmissions stuck in park.

Still, despite the obstacles, the cars were collected, slowly. By three in the morning, an immense stacking of cars split the highway a hundred yards west of the Red Gate. One wall done! Deanna then had the crane shifted to the Blue Gate. It was a painful process as the crane moved on its massive caterpillar treads with aching slowness, crawling at three miles-per-hour. Nearly an hour was wasted in the transition.

Deanna was out of her mind with worry and yet, the second wall fairly flew up compared to the first. Because of the delay in moving the crane, there were lines of cars ready to be stacked; more than was needed as it turned out. The crane operator worked as fast as he could as the people of the valley labored like ants, hauling car after car along the steep and winding mountain roads.

With thirty minutes to go before sunrise and the second wall built, Deanna again shifted the crane. She had wanted to build the first of the two backup walls a quarter mile down from the wall she had just finished, however General Johnston appeared and told her to hurry with all possible speed back to the Red Gate.

"That's where the hammer will fall, I know it," he said, casting nervous glances to the east where the sky was gradually turning to indigo. "How long to build the next wall?" he asked.

"Two and half hours," she had answered. Even with moving the crane back to the Red Gate, she felt her teams could put up another wall in that time. They had worked out many of the kinks concerning timing and spacing, and although the 'hauling' crews were tired from the long night, they still had spunk—they were so close to the front lines that they could hear the soldiers fighting and dying and it drove them past what they could normally have attained.

"To the Red Gate!" she ordered. When some of the civilian crews, who had just pushed two tons of rolling Detroit iron up a mile of hill, gave her an incredulous look, she added: "Let's leave the extra cars here; anything already up the slope stays."

There was a brief cheer and then the people turned around and started walking back down to the valley. Johnston watched, seemingly in pain. "Can you get them to hurry? Please? When the sun comes up..." He didn't need to finish his sentence. She knew that the enemy artillery would start raining down shells.

"I don't think stacked cars are going to stop artillery," she said.

115

"Of course not," he answered, over his should as he headed back to his Humvee. "Let me worry about the artillery and you worry about the walls."

Deanna had enough worry-room inside of her to agonize over both. She watched the general's Humvee speed back toward the valley with an ache in her gut. In all likelihood, they would never get the second wall up behind the Red Gate in time.

They had the crane halfway up the slope towards the Red Gate when the first artillery shell exploded just on the other side of the hill they were trudging up. The sound was terrifying. It was louder than anything she had ever heard and it sent a shiver of fear right into her guts.

Everyone threw themselves to the ground and huddled there, waiting for the next shell to strike. The next one came about a minute later and landed much further away.

"Ok, that wasn't so bad," Deanna said, getting to her feet. There were old leaves in her long, golden hair and when she went to pull them out, she saw her hands were shaking. She also saw that she was the only one still standing. "They, uh, missed. So, let's keep going. Come on." Only a few of the civilians climbed to their feet. Deanna forgot the leaves and strode over to the nearest person—it was the same balding, skinny fellow who had mentioned the telephone poles being cemented into the ground.

"Get up," she said to him. "They aren't shooting at us, they're shooting at the Red Gate and that's a quarter mile from here." When the man stood, it seemed to be a catalyst for the rest. The crane started slogging upwards again and the crews went back to the cars and began pushing. There were ten people per car bent well over and driving with the strong muscles of their legs and backs.

As they struggled on, they were passed by three trucks hauling cars, two with chains and one with a thick tow rope. The people gave the truck a long suspicious look. So far two chains had snapped that night sending cars careening out of control. One young woman, barely out of her teens had her leg broken, while on the second occasion, an entire crew was sent running to keep from being ground beneath the tires.

Once the truck was passed, they bent to their burden again. Groans escaped them as the car was slow to gain momentum on the slope, which was steeper than most. Deanna was close and so she added her strength to the effort.

Above them came the ripping sound of another shell. "Keep going!" Deanna ordered, as two of the pushers hesitated and the weight of the car on the rest increased. The shell landed well away from them, sending up a plume of smoke.

"What do we do if they start a forest fire?" a woman asked. It was a cool dawn and yet she was dripping sweat from her chin in a steady lip, lip, lip, as she pushed.

"We'll count ourselves lucky," Deanna answered. "Better a death from smoke inhalation than a death from them." They had just crested a hill and the sight before them was, as always, a horrible one. From above, it looked as though Highway 34 was a river of corpses that poured into a teeming reservoir of undead held back by the concrete wall that made up the Red Gate. The reservoir of dead was over thirty feet deep in places.

Even as they watched, the lone artillery piece hit just shy of the wall, landing in the great mound of bodies. The thunder of the explosion was muted, as was the impact of the shell.

As they pushed, the valley people waited and watched for the next shell to hit. Again it was a single blast and again it landed among the undead. "They got the range," squeaked the balding, skinny man. He was not wrong.

From across the tops of the mountains, they heard multiple thuds as though giants were dropping boulders for their own amusement. The air screamed with incoming shells and everyone slunk low just in case there was a wild miss. Two of the shells found the mark, hitting near the wall and sending bodies and part of bodies flying everywhere. One of the shells missed short, landing further back on the highway and killing thirty zombies. The fourth shell crashed into the side of a mountain half a mile away.

"Keep pushing!" Deanna commanded. She pushed for a few seconds to make sure that the rest were as well and then slapped the skinny man on the back. "Keep going. It'll be ok."

She turned to see how the other crews were progressing. All of them had lost a great deal of steam. She jogged down the hill, yelling encouragements to them. They responded but their fear weighed on them and their pace wasn't near what it had been. The Red Gate wall couldn't last. She saw the next salvo hit: three landed almost on the wall itself and the fourth was short.

The soldiers were now running from their positions on the wall and Deanna stopped what she was doing to squint down at them. She knew Grey would be one of the last to leave the wall; however when the final few sprinted away from the wall to the somewhat sketchy safety of the line of stacked cars, Grey wasn't among them.

"Thank God," she whispered, thinking he was safe.

Just then the crane drew up alongside of her. The operator, a jovial red-faced man, leaned out the window and pointed at the cloud of smoke lying over the wall. "If this keeps up, you know we're wasting our time here."

"The general assured me that he's going to take care of the guns." She pointed in the opposite direction, towards the valley and said, "Probably missiles or an attack helicopter or something like that." When it came to the different weapons systems available, she was generally clueless, but she knew about missiles and helicopters.

The crane operator looked a lot less jovial as he said: "I don't think we gots any of them." He shrugged and ducked back into the cab of the crane.

Deanna tried to tell herself that the man probably didn't know all the secret gadgets that the military kept hidden, and yet, she had seen precious little in the way of impressive army hardware. The 105mm howitzers that had been parked down in the valley had been frightening enough, right up until they had been destroyed.

She decided that she would simply trust General Johnston and ignore the explosions that erupted twice a minute for the next half hour. In that time, she directed the crane to where she wanted the third wall set up—this time deep in a gorge where the highway snaked around a sharp peak. She hoped that the mountain would shield the wall from the artillery fire...if it came to it.

Then she began directing the excruciatingly slow, hand-propelled traffic. It was imperative that each car was shoved into the exact proper position, forty feet from the crane, in order to keep the flow of work going. Whenever there was a miscue, the crane would take hold of the car incorrectly and it would dangle, oddly and dangerously. One car actually slipped from the grip of the crane and took out half the existing wall which then had to be rebuilt.

They were still trying to unjumble the cars when Neil came up in a Humvee. Deanna didn't wait for him to stop before she asked: "How's Grey doing? He's still alright, isn't he?" Neil hesitated and this, more than any artillery shell caused her heart to skip a beat. "What is it?" she asked, clutching at his arm and searching his face for answers.

"It's nothing," he replied, his eyes sliding down and to the side. "It's just that Captain Grey is heading up a team, uh, a team of the fittest men, soldiers actually. And their job is to go and take out those guns." He pointed, not at any guns, but at the horrible carnage being wrought among the horde of zombies piled before the Red Gate.

The repeated explosions had turned the area before the wall into a burning soup of charred blood and a black, viscous sludge made from who knew what parts of the zombies. Floating in the crud were arms and feet and other sundered parts. Those zombies that were still "alive" and who still had arms were doing a strange swim-crawl through it all, while those without just sort of bobbed in place.

Thankfully, there weren't many of these "live" ones left before the wall. The continuous explosions and the pall of smoke hanging over the area discouraged the main press of the horde to advance. This was an unforeseen blessing. The concrete wall itself, which had been built to stop a horde of up to ten thousand, had cracks running up and down it from top to bottom and any concerted effort by the zombies would have brought it straight down.

Deanna tore her eyes from the carnage and the soon-to-be-obliterated wall and stared at Neil in disbelief. "Grey did what?" she demanded. Before he could answer, she added: "He's attacking their camp you mean? In broad daylight? With how many men?"

He made a face, as though he had a sour stomach, before answering: "Twenty." Her eyes went as wide as they could go and he was quick to say: "I'm sorry, but it was the only way. If we had…"

"Twenty!" she exploded, cutting him off in mid-sentence. The number was so incredibly small that she couldn't really comprehend it. Had they been going in at night with the idea of a sneak attack she could envision the plan working, however in the daylight it was a suicide mission.

119

Neil began to stutter out excuses, but she wasn't listening. Her mind was shutting down—her love could be dying even then. She knew him; he would pit himself against any odds to get at those guns. And that meant he would die.

A bolt of hot anger rushed right through her and, before she knew it, she slugged Neil in the face. "How could you?" she seethed. "He was your friend!"

"He still *is* my friend," he countered, touching a delicate hand to his cheek. "And Sadie is my daughter; you're not the only one who has something to lose if they fail."

"You sent Sadie?" she asked in astonishment.

Neil shrugged. "She's a survivor, and she's tougher than anyone gives her credit for. Not to mention..." His words dribbled away as a series of explosions directly on the wall itself finally brought it down.

Chapter 14
Sadie Walcott

With the simple, and likely deadly, orders given, Grey nodded to Sadie, before he and Rogers bent low and began shuffling through the last of the underbrush. Before them there was almost no cover: waist-high grasses and a few stands of pine and aspen were it. When they ran out of trees, they began to crawl quickly through the grass. On their left, Dornier and O'Hannon were almost invisible moving through the forest that stretched nearly to the road. On their right, Riley and Morganstern worked their way along a stream bed with only the tops of their heads showing.

With the three groups so separated, Sadie realized that she could only act as a backup to one of them. She felt a strange pull towards Morganstern; she fought against it. "I love Nico," she said to herself and then wondered when the last time she had had even pictured his face. It had been so long that her memory of him was already dimming.

"I don't even have a picture of him to..." A gunshot stopped her tongue and sent an electric surge of adrenaline shooting through her body. She dropped into a crouch and peered through the underbrush, fully expecting to see a battle on the verge of breaking out.

The shot had come from the right where Morganstern and O'Hannon had crawled, but there wasn't a follow-up shot. Had they disturbed some poor man or woman of the Azael off relieving themselves?

No one seemed to take the gunshot as a warning of things to come. A few heads swung to look over the field, but for the most part, the Azael went on as if nothing had happened.

Thankfully, there were only a few people in and around the battery of guns, the great mass of the Azael were far up the road, well away from the thunder of the artillery which, even from three hundred yards away, was enough to rattle Sadie's eardrums.

When no great outcry occurred, Sadie finally began to move. She had dithered for almost a full minute without following any of the three teams, now she scampered low after Captain Grey and Rogers; theirs looked to be the most dangerous route and she felt she would be picking up one of their weapons sooner than she wished.

Afraid that through her inexperience she was going to give them away, she went along, squirming so low that she couldn't tell which way she was going exactly. The steady boom of the artillery drew her but she had no idea where anyone else was and there was no way she was going to lift her head to check.

Like some sort of blind snake, she slithered closer and closer to the boom of the big guns with the dread certainty that she had passed Grey and Rogers. Only the relatively tame chatter of small arms fire stopped her. Six guns seemed to go off all at once; shots left, right and center. The center guns were right in front of her; Captain Grey was very close, but unseen. She could tell it was him by the quick, controlled patter of his M4. He didn't waste a shot.

Putting her head back down, she crawled forward just as the grass above her parted with the whisper of passing bullets. They were coming so fiercely that the grass waved as if in a wind and small green shoots rained down over her prone body. She forced herself on, hugging the earth until she found herself just behind Grey as he crouched behind a good-sized log. It was being thumped heartily by incoming rounds and it sounded like some tribal drum being beaten rather than played.

"Hey!" Sadie yelled. There was no sense being quiet now, there was a veritable storm of noise all around them.

Grey glanced back, and instead of greeting her, he snapped: "Get your ass away from me! You want to get killed? Move to the side, damn it."

She wanted to be angry at the way he had spoken to her, however the moment she had moved a dozen feet to her right, the air above her was no longer filled with the passage of hot lead; it was a blessed relief. Someone on the other side was using a machine gun and along with the tat-tat-tat of the gun, there were blazing tracer rounds flashing by, looking like something out of a science-fiction movie.

Rogers was to her right, but slightly ahead of her. Because the land dipped a little, she could see him quite well. He too had found one of the half-buried logs in the field and was crouched down behind it. He was working his gun, a slightly bigger version of the M4, in an odd way. Instead of shouldering it and sighting down the barrel, he had it cocked slightly with the tip of the barrel pointed at an angle. He pulled a trigger half-way up the barrel and there was a *foomp* sound.

He ducked down, but Sadie sat up a little higher to see what he had done. A second later there was an explosion thirty yards or so distant from the howitzers. There was a flash and some smoke, but it seemed altogether insignificant compared to the huge guns, which had gone silent.

A bullet zipping by reminded her that she couldn't expose herself if she wanted to live through the next five minutes. She dropped and hugged the ground again in a firm embrace. "Too far!" she yelled over at Rogers. "It landed well past the guns." As she watched, he slid out one of the little bombs from the bandolier and shoved it into the open port of the tube that was attached beneath the barrel of the M16.

Again, he aimed the gun in his odd way and fired. Sadie risked a look to see where the shot fell, but didn't get a chance to see. The second she popped her head up, a tracer whipped within an inch of her face, blinding her. She dropped like a rock while all around her dirt and grass flew into the air. The bullets were missing her by the breadth of a hair. A scream that was beyond her control tore from her throat as she began to roll to get away from the barrage lancing in at her.

In mid-roll she saw the strangest sight: Captain Grey standing with the blue Colorado sky painted all around him. He was making himself a perfect target. For a full second, he stood there as he aimed his M4 with all the precision of a surgeon. Just as the air around him blurred with the passage of an unknown numbers of rounds, he fired.

Immediately, the machine gun went silent. Sadie did not see what had happened to the captain; the machine gun wasn't the only gun firing in her direction. A dozen were, and a dozen or more were firing at each of the soldiers, and the rest of the army of the Azael, five or six thousand men, were running down the highway to join the fight.

Sadie wanted to keep rolling right out of there. The "suicide" mission she had feared this to be was fast becoming a reality. Yet, she didn't run.

Above the din, she heard the odd sound of Rogers' grenade launcher and, against all reason, Sadie popped up in time to see the bomb explode on the highway sixty feet to the right of the howitzers and twenty feet in front of a row of parked five-tons.

"You're way off to the right of the guns!" Sadie yelled.

"I'm trying to hit the fucking trucks!" Rogers screamed back. He was crawling in her direction, while she was crawling in his. It was death to stay in any one place, but it wasn't smart to clump up and so she rolled back away. He stopped as well, as the land between them was suddenly torn up as machine gun bullets peppered the ground.

Someone new had manned the machine gun. It was going hot, blasting fire and metal from its muzzle. It was a nightmare weapon to Sadie, perhaps because the tracer rounds could be seen—it almost appeared as though the bullets were hunting her, searching for her in the tall grass.

Again, the daring captain exposed himself to kill the new gunner. He seemed to be able to aim by hearing alone. He stood, aimed and fired in about a second, and again the machine gun went quiet. However, the rest of the guns did not and a God-awful fury of rifle fire raked the area Grey had dropped down into.

In her terror, Sadie broke the cardinal rule and crawled on her hands and knees toward where she had last seen him. He was nowhere to be seen. The only sign he had been there was the blood. It was all over the ground, bright and wet.

"Grey!" she hissed just above a whisper, afraid that he wouldn't answer.

He didn't answer. Fueled by panic, she crawled as fast as she could, following a bloody path through the grass. She didn't have to go far. She found Grey lying on his back, staring up at the blue sky. He was sticky red from head to toe. With one shaking hand, he was clawing at his lower abdomen.

Forgetting the battle, she scurried up to him with tears in her eyes. "Grey," she said in a mumble as she fixated on the cascade of blood running off him. "Are you..."

"I'm fine," he grunted. "Help me get this belt off."

The request was so far out of the blue that she had to stare at his midsection for a moment to understand he meant the belt around his waist. She couldn't help wonder, why on earth he would want it. After a few seconds, during which she could only blink, dully, she moved his fumbling hand away, undid the buckle, and slid the belt from its loops. She held it out to him but he pushed it away, weakly.

"Don't give it to me. You've got to tie off my arm." Only then did she see that much of the blood on him was coming from a squirting wound in his bicep. "Lay it right over the top of that and cinch it down as tight as you can get it."

"Oh, right." In three seconds, she had worked the belt around his arm and pulled it as hard as she could until he grunted. "Where else are you hit?" She started scanning his bloody aspect: there was a gash on the side of his neck, a hole in his shirt, low down on his side, and there were two big dark wet splotches on his right leg, one on the side of his thigh and the other on his calf.

The calf wound looked to be the next worse and she started to pull back the leg of his pants when Grey pushed her away. "Don't worry about me... go spot for Rogers...We have to take out those guns... That's all that matters." He spoke in short bursts between gritted teeth. His pain was obvious.

Taking out the guns wasn't all that mattered to Sadie, but she knew Grey, she knew what a hero he was. He wasn't going to be 'babied" in the middle of a fight, especially when he had a mission to complete. Reluctantly, she left him and squirmed through the grass. She had gone maybe twenty yards when she heard the *foomp* sound that Rogers's grenade launcher made.

Acting on instinct, she lifted up just high enough out of the grass to see over the green tips. She was able to scan the fighting in a blink: to her left the forest where Dornier and O'Hannon had gone was being pounded from two directions at once; leaves and bark were flying in all directions. Eighty yards to her right, where Morganstern and O'Hannon were, nothing could be seen. There were so many bullets heading their way that the grass had been veritably trimmed almost to the level of the stream bed.

And much closer, she saw Rogers peeking his own head up to check to see where his grenade had landed.

There was a bang and a flash of light smack dab on the hood of the middle truck. Its windshield blew in and there was a cloud of sudden black smoke. The desperate need to explode the ordinance and get out of there let wishful thinking override prudence on both Sadie's and Rogers' part. Both were still there with their heads foolishly held out in the open, seconds later, each filled with the hope that the truck would blow sky high.

But there was no explosion.

Sadie recovered her wits first as bullets started hissing past her ears. As if in slow motion, she started to drop down again, her eyes flicking back to Rogers, hoping he was doing the same thing, instead he was still there for everyone to see. She wanted to scream at him to get undercover only she saw that there was something wrong with him. His eyes were staring at a horizon only the dead could see.

Slowly, he spun and she saw there was a hole just above his right eye and a larger one in the back of his head. With unhurried grace, he threw his arms wide and toppled back into the grass to stare eternally up at the sky.

A crackle of static filled her ears and deadened her mind. She was utterly numb between the ears save for one thought: *get that grenade launcher!*

Her life didn't matter, not just then. Getting the grenade launcher was the only thing that had any meaning to her. She burst out of the tall grass, not like a pheasant in fear of the hunter, she burst out like a cheetah. In two strides she was at full speed, outracing bullets that trailed in her wake.

She cleared thirty yards so quickly that she almost overran the corpse with the bandolier around its neck. She went into a baseball slide catching up the M16 with one hand while the other grabbed the bandolier. It hooked on Rogers' shoulder, and with her adrenaline pumping, she had him hauled halfway into a sitting position when he started to shudder, oddly.

For a moment she thought he was still alive somehow and she squeaked in fright and almost let go of the bandolier. Then something wet struck her in the face; it was a wet chunk of what had once been part of Rogers. Bullets had chased her to her present position and were now thudding into his corpse.

Again, without thinking, she hauled the body on top of her. It was the strangest feeling having a dead body shake and shudder as if it was trying to come back to life. This went on for a few seconds before she heard the rattle of Grey's M4—he was once again exposing himself for her sake.

Sadie heaved the body off of her, and went through a series of motions as if she had been actually trained with the weapon in her hands. She grabbed a 40mm grenade from the bandolier and shoved it into the chamber slung under the M16; with only a split-second peek at her target, she elevated the weapon as Rogers had and then pulled the trigger.

Foomp.

The round sailed down range and went long, exploding well past the three trucks. Immediately, she began rolling to her right, knowing that to stay meant she would suffer the same fate as Rogers. There was a thumping noise behind her and the eerie whispering of the bullets passing along the tips of the grass. Five minutes before she would've been scared shitless by the sound, now she ignored it completely.

The moment she stopped her roll, her hands worked, selecting another grenade, sliding it home, elevating the weapon, half as much as it had been.

Foomp.

The explosion was short this time. "One more," she said to herself as she rolled again. Who knew where she was in relation to everyone else and who knew if anyone other than Grey was still alive. Only his gun going in those pauses after she shot her weapon gave any evidence that he was.

Seven seconds of rolling and she was again working a round into the chamber. Her angles of firing had been too long and then too short—now, she needed it to go Goldilocks-style: just right. She popped up, chose an angle in the midrange and shot.

It was spot on. She knew it the second her finger had caressed the trigger. She knew, because it had to be. Her luck couldn't hold out forever and neither could Grey's, and if Morganstern were still alive he would need a miracle to remain so for another minute.

The *foomp* was followed by three seconds of waiting as the grenade sailed through the air. Against all wisdom, she lifted from her crouch, her eyes trying to follow the flight of the round. She lost track of it and was still squinting when everything in front of her went a skull-shocking white.

127

Her eyes crunched shut and still couldn't hold back the brilliance as tons of high explosive erupted in a stilted blast. There was a chain reaction as one 155mm shell set off another and then another and then another. Three hundred of them went up in three seconds.

The air shimmered and the earth shook. Sadie threw herself onto the ground as it rippled like an ocean wave, but that wasn't near enough to protect her from the amazing heat. When she breathed in, she felt as though she were breathing in the embers of a bonfire. The heat from the first set of explosions was tremendous but it was nothing compared to what came a second later as the other trucks erupted.

Like the first, another truck was filled with high explosives that made Sadie's eyes rattle in their sockets, however the next was filled with a combination of Napalm and white phosphorus. When it went up, it unleashed hell on earth. Even from a hundred and fifty yards away, the heat stretched the skin of her face tight against her cheek bones; it cracked her lips and she was sure her hair would ignite.

The very air was on fire; there was no way she could take a breath and there was no way that she wanted to. She rolled over and pressed her face into the cool dirt—a millisecond later, even that proved a pitiful shield against the unbearable heat. In an effort to keep her face from blistering into a puddle of pus, she grabbed handfuls of dirt and covered her exposed flesh.

There was no telling how long she remained in her partial burial plot before she realized that Captain Grey was probably being broiled alive, unable to even roll over to shield himself from the heat. With a grit she didn't know she possessed, she lurched to her feet. She was altogether unmindful of anyone shooting at her. There was no way anyone could have been. The intensity of the heat coming from what was left of the trucks made squinting down the barrel of a two hundred degree metal rifle impossible.

Sadie stood in a field engulfed in fire. Like a veteran, she slung the M16 across her shoulder and then staggered toward where she had last seen Grey, fearing what she would find.

Chapter 15

Deanna Russell

The artillery finally struck concrete. Neil, who had been yammering excuses about sending Grey and Sadie to their deaths, jumped and made a sound that was just shy of a girlish squeak, as the cracked and groaning cement wall holding back the ghastly pool of zombie soup and the endless horde, took three direct hits in as many seconds. The first two blasted out a crater so that when the third hit, it struck the wall itself fifteen feet up from the base.

Concrete blasted outward and for the space of a minute an ugly, brackish sludge poured through the hole, passing through to the west side of the wall and collecting in a hot spew at the base.

Deanna's eyes fixated on the hole. She could look at nothing else. She saw it crumble at the edges as more shells thudded home; gradually the break widened until it took up too much of the remaining support and the entire center of the wall collapsed under the weight of the massed bodies, the parts of bodies, and the terrific pounding it had taken.

Out came the entire pent-up sludge in a nauseating wave and with it came a horrendous stink. "Oh, my God," Neil whispered at the sight. He stood transfixed and slack-jawed. Deanna knew she had to appear equally revolted. A ball of puke began pressing up her throat from the pit of her stomach. She swallowed it back down with a shudder.

For ten minutes they watched as the enemy artillery continued to pound the area, increasing the destruction of the wall until there was nothing left standing.

To Deanna, the only good news was that the zombies weren't exactly roaring through the gap. They seemed confused by the violence more than anything and were milling around a few hundred yards away. Neil saw this and said, again, "Oh, my God."

Before Deanna could question the exclamation, he went running for the wall of cars that Deanna had had built earlier that night. As if against her will, Deanna ran as well and didn't know why. She jogged after him, unnerved, partly by the strange look in his eyes, but more so by the fact that the soldiers were abandoning the very wall the two of them were running toward.

Running *away* was the only thing that common sense dictated. If the tremendous and rock-solid concrete wall had succumbed to the destructive force of the artillery, then the much weaker wall of cars couldn't possibly last nearly as long.

"What are you doing, Neil?" she asked as she caught up to him.

"The wall won't last," he said in a pant.

She gave him a look that said: *No, fucking, duh!* However, he didn't see and so she had to say: "Exactly. So why are we running towards it? Shouldn't we be running from it like everyone else?"

"You can if you want," he said, and then they were at the wall. There were ladders leaning against it as if waiting for a group of white-spattered workmen to climb up and begin painting the structure. Neil went scampering up and for some reason Deanna felt compelled to climb up after him.

They climbed to a dizzying height, though it was not so dizzying as the climb she had undertaken a few weeks before when she and Neil had set the top of the River King's bridge on fire. That act had cemented the trust between them; it allowed her to climb up onto the pile of swaying cars when nothing else could have.

Despite having only three fingers on his left hand, Neil zipped right up the ladder and reached the top before Deanna hit the three-quarter mark. She didn't know what to expect from him, but she was shocked when he suddenly screamed at the top of his lungs: "Hey!" His voice bounced off the rocky walls of the canyon that the road was situated in and echoed back at them in faint waves. "Hey, you mother-fuckers!"

Deanna found herself shaking her head from side-to-side—what he was doing was well past crazy and so was their current perch. Deanna climbed up but didn't stand; she was squatted down on the hood of a light blue Kia Sedona, the fingers of her left hand tight on a windshield wiper. Neil was fearless, standing at his full height with his arms flung.

"What are we doing up here?" she asked.

"Protecting the wall," he answered and then yelled: "Come on, you stupid things! Come and get me!"

"Neil, what the hell are you doing?"

"Look at them," he said, pointing at the zombies. "They're just standing there. We need them to attack."

Deanna felt her head spinning as the wall was buffeted by a gust of wind; it was surprisingly unstable. "You're crazy!" she hissed, reaching for the ladder. The last thing anyone needed was for two hundred thousand zombies to launch themselves against the wall; it would fail, of that she was certain.

Just then an artillery shell whistled overhead. She spun, watching its progress and nearly lost her grip on the windshield wiper. The shell exploded against the rocky surface of the canyon wall behind them. It was the same wall protecting the third wall of cars that was even then in the process of being built.

Another shell exploded out to their right against a cliff face. For some reason this spurred Neil on and he shrieked curses louder than ever. He was starting to attract attention. Zombies, with their heads craned far back to look at the two of them, came charging through the hell that had been created by the artillery. Within a minute, thousands were surging toward them.

Neil screamed all the harder, sounding like a madman, while in the background was the whistling artillery shells that were being gradually dialed in to their position. Deanna shook her head, suddenly realizing that Neil really was crazy and, on top of that, the man she loved was probably even then dying in a hail of gunfire, and that it was just plain stupid to still be up there with artillery getting closer and closer, and with thousands of zombies, even then crowding around the base of the make-shift wall.

It was crazy but in her mind, there was nothing left to live for.

"Come on, you fuckers!" she yelled. Neil smiled at her.

"Exactly!" he cried. "It's the only way to hold them back. We need the zombies to protect the wall from the artillery. How do think the last wall lasted so long?"

"Oh," she said, suddenly understanding. The wall of cars wouldn't last five minutes once the artillery was spotted properly, unless there were mounds of bodies absorbing the greater part of each explosion. "Hey!" she cried at the top of her lungs. "Come and get us you stupid bitches." Like Neil, she stood up...and then nearly pitched straight off the Sedona as the wall of cars swayed even more alarmingly.

Neil didn't notice. He was still screaming and waving his arms. He stood with his legs wide apart like a sailor in a storm and for the next five minutes he seemed completely unfazed by the fact that his death could occur at any moment. Directly in front of him, the zombies built up higher and higher as they climbed over themselves to get at the two, seemingly deranged humans, while all around them explosions crept nearer.

Then the wall shook from a direct strike. Sixty feet from them, glass and metal went flying in a fiery detonation. Neil started pin-wheeling his arms to keep from falling into the horde. Deanna simply dropped into a low crouch and hooked one hand around the edge of metal where the hood met the frame of the minivan. The other hand she held out to Neil, which he grabbed, eagerly.

"I think we have reached the point where bravery outshines prudence," he said. "Let's get out of here."

With the immediate threat of a violent and sudden death upon her, she fairly flew down the ladder, but only beat Neil down by a second; he nearly landed on her as he leapt the final five feet. She paused for a heartbeat as the wall let out a strange metallic groan that made it seem alive and in pain, then Neil was pulling her away from the wall and, hand-in-hand, they went sprinting for the meager safety of the next wall.

Even with their efforts to swarm zombies to the second wall, Deanna knew it wouldn't remain standing for long. The weight of the zombies alone would collapse it and with the artillery pounding it, it was just a matter of time. The next wall would have to be braced better—if there was even going to be another wall, that is.

It seemed ludicrous to bother completing it. The reality of their situation was that the third wall would fail no matter what she did...unless, that is, Captain Grey could manage the impossible and blow up the enemy guns in the next few minutes.

Everyone on the other side of the barely begun third wall was cowering and casting glances back toward the valley, the one direction that offered an escape. This included the soldiers as well as the volunteers; they didn't think a miracle was possible. Only Neil was absolutely resolute.

"Everyone up!" he cried. "This wall's not going to build itself."

No one moved, not even Deanna. She knew that the wall couldn't last and that Grey couldn't take out the guns singlehandedly—they were doomed. She hesitated for a second until she realized that, if she ran and Grey somehow lived, she would be abandoning him. He would be coming home expecting a hero's welcome and all he would find is a valley overrun by the dead. What would he think of her if that happened? She would forever be a coward in his eyes.

"You heard the man," Deanna yelled, suddenly, striding forward. "Let's get moving. I'm going to need three times as many cars for this wall. I want it to be so sturdy nothing will be able to knock it down. Now, let's get moving!"

The people went to work, slowly at first and then gradually quicker as they got used to the explosions from the shells detonating so close. The hill that the roadway curved around protected them from accidental misses, but each knew that once the second wall came down, they'd be in the crosshairs next. It made them eager to rush their cars into position and then hurry back down to the valley.

The first wall of cars had taken two hours to build, but lasted only twenty-two minutes under the fire of the artillery. It came crashing down with glass flying and a sound like thunder. The zombies surged on through the chaos of twisted iron and the artillery sending deadly shards of metal in all directions.

For a few minutes, the artillery blasted everything in sight killing hundreds of zombies and keeping the horde from advancing. Then, as though a switch had been thrown, the artillery stopped. Everyone stared fearfully up to the skies, awaiting the next storm of metal from the howitzers. A minute passed and there was nothing.

Neil jumped up. "Keep working!" he yelled. "Get those cars in place." The first team in line shoved their car, a snow-white Lexus with California plates, into position beneath the jaws of the crane just as the eager zombies struck the last barrier between them and a couple of hundred humans. The wall of cars was only two high at this point and the entire thing shook from the impact of the beasts.

"Soldiers to the line!" Neil ordered.

Reluctantly the men went forward with their odd assortment of weapons at the ready. "Cheer up," Deanna told them. "Maybe Captain Grey has taken out their guns."

133

A grizzled sergeant shook his head. "I think we would have known. What's more likely is that whoever's spotting for them probably can't see us. I'd bet they're moving to a better spot."

"Or they don't think this wall will last," another soldier said, gloomily.

Deanna had every confidence that the wall would last if it wasn't destroyed by artillery, that is. She was making it double wide with the second row of cars perpendicular to the first for added strength. Strong or not, artillery would take it right down.

The artillery recommenced ten minutes later. The first few shots struck the hill in front of them—and the people cheered, thinking that they were out of reach. The next few landed on the hill itself, sending debris raining down—and the people fled. They ran with the wall half completed and the zombies beginning to pile up.

This was the end, Deanna knew. The crane had been abandoned. The cars left to roll off the edge of the road and into the trees. Even the military retreated. They double-timed it a few hundred yards down the road, leaving only Deanna and Neil standing on the hood of some banged up teal sedan.

Neil hopped down from the wall and put a hand out to her. "Come on. We can't stay. We..." He winced and ducked as a shell landed on their side of the wall. "We have to leave!" he yelled above the din as the artillery increased in fury. "We have to evacuate the valley."

She understood. There would be no chance to get another wall built when this one failed. The valley would then flood with the undead. There would be no fighting them: they didn't have the manpower or the ammo. Their only choice was to give up or run.

Deanna was tired of running. She'd been running ever since the apocalypse started a year before and every place she had run from had been worse than the place before, right up until she had met Captain Grey, that is. It had not been an auspicious beginning to a relationship: he'd had a gun against her head and a forearm that was like flesh-covered steel thrown across her throat.

And now he was most certainly dead. Sadie, too...and Emily...and Eve...and Jillybean and all the rest. All dead.

She shook her head and pulled out her Beretta. "I think I'll slow them down for you. You better..." Another explosion on the wrong side of the wall had her head ringing like a bell. There was smoke and dust covering the area. Squinting into the pall, she saw that the crane had been hit; part of its tread was flung out behind it like a tongue.

"You better get going," she said, finishing her sentence. "They need a leader. They don't need me."

"Son of a bitch!" he snapped, still with his hand held up to her. "Don't be an idiot..." Another explosion hit so close that it shattered the windows in the sedan, covering Neil in safety glass.

She wasn't being an idiot. A wave of depression and grief had washed over her and now she was three feet beneath its surface and no longer fighting it. She wasn't suicidal; however she had given up on the idea of running. Her only plan was to kill as many of the stiffs as she could and then...she didn't know what.

"Get going, Neil," she said and then shot her pistol at one of the grey-skinned beasts that had somehow managed to slither onto the hood of the car. The gunshot and the flying brain matter only added to the chaos of the battle. The air was dark with an irritating smoke that burned the eyes and her ears rung with the explosions and the *bang, bang, bang* of her gun. Zombies massed to get at her, surging over each other, mounding higher and higher. She saved her ammo, killing only those that made it to the top.

It was an amazing scene: tens of thousands of zombies fighting to get at her, explosions and flames and smoke and she was standing before it all, alone. It felt good to defy this great mass of death. It felt right.

But she was not alone. Huffing, Neil climbed up next to her. "I think I'll stay. If this wall falls, so does the valley, and so does our home. If it does, I won't really have anything left to fight for." They shared a look and they each saw the pain of loss in the other. It was a bond of sorrow.

Neil, always the optimist, tried to smile past it when part of the wall, fifty feet to their right, was hit dead-on by an artillery shell. There was a flash of intense light followed by a noise that sent spikes into Deanna's eardrums. The sedan beneath their feet shimmied and shook and both of them dropped to their hands and knees as a rain of debris fell like hail. Deanna's head rung from the explosion and it felt as though she was moving in slow motion as she turned to see the damage: there was a gaping wound in the wall of cars.

"We should do something about that," Neil cried. She could tell he was yelling his loudest and yet his words came to her muffled and strangely quiet. "Don't you th...hey, what's that?"

In the midst of more explosions, Neil stood staring eastward with his head cocked. Deanna did the same. Above the moans of the zombies and the echoes of the last explosions, the two of them could hear the sounds of another battle. It was far away over the eastern mountains. It was going so hot and furious that it seemed as though two armies were locked in a raging combat.

"That's Grey," she said in a whisper. Her voice held disbelief and awe. Only he could have come through, she thought. Louder, she cried in joyous victory: "That's Grey! That's Captain Grey!" Forgotten were the thousands of zombies and the partially built wall with the gaping hole in it. All she could think about was the fact that Grey was still alive.

Next to her Neil appeared less ecstatic. "We don't know if he has completed his mission or not," he cautioned. "However, we should proceed with the premise that he has. We need to fill that gap and we need to defend this wall."

Deanna scoffed at the idea that Grey could fail. "I'll take the hole, you try to get the soldiers and civilians back." As Neil climbed down from the two cars like an asthmatic ten-year-old who was never allowed to play outside, Deanna leapt from the roof of the sedan to the hood of a Range Rover with all the ease of a cat.

She couldn't stop smiling. Grey was alive! Deep in her heart, she hadn't believed it was possible. The idea gave her an energy she hadn't known in years and she leapt from car to car with a light and easy step.

When she got to the gap where the cars were tangled and twisted, she realized that it had been a mistake going to the hole in the wall. The zombies were fixated on her completely and by heading to the one weak spot in the wall, she had accidentally brought a flood of zombies right to it.

Bringing up her Beretta and squaring her shoulders in a proper fighting stance, she emptied the magazine into the horde, concentrating on those already in the gap. Bodies piled up, nicely. Still, she didn't have near enough bullets to close the gap with corpses; she had to rely on more than lead.

"Hey, you guys," she called, waving her arms as she walked back in the direction she had come.

The gap was all but forgotten as the zombies fought each other to get at her. A few dozen were shoved through the gap, however the vast majority followed along after her. She kept up a steady stream of nonsense words but it really wasn't needed; she was very human in their eyes and they were primed to kill, primed to eat her if she made even the smallest slip.

She didn't give them the chance. Every step was thought out and planted with assurance—she still had something to live for, after all.

Beyond the mountains the fight went on, and down the slope from her, Neil was pointing and stamping his feet in anger. He went so far as to drag some captain up toward the wall. Deanna could see him gesticulating, angrily. Clearly, they thought the wall a lost cause, artillery or no artillery.

She turned from the spectacle of Neil screaming up at a man who towered over him. With practiced ease, she reloaded the Beretta and aimed the gun at a stiff who had planted one foot on the face of his fellows and was clawing his way up onto the hood of a Jeep Liberty. Before she could pull the trigger, there was a strange, fantastic flash of light far away to the east.

It was so bright that for a long second it made the sun seem like a candle in comparison. She was shocked by the light and could only stare. Strangely, it had the same effect on the zombies. As though they were one tremendous being, they turned to stare as the brilliant, white light pierced their eyes.

Deanna threw an arm over her face to shield her eyes until the shock wave of the explosion struck her. The air pulsed and the cars shook; next to her the radio antenna of the car she was standing on, let out an eerie *zzzzing* sound.

137

"Oh, my gosh," she whispered. In the east, the blinding light faded to orange and then disappeared, to be replaced by a mushrooming cloud of black smoke. "He's done it," she said, again so low that not even the now-fixated zombies could hear. Suddenly, she was filled with a new fear: who could have lived through that blast?

Chapter 16
Jillybean

Brad had chosen an ideal spot from which to guide the artillery attack: low down, with the mountain ridges looming over them, a few hundred yards from the big wall. They were tucked up under a low, shrubby kind of tree that had prickled her something bad every time she had moved. It was good cover and, with the land thickly treed, they hadn't been bothered by the monsters at all.

Nor had the soldiers got them.

Just before sunrise, an entire troop of them had come jogging out of the darkness, running across the field in front of them and up toward the taller hills that overlooked the big concrete wall. They were heading exactly where Jillybean had said they would. Brad had given her a look and a grunt once they were gone, but said nothing.

She had honestly expected a 'thank you' though she didn't know what she was going to do with it once she got it. She certainly wasn't going to say 'You're welcome' or anything like it.

Brad's lack of manners made it a moot point.

Now, they were sitting watching the fireworks. As each shell passed over her head, Jillybean felt Eve grow stronger. *She* was winning. And so were the Azael. Their bombs from over the mountains had destroyed the first wall after little more than a half hour of explosions and fire and smoke. The second wall built of cars, seemed as if it had been constructed by one of her friends back in first grade.

The wind made it wobbly.

The first wall, with its sturdy concrete construction had been formidable, if not illogically placed. The second wall was just silly. She had even gone so far as to suggest to Brad that it was a ruse of some sort. Nothing else made sense considering the elements it was supposed to contend with.

Brad had lent her his binoculars so that she could study it. They were comically big on her face. "This isn't right," she had said. "They got all them cars sideways on. It's gonna fall right over."

And it had.

She watched through the binoculars as the wall went right over after what seemed like no time at all. "There it goes," she said, trying to figure out what had been the motivation for building such a useless wall. It had plopped right over and then the monsters went stumbling over the remains.

There it goes and there you go, Eve cackled inside of her. *When the monsters get into the valley, they're gonna eat all your friends and then you'll be all alone with no one to protect you.* Her evil laughter had filled Jillybean's head until the little girl reached up and pinched her own cheek hard enough to bring tears.

Jillybean then tried to find anything to distract her from Eve's constant voice and saw, in the destruction of the second wall, something entertaining enough to shift her focus. Brad had forgotten that it was his job to call off the artillery, it was still pounding away. She hid a secret grin behind her hand as the Azael's howitzers blasted the zombies into goo, sending chunks and limbs going everywhere, basically stopping the attack.

When he finally noticed, he didn't seem all that concerned that his own guns were doing a number on his monster army. "There's a lot more where they came from," he said with a shrug, pretending that the destruction of hundreds of the monsters and, more importantly, the loss of time and ammunition, was nothing to him.

"I think that's enough," Brad drawled into the radio as he casually leaned back among the sticker plants. He even put his hands behind his head, completely at his ease, content that the great, grey river of zombies was surging forward.

Jillybean watched with a queasy, guilty sickness eating at her belly. It made her want to throw up. It made Eve louder in her mind: *They are gonna destroy everything and they are gonna eat everyone. Sadie, Neil…even Captain Grey. They are gonna eat him right up! And it's all your fault, you traitor.*

A groan escaped Jillybean and the chain around her neck rattled as she leaned back from the horrible thought.

"Will you stop?" Brad snapped, rolling his eyes at her. "This was all preordained from the get-go. You know what preordained means, right? It means that this was a done deal months ago. The moment Augustus was able to claim Kansas, it was only a matter of time before he came after Colorado."

Her guilt could not be assuaged so easily. "Still," she insisted. "People are going to die and it's my fault."

Brad yawned and stretched before replying: "People were going to die no matter what. And really, there aren't going to be that many deaths. I'd say a lot fewer than you think. They aren't going to fight now that their walls are down. They'll run away. They'll go deep into the mountains; maybe to Canada or California. You'll see. When we get the stiffs cleared out of the valley, there won't be that many corpses."

Jillybean made no reply to that. Even if he was right, she was still guilty of betrayal, at the very least. The thought gnawed at her, and again Eve flared huge inside her, riding the wave of guilt almost to shore. *They are gonna get eated and it'll be all your fault!*

"Stop!" Jillybean hissed under her breath. The little girl looked around once more trying to find something to take her mind off of Eve and the tremendous guilt eating her insides. Next to her, Brad yawned again and put his legs out so that his boots poked out from beneath the shrubby tree they were hiding in.

She glanced at him for a second and then turned to look up at the ridge above them. There were birds wheeling in the sky above—just the thing to distract her. She grabbed the overly large binoculars and gazed upwards. The birds were nothing but crows, big and ugly. Even distance didn't help to make them appear more than what they were: scavengers, eaters of dead flesh.

They are gonna pick apart the leftovers! Eve laughed, gleefully.

The weight of guilt pulled Jillybean's chin down away from the sky and she found herself staring at the highway and the thousands of zombies. She followed the road with her eyes, past the two destroyed walls, as it snaked behind a steep, rocky hill.

When the road reappeared on the other side, it was wide, black, and empty. It shouldn't have been. There should have been zombies all over it. Brad was quick to notice as well. "Give me those," he said, snatching the binoculars off her face. He kept them held to his eyes for minutes before he mumbled: "What the fuck?"

Jillybean assumed the question had been directed towards her. "Maybe there's a bridge over a river or a small canyon that the Colorado people blew up and now the monsters are stuck."

Brad pulled the binoculars away from his face to reveal a sneer. "Don't you think the stiffs would be falling into this canyon? If so, then the rest of them would still be moving forward." He pointed at the line of monsters all along the road to their left; they were squishing into each other, but not really moving forward at all.

"Hmmm, you're right," she agreed. "Well then, maybe the Colorado people could have another wall built behind that hill. That would make sense, 'specially since that's where they shoulda builded the first one."

"Another wall?" Brad's lip curled at the thought. He grabbed the radio he had set aside. "Wally! This is Brad. I'm going to need some more firepower down here. There may be another wall."

There was a static-filled pause before Wally's cranky voice came back, chopped by the distance and the intervening mountains: "…you going…me some…ing coordinates?…I going to have to guess?"

"Asshole," Brad muttered, staring at the radio. He then thumbed the mike: "Watch your language, Wally! You forget who you're talking to. I'm going to make Baron for this. Now, drop those rounds about three hundred yards further than you had been."

Wally's response was so garbled that it couldn't be deciphered. Brad sighed in exasperation and then repeated: "Three hundred yards further on!"

They waited a minute and then thunder sounded from over the mountains. The shell missed, landing short, and so did the next two. "You need to shoot at a steeper angle!" Brad barked into the radio. There was no need to be quiet now; the zombies were completely fixated on the explosions, their normally blank faces showing something akin to religious awe.

Using the radio, Brad walked the artillery right up over the hill and very soon there was smoke brewing up from behind it and Jillybean, using the binoculars, could see people running away down the highway toward the broad valley.

Soon they'll be all dead, Eve said. *Soon you'll be a murderer just like me!*

Jillybean squeezed her eyes shut, hoping that Eve would just go away. The other girl inside her laughed at the feeble attempt. Next Jillybean tried to pinch herself again. It didn't work and Eve grew stronger.

"Fine," Jillybean seethed. "How about I strangle myself?" In despair, she threw herself to the end of her chain. The metal bit into her flesh as though it had hungry shining teeth; she gagged and choked, her world turning fuzzy and grey. She would have succeeded in killing herself if Brad hadn't reached out and pulled her back to the ground.

"What the hell are you doing?" he demanded. "Sit there and stop marking yourself up. You'll fuck up your resale value worse than it already is." At first, she didn't know what he was talking about, and then she touched her face and felt the swelling where she had been hit.

You're ugly, now, Eve said. *You're ugly and no one will want you.*

"Good," Jillybean said, under her breath. She didn't want to be sold anyway. Who would want that? Not her. She didn't want to be someone's slave.

Eve's laugh inside of her was booming. *You're already a slave. If you doubt me, ask yourself what's that around your neck?*

Jillybean felt the cold metal; the hard snake gathered under her chin. The heavy links weren't just tying her in place, they were weighing her soul down like an anchor. They were a constant reminder of her place in the new undead world.

"They're coming off right now," she seethed in an angry whisper. Brad was already back to ignoring her and didn't see her dig out the paperclip she had stolen the night before.

In no way was she an expert at picking locks, however she had seen the key that had gone with the cuffs and it had seemed a simple shape to copy. In seconds, she had bent the paperclip to approximate the key, stuck it into the lock and began working it back and forth, and side to side.

It clicked open just as the first gun shots could be heard from over the mountains, back the way they had come. Brad spun around, sending a cascade of small rocks bouncing down the hill in front of them. "What the fuck?"

Once again, Jillybean felt compelled to answer his rhetorical question: "Your place with all your men is under attack. That's what I think."

"No, fucking, duh," he snapped and raised the radio back to his mouth. "Wally? What's going on? Wally? Wally?" The radio remained quiet and lifeless, as did the artillery. For nearly a minute, Brad stood, staring east as the morning brightened and the unseen battle continued.

With his back to her, Jillybean didn't even have to sneak as she slipped the chain off. She let it slip into the carpet of dead leaves. The handcuffs were different. She heaved them as far down the hill as she could and gave a little jerk of surprise as they smacked into the back of the half-rotted head of a monster. It turned and caught her staring.

They were locked eye to eye for a full second before it started scrambling toward the shrubby tree. "Uh-oh," Jillybean said. She turned to Brad. "Excuse me, Mister Baron Brad, sir. There's a monster coming. I think it may have seen us."

"Huh?" He glanced behind him at the ugly creature in the tattered remains of a sundress. Its hair was scraggly and matted with leaves, and its filthy, bloodstained bra perfectly held its left breast, while the right hung free.

He scoffed at it. "It's just one stupid…"

It was then that Sadie's last shot with the grenade launcher detonated the munitions trucks in an ear-shattering explosion. The three of them, Jillybean, Brad and the monster, blinked at the harsh flash of light and then paused in place until the sky shook with the rumble of the explosion.

Jillybean didn't know what the sound was. She understood that it was a bomb of some sort, but she wasn't experienced enough to grasp the size of the explosion or the distances involved. For all she knew the bomb had gone off right on the other side of the ridge.

"Son of a bitch," Brad grumbled. "Those idiots! Come on, Jillybean. We got to go back."

"Why? What is it?"

"People being stupid," he answered and then started monster walking back the way they had come.

After a glance at the sun dress-wearing monster, Jillybean hurried to catch up. The way was steep and sure enough, when the monster came after them, it went tumbling away into the horde.

Trying to walk against the current of undead wasn't easy. When they could, they kept to the sloping hills just above the highway. It hurt walking on such a steep grade. Jillybean's ankles ached after a while and her lower leg, the leg that basically held her up, kept cramping into painful knots. When that happened, Brad would glare like a human, which really wasn't smart.

What was exceptionally difficult was when there wasn't a hill on either side. Frequently, and for long stretches, there were sharp, rock walls rising on one side of the road and scary drop-offs falling away from the other; which meant Brad and Jillybean were stuck forcing their way through the mob.

Brad had to lead in these circumstances and after the first two-hundred yard stretch, he made his way, huffing and puffing, up the next hill. When he left the monsters behind, he turned on Jillybean. "Where the hell is your collar? Huh? Where's the chain that was around your neck?"

"It was loose," she answered, without looking up. She was afraid that he would see the lie in her eyes if he was looking right into them when she told it. She was convinced that evil people were especially attuned to wrong doing of any sort when it occurred around them. She thought it was a sixth sense, or a superpower.

"It was also heavy, for reals. I took it off so that I could keep up with you. I wasn't going to run away, I swear. I could have if I wanted to, but I don't want you hurting those ladies on the bus."

His face was stormy, his brows down over his eyes and his lips were tight together and lined. The mud covering his face only added to the harshness of the effect. He stepped right up to her and threatened with a fist that looked as hard as one of the many boulders around them. "You had better not even think about running away. If you do, those women will suffer and it will be on your head."

Jillybean was now in a terrible place. She wasn't sure she could control her thinkings. What would happen if a thought about escaping just poked up out of nothing, all on its own? It happened to her a lot. Thoughts or ideas or even little conjectures would suddenly just pop into being inside her head even when she didn't mean them too. Sometimes she considered herself downright *afflicted* with thoughts.

As she stumbled along the sides of the hills, trying to keep up with Brad, she did her best to control her mind, which, as it turned out, wasn't easy at all. Her brain jumped from subject to subject, from bee to rock, to the spacing of trees for optimal growth, to the phases of the moon and the possible reasons it assumed the strange shapes it did. She pondered on the difference between oak leaves and pine needles, rounded pebbles and rough rocks, and why animals had tails and people did not.

And how to escape.

Her mind kept going there time and again, and, when it did, she would cast a furtive glance at Brad's back, sure she was seeing a stiffening in his muscles or a twitch in his fake monster gait. Every innocuous move he made convinced her that he knew what she was plotting, and before long, she was sweating from the stress she was under.

Fearing that she was dooming the innocent women back at the Azael camp, she tried her utmost to focus on holding her brain in check, and think of nothing whatsoever, however she had never tried to marshal her thoughts in such a way before and the strain was too great.

The river was the key to their escape. No one was watching it at all. The Azael seemed to think that it was too cold and too fast for anyone to try to cross, and besides, the far bank was a sheer, cliff face that ran up the grim flanks of the mountains. It was wet and clung-over with green moss; it couldn't be scaled by the weak and the inexperienced, and Jillybean was both. Crossing the river wasn't a means to escape; however, using its energy and direction was. She saw clearly how—they could use the seat cushions from the bus as flotation devices and, in the dead of night, could slip into the frigid, racing waters one at a time. It would be both scary and dangerous to use the big river, but it would work. They could be out on the plains by morning.

The plan popped straight into her head fully formed, causing Jillybean's stomach to knot up.

Brad took that moment to glance back at her and a most unzombie-like, guilty smile broke across her face. His eyes narrowed and a voice inside her screamed: *think of something else!*

She dropped her eyes to her hands and at first, she was unable to think of anything but the plan and the punishment for thinking of the plan—then she saw her fingers; five on one hand and an equal number on the other. Ten all together. They were the basic tools of counting for every child who had ever lived, and Jillybean could remember using them years ago to keep track of items she needed numbered.

This simple thought reminded her of her previous exploration into mathematics and, before she knew it, she was lost in concepts that should have been years beyond her. When next she focused her eyes on something, they were nudging passed the last of the zombies and gazing up at the tall angel-winged men on horseback.

"What happened?" Brad demanded. "What was that big explosion?"

"They got the munitions truck," one of the riders answered. "They got us with a fucking sneak attack."

Chapter 17
Sadie Walcott

When the twenty tons of high explosives and white phosphorus went up in a *snap-snap-snap* triple explosion, it incinerated a hundred men in a blink. It warped the barrels of the howitzers, twisting them so that they appeared to belong in a Dali painting and not on a battlefield. The five-ton trucks that had housed all the extra ordinance were reduced to fist-sized chunks of metal, rubber, and glass fused into bizarre shapes.

A minute before, the field had been waist-high with green, mountain grasses, now it was on fire from end-to-end. The men of the Azael were running away, those who were still alive, that is. With the tall grasses burnt down to the hard pan of the earth, an amazing number of contorted and shriveled bodies were visible scattered here and there.

Fearing that the injured Captain Grey was one of them, Sadie turned back to where she had left him and saw that yes, he was alive and yes, he was on fire. Feebly, he was beating at roiling orange flames running up his right leg. Without any consideration for her own safety, she was up and racing at him. In two seconds, she had cleared the twenty yards between them and, as she had no fire-fighting equipment with her, she threw herself bodily on his legs, smothering the flames with her torso, her hands, and the dirt she scraped up and threw on him.

If she was burned, she didn't notice. The flames eating Grey's uniform were out and that was all that mattered.

"You ok?" she asked. The two words ran together into one that sounded like: *U-k?*

It was a second before he could answer. His eyes were glassy and unfocussed; his head lolled as though he was drunk and his hands floundered around like a man looking for something lost in the dark. "Me?" he slurred. "Yeah…yeah, I'm good."

He wasn't good. The blast had caught him full on. His face had been flash-burned to a bright red, his brain concussed by the aftershock of the explosion and he had a new second-degree burn on his leg to go with the holes in his body from four different bullets.

"Leave me," he said, through cracked and parched lips.

"Fuck you," she said, and for the first time in weeks, despite the misery baking into the pores of her skin, she felt like herself. "Come on." She stood and looked around. Nothing was familiar; it was like she had been transported to some plain of hell. There was a tremendous crater where the trucks had been and the field had been transformed into a burning nightmare. The only things that made sense were the mountains. They pointed the way home.

She planted one foot next to Grey's shoulder, took hold of him with both hands and then heaved him to his feet, not noticing his weight which was twice her own. It was a feat, powered by adrenaline, she could never have replicated—Grey wasn't the only one who was feeling the effect of the blast—she was acting on instinct and that instinct told her she had to get out of there, fast.

He sagged against her and she accepted his weight draped across her shoulders as though he were little more than a child. "A little further," she said when he tripped not a dozen feet into their journey home. They were nonsense words. There was still ten miles between them and safety.

"One step at a time," she encouraged him. Gradually, she coaxed him across the fire-strewn field, avoiding the spots that were still raging. For some time, they seemed to be the only ones left alive on the face of the earth. Everything around them was either angry orange and searing, or black and sooty, billowing a haze of smoke that caused her to weaken and stumble.

Then, out of the smoke, another stumbling figure appeared. It was charred and hideous; she took it be a zombie that had been too close to the explosion. It came right for them without slowing. Her M16 was up and pointed so quickly the eye could barely follow the motion. As she braced for the jarring sensation guns always produced, her trigger finger squeezed down. Instead of the *bang!* she was expecting, the gun only produced a tiny *click*.

She was out of ammo!

Before she could throw Grey off of her and desperately attempt to flip the magazine around, the zombie spoke. "Hey, don't shoot. It's me, Morganstern."

"Oh," Sadie said. She couldn't be blamed for not knowing him. His apple cheeks were covered in soot, his normally soft, brown hair was plastered to his skull on one side of his head and stuck up in spikes on the other, while his uniform was filthy black in places and seared to a fine char in others. She could only guess at what sort of hell-creature she appeared to be. "Where's...uh, where's the other guy you were with?" she asked.

"Rob's dead," Morganstern said, breathing out the words. "Took one to the head. Here, let me help you." He came up under Grey's other arm and basically took all the weight off of her. She wasn't going to argue. The adrenaline rush of battle was fading and there was still a long way to go.

He took so much weight off her shoulders that she basically gave the captain over to him. She took his weapon and slung it across her back and then she did the same with Grey's. Next she flipped her magazine around and pulled back on the charging handle.

"I think I'm ready to..." A distant gunshot caused her to jerk around. She stared back across the field toward where the Azael had their camp strung out along Highway 34; there was a blinking light which was followed a second later by the sound of more gunfire. "Are they shooting at us?" she asked.

Morganstern started hauling Grey away, saying, over his shoulder: "Of course they are. Don't just stand there, come on."

She followed them deeper up the wooded slopes of the ridgeline and in seconds the burning field was out of sight and the gunfire tapered away to nothing. Then they were trudging back the way they had come, drinking in the cool air.

Grey was a bleary and mumbling load for Morganstern until they came upon a mountain stream that was only a few feet in width and a foot deep. It made a noise that was a cross between a gurgle and a chuckle.

"I need..." Grey said in a whisper before kneeling down next to the running waters. For two minutes, he guzzled the cold water and splashed himself until he was soaking wet. Then, gently, he peeled back the burnt uniform, exposing his lower right leg; the flesh was blistered and raw below the knee, but could have been worse. He grunted at what he saw and then made to stand, but went lightheaded and had to be held up by Morganstern.

"I'm good," Grey said, when his eyes could focus. He glanced back the way they had come and asked: "Where are Dornier and O'Hannon?"

Morganstern shook his head. "Don't know. Probably dead. They had stopped shooting about a minute before the explosion."

"We need to go back and see," Grey said. "We don't leave men behind."

Again Morganstern shook his head. "No, we can't, not this time. I'm sorry sir, but if they were uninjured, they would've been here by now. That means they're either too hurt to walk or they're dead. I can barely carry you and I don't think Sadie would be much help moving guys the size of Dornier and O'Hannon. If we go back, we go back to die, not to save anyone."

"Then leave me," Grey ordered. "You and Sadie go back."

"I'm not one of your soldiers to order about," Sadie told the captain, her fists planted firmly on her hips. "I'm not going back and neither is Morganstern. It's a stupid idea. Now, you two get going. I'll cover our retreat." She picked out a tree that was large enough to hide behind and then leaned up against it with her weapon pointing down the slope.

Grey let out an exasperated breath. "If you're going to do this, do it right. Where is your fallback position and how do you plan on getting to it without getting shot? Where are your fields of fire? The forest in front of you is too thick and while behind you it's too thin to provide cover. Come on, Sadie, use your head."

"Sorry," she mumbled. "I'm not used to doing this sort of thing. Maybe, you guys should show me a good spot."

"Sure," Morganstern said. "Don't listen to the captain, you're doing great so far."

With Grey leaning heavily on Morganstern, they led the way up the hill. Sadie walked with her head turned part way around; she could hear whispers coming from the woods behind them and she expected another shot to ring out at any second. It made her walk with a terrible itch between her shoulder blades where she figured the bullet would hit. The feeling was dreadful and her feet want to run, screaming away at top speed.

But she would not leave Grey to his fate.

Two hundred yards up the slope, Grey pointed at a fallen tree; its trunk was so big around that it would take two people to wrap their arms around its girth. "There's your field of fire right in front of you," Grey told her, pointing with his good arm at the relatively sparsely covered hillside they had just tromped up. "Wait until they're in the open area before shooting. Aim low and don't waste your ammo. They're going to want to flank you to the right. When they shift in that direction, wait until they show themselves through those trees before you fire. Then get low and scoot back around the bend of the hill. Got it?"

With her hands starting to shake, she didn't trust her voice. She nodded and gripped her gun tighter.

"I should take our weapons back," Morganstern said. "Just in case."

Just in case? She didn't like the sound of that, still she fumbled their guns off her back and, after handing them over, they left her, huddled against the downed tree. "They won't go far," she told herself. "It's not like they're going to abandon me or anything." She tried to laugh the thought away, but it persisted and she kept glancing over her shoulder to check their progress until they were out of sight.

Turning her attention back to the steep hill in front of her she was shocked to see men walking up the slope toward her. It was the Azael. Some were dressed in the flowing and wildly colorful scarves, while a few were in camouflage; none were foolish enough to come dressed in their angel costumes.

Sadie centered her sights on a group of three men in camo, thinking that once the shooting started they would be far harder to spot than the men in the scarves. Also, since they were walking so close together, she figured that if she missed her target, she might hit one of the others by mistake.

She didn't miss. The 5.56 mm round zipped across the sixty yards in a blink, catching a man just below his navel and blasting out through his right kidney. Without any hesitation, she snap-fired at the next man over without really aiming and, if he hadn't started to dive to his right, she would've missed him. He moved straight into the path of her bullet and caught it in the chest.

By the time she had brought the M16 back to the left, the Azael were throwing themselves to the dirt and scrounging for cover. The men in camo seemed to disappear, but two of the scarf-wearing men stood out in comparison to the yellow and brown grass. She fired four times at them; one of them cried out in pain and the other just lay there, unmoving except for his foot that twitched in an ugly manner.

Then bullets started blazing in her direction. The tree she was crouched behind thumped as bullets struck it. She could feel the vibration of each come up through her cheek. There were so many bullets hitting the trunk or flying right above it that Sadie was afraid to move.

But she had to. They would flank her if she didn't and there was little to protect her to the left and right. Having been in a few gun battles, she knew enough not to just jump up and start shooting. Keeping lower than the edge of the trunk, she skittered to her right where the branches of a nearby pine tree hung so low that they were almost touching the downed tree trunk.

Slowly, she stretched up over the trunk until she was able to see the entire hill below her. It was alive with flashes of fire and smoke. It crawled with men. Some were moving to her right where there was more cover, while others were hunkered down and sweeping the tree trunk with gunfire.

She brought the M16 up and blasted it at the men trying to flank her. They were about fifty yards distant and because of the terrain, her hyped-up state, and the fact that she was literally scared stiff by everyone trying to kill her, she missed with all five of her shots.

She pulled the trigger as fast as she could and then dropped down behind the trunk as a storm of lead flew her way. The pine tree that had given her cover was torn apart; branches and needles and chunks of bark fell all over her, thick as rain. The tree trunk rumbled and shook and splinters filled the air. A scream ripped from her throat; it was uncontrolled, adding to the near overwhelming panic that made her want to race out of there at full speed.

Only the realization that she still had a job to do kept her in place. Captain Grey and PFC Morganstern were counting on her. Their head start had been minutes only, and if Sadie ran away right then, they wouldn't make it another mile. She had to stay and fight, and yet she couldn't stay where she was much longer either. There were simply too many bullets whizzing all around her and the trunk, and the air inches above it. It was only a matter of time before one of those bullets would find its mark sooner or later.

Staying flat, she wormed her way back to her starting point and, with a quick breath, she hopped up and started shooting—at what she didn't really know. The trees and the mountains and her enemies were nothing but a blur of colors, and there was no time to aim at anything. She fired five or six times in the space of a second and a half, and likely didn't hit a thing.

But that was okay with Sadie. Since there were so many of them, killing three or four or even ten of them wouldn't do much in the long run. Her purpose there was to buy time. To that end, she wriggled a few feet further along the trunk, and this time, she didn't leap up to fire, she simply stuck the barrel of the M16 over the trunk and pulled the trigger three times.

She went up and down the forty feet of trunk, repeating this process four more times. On the fifth try, the trigger wouldn't budge; she was out of ammo...completely out. The only thing she had left to shoot with was the grenade launcher.

"Better than nothing," she said, as she worked one of the 40mm fragmentation grenades from the bandolier. There was an issue with the grenade launcher: she couldn't fire it at random to keep her enemies huddled behind cover. They would figure that out quickly and would grow bold and close on her too quickly. This meant that she would have to expose herself again. If she had testicles, they would have shriveled at the thought.

As it was, she felt a sudden lance of fear in her gut. The Azael had gotten used to her erratic movements and they were no longer simply reacting. Now they were shooting at random spots as close above the tree trunk as they could. Sadie knew there was a good chance that she would stand up into the path of a bullet.

"Fuck!" she growled, angrily. There was no lie to her anger; for too long she had been hunted and persecuted, and the reasons? Greed, lust, racism, and superstitious idiocy! She had a right to be furious. It was her enemies who had made her what she had become. It was their fault she was a killer…a murderer.

"Fuck!" she yelled again, psyching herself into doing something that commonsense told her was really, very stupid. With bullets zipping at her from almost every little clump of trees along a curving crescent in front of her, she popped up, sighted down the side of her gun at the thicker part of the forest on her right flank and pulled the odd forward trigger of the under-barrel grenade launcher.

Foomp! Bang!

There was a satisfying scream before the entire mountain side seemed to erupt in a million gun blasts. Sadie felt strangely exhilarated by the action of the grenade launcher. It was more…more manly-feeling, more of a savage weapon, than the simple *bang, bang, bang* of the M16.

She loaded the next round and did so with a grin.

This time she forced herself to wait half a minute before shooting the grenade. It wasn't out of fear, although her throat was so tight that she couldn't have swallowed a Tic-Tac. She waited because it seemed to confound her enemies. They blazed away at the trunk with more ferocity than before, changing their tempo and direction of fire, all with the purpose of tripping her up.

It made her grin. Strangely, once she started, she couldn't stop. The grin was simply glued to her features. Her face felt tight around it and, had she been thinking straight, she would have been worried about what it said about her mental state. Instead, she went with it. It was a death grin, like one found on the Jolly Roger, or on every Halloween mask ever made.

The next time she fired, she waited until the guns were going hot. She could tell they were afraid of the grenade launcher because their bullets were now passing four feet above the tree trunk. She was up and shooting before anyone could react. Again screams accompanied the explosion.

"Damn," she whispered, working another fat shell into the chamber, "I am good."

She was good. Destroying the howitzers had given her a boost of confidence that nothing else could have. She had accomplished what trained soldiers hadn't been able to.

"I'm good, and don't forget it," she said on her fifth shot. Her face ached with the maniacal grin frozen on her lips and her trigger finger was stiff from the recoil that went straight through her hand and up into her forearm with every shot.

She was just shaking out her hand when she saw movement to her right. In a flash of insight she knew she had been flanked. Her position behind the trunk, so impregnable for the last eleven minutes was now untenable. There was no cover down the slope on her right.

Immediately, she wriggled backward, passing through the underbrush like a lizard until she was on the back side of the hill. There was a great deal of excited gunfire coming from the right but, thankfully, they were shooting at where she had been and not where she currently was.

When she had crawled for a minute, she found herself in an area of forest so thick that she felt she could chance some speed. Up she jumped. In a blur, she began racing along the deer trail that Grey and Morganstern had been following. Branches swiped at her and roots tried to catch her flying feet, yet nothing could slow her.

She had sprinted two hundred yards and was feeling a good burn in her lungs when there was suddenly more gunfire to her left. At first, it didn't register she was being targeted. She foolishly thought she had left the Azael far behind, however, in all the time she had crouched behind the trunk, a large contingent of them had been racing along a ravine at the base of the ridge. They were now sweeping up the slope in a wave.

With leaves snapping off the trees all around her, and bullets whining off the rocks, Sadie started running in earnest. She sprinted as only she could and, with the steep slope, it felt as though she was outrunning the hot lead blazing through the air. She ran a hundred yards in Olympic time.

And yet she couldn't outrun everything. She sped up a little, tree-covered hill and was halfway down the other side before she realized that Captain Grey and Morganstern were standing on the path, and that there were people in the dell thirty yards to her left. The people were all armed to the teeth and a number of them were dressed in the colorful scarves of the Azael.

"Don't do it, Missy," one of the men said, as Sadie slipped her hand under the barrel of her M16. He had her in his sights and at that range, he couldn't miss. They were caught.

Chapter 18

Captain Grey

The world would not stop spinning. It went round and round whenever they let him stop for a breather, leaning against a pine tree with his face hard against the rough-edged bark. He would also rest when one of them stumbled on the tiny deer trail. It was almost always Grey doing the stumbling. There was a lancing, through and through quarter-inch tunnel in his left calf that bled freely, while his right, lower leg was one continuous blister that ached miserably.

His left arm hung and was practically useless. The fingers on that side were numb and weak from lack of blood flow. He was also shot through the side, just above his left hip bone. That wound wasn't bad. It barely bled compared to the other holes in his body and only hurt, miserably if he moved.

Unfortunately, they hadn't stopped moving, except to pause for a few gulps of air and they hadn't done that more than once or twice in the last hour. They just kept going with Grey, in spite of his injuries and his flagging stamina, forcing them on.

He pushed them right up until they were outflanked by the Azael who trapped them neat, as you please up, against the hard face of the ridgeline. There were a dozen of the Azael, maybe more, surrounding them. It was hard for Grey to focus enough to count because of the great black spots that had begun to swim before his eyes.

As the leader of the Azael swung an M4 around and barked orders about dropping weapons and turning about, it was all Grey could do to stay on his feet. He needed to rest badly. He also needed something to drink in a way he had never felt in his life.

Four years before, he had served in Iraq where the summers were arid and blistering, leaving him parched simply by walking to formation. It had not been an easy tour, going on patrols under the weight of a full combat load in a hundred and ten degree heat, and yet it was nothing compared to what he was feeling just then.

It's the burn, he thought to himself. It was the burn on his leg, coupled with the ten mile mountain run he had embarked on earlier…and the loss of blood. It had him reeling in place and when Morganstern and Sadie dropped their weapons and turned, Grey simply refused. He wasn't armed, and he was such a bloody mess they had to see he was practically harmless.

"Hands up!" the leader of the squad of Azael screamed. He was angry and keyed up, his finger on the trigger of his weapon.

"One second," Grey said. Slowly, he reached for his canteen as the screamer glared over his aimed rifle. "Just getting a drink," Grey told him as he put the canteen to his lips and chugged the water, relishing every drop. Right at that moment, he might have welcomed a bullet…a properly aimed bullet, that is.

The leader of the group was sloppy, not only in his stance, but in his entire attitude toward the situation. He appeared to be of two minds: on one hand, he was strangely excited, while on the other, he strove to give off an air of nonchalance, as though gun battles, explosions, and frantic chases were an everyday occurrence for him. All in all, it made it so that there was no telling what he would do, except shoot straight, that is; that didn't seem likely.

"He's unarmed," Morganstern told the man. "So why don't you relax and aim that gun somewhere else?"

The man did as asked, though from Captain Grey's perspective, he seemed to do so in slow-motion. The M4 swiveled like a minute hand on a clock, away from Grey and toward Morganstern. When the rifle was aimed midway between them, a sharp *crack!* sounded from off to their right. It was followed by an entire string of 'pops' from further up the ridgeline.

The leader with the M4 wore a look of confusion, right up until his face exploded outward, spraying the tall mountain grasses in front of him with blood and teeth.

Grey was the quickest of the three to drop to the ground. Just like at the stream, the quart of water from his canteen was like an instant infusion of energy. It wouldn't last and so he was determined to make the most of it while he could. He dropped to the dirt and, knowing that crawling with bad legs and a useless left arm wouldn't get him very far, he rolled like a log toward where the leader's lifeless corpse was face first in the dirt.

With bullets whipping from every direction, Grey took up the M4, one-handed as though it were the largest pistol ever made, and fired it at a blurry figure crouched behind a blocky boulder a few feet away. The man spasmed, his hands flaring out and his head pitching back. Grey shot him a second time as a precaution and then changed targets.

He sighted on a second of the Azael, but as he did so, a bullet went through the man's eye and blasted out the side of his head above his ear. Grey started sweeping his gun to the left but stopped as the man he had just witnessed being shot, unexpectedly, and unnaturally, stood up.

Battle was frequently full of amazing quirks that defied all explanation and this Azael man with the hole in his head was a perfect example. With his weapon lying in the grass and forgotten, he stood up with bullets flying all around him and simply walked away as though he had heard his mom calling him home to dinner. There was a lull in the shooting as everyone stared at the freakish sight, and it was likely they were all feeling the same queasiness in the pits of their stomachs, as Grey was.

The second that the forest hid the man from view, the fighting resumed in a furious exchange with all pretense toward civility or humanity cast away by either side.

By the disciplined pattern of the shooting from up the hill, Grey knew that it was his men arrayed upslope from them. In spite of their exhaustion or injuries, six of them had stuck doggedly to the trail and now were in a perfect position to spring an ambush.

Even with their initial attack, which saw a good number of the Azael drop to the ground lifeless, the soldiers were outnumbered three to one. What was worse, they were limited by the small amount of ammunition they carried. The Azael, who weren't hampered by a lack of ammo, ripped-up the hillside, going full auto in many cases, keeping the soldiers pinned down or scurrying back and forth from cover to cover.

And yet the soldiers weren't new to firefights. They chose their moments, they laid down cover fire, they actually took the time to aim, and they were fearless. The fearful man hurries his shots, sometimes missing by yards in his desire to get back down behind cover where it was safe. The soldiers, and that included Grey and Morganstern, were amazingly steady in the face of danger. And they rarely missed.

159

For a good thirty seconds, the Azael were too confused by the sudden onslaught to realize that Grey had managed to find a weapon. He killed three more men before they got wise. Their return fire was appalling in its volume. The bullets came like hot rain and only a slight gully kept him from being killed ten times over. As it was, he received two more nicks: one high up on his right shoulder from a bullet that traveled down the barrel of the M4 and another that creased his lower right leg.

He thought the leg injury was worse than it was as his leg felt almost instantly wet. When he glanced down, he saw that the bullet had ripped open a blister the size of his fist and that it was only interstitial fluids that were running down his calf.

A grunt that implied *interesting* escaped him and then as the dirt all around the gulley kicked up, he lost all interest in the wound. With rolling now out of the question, he started thrusting forward using just his right elbow and the toes of his right foot. After a minute, he left the shooting behind him and took a quick peek above the grass.

He counted fifteen of the Azael remaining. Up the slope, four of his men were still in the fight, while there was only silence from where Grey had last seen Morganstern. Poor odds indeed, especially as the captain wasn't able to move and aim with anything close to his full capabilities.

Hunkering back down, he clicked his weapon over to three-round burst before lifting back up so that he was just above the tips of the grass. Again, he fired his weapon pistol style, this time at a clump of men squatting behind a row of thigh-high boulders that stuck out of the ground like the spine of a dinosaur.

At least one was hit. There was a cry as the men dove into the heather sending a scattering of shots his way; all missing high. Grey was already back down in the rut, kicking and scrounging forward, leaving a trail of blood behind him. Someone on the hill fired on the same group of men, complementing Grey and hitting another.

Even as one of the soldiers on the hill cheered, one of the Azael lifted his weapon up from behind a termite-riddled log and emptied his magazine, hitting the soldier more by accident than by any skill. Before Grey could come to grips with the latest loss, there was a sudden rattle of gunfire east of them. It was answered by what sounded like a thousand guns erupting all at once.

"What the hell?" he groused, wondering what fresh craziness was happening. A separate and very one-sided battle was playing out but who was shooting who, he didn't know. He hoped that the two groups of Azael had blundered into each other and were now killing themselves.

It would be their only chance, he figured.

Only, he hadn't figured on Sadie. She popped up suddenly, aiming her M16—*Foomp! Bang!*

The blast was so close that Grey had to shield his eyes from the effect of the explosion. Three seconds later: *Foomp! Bang!* Grey hugged the earth as shards of metal zinged about. He wasn't the only one. All of the Azael were cringing instead of fighting. Even when there was a pause while Sadie reloaded, they were afraid to lift their heads.

Grey needed them to move. He needed them running as if their life depended on it. After Sadie's third shot, he leapt up and cried: "Now! Kill the Azael. Kill all of them!" The next few moments were a blur. His eyes were both angry and crazed, and his face, streaked with mud and blood was that of a wild creature. He looked and acted like a man possessed; his injuries were altogether forgotten as he charged.

The remaining Azael broke and fled, many flinging aside their weapons. Grey shot after them until his gun was spent. When it clicked dry, it dropped from his hand, forgotten; there were quite a few guns lying about and quite a few men as well. Some were stretched out in calm repose as though sleeping, the holes in their bodies barely visible, some were simply the pale white of cadavers laid out on morgue slabs, and some were contorted, mangled and bloody, evidence of their hard deaths.

He was sure some of the men were faking, holding their bodies rigid to keep from shaking, hoping that they wouldn't be found out. With the firing continuing sixty yards to the east, Grey didn't have time to hunt them out. Nor did he have the inclination to. The brief flare of energy that had carried him through the battle was ebbing, leaving him feeling shaky and weak.

"Let's get moving," he called out. "What's our casualty situation?" Up the hill, three men stood and glanced around before one held up three fingers. Three more men he had led to their deaths. Three more souls he was responsible for. Grey buried the thought somewhere deep.

"We can't leave Morganstern," Sadie said, as she came up. Like Grey, she was burying things deep. She held her chin tilted up slightly and wouldn't look at the corpses sprawled around them. "He's fighting, like a hundred of them, singlehandedly. I told them I had passed by a bunch of guys with guns and he said something about flanks or I don't know what, and then he left."

"You did great," Grey told her, before squinting up at his remaining men. Their camouflage was so well applied that he only recognized one of them. "Rider, pull Morganstern back, and you two," he pointed at the other pair, "Set up a secondary ambush site right here. We'll leapfrog our way back to the valley. Remember, don't get bogged down. Kill a couple of them and move. One team up, one team back. Bound past each other with enough intervals to lay down cover fire."

As the men looked for cover, Sadie waited for instructions with her face impassive and hard. She seemed to think that he was going to send her into battle and he planned to, but only as a last resort. His soldiers were trained to act together in perfect harmony. Two of them would wait in hiding, firing when the enemy closed to within fifty yards and when the return fire became too hot, they would retreat past the back team, who would now repeat the process: hide, ambush, fire and retreat.

It took practice to perfect. If one of the team members left their firing spot early, he would leave his friend alone and unprotected, and if he didn't leave quick enough, he risked being surrounded, unsupported and killed. Grey knew that Sadie's courage was easily greater than her experience.

"I'm going to need your help to get out of here," he told her. "But first, grab as much ammo as you can carry. We'll act as a supply point for the men."

As Sadie began rushing around, stooping here and there among the dead, picking up magazines and checking their loads, Grey tried his best not to faint. In the grass next to him was a dead Azael, strapped to his bloody shoulders was a bulky backpack that was spilling fully loaded 30 round magazines onto the ground. Grey tried to stoop to replenish his supply and nearly passed out. The world spun as it had before and he fell against a tree; it was the only thing that kept him on his feet.

Forget the ammo, he told himself, realizing that he was no longer capable of fighting. It would take everything he had just to survive.

Of course, survival was secondary. Leading his remaining men out of danger was paramount. They had done their job; their mission had been a success and Grey wasn't going to let them die out there if he could help it. And that meant he wasn't going to burden them with the weight of his body by fainting.

Going from tree to tree, Grey started hobbling on a diagonal up the slope toward the deer trail they had been following. Sadie hurried to catch up. She had pulled the chest rig off of the dead Azael and had filled it with ammo. She 'clinked' as she walked, something that he normally would have frowned at. Frowning took more energy than he had to spare.

She put a shoulder under his good arm and tried to heft him up. "Other side," he said. With his good arm over her shoulder, he was virtually useless; he couldn't hold a gun or help to pull himself along, or even catch himself if and when he fell. There would be no getting around falling—the land was as rugged as almost anywhere on earth.

While he held onto another pine, she slid around to his left. When she lifted his arm, the pain was immediate and yet he only grinned through the waves of agony. His men, and Sadie, needed to see that he was a rock. Their morale would sink if they saw him struggling.

He wanted to tell himself that his injuries weren't so bad and, after moving a hundred yards, he found that his burned right lower leg grew stronger as the blood flowed in his veins. The same was partially true with his left leg as well. His calf muscle was a gory mess and useless, but at least the blood flowed; his boot was filled with the stuff so that every step was accompanied by a squishing sound that had Sadie looking both anxious for him as well as revolted.

He said nothing and made no noise of complaint as they trudged along one step at a time. The Azael were hot on their trail, revenge driving them despite the casualties they were suffering. The soldiers, using every bit of natural cover available, were holding back hundreds of enemy fighters through sheer courage and marksmanship. Working in pairs, they were constantly in motion, going back and forth, keeping up a drumbeat of fire that was always answered by a firestorm.

Gradually, Grey became numb from exhaustion. The spurt of energy from the water was long gone and his feet began to stumble so that Sadie was forced to take more and more of his weight on her shoulder. She didn't complain. For an hour, nothing changed for Grey except the steepness of the slope they were on and the number of bodies that they left behind.

To the east, the sun arced over the mountains while in the air, bullets passed each other and the sound of the guns echoed, bouncing from one stark mountainside to another.

Grey got used to seeing his remaining soldiers huffing and puffing past him to find their next ambush point. At one time or another they each came to Sadie for more ammo—it was going fast. They were weary and getting sloppy, missing their shots with greater frequency.

Eventually, Morganstern jogged by alone, his face set to a purposefully expressionless blank. Grey grabbed his arm. "Where's Rider?" It was a stupid question. Rider wasn't taking a leak or a smoke break.

"Dead," Morganstern replied. "One of them got off a lucky shot." He didn't have time to elaborate, the Azael were pressing too close. Some were on the string of hills to the north and were taking long distance potshots at the three of them.

Morganstern took up a lone position behind a boulder that had good cover on his left to protect him from the flanking shots. At the moment, the incoming fire was sporadic and poorly aimed. It was a mere nuisance, but it likely wouldn't remain that way as the Azael grew bolder.

Ten minutes later, they lost another soldier. He came hobbling up the trail supported by his teammate; there was blood turning his camouflaged trousers black. "It's nothing," he said in a whisper. "I just caught one in the leg. It doesn't even hurt."

It wasn't nothing. His face was stark white beneath the mud and his blue eyes were so drained of color that they were the color of a pond ice. On the trail behind them, there was an alarming amount of blood. "Let me see," Grey said.

The wounded soldier didn't so much sit down as he allowed his legs to buckle beneath him. In a second, he was on the ground staring up at the sky and looking confused as though he thought the sun was the wrong shape or the wrong color perhaps. "It's nothing," he said again, only this time his voice was softer.

He pushed aside the soldier's shaking hands and a fountain of blood came spurting from the wound; Grey saw right away that he would soon be dead. The femoral artery had been shredded—it was a death sentence. In vain, Grey pushed the heel of his palm onto the wound and leaned his entire weight down. In seconds, there was a pool of dark blood covering his hand; Grey estimated that the man was losing a quart of blood a minute and, in the situation they were in, there was nothing more he could do.

"Why is the sun like that?" the soldier mumbled. "It's dim…what's that mean?"

"It means we're almost home," Grey told him. He wore a warm smile that hid the misery bubbling up from his soul. The soldier's coming death was another on his head. His men could have escaped by now if they hadn't been lugging him about. He turned to the other, still-unknown soldier. "I'm going to cover your retreat. Take Morganstern and Sadie and get over that ridge and when you get to Estes, tell them…tell them that we did our jobs.

The soldier's lips twisted and his eyes went hard. He wanted to argue with his captain; however, he was a good soldier; he wasn't going to disobey a direct order. Sadie was a different story altogether.

"Hell no!" she spat. "We're getting out of this together. The valley needs you, Grey. Especially now. The valley needs a hero and a leader. If anyone's going to stay, it'll be me. I'm practically useless. We all know it."

Just then Morganstern came out of the forest. His brown eyes clouded with sadness as he looked at the dying soldier. When he saw Sadie's imperious face and Grey's tired one, he took charge. "You're being loud," he said. "And they're right on my tail, about sixty yards back. You guys have to get moving. I'll stay with Beeman and buy us some time."

"Beeman," Grey said the word as a ghost might, he breathed it out slowly, vaguely. How had he not recognized Sergeant Charles Beeman? How was that possible?

They had stood side by side through a dozen battles; they had laughed together and bled together. They hadn't been the best of friends since they had been in different companies; however the odd, unpredictable nature of battle had frequently thrust them together. Grey could remember one star-filled night north of Santa Fe when they had sat in adjacent foxholes, trading stories, mostly of women from back before the apocalypse and playing remember when.

They had also competed in a juvenile game of one-upmanship, trying to outdo the other telling farfetched tales. Grey remembered he had grown quiet after a while thinking about all the death he had seen and of everything he had lost in so short a period of time. Beeman had cheered him up in the strangest way.

"Bet I can spot more shootin' stars than you," he said. "Me and my brothers used to have this competition 'bout who could see more."

So they fell into calling them out as they streaked across the sky. There were many dozens to see that night and, although Grey had a quick eye and got into the friendly game, he lost and lost big.

"Hey, Beeman, it's going to be ok," Grey said as the man began to gasp for breath. "Maybe just close your eyes and think about those shooting stars. Remember them?"

"Yeah...I do," he answered, slowly.

Grey watched him for another second and then said. "I got this. The rest of you get out of here, that's an order. Morganstern, carry Sadie if you have to."

Sadie glared at Morganstern, warning him with a dark look not to touch her, making it obvious that she was going to fight the order tooth and nail. They locked eyes, communicating something between them and before Grey knew what was happening, Morganstern had a firm grip on his chest rig and had hauled him to his feet.

Standing so quickly caused the world around Grey to go hazy as the blood drained from his head and his legs went wobbly. It was a sign that he was heading into a hypovolemic state and that he would be in shock in the near future and dead not much longer after that. "What the hell are you doing, Morganstern? You have your orders."

"I don't take orders from dead men," the young soldier said.

Chapter 19

Captain Grey

Grey tried to push away from Morganstern, however he lacked the energy to both stay on his feet and fight the young buck. "Let me go," he seethed.

Morganstern refused the order with a simple: "No. If you stay here, you'll die. I have a fighting chance at least. Now, everyone get out of here. Sadie, help the captain. Rutledge, take up a position in that stand of trees and together we'll cover our retreat."

Sadie didn't wait for the argument brewing on the captain's lips to materialize. With her usual fiery determination, she started hauling Grey along against his will. He didn't have the strength to fight her either, he could barely keep his feet moving. Behind them, the shooting started in right away. Morganstern's lone rifle sounded and was answered by the fire of a hundred enemies. The firing seemed to come from three directions at once. Sadie looked back, fear in her eyes.

"Please make it," she whispered.

"He'll be fine," Grey lied. "He's a good soldier." Good soldier or not, Grey knew his chances of breaking contact when engaged with so many opponents were slim.

Morganstern proved elusive and a difficult target, however. He kept up a steady rhythm with his M4 for half a minute and then somehow managed to scramble away with bullets flying all around him.

He jogged past Sadie and Grey to crouch down among some low fern-like plants, thirty feet off the trail, managing to blend wonderfully with his surroundings so that just the smile he had for Sadie was the only truly human appearing part of him.

There was a lull in the fighting as the Azael came on slower, nervous about where the next shot was going to come from. They were spread out all along the hillside, moving steadily and somewhat predictably forward.

Rutledge, a man Grey had never spoken to until that morning, fired three times, killing with every shot, and then was on the move…but too quickly. In his haste to get away, he stumbled on a root and his gun flew out of his hands. He scrambled to retrieve it but, by the time he did, bullets were flicking over his head at knee height.

From up the slope of the ridge, Grey and Sadie had a perfect view of him scrabbling in the dirt, desperate to get to cover. A little below them, Morganstern began laying down a stream of lead, raking the trees and rocks across from him, trying to take the focus off of Rutledge. In seconds, he was forced to duck away from the answering barrage heading in at him.

Like a noob, Grey was doing nothing but watching the spectacle and was surprised when Sadie suddenly shoved him up against an outcropping of rock. She pulled the M16 from her back, loaded one of the 40mm grenades and was just in the process of pulling the trigger when Grey stopped her.

"Wait! You're aiming too low. You have to loft those shells or you might drop them on Rutledge." She banked the launcher up until he said: "There; fire!"

Foomp! The grenade sailed in an arc to land with a *Bang!* thirty yards past Rutledge and into a stand of trees.

"Good shot! Fire for effect," Grey told her.

She blinked at him. "What kind of effect are you talking about?"

Right. He had forgotten she wasn't a soldier and didn't know the jargon. "It means to fire in the same vicinity, you know, for maximum effectiveness."

"Oh," she said. "Why didn't you just say so?" She began working the grenade launcher, thumping the rounds down the trail they had been climbing. The explosions and the *zing* of flying metal kept the Azael hunkered down, however, she had only three grenades and very quickly she was out of ammo. And worse, Rutledge hadn't taken the opportunity to get away. He was still caught on the uneven ground without real cover.

In seconds, the Azael were shooting at him again and it wasn't long before Rutledge was shot. "Crap! I'm hit," he yelled. "Shit! Stop shooting. Ah, damn it, stop shooting!"

Sadie and Morganstern immediately let up and so did a number of the Azael, though not all of them. Eleven or twelve kept firing, and quickly, Rutledge gave a second cry and then slumped, face first into the dirt.

"You son of a bitches!" Sadie raged. She threw herself down between two jagged hunks of exposed rock and started blasting away, her anger growing with each shot.

Grey's energy dissipated in the same proportion. By the time Morganstern, running low and dodging side to side, arrived, Grey could barely stand.

Morganstern took one glance at his captain's ashen face and whispered: "Shit." He then chanced a look back the way he had come at the Azael as they ran in short bounds, going from cover to cover, coming ever closer. "Sadie, I don't think he can walk anymore. You're going to have to cover us. Can you handle that?"

Without hesitation or looking up from the sights of her gun, she replied: "Yeah, get going and don't stop for anything. I'll keep up."

Leave me behind, Grey wanted to say, however he was too tired to make the effort. Only a whisper of breath came out and he could do nothing but watch as Morganstern stooped and hefted his bulk onto his shoulders in a fireman's carry.

There was no discussion of tactics, signals or even of their route. This was how Sadie operated, by the seat of her pants, and it went against everything Grey had ever been taught. Morganstern should have known better; Grey wanted to call a halt and bitch him out, only he couldn't. It was taking everything he had just to stay conscious. The world went in and out, sometimes in focus, but more and more it appeared to be made up of a swirling fog of mashing hues of green and brown.

Even Morganstern became insubstantial to Grey. At first all Grey could see of him were his legs however, these soon blurred into the background and his human shape lost all meaning. The only thing about the young man that made sense was his ragged breathing. It was very loud in Grey's ears as though the PFC had the lungs of a giant—a very sick giant.

He started off with a steady rhythm, but as they mounted the last ridgeline looming over the Estes Valley, Morganstern's breathing degenerated into an awful, strident gasp. Up and up they went until the soldier reeled from exhaustion and was plodding along so slowly, bent under the mass of his captain, that it was all Sadie could do to keep the Azael off of them.

At some point, Grey blanked out. He wasn't unconscious; he could still hear the hoarse breathing and the gunshots, some close, some far, and he could still hear the near misses as the bullets whined off of the rocks around them. Yet none of that held much significance to him anymore. He was barely hanging onto the last embers of life.

Then something abruptly changed.

A brisk, chill wind suddenly struck him, its icy fingers slipping over the wet blood that ran down his back. His eyes fluttered open and he found himself in a little dell carved out of the side of the mountain. Over the lip of rock to the east was the ragged slope they had climbed and to the west was a crag in the ridgeline through which he could see the Estes Valley. It was maybe four miles away and there were a thousand smaller hills and peaks between them, but even from that distance, he could see that it was still and quiet and peaceful. The zombies hadn't overrun it yet.

He had done his job and now he felt he could die in peace.

It seemed as though Morganstern thought so as well. Without warning, he dropped Grey onto the hard earth. It was a few inches of dirt covering over a mountain of rock and all Grey could think was that he wouldn't be buried when he died. He'd be left for the scavengers; and that was alright with him.

"Circle of life, right Morganstern?" When the PFC didn't answer, Grey cracked an eye and found himself staring up at the bluest sky he had ever seen. With more of an effort, he said again: "It's the circle of life, Morganstern. It's ok. It's ok to leave me right here."

Morganstern did not answer.

Grey pushed himself over and found the young man flat on his back, staring up just as he had been. His breathing was beginning to calm already. After a minute, Grey said: "Get up. Sadie needs you"

"I can't feel my legs," Morganstern answered in a dreamy whisper.

After the herculean effort, it was no wonder. "I can't either," Grey told him. It wasn't an exaggeration. The pain was gone, but so was the feeling in his extremities. He could see his fingers move, but the sensation didn't register. "Come on, Morganstern, get up. She won't be able to hold them back much longer."

"My legs…are they…are they there. I swear it feels like they're gone."

"They're there," Grey said, forcing himself to a sitting position. The world no longer spun, it just seemed to disappear a few feet away from his focus. He was very aware of his pulse. It was quick in his ears, as fast as a rabbit's. He understood: his heart was working overtime trying to keep up with his body's needs by pushing the remaining blood in his system around as fast as possible. There just wasn't a lot of blood left in him.

"Come on, Morgan…" Grey's words stopped midsentence as he saw blood creeping in rivulets along the rocks beneath Morganstern's back. Grey tried to get to the soldier, but lacked the strength. He inched closer a couple of feet, but couldn't go on.

Just then Sadie, who was sweating so much that the mud she had daubed on her face was streaked in wavy lines, darted up the trail with bullets chasing her. Before she glanced around, she threw herself against one of the bigger rocks and switched out the magazine in her weapon for a full one. Only then did she look up to see the situation in front of her.

"What is this?" she asked, her eyes taking in Morganstern's ghostly appearance and the little streams of crimson flowing along the rocky surface of the dell they were in. The blood flowed into a natural basin of sorts and was already several inches deep.

They both knew what it meant.

"It's a sign, Sadie," Grey told her. "It's a sign for you to get going. You've done everything anyone could have asked of you and more, but now it's time to go."

"Maybe it's not as bad as it looks," she said, letting her M16 clatter to the ground and rushing to Morganstern's side. Gently, she slid a hand under his back and probed for a second before her face broke into harsh lines. Grief etched grooves across her forehead and down her cheeks.

Morganstern seemed to only just see her. He spoke her name in a whisper: "Sadie...I liked you. Did...you know that? I wanted to ask..." He swallowed, thickly and before he could finish, his eyes rolled in his head.

"Hey, Morganstern," Sadie said, anxiously, giving him a shake. "Hey..." She turned to Grey and asked: "What's his first name?"

Grey might have known the answer at one time but just then his ability to concentrate or dig memories out of his skull was practically nil. Morganstern came around long enough to answer. "Abraham....Abraham Morganstern." He smiled at her showing shockingly white teeth in his pale face. "It's a...it's a, old man's name. I was supposed to be an old man one day...and I was...supposed to sit...on a porch...with an... old lady..."

His words trailed away and the smile faded to nothing and his eyes turned glassy and vacant. He died with Sadie crying over him.

171

"You have to get going," Grey told her. "Give me your weapon and go. It's time. Just pull me close to those rocks and I'll give you a few minutes." She didn't argue. He could no longer walk and she couldn't carry him. The time for heroics was over. It was a time for fleeing or dying and they both knew it could be no other way.

She took hold of his shirt and, as he kicked with his burned leg, she pulled. Together they got him to the lip of the dell where bullets were chipping the rocks and flecks of quartz and granite skipped into the sky.

There were many words that should've been said, however, Grey was stoic in nature, and as always, Sadie matched the moment. Though her eyes sparkled with tears, she only squeezed his hands to say goodbye. It was more than enough for Grey.

"Don't look back," he ordered.

Sadie's teeth set hard against themselves and her lips peeled back, but she didn't argue. She handed him her last three magazines and then jogged away, heading the last hundred yards up to the top of the ridgeline.

He watched her for a moment, regretting that he hadn't said more to her or that he hadn't given her a message to take back to Deanna. But that had never been his style. It likely would have taken him ten minutes to come up with two very inadequate sentences, and he didn't even have one minute. Already he could hear the scrape of boots on rock just down the slope. They were coming for him.

With his left arm, dangling uselessly, Grey brought the M16 up to his shoulder, resting it on the lip of the dell to keep it steady. The closest man was exactly twenty-three feet away. He was so close that Grey could see the beads of sweat on his upper lip and could hear his breath wheeze in and out of his lungs.

He was a smoker; the climb had taken a lot out of him and he was slow to aim. Grey was not. Even with a useless arm and his life dribbling out of his many wounds, one drop at a time, Grey was a natural born killer. They both fired at the same time. Grey didn't miss.

One down, he thought, *two hundred to go*.

The odds of winning this fight were impossible. The odds of giving Sadie a five-minute head start were very likely just as long as he could stay conscious. Grey fought the swirling in his head and ignored his pulse racing faster and faster and did his best not to think about how his blood was already trickling down the rocks to mingle with Morganstern's blood.

He concentrated on what he did best. He was the sharpest of the sharpshooters and brought the Azael down one by one and kept firing right up until they flanked him, cresting the very hill that Sadie had jogged up—five minutes before.

A man in the swirling scarves of the Azael suddenly appeared on a rock outcropping fifty feet above Grey. He couldn't miss and Grey was too weak to even attempt to try to evade the bullets that came raining down on him. It was now his turn to die.

Chapter 20
Jillybean

The long pursuit and the running gun battle could be heard for miles. To Jillybean it sounded like distant workmen wielding giant hammers and building houses that had to be as high as heaven.

She didn't know who to root for—though in her mind she referred to it as "voting" for one side or the other. Of course, she wanted the Azael to lose, but she knew they wouldn't. The monsters were unstoppable; there were simply too many of them. And if, by some miracle, they could be overcome, there were still the Azael to battle. They were a bloodthirsty lot, full of bad manners and ugly looks.

For some reason many of them seemed to think Jillybean had been involved in the attack in some way. They pointed at her as she passed and whispered behind their hands. There were rumors flying about concerning her and she caught many unpleasant words such as *schizo* and *possessed*. Much to her dismay, she even heard *idiot-savant*. She didn't know the meaning of the term, however anything with the word 'idiot' in it couldn't be good.

Brad went in search of the king and his ragged court straight away and dragged Jillybean along. "They're going to need us," he said. "I swear these guys are useless sometimes." The little girl only nodded and didn't say anything. She hoped to goodness that they wouldn't need her. The guilt she was feeling at what she had done was already like a sickness inside of her. It made her want to puke.

Seeing the destruction around the howitzers didn't help, either. Everything was black and the air was hazy with the foulest smelling smoke that Jillybean had ever smelled. The explosion and subsequent fire had seared the high grasses, that had once swayed in the field, right down to their roots so that the charred bodies, lying here and there in clumps of two or three, were obvious, even at a distance.

The king and his brothers and the lesser dignitaries of the Azael stood just up the road from the carnage. They all appeared on the verge of murder, especially the king. His eyes blazed when he saw Brad. "Tell me that the wall is down," he demanded.

Brad bowed low before answering: "We destroyed not just one wall, but two. I fought my way through a hundred thousand zombies and risked my life ten times over to guarantee success."

"Then explain why the stiffs aren't moving!" Duke Paulus cried. Jillybean noted that he was no longer the smiling, confident man he had been the night before. His face was decidedly pinched and his eyes were a little mad as if *he* were the schizo.

"I would think the explanation was obvious," Brad replied. "But why is everyone looking at me for an explanation. I did my job and I did it exactly as King Augustus asked. If you're looking for a scapegoat, you don't have to look any further than the man who screwed up and forgot to arrange the least amount of security for his guns."

Paulus began to snarl curses, but before he could force out a coherent sentence, Duke Menis limped forward to stand beside Jillybean. "He's not wrong, Paulus. You screwed up, not them. They did everything I said they would and more. Who knew there were secondary walls?"

"If we had sent men to the top of some of those peaks like I said to, we would've known that and more," Paulus countered.

The king snapped his fingers before Menis could answer. "Stop it! No one has yet to explain why the stiffs aren't moving. If you blew up two walls on that God-forsaken highway, what's holding them back?"

Brad shrugged and stated what should've been obvious: "A third wall. It was protected by a very steep hill, but we were in the process of knocking it down when the howitzers blew up. A few more minutes and the valley would have been ours."

Augustus turned his gaze back to the west and stared at the mountains. "So, what do we do?"

Brad opened his mouth to speak, but Menis gave him a sharp elbow and answered: "I recommend we keep the pressure up with the stiffs. We keep driving them, and driving them. Our enemies are tired and the wall across 34 is damaged. It will only be a matter of time."

"Wrong!" Paulus declared. "We need to bring the fight to them. We have the numbers. With the stiffs pinning them down, we can sweep over the same mountains they attacked us from and come down on them like an avenging fury."

One of the other brothers shook his shaggy head. He was the hairiest of them all, so hairy that Jillybean thought he must be some sort of Bigfoot. "I doubt that will work. One of my men just gave me a count of the dead. So far we've recovered eight of their bodies and guess how many of ours."

"Sixty?" someone ventured.

"Nope," the hairy brother said and then waited expectantly for more guesses.

King Augustus was in no mood for guessing games. "Just tell us, damn it! How many?"

The hairiest of the brothers suddenly realized he had put himself in the position of 'bearer of bad news' and he didn't relish it. He pointed Paulus' way as he said, "Because there was no security, we lost a hundred and eighty-four." This caused the assembled group to gasp all except Paulus, who again began to splutter.

"I wasn't in charge of security. I was in charge of the guns. I was the one who found them and the men who could shoot them. I wasn't..."

Menis waved his hand, dismissively. "It doesn't matter now, does it? Our guns are gone. What matters is that we don't throw good men into a bad situation. One hundred and eighty-four dead versus just eight of theirs? That's unsustainable and the surest way to see our army dissolve into nothing."

"What does the girl think about all of this?" the extra hairy man asked.

Jillybean tried to shrink away from the question, but Menis held her in place. She had been worried they would turn to her eventually and, as much as she didn't want to, she had to answer. The fate of thirty-two women depended on her and she knew she wasn't strong enough to see them tortured right in front of her. Eve would take her over for sure and then there would be no knowing what evil would occur.

"I wouldn't attack if I was you guys," she answered. "They'll know you're coming and this sort of hilly land with all these big rocks is easy to defend, which is good for you because they're gonna attack you again. At least I think so. Captain Grey isn't the type of fighter-man who is gonna sit around and wait to be attacked. He'll come for you, starting with the angel-horsemen pushing the monsters on this road. He'll want to stop them real bad because if they're all dead, the monsters will go away. You know?"

King Augustus eyed her shrewdly as the last embers of the pursuit of Grey and Sadie sounded in a brief fury of gunshots. When all was silent from the mountains, he smirked and said, "We'll take both routes," he said. "We'll stand on the defensive along that ridgeline." He pointed to a stiff, forbidding wall of earth and rock stretching into the distance to the west of them. "With the heights under our control, they won't dare attack us. And, at the same time, we will protect our drivers so that they can keep pushing the stiffs."

The brothers nodded and stroked their beards in appreciation as if this was a stroke of genius on his part when it was exactly the advice Jillybean had just given.

"Remember, they can't last forever," Augustus added, pacing back and forth. "We'll keep grinding forward. We'll keep wearing them down until they can't take it anymore! This was the plan to begin with and one minor setback with the big guns shouldn't upset that. Tell your men that. Tell them we are on schedule. Tell them that it's just a matter of time before the walls fall and our armies surge forward to victory! We will plunder the valley and take it for ourselves! It will be ours!"

The men and women roared their excitement.

Orders were given and men rushed about and each went to their posts with a fire in their eyes. Jillybean watched with a tummy ache eating her up. It felt as though she had feasted on a banquet piled high with guilt. Course upon course of it until the guilt crept up her throat and threatened to come spewing out with the slightest hiccup.

With so many people going this way and that, the little girl wanted to slink away and hide under one of the seats on the bus. She missed Ipes terribly just then. He would've known exactly what to do. He would've helped her steer the course between betrayal and ultimate victory for her friends. Without him, she knew they were doomed.

Duke Menis caught her as she tried to slip away unseen. "Where do you think you're going?"

"I...I just was going to, uh, the b-bus."

Brad had left to set up a defensive line along the hills above the drivers on I-34, leaving Jillybean under the care of the duke —a most repulsive thought to the little girl. He offered her a smile; the look she returned was part misery, and part *giving up*; her face was tight and tense, like a CEO fighting against the pain of a stress-induced ulcer.

"Try to relax, Jillybean," he said, throwing an arm around her thin shoulders. "It's a done deal and has been from the start. With or without you, those walls will fall and we will be victorious. It's just a matter of time. I think I might want to take Estes for myself. I'm due you know. I took that crappy little town in Kansas as a favor to my brother, but I think I want something better; something bigger."

He smiled down on her as if expecting some sort of acknowledgement or approval of the idea. "I guess that sounds good," she lied. What actually sounded "good" to her was the Azael leaving as fast as they could and never coming back.

"Yes, it does sound good," he said. "Good walls, a good defensive network, fertile land to grow crops, plenty of space, a place to grow a community. It sounds ideal if you ask me."

Jillybean wanted to point out that everything he had just mentioned had already been in place before the Azael arrived. She hid her gritted teeth behind a thin-lipped smile and could only nod.

Menis didn't see her minor deception. The hand on her shoulder squeezed. "I've been thinking of keeping you for myself, Jillybean. If I get Estes, I'll need someone who can give me good advice. What do you think about that?"

The idea was appalling to her.

Had he forgotten how much pain he had caused her and the people she cared about? Had he forgotten how he had urged Brad to hurt Kay? Had he forgotten that she was only helping him because her guilt was a disease eating her alive?

We could kill him, Eve said in her ear. It was as though Eve was standing just behind her; Jillybean could almost feel the imaginary breath tickle her ear. She did her best not to react to the words. It was easy. The idea wasn't exactly original. The thought had crossed the little girl's mind a minute before and this time it hadn't come from someone other than her.

She wanted to kill Menis, plain and simple.

He was a bad man. Really, he was worse than that. He was evil, worse than any monster. They, at least, had an excuse: they couldn't think. They were monsters and monsters only knew how to attack and how to feast on the flesh of people. Menis knew better. He was a man, a thinking human person.

He deserved to die. Just like the other bad guys: Abraham, Cassie, the bounty hunters. They all needed to die.

But she couldn't kill the duke. The rest of the Azael would know and they would hurt the women on the bus.

Then do it smart, Eve said, with what was practically a giggle. *Kill him and hide his body in a ditch or, better yet, let it float down the river. It'll be in Kansas before anyone knows.*

It wouldn't take much. Menis was far too trusting not only in Jillybean but also in his own abilities as a fighter. But Jillybean wouldn't fight him. That was just stupid. She was a tiny thing and knew it. Her strength lay in her mind not in her muscles. Still, she could kill him easy. She could kill him even without Eve's help.

The thought, true though it was, and not yet acted upon, only added to the guilt weighing her soul down.

"I would like that," she said to the duke, after only the briefest pauses. "I think I could help you pretty good." *And kill you pretty good*, a voice in her mind said. It wasn't Eve's voice, which meant that it was either another personality speaking or her own mind saying the impossible. She didn't know which it was and that was more frightening than anything.

A pained grin, one that spoke volumes concerning her erratic mental state, broke across her features. The duke missed it along with the many deadly clues that her young mind and inexperienced face gave away. Foolishly, he said, "Excellent. That's just excellent. We make a good team, you and I."

It seemed as if there were two avenues open to her: meek compliance down one lane, and down the other: anger, hate, revenge, murder. Neither appealed to her and yet she couldn't find any middle ground. "Yeah, I guess so, Mister Duke Sir," she replied, not allowing herself to go one way or the other.

"And as an added bonus, when I get Deanna back, you'll have a friend here in Estes. Won't that be something?"

Jillybean gave him another thin-lipped grin. Yes, it would be something having Deanna around, someone to constantly remind Jillybean of her treachery. *We could kill her, too*, Eve said, in a deadly serious tone. *Wipe the slate completely clean and then no one will know what evil, nasty things you did.*

There was a certain appeal to the idea. If there was no one around to remind her of the things she had done, she could hide from the guilt eating her up. She could lock the guilt up behind one of those doors in the depths of her mind and never have to think about it again.

That's a great idea, Eve said. *No one will know except you and me.* An avalanche of pictures splashed across her consciousness: Jillybean shooting the bounty hunter, David Wolff in the eye and seeing the tunnel into his brain and the whiff of smoke coming from it; Jillybean unleashing the zombie army on New Eden; Jillybean blowing up the barge and the ferry boats and the bridge; Jillybean tossing a grenade at Neil as he crouched in the grass; Jillybean, wearing a cruel smile as she shot Ernest, and then again, as she gunned down the River King's men, shooting them in the back.

A cloud of guilt engulfed the little girl. It invaded her lungs and lay so heavily upon her that her shoulders slumped. Eve was slowly getting stronger again and it wasn't fear invigorating her this time, it was the guilt. Jillybean knew it and yet she was powerless against it.

Fear could be fought against, it could be overcome by challenging it. She didn't think she could fight against guilt.

You could try, Eve suggested. *Just tell yourself that all those people you killed don't matter at all. Tell yourself that it was ok to kill them...of course you'd have to lie to yourself and pretend that they were all evil, right? Because they weren't all evil, were they? You didn't even know most of them.*

"They were all bad guys," Jillybean whispered, turning from the duke.

Even that guard on the barge? He could have shot you, but he didn't and you blew him up. And what about those people in Estes? If it wasn't for you helping the Azael, their big wall would still be up and they wouldn't be fighting for their lives behind a few stacked cars. So, tell yourself those lies and keep on killing and pretty soon no one will be able to tell you and me apart. Would you like that? Would you like to be me without all the whiny guilt?

A shiver ran straight up Jillybean's back and Eve giggled again. *She* watched out of Jillybean's eyes and knew her time was coming. There would be more blood to shed and more bombs to explode and more fires to brighten her world, and all of it would be like an anchor tied around stupid Jillybean's legs and she'd sink down into the black where she belonged.

Jillybean heard these thoughts and knew Eve was right.

Chapter 21
Sadie Walcott

Just at that moment, with Grey's M16 cracking steadily away, Sadie's guilt matched Jillybean's in its intensity. She had left a good man behind to die. It was a hard truth to face and, lucky for her, she had plenty of excuses. They repeated themselves over and over like a skipping record: the captain was going to die anyway, he was too big to carry, and she would have been throwing her life away by staying.

The excuses were all worthless and served to inflame her guilt rather than assuage it. She sobbed as she ran, her eyes blurred by tears. She could barely see her feet dancing from rock to rock and the camouflaged man with the M4 who was standing thirty yards away, catching his breath after a long climb, she mistook for a bush.

He was surprised, as well, by her sudden appearance. His gun came up and he fired a three round burst, missing high as she flung herself behind one of the boulders jutting up from the top of the ridgeline. The boulder was an oblong that protruded out of the earth to the not so staggering height of four feet.

It was crappy cover in Sadie's opinion, and wouldn't keep her safe for more than a few seconds. The shooter, and his friends—she could hear an excited whispering coming from further up the trail suggesting there were a lot more of them—would be able to flank her simply by moving to their right by about thirty feet where there was a lane between the rocks as wide and open as a sidewalk.

Unsnapping two buckles, she had the empty chest rig off in half a second. She swirled it once over her head before flinging it to her left; at the same time, she broke right. After the long morning of running up and down the mountains and fighting for her life, her legs were heavy and she moved without her usual blazing speed, as she headed for the edge of the ridgeline to the west.

She had no idea if there was any safety in that direction, in fact she was pretty sure a steep drop into nothing was likely waiting for her, and yet the alternative: capture at the hands of the Azael and sold off to whichever of her enemies bid the highest, was so much worse.

Behind her the chest rig danced in mid-air as bullets caught it and spun it away. Then the gun was turned on her. Out of the corner of her eye, she saw it blaze and the air was filled with the sizzle of lead. Eight feet from the edge of the ridgeline, she planted her left foot and hurtled over the rim.

The drop was nowhere near as steep as was needed for the fall to kill her. She landed twenty feet down the hill and with gravity pulling her urgently on, she immediately began to tumble in a flailing ball of arms and legs. Her momentum was slowed as she resembled a pinball bouncing from tree to tree until, with dirt and leaves collecting down the back of her shirt, she slid the final twenty feet, belly up with a perfect view of the sky.

The view was ruined as the black bore of an assault rifle was shoved into her face within a second of her grinding to a halt. She couldn't seem to look past it. "Go ahead, pull the trigger, dickweed," she said through gritted teeth. "See what I care."

There was a moment of uncertainty and she forced her eyes from the bore of the weapon. Standing above her, looking strangely tall and long as if they had been pulled like taffy, were four men.

"What the hell?" one of them asked, clearly surprised at having a girl fly from the top of the ridge to land at his feet. He glanced up at the way she had come, back down at her and then toward his friends; Sadie could look straight up his nose when he did. His nostrils seemed to be in the same odd proportion as the rest of him so that his nose hung everything below it in a shelf of gloom.

"It's that girl," another said. "Captain Grey's friend." The way he said Grey's name was with more than a touch of familiarity. He stuck out a hand to Sadie and when she only looked up the very long arm it was attached to with clearly puzzled features, he asked: "Are you ok? Did you hit your head?"

She was sure she had and yet her head wasn't ringing or in pain, nor was her hearing affected or her sight impaired, beyond the odd angle that she found herself in, which made everything seem elongated. She even recognized one of them.

"Lieutenant Boyd," she said, noting the bandage that had kept him from joining the twenty person team that morning. These men weren't with the Azael, they were from the valley! "What are you doing here?"

"General Johnston decided to send a supplemental force to help with extraction," the lieutenant answered as he lifted her to her feet. "Where is everyone else?" From over the ridgeline she could hear the last shots of Captain Grey.

"That's the Captain!" she cried. "He's hurt and won't last much longer." The men had been standing on the deer trail they had followed that morning. She knew it looped a hundred yards out of the way to the north before coming back to cross right above them. "Come on!" she urged and then attacked the very slope she had just fallen down.

She was unencumbered and, though she was tired, she was filled with a new hope and a new energy. Able to use both hands, she went from tree to tree, making it to the top well before Lieutenant Boyd and the others. Five soldiers who had been on point and ahead of the rest, waited for her there, two with their guns trained on her. She ignored the possibility of death at their hands.

"Captain Grey's in trouble. Follow me." Weaponless, she ran back the way she had come, sprinting so fast that her chest burned. There was no way she could make it in time. It had been five minutes since she had left him with the Azael closing in on his position. They had to have surrounded him by then.

Sure enough, a half mile away she could see the Azael climbing the rocks just above where she had left Grey to die and one was already standing and bringing his weapon up to his shoulder. He looked like an ant with the distance and she knew that only the best marksman with finely tuned, scoped rifles could hit a man from that range. She had to hope that one of these soldiers was that good a shot.

She pointed at a sergeant who seemed the most experienced. "You! Kill that man!" She swung her arm towards the Azael. "The rest of you with me." At a sprint, she took off without looking to see if any of them were keeping up. Happily, the sergeant began to shoot his rifle, though he didn't sound like a marksman.

In her mind, she equated the word marksman with *sniper*, and that she equated with *assassin*, which she pictured as a cruel and coldly calculating man. She expected the soldier to fire single shots and kill with each, instead he shot at the Azael with a spray of bullets, emptying his gun in seconds. Whether the man was killed or even hit, she didn't know. He did drop down, out of sight which she considered a win.

It meant Grey had a chance. She raced along the deer trail, feeling the cool wind burn in her lungs as her legs began to stiffen and her heart thundered. Tree branches whipped by, sometimes within inches of laying an eye wide open, but she paid the branches no mind. Dodging them was a waste of energy and she didn't have any to waste.

She ran full out for three minutes and felt each painful second. Then she crossed over the last rise on the ridgeline and there, below her was the dell where she had left Captain Grey to die in. He wasn't dead yet. He was curled behind a rock the size of an end table, trading shots with a dozen of the Azael who were ranged in a semi-circle on the south side of the ridge.

Around her, the soldiers who had made the run with her, threw themselves behind cover, but she did not. She stood in the open with her arm outstretched and pointing, as if her finger was a weapon itself. Immediately the Azael turned their guns on her and sent a cascade of bullets flying her way. She didn't even flinch, though why she stood there so exposed was beyond her. A part of her felt invulnerable. So many of her friends had died and yet, impossibly, she had always lived—even when Cassie had killed her by drowning her in the East River, Sadie had managed to live. It made no sense, unless she was fated to be the last person left alive on the planet, something that seemed horribly sad to Sadie.

It took one of the soldiers to save her from her own delusions or survivor's guilt or whatever it was making her stand there waiting to be killed. He was rugged as most of them were, and wore a day's worth of stubble on his cheeks, and he was not at all gentle about saving Sadie's life. One moment she was standing there like a fool and the next she was dragged down like a wounded gazelle. She went face first into the dirt with a heavy knee planted square in her back.

"Get off!" she gasped, in a wheezy breath as she struggled against his bulk. The knee made it impossible for her to take a full breath or to move at all.

"It's for your own good," the soldier told her. "Now, hold still so I can aim." He fired three times from the unpleasant kneeling position before ducking back down and sliding off of her. Just in case, he kept one hand tight on the collar of her shirt.

She gulped down air until she could spit out: "I have to get to Captain Grey. He's hurt."

"You're going to have to give it a minute. He's caught in a crossfire. Anyone who tries to go out there won't last ten seconds."

He was right, the Azael were flocking towards the dell from the south and the east, while the soldiers were racing in from the north. Grey was in the exact middle of the battle, bleeding out onto the rocks. A few feet from him lay Morganstern's corpse. He looked like he was sleeping despite the hurricane of metal passing three feet over his head.

At first it looked as though the Azael were winning the battle. There were twice as many of them and they didn't seem to care how much ammunition they expended. The sound was amazing and terrifying.

The soldiers were far more disciplined and circumspect. They rarely fired more than a single shot at a time and they never rushed their shots. They seemed far too relaxed in Sadie's opinion. One man would pop up from cover, take a shot and disappear again, then another man would take his turn. Worse, their shots weren't particularly well aimed.

"What the hell are they doing?" Sadie demanded of the soldier who had pulled her down. "They aren't even hitting anything."

"Look again," the soldier grunted. "Look behind us."

She turned, and at first didn't see anything and then just as one of the closer soldiers popped up and fired, someone unseen fired from beneath a fallen log. Sadie spun to see one of the Azael suddenly pitch forward.

"And look to your right," the soldier next to her said. "Down the hill a bit." A quick peek showed her a squad of men scurrying along the ridge while behind them three men had their guns aimed waiting for any enemy to show their faces. "We hold their attention here, while those men flank them. Then while the enemy is engaged on the right, we move a force up on the left."

"And what do I do?"

"Nothing," he answered. "Except don't get killed."

Doing nothing wasn't her style, especially when her friend was hurt and dying fifty yards away. Sadie watched the battle unfold and, when the Azael's right flank was engaged, she moved up with the men assaulting the left. One of the soldiers gave her a quizzical look as she moved forward, empty handed in a crouch.

"What the hell do you think you're doing?" he asked.

185

"Waiting my turn," she answered. She understood the tactics involved, however she was consumed by the idea that Grey would die before she had chance to get to him. It made her reckless and she was only waiting on the chance to be completely stupid.

That moment occurred when the first of the soldiers was shot. He was hit in the right shoulder, and though he bled like a stuck pig, he seemed more angry than in pain. "Lucky, fucking shot!" he yelled. He was just in the process of switching his weapon to his left hand to continue fighting when Sadie leapt up and charged over to him.

"Hey, chill," he said. "It's just a flesh wound. No reason to be a fucking hero." In answer she grabbed his M4. "What the fuck!" he cried and tried to snatch it back.

The wound was worse than he let on and Sadie pushed his left hand away with ease. She even grabbed two extra magazines from the soldier's chest rig. "I won't hurt it, don't worry," she said, indicating the gun.

Before he could find words that weren't curses, she was up and sprinting. In the last five minutes her muscles had a chance to rest and now she was almost at full speed as she leapt down into the dell where Grey was lying. The Azael gunned for her, but as they did so, they opened themselves up to a withering hail of bullets from the soldiers who fired with near impunity.

A dozen Azael were killed in Sadie's sprint and she made it to the rock Grey was huddled behind, unscratched, though she had lost the tip of one of her spiked locks to a very near miss.

Grey stared at her with glazed-over eyes. "Sadie." His voice was hoarse and so quiet that the gunshots going off all around them nearly drowned out the one word salutation.

"Hey." She didn't know what else to say. *How are you doing?* seemed moronic, as did: *What's up?*

He replied: "Hey. What…what's going on?"

This lack of awareness was a bad sign. It was a sign that shock was setting in. His body was reacting to the massive bleeding by shunting blood from his extremities and to his core. Loss of mental acuity was a classic symptom as was the shaking in his hands. He held his hands close to his chest as though he were freezing.

"You're going to be ok. You hear me? Just stay still and…" She stopped as she saw the pool of blood he was lying in. It was perfectly smooth as if someone had spilled a gallon of paint. The first thing she thought was that he had been shot again—and he had been. There was a fresh groove notched in his forearm, but that wasn't where all the blood was coming from.

Desperately, she searched his body, looking for a new bleed and discovering that the bandage holding his bicep together had slipped off. "Ok…Ok I see the problem," she told him. "I can fix this."

Fixing the bandage meant exposing herself. She didn't hesitate. Sitting up with bullets snapping off the boulder and cracking the air all around her, she shoved the bandage back over the gash in his arm and then leaned her knee on it, causing him to groan.

"Stop being a baby," she said as something tickled the nape of her neck. A bullet had passed so close it had parted the wispy little hairs hanging down her neck which had been in need of cutting for weeks now. It caused a chain reaction as an involuntary shiver went down her back as her subconscious envisioned what would have happened if the bullet had been a half inch lower. It would have severed her spinal column at the base of her skull, paralyzing her but leaving her perfectly aware of her surroundings.

People would come and look down on her. They would shake their heads and say: *What a shame* or *What a waste of a fine piece of ass*. They would discuss hauling her carcass back down to the valley, but it wouldn't be more than just talk. None of them would want to be burdened with the extra weight, so they would all agree that it made better sense to put her "out of her misery" even though she wouldn't really be in any pain.

She would try to scream and plead for her life, but one of them would squat next to her and say: *Sorry about this*, before sticking a handgun to her head. She didn't know if she would even hear the report of the gun or see the flash, yet the result would be the same.

In a flash of goose bumps, the shiver went down her body in a wave. She ignored it as best as she could as she cinched the belt back in place and when Grey grunted again in pain, she ignored that too, knowing he would be embarrassed if he knew he was making what he would consider a sound of weakness.

"There," she said, when the bandage was in place. She ducked down out of the path of the bullets. "Feel better?"

"It…it's great," he said, trying to smile. It was crooked on one side; another bad sign.

She smiled back, hoping that it conveyed reassurance instead of fear for him. She wanted to say something that would be full of meaning but couldn't seem to put two coherent words together before someone came rushing up. It was a soldier splashed with more sweat than camo paint.

He slammed square into Sadie, crushing her down, so that his entire weight was practically on top of her. "It's ok, I got this," he said.

"Got what?"

The soldier didn't answer. In the meager cover afforded by the rock, he unzipped a medkit and pulled out an IV bag of normal saline. "Open that," he said, shoving the bag at Sadie. Around the bag was a tough outer shell of plastic which she tore open with her teeth.

"Here you go." She tried to hand the bag back, but he wouldn't take it. He was busy trying to thread a needle into one of Grey's veins that usually looked like subcutaneous pipes but which now were only blue lines barely showing through his skin. After much digging with the needle, the soldier said: "There it is." He then withdrew the needle, leaving only the catheter to which he attached the IV tubing and then ran the fluid into the captain's arm, full bore.

"Keep that up in the air," he told Sadie, indicating the IV bag. "It runs on gravity. Also, tell me when it gets low."

Sadie lifted the bag until her hand was just at the height of the rock they were crouched behind. She worried that her arm would get tired, however the bag drained so quickly that she didn't have time to tire. After only a minute, she tapped the soldier on the back. "It's almost out."

He was huddled over the captain, his hands wet and shiny with blood. "I'm a little busy here. Just grab another and plug it in. It's not hard to do."

She had to almost climb over the soldier to get to the med bag. As she did, she saw him trying to tie off the bleeder in Grey's arm. The artery was a slick little thing and was constantly obscured by the fresh blood pooling in the wound. "Damn it! I can't get this. It keeps slipping. I'm going to need your help, ma'am. But first get the IV hooked up."

That took all of two seconds and then she and the soldier shifted positions so that they were kneeling side by side over Grey. Sadie felt entirely too exposed. The full length of her right side wasn't protected by the rock. "What do you want me to do?"

"Hold these clamps steady. Don't let them move." On both sides of the lacerated artery the soldier had attached bright steel clamps. To get at them, and allow the soldier to work, she had to entwine her arms through his. With her elbows resting on bare rock, it was a painful position. She didn't complain.

While the battle raged around them, the soldier struggled to sew up the artery, but after a few minutes he yelled in frustration. "I can't fucking get it!" The problem was his hands. They were too large and thick. One got in the way of the other and they both made visualizing the wound practically impossible.

"Let me," Sadie said. She had no idea how to properly place sutures and the last time she had sewn anything had been in the seventh grade when she had made sock puppets in a lame home economics class, still she understood the concept and her hands though filthy, were small and nimble.

In seconds she had hooked the suture needle through both ends of the artery. "Ok, good," the soldier said. "Form a loop...yes. Now push the needle through and pull, gently...gently! Now do another right next to the first."

It took eight minutes to stop the bleeding and another two in order to clean out the wound with alcohol and bandage it with a new field dressing. By the time she was able to look up, she noticed that the battle had shifted down the hill—the Azael were running away. "Stay with him," the soldier said, handing over the last IV bag in his medkit. "Elevate his feet; keep the IV running and make sure he's warm. I'll be back."

Sadie watched him leave and then, seconds later, found that she had been staring at nothing instead of following his instructions. She put the IV bag on the rock and turned it down halfway so that it wouldn't run out so quickly. She then dragged a tree branch over and propped Grey's legs on it. Finally, she scooped up leaves and dumped them over Grey's prone body to keep him warm—he hadn't stirred or even groaned in all the time she had been working on him.

189

He still had a feeble, thready pulse which meant he was alive. It was almost the only sign. His respirations were so shallow that she could barely tell he was breathing at all and his skin was ashen, cool and slightly damp. To keep him warm, she laid down next to him and flung an arm across his broad chest.

She found herself staring again, her eyes fuzzy in a state of semi-focus. They were locked, in a vacant sort of way, on the black face of Grey's watch. It was a few seconds before she realized it was almost nine in the morning. That caused her to say, "Huh?"

It felt much later; hours later. She had never been so thoroughly exhausted in all her life. She didn't even know if she could stand, not that she wanted to. She wanted to sleep, badly, but there was no way she could. The soldiers were going to be back soon and she didn't want to embarrass herself by being caught sleeping. It seemed weak and she didn't want to be looked on as weak.

It was a fight to keep her eyes open, a fight that she lost, and just as her lids began to droop beyond her control, she remembered the old commercials the Army used to run when she was very little. Their catch phrase back then was: *We do more before nine a.m. than most people do in a day*. She never realized how true that was until that moment.

And then she was fast asleep, cuddled up to Captain Grey in the middle of a battlefield.

Chapter 22
Neil Martin

If anyone was as tired as Sadie, it was Neil Martin. He had been up for a day and a half straight with zero sleep and almost no rest. There had been too much to do to even consider sitting and putting his tired feet up for even a minute. In fact, he'd had to go to the bathroom for the last five hours and was only just breaking away.

He stood in the bathroom that sat adjacent to his new office, with his head canted back as a steady stream, one that lasted almost four minutes, flowed out of him. He almost didn't want it to end. "There's more work to do," he told the empty room. After the briefest of hand washes during which he spent most of the time staring at the ruin of his face and noting how old his bloodshot eyes appeared, he left the bathroom only to run into Deanna Russell, who accosted him immediately.

"Any word yet?" she asked, her pretty face worn down by anxiety. "They've been gone for hours and the guns stopped ages ago."

Neil felt awkward standing less than a foot from the bathroom door with his hands still damp and Deanna almost nose to nose with him. He edged to his right, hurried into his office and put his desk between them, saying: "Oh, hey, Deanna. Yes, I did hear something about an hour ago. It was a real brief radio message because of the static. They said the mission was a success and that they're bringing back six casualties and one deceased. I'm sure it's not Captain Grey."

"Just six hurt?" She relaxed, visibly. "And only one dead? Ok...ok, it wouldn't be him. He's too good. And...and it wouldn't be Sadie either. You know how slick she can be."

"Yes, she is pretty slick," Neil agreed. He wasn't worried about her now. He had been earlier as the mountain gun battle had stretched over two hours, gradually getting closer and closer, but once he heard the garbled message crackle over the radio he had calmed just as Deanna had. Sadie was indeed slick and she knew her limitations. She wouldn't risk her life for nothing.

Deanna grinned suddenly, something she hadn't done in hours, not since the explosion that had destroyed the howitzers. It brought back her beauty, full force and it seemed ten years dropped from her face. "Ok, that's all I wanted to know," she said, turning away. Neil grabbed her arm.

"Whoa, slow down. How are the walls holding up?"

"Oh, right. Sorry, my head has been spinning and I've been on the go for hours. Red Gate 3 is holding steady. From what Oliver says the tracks on the crane are 'done in,' whatever that means. I suppose that means it won't be going anywhere, but at least the crane part still works so the wall is very strong and so is Red Gate 4. It looks strange so close to the other one but it was as far as the crane could reach."

She smiled again and Neil inclined his head slightly, waiting for her to continue. "And the other walls?" he finally asked.

"Right, sorry. The Blue Gate is going to fall sometime this afternoon, at least that's according to Captain Tully. He says the mound of undead will broach the wall by 3p.m. He tried to show me the math, but I didn't really pay attention. All I cared about was that the wall is going to be breached. The second wall we built with the crane is only 'okay.' We placed the cars sideways on and there's no way of knowing if it will hold when the zombies reach the highest level. We used a bucket loader and propped it up with more cars but we could only stack them three high, so it just might tip."

Neil nodded, remembering how the second wall behind the Red Gate had toppled with surprising ease under the weight of the zombies and the pounding of the howitzers.

"With that in mind, we have built three smaller walls behind Blue Gate 2," Deanna went on. "Each should hold up the zombies for five to six hours depending on if we get to use guns or not."

"Not," Neil was quick to say.

This caused a quick look of pain to cross her features. "We're going to need them in the river tonight. General Johnston says there's no way to hold it without using guns."

"I agree with using them at the river, but nowhere else. We'll just have to figure out something. Any other hot spots that need to be handled?"

"If you recall, other than the river, we had one overflow spot at the Red Gate, but since the main wall went down, that stream of zombies have merged with the main group. It's at the Blue Gate where we still have zombies coming down out of a couple little ravines. Thankfully, neither has crested badly and, from what I saw, we are getting only thirty or forty an hour. It's not bad at all."

Neil raised his left, partially chewed off eyebrow. "Not bad at all? How come I find that hard to believe?" He had visited each of the battle zones already three times, twice during the night when everything was dark and quite scary, and once after the big explosion when he and Dianna had been alone, standing against a wave of zombies on the partially built third wall behind the Red Gate. On each visit, the number of zombies was definitely in the 'very bad' category.

"It's true, the numbers have really slacked off. You know how much the zombies hate hills, especially steep ones. General Johnston thinks that since the zombies can't go forward or back, they're only milling about on the two highways and that unless something on the Azael side changes, the overflow will keep slacking."

"Ok that's the good news. What's the bad?" There was always bad news. Neil had come to grips with this reality in the last year.

Deanna didn't hesitate with an answer. "Everyone is exhausted. The civilians aren't used to such hard labor on four hours of sleep. They're starting to get sloppy and starting to make mistakes. There's been a bunch of near misses and one not-so near miss. This guy named Mason had his leg broken when someone bumped into the jack holding up the car he was working under."

A broken leg? Neil wanted to roll his eyes. Soldiers were dying on the front lines and a broken leg just didn't compare. "I'd like to tell them to just suck it up and keep..." Just then a young woman with mussed hair and a wrinkled white blouse busted into the room. She looked like she had just been pulled from a deep sleep.

"Sorry, Mr. Martin. I just got a message from the second team. They're inbound with an ETA of twenty minutes. They say they need two operating rooms ready to go and as much O negative blood as we have on hand."

Next to Neil, Deanna went white and she put a delicate hand on the pine-knotted desk he had inherited from General Johnston. "It's Grey," she said in a whisper. "He has O negative. I saw it on his dog tags."

Neil knew it as well, just as he knew all eighteen people in the valley who possessed what was an inexplicably rare blood type. According to Margaret Yuan, there should have been at least two hundred people with O negative blood in the valley, but for some unknown reason they had only found eighteen and two of those were also carriers of hepatitis.

He knew all of this because Marybeth Gates was O negative and in the last eight days she had received eight and a half gallons of blood. It was the only thing keeping her alive. The wound in her liver refused to clot or heal and it would not stop bleeding; a drainage tube stuck out from the side of her body and hung down the edge of her bed where it filled a mop bucket that had to be dumped twice a day.

She went through three liters on a daily basis and the donors were starting to run dry especially with the battle raging. No one had the time or the energy to give blood.

"Thanks, Shelly," Neil said, with a nod, dismissing the radio operator. He started for the door at a quick walk. Deanna with her long legs matched him easily; there were tears brimming in her eyes. "He'll be fine. You don't know him very well if you think a little raid like this will do much more than slow him down. There was this one time I saw him get shot right in the chest. All it did was bring up a burp."

He tried a little smile for her, but she was too deep in fear for Grey for it to register. They exited the hotel, and though they walked south, they both had their heads turned to the east, towards the mountains and the direction of that morning's battle. They saw nothing but the craggy peaks and the pine strewn slopes.

Deanna kept watching even as they got in Neil's Humvee and sped for the hospital. The hospital was actually a glorified clinic in which colds, sniffles and the occasional turned ankle had been the order of the day back before the apocalypse. Two of the rooms had since been scrubbed with ethyl alcohol until they smelled so sharp that it watered the eyes; these were the operating rooms and so far they had been little used.

In the reception area, Neil and Deanna found Margaret Yuan playing cards with a slight woman who had been a certified nursing assistant at one time. Other than the handful of Army trained rangers like Captain Grey, this was the extent of the medical personnel in the valley. The apocalypse had been particularly hard on the first responders and hospital workers.

Margaret's narrow eyes went to slits at the sight of Deanna's tear-stained face and Neil's pinched look. "Casualties?"

"Yep," Neil said. "We're going to need both O.R.s up and going. And we're going to need all the O negative you have."

"O Negative?" Margaret asked, slipping her dark eyes in Deanna's direction. "It's Captain Grey, isn't it? Oh, damn, I knew it. He's donated quite a bit to Mrs. Gates, but there's not much left and no one has come in today at all to donate."

Neil had guessed as much. "How much do you have left?"

"One liter," was her quick reply. She gave him a look which he interpreted to mean: *there's going to be trouble.*

Deanna saw the look pass between them and alarm registered in her face. "What is it? Is there not enough blood? That's ok. Grey can have some of mine. I haven't donated anything so far."

Margaret sighed. "It's not that easy. Captain Grey has a particular type of blood: O negative. Unfortunately, it means he can only receive O Negative blood and nothing else. Do you have O negative?"

She shook her head as her lip started to quiver. "B positive."

"Yeah, that's the problem," Margaret said. "B positive will kill him. Another problem is that we have an odd deficiency in the number of people with O negative. It's always relatively rare, making up about eight percent of the population, but for some reason we have even less than that in the valley. Eighteen altogether and that includes Mrs. Gates and Captain Grey."

Deanna's lip stopped quivering and she stepped toward Margaret; standing half a head taller than her, Deanna stared down and said in a chilling tone: "Who are the other sixteen? We'll get the blood from them."

Margaret glanced at Neil as if asking for help. Neil touched Deanna on the shoulder, fully expecting her to snap at him, but she only turned toward him, slowly. "Let's see how Grey's doing before we freak out," he said. "In the meantime, we'll turn down Marybeth's IV and I'm going to need a list of the O negative donors."

"You want me to turn down Marybeth's IV? She'll bottom out if we do."

"Give her normal saline," Neil replied, with the cold necessity of leadership. "It'll hold her over until we can get some more blood. If you have an issue with it, I'll do it." Margaret had an issue and Neil knew exactly what it was: Michael Gates was protective of his wife, almost to a dangerous degree.

Knowing this, Neil attempted to find donors first, which was easier said than done. The donors were either locked in combat with the zombies, recovering from what felt like endless and soul-draining shifts, or were tapped out having given all the blood that was safe to give.

Ten minutes later, after having his tiny staff radio everyone they could to find a donor, Neil walked into Marybeth's room as if he had walked into a memory of the day before or the day before that or the day before that. He had visited her every day since coming to the valley and the scene was always the same: Marybeth lying in bed, sleeping or staring listlessly out the window, while her husband Michael sat in a steel folding chair that was slowly coming apart beneath his bulk, and in the next chair, a much more comfortable piece of office furniture, was their daughter Ann, who was also O negative and who was so pale from the amount of blood she had given that she was almost translucent.

"How's the battle going?" Michael asked. There was a shadow of remorse about him. Neil could tell he felt guilty about not taking up a position on the walls.

"Stable," Neil answered passing him a slight smile as his eyes shifted to the IV dripping into his wife's arm. It was almost out. "Here, let me slow this down a bit. I'm afraid Margaret's going to be busy for the next couple of hours. We've had some casualties. You understand, I'm sure." Neil slid the runner down, slowing the blood coming from the drip chamber to the slowest possible dribble.

Michael reached out and slid it back. "That's ok. I know where they keep the extras. I'm getting to be something of an expert." He laughed a little chuckle that neither Marybeth or his daughter heard; they were both deep asleep as their bodies fought to heal and return to homeostasis.

Neil's smile remained locked, it felt rigged in place by chicken wire as if it was little more than a child's school project. He slid the runner back down. "I'm sorry, but I guess it's not that easy. We're having an issue with the blood supply. Some of the guys are busy with the battle, so it makes the most sense to slow this down. I'll get some normal saline when this runs…"

A hard look passed across Michael's normally pleasant features. "What's wrong? It's not the donors, I have their schedules. I know who's ready in the rotation and I know that it'll only take an hour, so what's wrong?"

From the doorway, Deanna said: "It's Captain Grey. He's hurt, badly. He needs this." In her hand was the last bag of O negative blood.

"What the hell are you doing with that?" Michael cried, jumping up. "That's Marybeth's!"

As Deanna hid the blood bag behind her back, Neil threw his slight form between them, holding his hand out to Michael as though he was trying to stop traffic at the crosswalk of a school. "Stop it, Michael! It's not hers. It belongs to the people of the valley and will be distributed as needed by the supervising physician of this facility."

"Who just happens to be under your command," Michael said, coldly. "I know what this is all about. Grey's your friend and you're putting him over Marybeth."

"Wrong," Neil snapped. "Grey may be my friend, but so is Marybeth and so are you. I'm just trying…" He lowered the volume of his voice, "I'm trying to do what's right. We don't know what sort of shape Grey is in and Marybeth…"

A silence drew out in the room, one that was long and painful. Neil couldn't finish the sentence he had started. He couldn't say: *Marybeth has had her chance and now it's gone, so let her go*. That would be too cruel.

The sentence went unfinished perhaps because Michael couldn't stomach its obvious completion either. Neil cleared his throat. "We can ask the donors for more blood. But right now I need this blood, just in case. We'll give Marybeth normal saline until we know what's going on. She'll be fine." This was a lie and a sadly obvious one.

"I'll give her more of my blood," Ann said. Sometime during the brief argument, she had woken but hadn't moved a muscle. Neil wondered if she had the energy to. Whenever he saw her, he was reminded of the character Lucy from Bram Stoker's *Dracula*, who wasted away while having her blood drained night after night. The bones of Ann's face were beginning to appear as hard lines beneath her once soft skin.

Michael was pained at the idea and actually moaned aloud. He was just opening his mouth, probably to tell her that she couldn't, when the sound of racing Humvees came to them. Deanna was out the door in a blink with Neil close behind. She ran with the bag of blood cradled to her chest as though it were a baby and even turned to hit the door with her back to protect it.

In the parking lot were three Humvees, each still rocking from a sudden stop. From two of them, wounded soldiers, with the help of their friends, eased gingerly out. The third Hummer had an open back hatch where a stretcher stuck about a third of the way out. Neil could see a set of lower legs on the stretcher. The pants the soldier wore were no longer the soft green swirl of normal camouflage. One leg was dark with old blood and the other was blackened like a log pulled from a fire.

Keeping out of the soldiers' way, Deanna moved sideways, crablike, until she could see into the back of the Humvee. She squinted, trying to peer into the dark space and then her face broke. Neil started to head in her direction when a fast-moving black blur crashed into him.

It was Sadie. She was tear-streaked and covered in mud and crusted blood. "Are you alriii..." Her hug crushed his ribs and sent the air right out of him in a formless rush. She sobbed against him. When he could find breath he asked, "Are you hurt?"

"No," she said, pulling back, her tears ending so abruptly that it was a little frightening. "I never get hurt. It's everyone else who gets hurt and dies." Her big, dark eyes were glassy as she stared at nothing.

Just then the soldiers pulled Grey from the back of the Humvee. He was a mess, covered in blood from head to toe, his head lolling from side to side as he was rushed inside. Neil, Deanna and Sadie tried to go in as well, however Margaret Yuan stopped them.

She took the liter of blood from Deanna's hands, saying: "Find us more or he won't make it."

Chapter 23

Neil Martin

Because she was so haggard and drawn, Neil sent Sadie away to sleep. Deanna went to hunt down the O negative donors. There were many tasks that were far more important to the community as a whole, however Neil knew she had become singularly focused and nothing short of all the walls coming down simultaneously would have kept her from getting the blood needed to keep Grey alive.

Neil wished he could be so laser focused on one thing; it would have made his life a lot easier. Instead, after a complaint from one of the officers, he had to make sure the team who was pulling water from the lake for forty-two hundred people was staying on task and running at optimum efficiency.

Next, again because of complaints, this time from hungry soldiers, he had to check on the food situation. The man in charge said he couldn't move the food from the storage facility because of a lack of fuel—and the fuel team said they were maxed out, working at full capacity because of the importance given to constructing the endless series of walls that marched down out of the mountains towards the valley.

Then there were the teams hauling firewood who warned Neil that they were undermanned and that the coming night would get extra dangerous if the fires weren't kept lit.

"Wouldn't it be easier if we just hauled a few generators to each site?" Neil asked. "There are spotlights at the Department of Transportation depot out on Mule Trail Road."

Instead of being grateful at the idea, the man in charge of the wood hauling teams threw his hands in the air. "Why didn't you tell us that last night? Look at all this fucking wood." There were huge stacks of it, enough to keep dozens of campfires burning.

"No reason to be a jerk about it," Neil snapped. "If I had thought of it earlier, I would have said something then. Now, pick thirty people and go get the generators and the lights. The rest need to be released to me."

Neil divided the three hundred men and women and sent a few to the teams involved with hauling water, fuel and food. Most of the rest he sent to the wall building team. He kept twenty behind and set them on a new and unsavory task—the areas around the walls were becoming frightfully unsanitary. The hundreds of soldiers fighting at each section had to relieve themselves somewhere and the smell was becoming unbearable.

The *Crap Team,* as they called themselves, was sent to find enough port-a-potties, again housed in the Department of Transportation depot, to keep eighteen hundred fighting men from despoiling the environment any more than it was. The *Crap Team* grumbled, of course but Neil shut them up. "Anyone who doesn't want this assignment can grab a baseball bat and go man one of the walls. Those are your choices."

No one changed jobs.

It was after three in the afternoon when Neil felt the situation was well enough under control for him to go back and check on Captain Grey and the other injured soldiers, and, of course, Marybeth. He paused outside the clinic, afraid to go in, afraid that death awaited him on the other side of the doors.

As he stood there, Michael Gates came stomping out, his eyes red and bulging, his large hands opening and closing. He saw Neil and his anger looked to double. "This is your fault!" He strode up to tower over Neil in a rage and grabbed him by his sweater vest in his two meaty hands.

Neil made no move to defend himself. He was the first to admit he wasn't a fighter and he would readily agree to the fact that Michael owed him more than a beating. If anyone had tried to stop Sadie from getting proper care, Neil's claws, small and dull as they were, would have come out.

Assuming that the worst had occurred, Neil said: "I'm sorry for your loss, Michael. Marybeth was the finest of women I've ever known. I wish I could have said goodbye."

Michael's anger lost some of its fire, and instead of punching the smaller man, he threw Neil to the ground. "She's not dead, no thanks to you. She's still fighting. I'm going to get more blood even if I have to beat it out of someone." As angry as he was, this sounded like an idle threat and Neil guessed he was actually going out to beg the donors in person.

"Can I stop in to see her?" Neil asked, squinting up.

The fire came back into Michael's face and he stood, threateningly over Neil. "You stay away from her. If I catch you in her room, I'll take your head off." Michael then jumped in Neil's Humvee, hit the starter button and sped out of the clinic parking lot.

"You sure showed him," a voice said from the side of the clinic. It was a soldier with a bloody shirt and a poorly bandaged arm. He stood leaning against the building smoking a cigarette and smirking as Neil picked himself up.

Another voice, this time speaking from just inside the clinic door said: "He did the right thing. There was no honor in this fight. No purpose could have been served by more bloodshed." It was General Johnston and, despite his words which were true enough, Neil felt a ripple of humiliation go through him.

"Michael is my friend," Neil told them. "I wouldn't fight him, no matter what the reason. Now, if you'll excuse me." He started towards the door but the general didn't relinquish his position and stood, barring the way.

"You didn't ask me how the battle is going," the general stated. "Aren't you curious?"

Neil shrugged. "I've been to the front lines. I've seen the situations involved with each and I'm doing everything in my power to support the military. I figured if there was an issue with containment you would have told me. Am I to assume by your presence that you are losing containment on one of the walls?"

"No...I guess I should say yes. We are withdrawing from the Blue Gate in half an hour, once the demolition charges are in place."

"You're going to blow up the wall?"

Johnston grinned. "Oh, yeah. It's going to be a big show. We can't use our artillery except for one damaged piece so I figure we would use up some of our horded munitions. We'll wait until the wall has finally been topped and once enough of the stiffs drop off the other side that the fall is no longer hurting them, we'll light it up...but that's not why I'm here."

"Here to visit the wounded?"

He nodded. "Same as you. It's one of the worst aspects of the job, but at least, for the most part, there aren't any grieving widows to console. That is a horror beyond the telling." Neil glanced into the building but before he could ask, Johnston said: "Captain Grey just got out of surgery, or what passes for surgery around here. He's alive, but still unconscious. I'm more than a little nervous about that, but I suppose that's what happens when you have so many holes where they don't belong. I have to get going but do come by and watch us knock down the wall. It'll be a blast."

With a chuckle, General Johnston skipped down the stairs and quick-marched to his Humvee in the parking lot. Neil watched him go and then hesitated turning back to the door; he was dreading going up into the clinic. He didn't want to see his friend bandaged and deathly pale, and he didn't want to have to say nice, consoling words to Deanna, such as: *He'll be fine. He's a trooper,* and *Nothing will keep him down for long.* The words would be lies at worst or just hopeful platitudes at best.

And, despite his asking, he really didn't want to see Marybeth. It had been hard enough to visit her when she had simply been mortally wounded during an escape he had led; now he was her killer, the man who 'pulled her plug' so to speak. He was sure General Johnston had never had to do anything like that.

Steeling himself, mostly by holding his breath and contorting his already maimed face, Neil strode into the clinic heading for Marybeth's room. He wanted to get the worst over with and it was better to see her without Michael threatening to break his neck. As noiselessly as possible, he slipped into her room.

Ann was there, fast asleep, curled up in a chair with her woody brown hair loose and thrown over face like a cowl blocking the overhead fluorescents. The chair was parked next to Marybeth's hospital bed.

Marybeth's eyes, a dull blue, were open and staring at Neil. He froze, half in the doorway and half out; he'd been hoping to sneak in, murmur a quick apology to her comatose body and then slip away with his conscience at least partially soothed. They stared at each other for a long moment; she regarded him passively, not moving a muscle, while he looked at her with his insides coiling and a tic working at his right eye. Only when he opened his mouth to speak did she move: her head eased from side to side, moving only about an inch in either direction away from center.

He was to be quiet. Perhaps she didn't want to hear his lame and feeble sounding apology. Perhaps she didn't want him to wake Ann. Marybeth lifted a finger and tapped her bed, beckoning him.

Neil tip-toed to her bedside and saw that her IV bag was filled with normal saline; a donor, other than Ann hadn't been found, either that or all the blood had gone to Captain Grey. Neil couldn't help himself. "I'm sorry," he whispered. "We don't have enough blood..."

She began shaking her head, telling him again to be quiet. "Are we going to win?" she asked, in a brittle voice that had all the strength of an infant's.

Neil's answer was entirely reflex: "Yes, of course." She shook her head again in that tiny way. What did she want? Neil wondered. The truth? Or a lie that would make her feel good about the family she was leaving behind as she slipped into death?

"It doesn't matter if we win or not," Neil told her, hoping to strike a middle ground. "You don't need to worry about that. We are doing everything possible to keep you and your family safe."

"Tell me the truth." Her eye color might have been a dull blue, but there was still a spark of life in them. Answering her question wasn't so easy since Neil didn't know what the truth was. He had come to assume that the military would either fight off the zombies or contain them in some way. But were either of those happening?

The realistic answer was no. When the big wall fell at the Blue Gate, they would find themselves working on borrowed time. Each of the smaller walls would be stop gap measures only, holding the beasts back until new mounds of corpses would grow so large in width, depth, and length that, when one of the beasts was struck down, there would be nowhere for it to go but on the valley side of the wall.

When that happened, it was only a matter of time before the fighting conditions became too difficult and too dangerous and the men would have to abandon the wall and retreat to the next wall and these were only twelve feet in height in parts. They wouldn't last nearly so long and then the men would have to retreat again and again.

How many walls could they realistically make? There were at least a thousand cars in the valley. That would make seven walls, maybe eight. That would mean three or four days of constant fighting and dying on the part of the soldiers, and four days of constant drudgery on the part of civilians before they would be forced to give up the valley and retreat to who knew where. That is unless someone could think of some other way to stop the beasts.

"No," he told her. "We aren't going to win." Saying it aloud, actually admitting it to himself had a disconcerting effect. He suddenly felt bone-tired as if he could lean back and sleep right there, right that second. It seemed as though his body had taken the admission as an excuse to shut down. His eyes suddenly felt heavy and he fought to stifle a yawn that threatened to overtake him. It would have been rude as Marybeth had opened her mouth to speak.

She took a few seconds to say: "Stop…stop the IV."

Neil's eyes were drawn to the bag, hanging above her bed. It was half full and dripping steadily. Stopping it would kill her, perhaps not right away, but if no one noticed that the fluids were no longer running into her body, it wouldn't take long.

"Someone else is going to need it more than me," she said. "I'm done, I know it, but Michael won't accept the truth and Ann will end up draining herself to the point of death, all for nothing." Neil was having trouble grasping her words which seemed to be gaining in strength rather than losing it.

"I can't," Neil told her. "That's murder."

"If I do it, it's suicide," Marybeth said. "That's a sin that can't be forgiven. You have to do it, Neil, you're the only one who is mentally strong enough to do it. My family won't and neither will the doctor. I'm ok with this, Neil, really. Just do it. Now, before anyone comes in or Ann wakes up."

He wanted to cough or bump the bed or do anything to wake Ann up so he could shrug his shoulders at Marybeth, wish her good luck and scoot out of the room, but he didn't. With a sick, oily feeling in his belly, he reached out to the IV tubing where the clamp sat six inches below the drip chamber. He rolled it all the way down so that the fluid no longer moved. He did this with his eyes on Ann, certain that she would flick her eyes open and catch him in the process of killing her mother.

She didn't stir and Neil finished the act that would kill Marybeth.

"Thank you," Marybeth said, already sounding quieter. "You're a good man, Neil. Michael will remember that before it's all said and done. Now, you better go." Neil wanted to run out of the room but he stayed and squeezed her soft hand; it was cold as a morgue slab. He consciously kept from wiping his hand on his pants as he walked away from her. At the door they smiled at each other and then he was through it only to run into Margaret Yuan's assistant. She tried to get past Neil.

"She's just fallen asleep," Neil said, holding his hands out. "You understand how it is in hospitals, everyone constantly coming in and out. A person is supposed to rest and to heal but how can they with all the interruptions? Am I right? Why don't you show me to Captain Grey's room?" He was babbling.

Neil took the girl by the arm. She grinned at him and it was the same grin he'd been getting since he came into the valley. It was an uneasy grin, one that suggested she was sickened by his mangled face or was grossed out by his chewed off fingers. Quickly, he let go of her arm and let her walk next to him.

They walked in a stiff silence which lasted even after they had entered Grey's room. Neil expected Grey's every orifice to be plugged with a menagerie of tubes, but he could only see the one that ran into his arm, it was filled with O negative blood and Neil felt his stomach grip from the guilt.

In a chair in the corner, Sadie was sleeping full on, her head back, her legs flung and her arms dangling. She had taken little time to wash off some of the blood that had been covering her, mostly just from her hands and face. Otherwise she was a mess.

Deanna stood next to Grey's bed and she was on the other end of the spectrum: she had somehow recovered from all the stress she'd been under, and if she was exhausted it didn't show; she seemed completely at peace. "He's going to live," she told Neil before he could ask. "I know it. And he'll be good as new, only he'll have a few more scars to brag about."

Neil turned to the C.N.A. "Is that what the doctor said? Is he going to be ok?"

"She thinks that if he wakes up in the next day, he should be ok," she answered. "But he did lose a lot of blood. It was really very close there for a bit, so I don't know."

Deanna became adamant and her words took on a sharper edge. "He'll wake up soon, I can feel it in my bones. Mark my words."

"I'm sure he will," Neil said, not just to placate Deanna but also because he actually believed it. "Knowing him he'll be up tomorrow for some light P.T."

The girl didn't hear this as the joke Neil intended. "He can't exercise! Those stitches in his arm are very weak. The artery was shredded up. So, whatever you do, don't let him move, don't even let him walk to the bathroom. The doctor thinks he should remain bedridden for at least two weeks or the artery might rupture and she doesn't know if she can repair it again."

"Of course," Deanna agreed, without question or even blinking an eye. She was in love and was in some sort of happy, euphoric state simply because Grey was still alive. She wasn't thinking. They didn't have two weeks. They had four days at the most and they had to be gone by that fourth day, gone and traveling further up into the mountains where the land was unforgiving and the air thin and frigid even in the deepest part of summer and where there would be little food and less shelter.

Neil stared down at his friend, thinking that it was a blessing he was unconscious. Grey would know the score, he could do the simple math: one plus one and he was dead. With their very limited fuel, he would know that all unnecessary items would have to be abandoned. Neil was sure he would count himself as unnecessary and would insist on being left behind, perhaps with a pistol and a single magazine.

Of course, everyone would insist he come along, taking up valuable room on one of the dozen or so heavy trucks that the people of the valley possessed. But how far would he make it? The roads coming up from the foothills hadn't just been pothole ridden, they had been dangerous. Landslides, avalanches and just plain erosion had turned the mountain road into an obstacle course. There had been places where the road had just disappeared and they had climbed down steep ravines or over piles of rubble. People and gear had been tossed around like crazy.

And they weren't even that high up yet. What would the mountain passes look like? A nightmare, Neil was sure.

Grey was going to die, because Neil wasn't smart enough to save him. Another life on his conscience.

As these thoughts ran through Neil's mind, Sadie appeared suddenly at his elbow, making him jump. She didn't smile as she once would have. She only gazed down on the captain with a strange, unreadable look in her dark eyes.

More by accident than design, she looked, once again, thoroughly Goth. Her eyes were shadowed in dried blood and dark circles; her fingernails were black with a combination of dirt, ash and blood; her hair was once more standing in spikes held upright with dried blood. Flakes of it had fallen to land on her cheeks like morbid freckles.

Neil saw her appearance but with the weight of his new responsibilities and his fresh double helping of guilt, he couldn't summon the energy to look beyond it and worry about her mental state. She was alive and that's what counted; everything else would have to work itself out when there was time.

Unless, once again, someone could think of something to either stop the zombies or stop the Azael. "What would Jillybean do?" he said, under his breath.

"What's that?" Deanna asked.

"Nothing. I got to go. The general is going to blow up the big wall at the Blue Gate once it's breached and I should be there." He didn't really need to be, however he was hoping that an explosion would jar a Jillybean type idea into his head. He was sure that she would have some sort of explosion-based solution to their problem.

With his Humvee having been "borrowed" by Michael, Neil commandeered another one from the clinic parking lot. Sadie was in the passenger seat before he had shut his door. Their eyes met and nothing needed to be said. She would come with him and share his pain and protect him if needed, no questions asked.

Neil drove with a sense of urgency to the Blue Gate, well actually to the secondary wall a hundred yards behind it: Blue Gate 2. It was crowded with ragged, unshaven soldiers who rested with their strange weapons across their thighs. There were baseball bats, sharpened mop handles, sawn-off pool cues and fat-headed hammers that were caked in old blood.

There were civilian workers present as well. These were forced to watch from further back, sitting up on the steep hills surrounding the road. They seemed eager for a show.

As Governor, Neil was given VIP status and was escorted by a sergeant to the middle of the wall. After some barked orders by the sergeant, a way was cleared and Neil climbed up to stand in the center of the wall that Deanna had built while the crane had still been running. It was tall and frightfully unsteady. If he felt he could have bowed out of the ceremony, he would have, but he thought he needed to be as close as possible in hopes of triggering an idea.

He stood with an old, finned caddy shaking beneath his feet. Next to him on his right, Sadie straddled the space between the caddy and a Volkswagen Jetta while, on his left, was the general, watching as the zombies fell from the great height of the now abandoned Blue Gate 1.

The undead dropped down, stepping off into nothing as if expecting the thin air to support their weight. To Neil they appeared comically surprised and continued to walk their feet in the air as they fell. Sadie grunted once when it first started. It was what passed for a laugh for her.

"Would you like to do the honors?" the general asked, holding out a small black box with a switch on it.

Neil shook his head. "No. I don't get any pleasure from this sort of thing. Death, even their death is a sad thing."

The general didn't bat an eye, nor did his pleasant expression change in the least and his hand holding the detonator out to Neil didn't budge. "Some things we do because we have to and not for pleasure. The men will be cheered to see their new leader do the honors. Remember, half your job is as figurehead."

Holding back a sigh, Neil took the detonator and held it up. "Who wants some fireworks?" he cried.

The weary soldiers, desperate for something to break up the awful monotony of killing, cheered in a great voice. It was taken up by the civilians swarming the hills until the man-carved valley echoed with their cry. Neil waited until the sound had begun to slacken before he thumbed down the switch.

The general's engineers had linked three hundred rounds of 105MM ammo to explode in one tremendous thunderclap. When Neil hit the button, the back face of the concrete wall blasted up and out, flinging huge chunks of concrete into the air, some of which smashed into the wall of cars a hundred yards away. Neil did his best not to flinch as concrete starred windshields and dented the car he was standing on.

When the wall let go, the mound of zombies, a fantastic mass of corpses, gushed forward, spilling out as though someone had kicked over a pail filled with worms. The grotesque sight killed the cheers and, just like that, the celebration was over. The civilians came down off the hills and went back to their tasks and the soldiers took last sips from water bottles or puffed cigarettes as the tens of thousands of zombies that had been held back by the mound and the wall surged forward, their all-encompassing hunger driving them on.

"Take a good look," General Johnston said, as the first of the zombies rushed across to the wall of cars. When the first hit, the entire structure shuddered. "This wall won't last. You can see that, right?"

Sadie spoke for the first time that afternoon. "We're not blind."

"Good," Johnston said. "Then you know that the inevitable can't be staved off for long. When this falls, we'll retreat to the next and, as you can see, it's a lot less impressive." The three of them, glanced back at the next wall; it was only three cars high. "And when that one falls we'll retreat again and again and so on. But there is a limit that we have to consider both in material and human stamina."

"What are you saying?" Sadie asked with acid in her voice.

"He's saying that we have to consider abandoning the valley," Neil said.

Sadie's eyes blazed and she stepped across to the caddy, so that the three of them shared the dented in hood. "I can't believe what I'm hearing. You want to give up the very thing you sent a dozen men to die for this morning? Why? Why sacrifice those men for nothing?"

"They didn't die for nothing," the general explained. "They bought us valuable time so that when we do retreat, we can do so in relative safety and not with artillery sending us running out of here empty-handed. At least now we can make an orderly retreat and salvage a lot of our necessities."

A category in which Grey didn't belong, Neil thought. The guilt, which had been held to a simmer with the explosions and the rickety Cadillac, was on him again full force. "And if we can think of some way to delay them? Have you considered sending out more assault teams? If we stop their horsemen driving the zombies on, the pressure on the stiffs will slack off and..."

Johnston cut in: "We have already thought of that. I sent out teams hours ago, but unfortunately, our enemies have finally wised up and are now protecting their men and positions with proper numbers. The hills above their camp and above their driving teams are now too well defended for another assault to be successful. Believe me, if I could save this valley I would, but we can't. That's the simple truth."

The fury roiling in Sadie became too great and she stomped her foot on the caddy's windscreen, cracking it, sending white lines shooting out from her heel. "No! I refuse to believe Morganstern died so that we could have a few more hours to pick through our crap. I won't believe that."

"Would you believe he died in order to give us enough time to realize the truth?" Johnston asked in that deep, soothing voice of his. "We were so focused on defending our walls that we... that I didn't look at the big picture. That was a mistake, and if we keep going, blindly defending these walls, it'll only end up costing more lives. The truth is we need to leave. We have to."

Leaving would cost at least one more life: Captain Grey's. Sadie knew it and, with her eyes, she implored Neil to say something. The problem was that the explosion that marked the end of the Blue Gate and perhaps the entire valley, hadn't triggered anything in him. He was just as clueless as how to save the valley as he had been thirty minutes before. He had failed and now Grey would die.

Chapter 24
Sadie Walcott

The ladder down from the swaying wall of cars shook and rattled as her feet clunked on the rungs. Neil was above her, moving far more slowly. He was, as always when it came to heights, methodical, making sure each hand had its proper grip before moving on. That was his way. He was smart, but not a risk taker, nor was he the most inventive of men.

There was a way to save the valley, Sadie knew it in her bones and the reason she knew it was because of Jillybean. In every given situation, the little girl always saw the one thing that no one else could. If she was here in the valley, she would have scratched the side of her nose or picked the panties out of her bottom and without much effort would've said: *Have you tried this or that?* in that infuriatingly innocent way of hers, and *voila*, the valley would be saved and the Azael sent running for their lives.

In Sadie's mind it was as simple as that. There was a way to save them, somebody just had to come up with an idea.

At the bottom of the ladder, Sadie turned in a slow circle, her eyes staring hard at everyone and everything, trying to force inspiration into her sluggish mind. "What if we tried..." she asked, hoping that the end of the question would just fill itself in with the answer she needed. The answer didn't come.

Above her, Neil called down: "You okay?"

A growl escaped her throat and she stomped away. There were soldiers around her. They were the usual tired and blood-bedraggled men. She stared into their eyes, looking for any spark of intelligence greater than her own, trying to find someone who could furnish the ending to her unfinished question: *What if we tried...* The only problem was that her IQ was well above the average, though she would never admit that to herself, and the men around her seemed either too dimwitted or too fatigued to think straight.

When none of the soldiers satisfied, she moved on to the civilians and they were even worse. For a year they had been coddled and protected like no other group on the planet. They weren't used to the nerve-rending stress of living with a true zombie threat hanging over their heads. And they weren't used to back-breaking labor while in survival mode twenty-four hours a day.

Half of them walked around with their shoulders so stooped you would think they were trying to drag their knuckles along the ground as they moved. The other half were simply too afraid to come up with complex plans. These people cast uneasy glances up at the hills or they went about with their hands tucked in close to their chests and their lips quivering.

No one seemed to have that spark Sadie had come to rely on in Jillybean.

Sadie looked around for Neil, however he had been stopped by the flow of soldiers and civilians, all of whom were looking to be reassured that everything was going to be ok. His smile was a lie that she recognized from fifty feet. She could also see the pain in his eyes at having to wear that awful smile.

Deflated, she went to the Humvee Neil had appropriated and, without a single qualm, hopped in and sped out of there.

She knew one person whose intellect was more than a match for anyone she had ever met, besides Jillybean that is… she just hoped he was conscious.

Sadie slipped through the clinic doors ever so quietly. There were people dying in the building after all—or at least there was one dying person, Marybeth. She didn't think anything could kill Captain Grey; in her eyes he was too tough for the Grim Reaper.

Deanna was still by his bedside and the captain was still zonked out. "How did it go?" Deanna asked. "I feel a little shabby about not being there for Neil. I am supposed to be Lieutenant Governor after all."

"I wouldn't worry about that if I was you. And the explosion was...it was impressive, I guess, and eye opening." Sadie paused for a second, wondering if telling Deanna about the plans to evacuate the valley was a good idea. *She'll find out soon enough*, Sadie decided.

The older woman caught the pause and the odd choice of words. "Eye opening? How so?"

"After the wall came down General Johnston basically said that the military won't be able to defend us for long. He wants to abandon the valley. Which means..."

Deanna's eyes swung from the girl to the unconscious captain. "It means Grey will die. They know that right? Neil knows that. He was right here when the C.N.A said so."

Neil knew. Sadie guessed it was why he looked so miserable when he was glad-handing it with the people. For the "greater good" she knew he would pack up whatever he could and march at the head of his new clan of renegades acting as a modern-day Moses looking for the promised land. But Sadie knew that they were already in their promised land, they just had to defend it.

"He knows," Sadie agreed, "But he's confused. He will only consider what route will keep the greatest number of people alive in the short term. He doesn't see that endless running will only end in ultimate disaster. There's nowhere that is really safe. Nowhere that's better than this."

Deanna's eyes shifted away. "I don't know about that. It's not safe here, not really, but that doesn't mean we can't hold out for a few more days. Five might work, but they have to try. They just can't give up on the valley so easily."

Sadie saw that Deanna was blinded by love. She would allow a hundred men to die in order to save Grey. It was a selfish love, but then, Sadie thought, most love was. And what was the basis for her own motivations? She had felt an ugly, visceral reaction to the idea of giving up the valley so easily after so many lives had been cut short defending it. Beyond that, why did she want to stay? Did she really think this was it? The last refuge left in America?

In short, yes.

During the last year, she had crisscrossed the country, fleeing from place to place and only finding disappointment and pain, betrayal and bloodshed. So far, the valley had been the one place she had found where the people were truly good and where their leaders weren't deluded or barbarous. Even the land itself, with its fertile soil and its natural barriers, screamed to be defended.

"What we need is a way to convince Neil..." Just then the door opened and Neil Martin strode in, so much different than the first time Sadie met him when he had been as timid as a mouse.

"Convince Neil of what?" he asked, pleasantly, not at all upset that Sadie had abandoned him at the wall.

"To give us more time," Deanna said right away, even though that wasn't what Sadie was thinking. "Just a few days is all we need. Grey's life depends on it. And you owe him. As...as a friend, you owe it to him to do everything possible to save his life." She advanced on Neil as she spoke, her hands out to him.

Neil looked distinctly uneasy. With a strange crooked smile on his face, he glanced back at the door as if he was contemplating running away or perhaps he was afraid that someone one was going to run in.

When neither occurred, he turned to Deanna. "You have to know I understand what you're going through. I really never expected Grey to come back in this condition. I just thought he'd come back the same gruff soldier he left as. But...but that doesn't really matter, does it? What matters is that this valley can't be defended. It's that simple. Whether it's three days or four, the zombies will get through and then it will be running and screaming and chaos. Our only choice is to anticipate this, pack up what we can, and get out before it happens."

"Or we figure out a way to stay," Sadie said. "We figure out a way to fight them to a standstill until the Azael give up and go home. It's possible, I'm sure it is." She didn't add: If Jillybean were here she'd have thought of a way long ago.

"We're doing everything we can already," Neil countered. "If you have a better way to fight them, let me know, I'd gladly present it to the general, but I'm not going to him with wishful thinking. The Azael aren't just going to give up and go away."

Sadie countered: "We don't know that for sure. Just think, they probably didn't bring much food with them, maybe a few days' worth only. And I bet their water situation is way worse. I bet they were counting on the rivers. The Big Thompson is polluted, we should consider throwing in a bunch of zombies corpses in the Little Thompson, as well."

"That's a great idea!" Deanna said, in an excited whisper. "We can use germ warfare to get the Azael so sick they won't be able to fight. What else can we use?"

"I don't know," Sadie answered. "I don't know anything about war, but he does." She pointed at Grey. "We need to wake him up." Deanna began shaking her head, but Sadie ignored her. She went to Grey's bedside; he didn't look peaceful, he looked tired, even in sleep.

"Grey," Sadie said, shaking him gently on his shoulder. She glanced back and saw Deanna waiting apprehensively, seeming afraid for Sadie to wake him and afraid that she wouldn't be able to. "Come on, Grey, Wake up. Hey, what's his first name? I know it's not *captain*."

"James," Deanna told her. "I tried to call him Jimmy once and he got so mad that he threatened to throw me in the lake. God, that was just like three days ago but it feels like a month."

Sadie bent over Grey a second time and started shaking his good right arm saying: "James," over and over until his eyes fluttered and he began a confused blinking. When his eyes could focus, Sadie said: "Hey, Jimmy."

He glared for a second and then turned to stare around the room until he saw Deanna, who was crying. "Don't cry," he said in a course, dry whisper. "We won. Sadie blew up the guns. Shame about Morganstern and...and...and, who else was there?" His brown eyes had slowly come to focus again on Sadie, seeming to look to her for answers, but just then her mind drew a blank. She knew Morganstern's name and then there was the guy who had been pinned down and was killed by the Azael after he was already shot. She couldn't remember his name, which she thought was a little unsettling. Nor could she remember the soldier's name who had been carrying the M16 with the grenade launcher.

"There were a lot of guys," Sadie said, her vision blurring; she tried to grin through the tears that had sprung up. "But don't worry about them just now."

Deanna stepped forward and grabbed his right hand, the tears on her face coming quicker now. She bent and kissed his lips. "How do you feel? Are you in pain? Can I get you anything?"

"Water," he said, and swallowed audibly. Deanna hurried out the door, letting it swing shut with a bang. In the fifteen seconds she was gone, there was silence in the room that wasn't at all awkward between the long time companions, though they each jumped a little when Deanna came rushing back to hold a small cup to Grey's lips.

He took only a couple of sips before he shook his head and said, "That's good."

Sadie was anxious to ask him how they could win the war against the Azael; however she didn't want to rush her question. He was still too groggy and if he only shrugged or couldn't otherwise answer, she knew that Neil would take that as an admission that winning wasn't possible.

Neil spoke first: "We have a bit of a problem and a large part of it concerns you." This brought Grey around and the shrewd look that Sadie had come to know was back. "The bad news is that despite yours and Sadie's heroics in destroying the enemy's artillery, our walls aren't holding the zombies back and it's only a matter of time before they come down or are breached."

"And how can that possibly concern me more than it does anyone else?" Grey asked.

"Because it behooves us to plan ahead and to act prior to the event, which means we will be evacuating the very youngest and oldest and anyone infirm or injured. I know this isn't news to you, however, the problem stems from the fact that Ms. Yuan seems to think your injuries are too grievous for you to be moved for quite some time."

Grey looked surprised at this and glanced down at his body as though expecting to see missing limbs. He tried to move his arms and legs under the hospital blanket and grimaced. "Please, let me see," he said to Deanna. She pulled back the cover to reveal his body adorned in fresh, white bandages. He grunted. "A couple of bullet wounds and a not-so-bad burn is hardly fatal."

"It's your arm," Deanna explained. "The artery was in ribbons and Margaret is afraid that her stitches won't hold if you move it. You could bleed out quickly and there isn't very much blood left for a transfusion, really, there's only one liter of O negative and that I scrounged this morning."

"What about Marybeth?" Grey asked. "She needs more than that."

A muscle jumped at the end of Neil's lip as he stammered: "I-I'm afraid I've had to restrict Marybeth's access to blood. With the battle raging as it is, the donors are too exhausted and too busy. Really, we were lucky to get this last liter."

"Give it to Marybeth," Grey demanded through clenched teeth. "I'm clearly on the mend. I don't need it."

Deanna wouldn't hear of it. "You're fine at the moment, but what happens if the stitches tear? You'll die in minutes without the blood."

"That's not necessarily true," he answered. "But what is completely true is that Marybeth is going to die without the transfusions. Normal saline won't cut it. So. Give. Her. The blood."

Neil wasn't put off by Grey's growling voice as it was only a shadow of its former self. In fact, his own voice rose sharply as if he were dressing down a very junior colleague. "No, not yet, not until we get at least three liters. I think we can all agree that she is not going to make it and I won't have such a precious commodity basically run down the sink for no good reason. That's my final word on this, Grey."

Sadie jumped in, quickly as Grey's face grew stony. "Hey, let's put a pin in that for now, alright," she said. "One liter won't save Marybeth so let's figure out a long-term solution, one that doesn't revolve around running away. We need a solution that will save not only this valley but also Marybeth and you as well Captain Grey. We need a way to fight the zombies to a standstill."

"A standstill? To what end?" Grey asked after giving Neil a last, hard look. "They need to be destroyed."

"Maybe not," Sadie said. "If we hold out long enough, the Azael will give up and go away. They're not real military people. I bet they haven't planned for a long stay, sitting on the side of a mountain road. Their food situation is going to get critical soon and I bet their water supply is worse, especially if we dump a bunch of dead zombies in the rivers to poison them."

Grey smirked and there was a shade of evil to it that darkened his features. "I like it, but how are you going to stop the zombies? I gather from Neil's nervous-nelly look that he doesn't think it's possible."

"It isn't possible, or it's highly unlikely," Neil said, ignoring the nervous-nelly comment. "That's why we're working on a contingency plan that, yes, involves retreating into the mountains."

"We were hoping you could think of some new way to stop the zombies," Sadie said to Grey. "The walls we've built won't hold. We had this crane that got bombed and so now the walls are barely twelve feet high. And you know our ammo situation. We just don't have enough bullets to kill them all. So…" Her lip quivered on its way from an uncertain grin to a hopeful smile.

"So…" Grey said, settling back in his bed to stare up at the ceiling. "No ammo, hmmm, and no walls." He hissed between his teeth and then his lips pursed. "Are the back loaders still operational?"

Neil replied slowly, cautiously: "Yes."

"Have you tried digging trenches before the walls? A ten foot moat will be the equivalent of adding ten feet to the height of the wall."

"We haven't," Neil said. "Huh? That's crazy we hadn't thought about that before. Do you have any other Jillybean-esque ideas?"

Grey was silent for a long time and then a spasm of anger crossed his features. "No, nothing's coming to me. The zombies don't have many weaknesses. We have a little CS gas, but it wouldn't faze them in the least. Now, if we had mustard gas, we could burn the eyes right out of their heads."

"Is there another way to blind them?" Deanna asked. "Maybe really powerful lights would do it. Do you guys have any lasers?" she asked, excitedly.

"Like in the movies?" Grey asked, smiling at her. "No, we don't have any lasers and we don't have sonic beams either."

Sadie started tapping the metal frame of Grey's bed, her brain trying to eke out an idea. "Can you make one? Are they hard to make?" Grey gave her a look that suggested the idea was preposterous. She went on, thinking aloud: "Well what do we have that will hurt them, besides weapons and stuff like that? What affects them? Poison?"

Grey started to shrug and then grimaced and glanced down at his injured left arm. "No," he said, his voice quivering with pain. "We brought only what we had to. We have a bit of C4 and some artillery and a few hundred rounds of mortar ammo, mostly flares, nothing that'll do any lasting harm, though it might dazzle them a bit."

There was a moment of silence that was interrupted as Neil thumped his fist down on Grey's mattress. "Yes, we could dazzle them," he said, his scarred face lit up with a grin. He turned to Sadie and asked: "Remember when Ram died? Remember the fire that Jillybean set?"

A thousand years could pass and Sadie wouldn't forget the flames that reached twenty stories into the sky or the smoke that went forty more. Nor would she ever forget the heat that stretched the skin of her face as tight as a drum. It had been so hot she had feared that her hair would spontaneously ignite.

"I remember," she said. "Do you have some way to replicate that fire? Wouldn't it take up all of our fuel reserves?" Even she thought that was a bad idea; retreat had to be in their contingency plans at some point.

"I don't think we need the exact same sized fire. I mean, if we could turn them to ash I would do it in a heartbeat, but we don't have those sorts of resources available. But we may not need that sized fire. When the boat was first going up in flames, and Jillybean was running around trying to save me, Ram was, for want of a better word, mesmerized by the fire. He couldn't take his eyes off of it."

Sadie had a flash of memory: Jillybean lighting a house on fire in a Philadelphia suburb to help them escape. Sadie had looked back on their way through the backyard—the zombies in the house had been standing, rooted in place as the fire in the living room had slowly engulfed the house. They hadn't done anything to save themselves.

Then a second memory flicked across her conscious mind: The fire Jillybean had set on the fuel truck outside the hangar when a thousand zombies had surrounded Neil, Grey, Deanna and herself. It had gone up like a bomb and the flames spun tornadoes of light and smoke into the air, a hundred feet high. The zombies had stood, transfixed as if witnessing a holy event.

"We could build bonfires," she said, "big ones on platforms."

"Or right on the walls themselves," Deanna said. "The closer the better. The fires we had been using to light things were too small." She grinned all of a sudden, her teeth looking so very white and her eyes just as bright. Grey couldn't stop staring at her and Sadie thought that was just the finest thing ever. They were in love and that was a great thing.

But then the captain's eyes dulled slightly and his smile softened and grew less. Deanna was quick to assume a motherly role: "Maybe you and Neil should go get those trenches dug and those fires started."

"Of course," Neil said. Before he left, he grabbed Grey's good shoulder and squeezed. "Who needs Jillybean, right?"

"We do," Grey answered in a snap. "She would've seen these simple things right away. We shouldn't have allowed her to leave like we did."

Neil paused in the doorway, feeling the edge of the door with his thumb. "You're probably right, but that's water under the bridge now. It's not something we should bother dwelling on. You get better, quick." He gave Sadie a look and jerked his head toward the door.

She followed him out into the hall where the two of them were almost run over by a sprinting Margaret Yuan, who was decked out in full scrubs, her gloved and bloody hands held out before her. Sadie flattened herself against the wall as Margaret smashed opened a door with her foot and charged through.

"Was that Marybeth's room?" Sadie asked, taking a step in its direction. Neil pulled her back by the elbow.

"Yes, and don't go in there. Let Margaret do her job, we'll do ours." He hurried her out of the hospital with his eyes darting from side to side as if they had just robbed a bank and were making a getaway.

Chapter 25
Neil Martin

Had Marybeth died so quickly? Neil wondered as he speed-walked out of the clinic, dragging Sadie after him as if Marybeth's ghost were hot on their tail. Neil didn't look back, afraid not only of said ghost, but also that Michael would come storming out. Neil wasn't truly afraid of the man. He just couldn't abide the idea of looking him in the eye, he was sure his heart would shrivel to nothing in his chest if he did.

In the parking lot was his official Humvee that Michael had taken earlier. It was a command and control vehicle sporting two radio antennae whips, a strange dome on top and a useless laptop on the console between the back seats. Neil purposely ignored it and headed for the same Hummer that he had used earlier. He hoped that no one would know that he had been at the scene of the crime.

Thankfully, Sadie's mind was elsewhere and she didn't notice what he thought was painfully obvious. How could she not see she was traveling with a murderer? That's what he was. He hadn't thought of himself as such when he had denied Marybeth the blood earlier; that had been a decision made in his official capacity. Sure, he had felt guilt over it, but it was nothing compared to what he was feeling just then.

She had asked for it, he told himself. His conscience didn't care.

She had practically begged to be killed, he added silently. Still the guilt burned.

I did her a favor. Premeditated murder is a favor? Not hardly. As governor, he could have ordered the O negative donors to stand in line to be drained of their last reserves.

Neil knew he shouldn't feel the weight of such guilt, but that was logic speaking and guilt was simply far more powerful. It grew even greater when his mind switched to a second, very rich vein: Jillybean. Why had Grey said that about not allowing her to leave like that? He had used the pronoun 'we' but everyone knew it was Neil who had allowed her to sacrifice herself.

A seven-year-old, sacrificing herself for an entire company of adults. It was preposterous and stupid and morally bankrupt and perhaps it was even a little evil.

"Hey!" Sadie suddenly cried. "What are you doing? Slow down."

Somehow the Humvee was barreling through the valley at seventy miles an hour with Neil at the helm, his hands like vice-grips on the steering wheel and his eyes growing dewy with tears.

"Oh, sorry. I was just in a zone, I guess." At seventy miles an hour, they had crossed the valley in two minutes and were already winding their way up route 36 towards where the Blue Gate had once stood. They passed teams of men and women, some pushing cars, some hauling food or water. Neil waved like any politician would and tried to appear confident in spite of the greasy feeling inside of him. Guilty or not, it was important that the people saw him as confident and brave. Any sign of weakness would have a terrible effect on morale.

They had to leave the Humvee at the first of the smaller walls and go on foot from there. It wasn't far and soon they were at Blue Gate 2, the much bigger and much flimsier wall of cars they had been standing on only an hour before.

General Johnston came zipping down the ladder like a ten-year-old boy and greeted Neil and Sadie with his usual white-toothed smile. "You two disappeared so quick we didn't have a chance to talk logistics. Though it's only logical that we first decide on a destination. The contingency plans we drew up last year..."

"We aren't going," Neil said, interrupting. "At least not yet. If we delay the Azael as long as possible, there is a chance that we just might win." He went on to explain the idea they had worked up. Johnston made a grumbly sound in throat and then turned away to look up into the hills.

"Maybe," he said, mostly to himself.

Sadie walked around in front of him and planted herself there. "It will work, and when it does, I doubt we'll ever be bothered by the Azael again. If we run, we'll probably never stop running."

"Your plan has holes, namely what to do with half a million stiffs. If the Azael leave, which I doubt they will, we'll still have the stiffs on us. But that's almost a moot point. My guess is that if we stall for too long, the Azael will come against us in force and it will be hard to stop them with so many of my men fighting off the zombies."

"It'll be hard, but not impossible," Sadie said. "I've fought with your men. They're incredible. They fight like lions."

The general grinned at the flattery and then sighed. "This is your parade, Neil. You're the governor, but have you considered how many lives will be lost if we try to hold out?"

"I have, and I've considered the fact that moving forty-two hundred people across those mountains to who knows where may end up costing even more lives. How are we going to feed them all? I've seen the stores of food we have left. It's a couple of weeks' worth at most. Here, we have an entire valley filled with food almost ready to harvest."

"And if we fail, we'll have even less," the general snapped, angrily. He immediately regretted it. "I'm sorry, that was uncalled for. Neil, I will do as you ask but you should still prepare for the worst. As a precaution, we should send a scouting party out to Steamboat Springs. Also, we'll need to start loading the five-ton trucks with the essentials. And we'll need to start moving the cattle if we are to have any chance of saving them if things don't go our way."

Neil agreed, consigning himself to another long, long day of work. Actually, it was a couple of days of near nonstop running around, most of which was work related and the rest relegated to avoiding Michael Gates. Marybeth had died seconds after Neil and Sadie had, for want of a better word, fled the clinic. Michael had ranted about "foul play" to anyone who would listen, but few people had the time or energy to, and what was more, even fewer cared. That Marybeth was going to die had been a foregone conclusion to everyone except Michael.

Since a confrontation was the last thing he wanted, Neil tried to keep as low a profile as he could. He scheduled meetings in odd spots: the forest on the western end of the valley, or at Lake Estes on the little beach that could barely fit a hundred bodies laying out to catch the warm sun, back in the day, or at the Department of Transportation depot which was always deserted.

And he had Sadie run interference for him. She didn't question this despite the rumors floating around that *somebody* had switched off Marybeth's IV, and despite how odd Neil looked and acted whenever the subject came up—he was always very quick to change the subject, though this wasn't hard to do.

There were a thousand things that had to be done and ten thousand discussions in order to get them done.

The first thing Neil accomplished was the digging of moats in front of the smaller walls. The backhoes and the front end loaders worked nonstop for eight hours in front of what was being called Blue Gate 3, in order to make it a much more impressive barrier. The ditch was thirteen feet deep, twenty feet wide, and a hundred and forty-seven feet long.

It was calculated that it would hold the squished remains of ten thousand zombies, once there were tens of thousands more piled on top of them compressing them into goo. It was tested minutes after its completion as Blue Gate 2, the feeble first attempt by Deanna at wall building, collapsed. They had hoped Blue Gate 2 would hold for twenty-four hours, but it was so rickety that the General pulled his troops off as the last embers of twilight became the first gloom of full night.

Two hours later, the weight of the zombies mounded before it became too much. The center went first, falling over with a tremendous crash, and then, seconds later, the entire thing came down releasing an avalanche of bodies, body parts and a hellacious brown sludge that had everyone turning away or risk becoming violently ill.

"Light the tower," Neil called out the moment Blue Gate 2 came down.

The tower had been high on Neil's list of things that had to be done *right that second*. It was a welded structure of pipes supporting a platform of corrugated metal that stood thirty feet high and just three feet from the back of Blue Gate 3. Only once it was completed and the wood arranged on it in the form of a teepee did someone point out that there would be no way to feed the fire once it got going save by chucking more wood up on it from the top of the wall of cars.

Neil came very close to cursing yet managed to hold onto his fake politician's smile, though it wasn't nearly so wide as it had been. The solution was to build a second tower behind the first. This one was taller than the first and resembled the Eiffel Tower in its shape. To feed the fire, it took ten men clinging to the metal work, almost one atop the other, each handing up the next cut of wood until the last man, thirty-five feet in the air, leaned out and dropped the wood into the roaring flames.

Everyone figured the job would be hell and yet there was no shortage of volunteers. The smallest men were chosen since the structure hadn't been built by an engineer. A fellow named Barry who had welding experience flung it together as fast as he could, which turned out to be just in time for Blue Gate 2 to fail.

The zombies slogged over the piled bodies and parts of bodies, and in minutes, nothing could be seen of Blue Gate 2. It was just an uneven hill covered in the undead as they surged forward. The pit before the new wall was half filled before the tower lit properly and then night was turned to day by the tremendous bonfire.

The soldiers shied back from it, squinting from the heat and the sharp light; the zombies simply stared in awe—at least those in front did. The ones further behind saw it as a beacon and they trudged onwards, eagerly pushing those in front of them. Those that stumbled were crushed beneath the feet of the rest, and there were many thousands who stumbled as they tried to make their way over the remains of Blue Gate 2.

"Is it working?" Sadie asked.

"It's hard to tell," Neil answered.

"It's slowing them down a little," General Johnston said, "And that's a win if you ask me." Three hundred soldiers stood watching the zombies and everything was strangely quiet save for the crackling of the fire. An hour passed and the moat slowly filled, but it wasn't like it had been before where the zombies tore at everything in a fury to get at the humans.

It almost seemed orderly how the dead crushed one another. The press from behind was continuous and there were enough lame and one-footed zombies to ensure that falls would occur three or four times a minute. They didn't just happen in the moat, it occurred all over and to Neil it looked as though the river canyon in which this part of I-36 had been laid out, was slowly filling higher and higher with the undead. The ones that weren't crushed only stared upward at the great ball of fire in the sky.

Hours went by in which the bonfire had to be replenished over and over again by sweaty, ash-faced men, however by ten that night General Johnston said: "I can't believe that it's working." Everyone began to grin—all save Neil. He had too much to do.

The back hoes were sent to start digging a new moat in front of Blue Gate 4, just in case it started raining and the bonfire went out. He also had to deal with the two hotspots diverging from the overflow at Blue Gate 3. They had both picked up and men had to be shifted, including Barry the welder, who started in right away with another pair of towers. These went up in a matter of hours since they didn't have to be nearly as high.

At the first hotspot, the bonfire tower stood fifteen feet tall and the second "feeder" tower was seventeen feet. The moment the bonfire was lit, things became a snap for the men. The zombies would forget them entirely and become transfixed by the flames. In minutes they were butchered with ease.

Neil then sent Barry on to the Big Thompson River where the sound of gunshots had been going on all night. Meanwhile, Neil went to Red Gate 3 with Sadie trailing after him. The battle here was in full swing. A major greeted them just before Red Gate 4, which was an impressively massive wall of cars.

This wall had the luxury of time as it had been constructed. The derelict crane sat between the two walls and, in hindsight, Neil wished that they'd had the forethought to drag it out of there, but events had happened too quickly and no one had known if Red Gate 3 would hold.

It had done a marvelous job, but it would not last. "Take me up there," Neil said to the major. "I need to see the battle for myself." The major gave Neil a peculiar look that implied he didn't think Neil was up for it—and he was likely right.

Neil swallowed his fear of heights and mounted the wall, not by ladders, but by what the men called the "giant steps." On the safe side of the wall, the crane had stacked cars, first one, then two atop each other, then three high, and so on until the last was a dizzying fourteen cars tall. The steps had to be climbed or scrambled up, and the last put them so high up that Neil, afraid that a gust of wind would pluck him off the heights and send him screaming down to the road below, wouldn't stand up straight. He stood in a crouch and made sure each foot he planted was square on a hood or trunk and not on the roof of the cars which dented inwards under his weight and caused him to wobble.

He might have whimpered a bit because the major told him: "Everyone is like that at first, but you get used to it after a while." Sadie acclimated to the height, and the frightening drop, in seconds. She stepped across to the main wall, which was made up of two rows of stacked cars pointing nose-on towards the zombies instead of broad-side. This made a much sturdier platform, but it remained to be seen if it would hold up under the weight of the mounting hill of corpses.

The hill of dead had already reached to the lower lip of the wall, however the mound leading up to the hill wasn't as fully formed as had been the case when Blue Gate 2 had been overwhelmed. There was still a gentle slope that the slain zombies would roll down. It would be when the mound reached critical mass and there was nowhere for the dead to go, that the wall's strength would be truly tested. The weight on it would be enormous.

Following Sadie's lead, and yet still shy, Neil placed a tentative foot on the wall and then strode across, still in a crouch and now fighting against a wave of vertigo. A soldier, who was resting on a windscreen as if he was at a drive-in movie rather than a war zone set fifty feet in the air, put out a steadying hand.

"These the reinforcements?" the soldier asked. Neil didn't care for the over the top note of shock in the man's voice, however he understood it. Sadie was small and slim and, while Neil was slightly bigger, he was also, in spite of the dark, clearly on the verge of wetting himself.

"No," the major answered, sharply, suggesting by his tone that the soldier would be wise to shut his mouth. "This is the governor and his assistant. He wanted to see the fighting for himself."

The soldier looked Neil over. "That's good, I guess. You know, Governor, if you step over to the trunk of that next car, you'll feel a lot better."

Neil made the move, scary as it was and found that the soldier was right. The car he stood upon was exceedingly steady and his fear of falling completely vanished only to be replaced by a fear of being swallowed alive by the wave of zombies crashing up against the wall. It was a lesser fear in truth and one that he felt he could manage. "Thanks. This is much better," he said, standing to his full, and not very commanding, height.

"Told ya. Hey, I heard that you and that girl stayed on this wall when everyone else ran away," the soldier remarked, giving the underside of his scruffy chin a good scratching. "Is that true?"

"It was a different woman, actually, but yes. And this, this is Sadie Walcott, daughter of the River King. She was the one who blew up the howitzers this morning and then saved Captain Grey's life. If you ask me, she would make a fine replacement for any of you men." Instead of beaming in a show of gratitude as she normally would have, Sadie turned away.

The soldier reappraised Sadie with a raised eyebrow. "Cool," was all he said.

The major also gave Sadie a second, brief look, accompanied by a grunt of appreciation. He then directed Neil closer to the thin line of men who stood at the brink of the great hill. They fought with an assortment of weapons and these were even stranger than some of the others Neil had seen. Long poles of metal or two-by-fours that stood higher than any man, were the preferred weapons.

The soldiers would bring them back, high over their heads and then send them whistling down to crush zombie skulls, sending brains and blood flying. Even near misses were enough to stun one of the beasts and that was as good as a kill.

As Neil watched, he saw a young man swinging what looked like the runner of a bed frame. It glanced off the side of a zombie head, denting it but not caving it in. The runner tore the creature's ear practically off and thudded home, breaking its collar bone. The beast lost its grip, teetered at the top of the tremendous pile of previously killed zombies and then was pulled back by others climbing with single-minded determination. Very soon the one-eared zombie was lost under the pile.

"That soldier mentioned reinforcements," Neil said. "Have you had a lot of casualties?"

"Three tonight," answered the major. "One bite and two pull downs." At Neil's questioning look, the major added: "A pull down is when a man slips or has his weapon snagged or yanked and he falls down there." He pointed at the hill which squiggled and writhed and slowly grew larger. "When that happens, our mercy shooters take care of the man."

The major inclined his head toward a soldier who stood at the center of the wall with a long-barreled deer rifle in his hands. Next to him, sitting on the roof of a jeep and eating a sandwich, was a man with a canon-like spotlight. Nothing more needed to be said about what would happen if one of the men accidentally fell in among the zombies. There could be no rescue once that happened and yet the men swung their modern-day halberds without fear.

Neil's next question, having been sparked by a sudden groan of metal coming from somewhere deep in the wall beneath his feet was: "How long will the wall hold?"

The soldier who'd been reclining on the windshield laughed as Neil flung his arms out in alarm. "You just have to ignore that. It happens all the time."

The major seemed to take no notice of the groaning metal or of the soldier. Casually, he checked his watch, glanced down at the mound of corpses that stretched from one steep ridge line to another, and then shrugged. "I'd categorize that hill as a decent sledding hill. When the slope is practically gone and it reaches 'kiddy-hill' status, that's when I think it'll be time to pick up stakes and go."

"But it might go sooner than that," the soldier said. "It could go anytime. That's why no one hangs out at the base anymore. Hell, even that ol' duff who was running the crane has packed it in."

It could go anytime...Neil didn't like the sound of that. "Ok, I think I've seen enough." He went back into his crouch as he made his way down the "giant steps" and he did his best to ignore the desire to kiss the earth when he was finally down. Sadie went down with the ease of a mountain goat and beat him down to the ground by half a minute, though again her customary smile was gone.

"The wall's already leaning," she mentioned. She stood at its base, looking up. Although he didn't want to, Neil felt that it was his job to look as well. The second he did, the wall groaned once more, sending a shiver up his back. The major looked as well and didn't seem all that concerned.

"Same, same," he said. "Nothing to fret over, yet."

The wall came down at eight the next morning. Neil watched as he took his breakfast high atop of Red Gate 4. He hadn't slept a wink the night before and was so tired that he was only slightly alarmed when a stiff breeze shook the wall under him. Red Gate 3 had been abandoned two hours before and just like at the Blue Gate, there was a festival type atmosphere among the soldiers.

The men made bets as to when it would fall or how far the top cars would roll. Some snoozed in the new sun and others did their level best to chat up Sadie, who had fallen asleep in Neil's Humvee sometime around three in the morning and was a good deal more awake than he was. Just like at the Blue Gate, the unimpeded zombies crawled to the top and then dropped like stones to smack into the road below. There was a very large pile of the beasts, most of whom were still alive but broken in many place, when the wall of cars finally came down.

There was a roar from the soldiers that Neil didn't understand. There was now one less barrier the zombies had to cross. Still, he supposed, there was some excitement in seeing such an unusual and large-scale demolition occur. And there were real things to cheer about: not a single wall had fallen during the night and the casualties had been exceptionally light.

Neil decided a nap was in order and he left Sadie in charge. He would have preferred to have Deanna running things but she was still bedside with Captain Grey. Neil probably could have asked her to come back to work, but his guilt was too great for him to venture back into the hospital.

Worried that Michael would find him if he went back to his own place, Neil found an open room at the Holiday Inn and threw himself down on a dusty bed and fell asleep so quickly that he couldn't remember actually closing his eyes. A few hours later, though, it took an act of will to get them open.

He glanced at his watch and saw the time was two in the afternoon. He was so out of it that he was only slightly curious as to what exactly had woken him—then he heard the thin crackle of gunfire. It was intermittent, coming and going, and it quickly drove the sleep out of his head.

Within seconds, he was out the door and staring, fearfully eastward in the direction the shots were coming from, expecting to see the hills swarming with enemies, but only seeing trees and rocks, which was to be expected because of: A, the distance and B, the fact that the shots were so infrequent and isolated that it meant this wasn't a major battle.

Still, he was nervous enough to seek out the source, which turned out to be the defensive line astride the Big Thompson River. General Johnston beat him to the trouble spot and looked as though he was going to drill holes in a young lieutenant with just his eyes. The young man was wilting under the pressure as he tried to explain the situation: the bonfires weren't working anymore.

The brilliant Colorado sunshine had dampened the effects of the bonfires so that they were practically useless and now the river below the Red Gate was becoming congested with the undead, and was once again the most dangerous place to be in the valley. Accordingly, General Johnston shifted forces.

This was the first crisis of the day and, for the valley, that amounted to a very good thing. For the next few days the walls held steady while the sun blasted down. It was uncommonly hot, even for July and the men fought to exhaustion while the civilians labored away. With their limited fuel supplies reserved for what could be a long retreat, the civilians were forced into back-breaking labor.

Carting water was a never-ending dreary chore. The civilians hauled jugs, two or three at a time, up steeply sloped roads. The new demand for firewood was nearly as bad since every aspect of the wood gathering had to be carried out by hand: hewing trees, sawing their trunks, splitting logs, and then hauling the wood to the various walls and hotspots took half the labor force.

Still, no civilian wanted to trade places with the soldiers. The men fought at dizzying heights where a slip meant a horrible death, or they fought in the icy river that numbed them to the bone and made their movements slow and unsteady. What was worse than swinging a heavy length of pipe for six hour stretches until their hands bled, was the smell and the flies.

At times the flies swarmed in clouds so dense that the sun was hidden and the hum generated by the millions of tiny wings could drive a person mad. While the smell of the tens of thousands of decaying bodies, bloated and putrefying in the hot sun, quite literally caused grown men to pass out.

Yet the people of the valley, both the soldiers and civilians, toiled heroically and if there was ever a complaint, the complainer was usually frowned upon and, on at least one occasion, was punched in the face.

Neil seemed to be everywhere, always encouraging, always supportive, always trying to find a solution to the hundreds of problems that sprang up on a daily basis. The people rallied to him; it wasn't an uncommon occurrence for him to be cheered when he showed up. It was the general consensus that the people of the valley were "winning," however, that was defined. Two things were certain, they weren't running away and they were holding their own.

Five days of hard work slogged by but at noon of that fifth day things changed for the worse. The Azael, sick of waiting for the zombies to break through to the valley, attacked in force, driving in the thin line of soldiers that held a portion of the eastern ridgeline. With the sounds of a thousand guns going off in the hills, men were pulled from the all-important job of securing the walls in order to beat off this new attack. Neil didn't hesitate to jump in his Humvee, fully intending to head to the scene.

It wasn't until the barrel of a Beretta jabbed him in the temple that he realize this really was "his" Humvee, the same one that had been stolen from him by Michael Gates days before, the same one he had been avoiding like the plague.

"You killed my wife," Michael breathed into his ear. There was whiskey on his tongue that did not blend well with the powerful stench of unwashed armpits. "Say it, you piece of shit. Say that you killed her."

The guilt had been on him for days, and it was actually somewhat of a relief when Neil said: "Yes, I did."

Chapter 26
Jillybean

For the Azael, the days passed in sullen fear and dwindling expectation. After the destruction of their big guns, they prepared for the next "big" attack by fortifying the hills above their two little sections of the river gorges. They dug fox holes that were plain to see and built walls of fallen trees, generally being too lazy to cut down live trees.

Jillybean watched their progress and found it laughable. The log structures were so clearly manmade that they drew the eye, and the foxholes could be spotted from a hundred yards away since the Azael lazily piled the dirt in big mounds right in front of them. The fresh turned dirt stood out against the pine backdrop as blatant as sin.

Even when they bothered to camouflage their positions the effect again suffered from their laziness. Instead of cutting fresh limbs to drape over their holes, they used fallen limbs; the big patches of brown leaves or strange arrays of dead sticks didn't blend naturally.

Then there was the trash that accumulated more and more every day. It was glaringly obvious from a distance, while at night the soft orange embers given off by the chain-smoking sentries could be seen at a quarter mile. Anyone walking up on the hill would see what appeared to be a long line of fire flies strung across the top of the ridge. But no one...no enemy, actually did walk up the hill.

Each morning there came from the collected Azael a mix of curses and sighs of relief. They hadn't been attacked, thus the sighs, but on the other hand, the zombies hadn't progressed more than a bare fifty yards, which brought out the curses.

By the third day people began to walk about with an air of ugly hanging over their heads; scowls accompanied the curses and tempers were short—they were not enjoying life tenting it on the highway, eating lukewarm cans of beans and drinking stale water that had to be hauled up from Horseshoe Lake, twenty miles away, because the red taint running down the rivers.

On the fourth day no one sighed with relief that they hadn't been attacked. Everyone guessed that if they hadn't been attack by then, they weren't going to be. This meant the focus was squarely on the progress of the zombies which was more than disappointing and the curses were, thusly all the greater.

People began to mutter among themselves and blame was splashed about wetting even the princes of the Azael and, of course, Jillybean as well. One of the chief blamers was the king who called for the little girl. She arrived accompanied by Duke Menis, who considered her to be his personal property, or maybe, a pet that could do tricks. Kay was brought along as well to ensure that Jillybean cooperated. For the last five days, the higher ranking men had availed themselves of the women on the bus, studiously ignoring Kay and her battered face.

Regardless, whenever a prospective 'lover' came onto the bus, Kay sat on her seat with her knees drawn up like a child who thinks the floor is lava, and yet it wasn't just this overly defensive façade that Kay strived for, or her bent nose and scarred face that kept the men away. It was also Jillybean, who sat next to her and who could wilt even the strongest libido with the unsettling way she looked at a man; she seemed capable of looking straight into their perverted souls.

Kay made sure to keep her close except when she was called upon by the royal Azael, then she did her best to find an excuse to be somewhere else. On that fifth day the duke grabbed Kay by the hair and growled: "Stop your whining or you'll never need a dentist again." She dropped her chin and skulked along behind the duke until they were in the presence of the king where, to her immense relief, she was forgotten.

The king was seated with his brothers around a number of folding tables which were covered with rings of moisture from a case of beer that was being consumed. The king had five empties in front of him, a fresh one in his hand and his cold, unfeeling eyes on Jillybean. "You said they were going to attack," he growled.

Without realizing it, Jillybean stepped back. The duke shoved her forward, and she stumbled. There was mean laughter. It coaxed Eve out from the dark, wet grotto of Jillybean's mind. The *other girl* began a whispered hissing that made her skin crawl. There were words in the hissing but Jillybean couldn't quite make them out, though she was sure that they were evil words, murderous words.

Jillybean squeezed her eyes shut and forced the fear out of her body. After a breath she boldly answered the king: "Yes I did, and they would have if they were smart and I think they are. It suggests…" She bit off her sentence, realizing she was again offering information that hadn't been demanded. She was under no obligation to do so.

"It suggests what?" the duke asked, grabbing her arm and giving it a shake so that Jillybean was nearly thrown off her feet.

She wanted to glare. She wanted to give in to the other girl inside her who was still hissing, although in a quieter little snake sort of voice, advocating for daggers in the night, razors across the soft part of their throats, or a "found" grenade finding its way into the king's tent in the darkest part of the night.

In spite of the evil coming off it in waves, it wasn't easy ignoring that voice just then.

The voice made sense. These were her enemies. These were people who deserved to die. But she was not a killer, she was a good girl; that's what her daddy and mommy had always told her. And she believed it. Too bad being good was so difficult. Killing was easier. Killing was primal. Killing was a solution to so many problems and Jillybean felt the urge to give in. She bit it back.

"It suggests that they are weaker than we know," Jillybean said after a brief pause.

"My thoughts exactly," the king said, stroking his beard and gazing at each of his brothers in turn, with his shrewd eyes taking their measure. "I'm beginning to think we should attack."

What a coward, Jillybean thought. *He can't make a decision without the moral support of the people he views as inferior.* She was pretty sure that it was her own mind thinking this, however there was a tinge of Eve to it...a tinge of evil. It wasn't pleasant at all.

The brothers in turn, knowing that he was looking for their opinion, did their best to pass the buck. While many of the six brothers shifted their eyes away, Paulus suggested that Menis had been saying the same thing just the day before. *That's right*, two others said, simultaneously as the rest nodded eagerly.

Menis grinned in a sickly, sour manner and amended his previous words: "I only suggested that we should attack under optimal circumstances."

The king hesitated, seeing that there wasn't a real advocate for attack among his brothers, and again Jillybean mentally labeled him a coward, though a second later she wondered if that was really fair. He hadn't been born a king, and nor had he had any real training as one. He understood only bullying, threats, and overwhelming power, none of which had caused the brave men and women of the Estes Valley to capitulate as expected.

King Augustus faced real leaders. Both Grey and General Johnston had been trained to lead men into battle, sometimes, to lead them to their deaths.

Into the silence, Jillybean said: "Hmm," realizing that all of their past enemies: Yuri in New York, Abraham in New Eden, the River King, and now Augustus, had just been normal men a year before. They had been like her daddy, or like the mailman who came around every day wearing a pith helmet, or like the sweaty, crack-bearing plumber who fixed their sink once.

This prompted an internal question: was her enemies' collective evil a natural and, perhaps, an expected thing? Was this a normal reaction in men thrust into power without warning?

She was sure that she would not be able to glean the answer from history because as far as she knew there had never been a zombie apocalypse before. She could only ferret out the answer from what she knew of humans in general, which suggested the evil she was experiencing should have been predicted, though certainly not condoned.

The Azael were governed by fear: they feared the zombies, of course, but they also feared their neighbors whether enemies or not. And they feared running out of supplies and they feared that someone would take what they had by force. That fear made them aggressive and they had, not really chosen, but rather accepted Augustus perhaps because of his uber-aggressiveness.

The king was staring at her and it was a few moments before she noticed. "You have something to add?" She dropped her eyes to the highway and meekly shook her head. "Well fuck," the king said, sighing moodily. Remembering his beer, he drained it as if it was water and then chucked the empty aside. "What we're doing isn't getting us anywhere, so here's the plan: we'll attack. They are weak, they have to be. Since you started this mess, Menis your men will lead the attack. And, since Paulus fucked up with the guns, his men will reinforce yours."

Now that he was committed, Menis became suddenly, and strangely eager. "As you wish, brother. I'll have a thousand men ready in thirty minutes." He grabbed Jillybean and went stumping off at a fast clip with Kay trailing along, forgotten by everyone and glad for it.

Menis went right for his tent where a number of people, Brad included, were sitting in a group playing with a deck of cards and some round disks—they weren't playing Go Fish, the only card game Jillybean knew. They all jumped up as Menis began shouting: "Assemble the men!" Jillybean pictured plastic soldiers in pieces that had to be snapped together.

She made sure to keep out of the way as a great commotion struck the camp. The Azael were running all about and no one seemed to care if Jillybean was stepped on or had her head smacked with the butt of a rifle. Menis stood for a moment watching before he ducked into his tent only to come out seconds later with a gun and a map, both of which he threw down on the card strewn table.

"Do you know anything about warfare?" he asked Jillybean after pouring over the map.

"No mister, Duke Sir," she answered. "I don't understand war at all. Why would people kill each other for no reason? It doesn't make sense. There are other places for the Azael to live besides..."

The duke threw a handful of poker chips at Jillybean. "If you aren't going to be any help, shut the fuck up."

Jillybean mumbled a: "Yes sir."

She didn't want to help him anyway and wished she could go back to the bus which was the closest thing to a home she'd had since she had left her house in Philadelphia months before. She had left behind the great big doll house and Todd the turtle, and her mom who was still lying in her bed, and would forever.

It had been a mistake to ever leave her house. They shouldn't have gone to New Eden in order to try to save Sarah. Not only had Sarah died, but Nico had died as well. A lot of people had died in all that time since she had left home. The thought made Jillybean very sad and she dwelt in her sadness as the duke's soldiers came together to form five long rectangles of men standing shoulder to shoulder down the road from them.

The duke stood in front of them and he yelled stuff that Jillybean couldn't hear and he pointed away to the west at things Jillybean couldn't see. The five groups then turned to the right in an uncoordinated fashion and began marching.

"Hope they forget about us," Kay said, in a soft voice, though no one was around except the creepy, bone-thin cook who had poisoned Deanna.

The two were not forgotten. They were forced to walk along behind the Azael and were yelled at by the duke if they ever fell too far back. Since he still had a terrible limp, he rode an ATV as far as he could but was forced to give it up when they came to the last ridge controlled by the Azael. He then had to climb like everyone else.

Jillybean found the steep hill a challenge, but not a particularly difficult one, since she carried nothing at all while the soldiers huffed along under the weight of their weapons and hundreds of rounds of ammo. They also carried water and food, shovels and flashlights and all sorts of items that only weighed them down.

Finally, with the sun straight up above and the air hot enough to melt butter right into nothing, they topped the rise and stood looking across at another ridgeline a mile away. Other than a few hills, it was the last barrier between them and the Estes Valley.

Had Jillybean been in charge, she would have advocated for a night attack. She held Captain Grey and, as an extension, all the soldiers of the valley in such high regard that she didn't think it was at all smart to cross the relatively open land between the two ridge lines in the full light of day.

She wasn't the only one who thought this either. Practically all the soldiers cast fearful glances up at the looming line of hills as they walked. Lucky for them, they had a good leader in Brad Crane who was first down their side of the ridge; he kept to where the scrubby pines were thickest.

They were also lucky in another sense. Five days of quiet on this front had caused the soldiers of the valley to become over-confident. They especially didn't expect an attack in the day and a few of the men on duty were nodding off and more were shooting the shit with their friends in the next foxhole. The ridge was also lightly defended. There were a bare thirty men holding the half mile of ridge up which the Azael were scrambling.

The leading group of Azael got within a hundred yards before a rock was dislodged by one of the men. It went clattering down the hillside, almost hitting a man who made the mistake of cursing loudly.

A rock skittering down the slope was one thing; it happened all the time and made for some very anxiety-ridden nights, but a voice as well? That got the soldiers' attention and the first Azael was spotted seconds later.

The valley soldiers fired, killing three men in as many seconds. The return fire from half of the duke's men was a storm of lead that withered plants, scorched the air and had the soldiers throwing themselves down into their holes.

Led by Brad Crane, the men of the Azael scrambled up the hill while they could, hoping to get close before the soldiers recovered from their shock. They were within fifty yards when the ridge came alive with gunfire, though it was with nowhere near the same intensity, the fire was effectively aimed and men dropped with every shot and the attack stalled.

"Move!" screamed the duke. "Get your asses up that hill!"

He yelled and kicked at his men and even fired his rifle into the dirt next to one of them and, gradually, he got them moving again. The press of men upwards became too much for the thin line of soldiers and it wasn't long before their courage broke and they ran, leaving a gap square in the middle of the defensive line.

The Azael rushed up, cheering, excited that they had been able to crack the first line of defense with such ease; barely forty of them had been killed, they had been expecting five times that number. They stood on the ridge as if they had conquered a mountain and their inexperience was never more fully on display. Instead of racing down the far side of the ridge to fully exploit the gap, they rested, leaving both of their flanks unguarded.

The center of the hill was taken but there were still enemies to deal with both north and south. The valley men crept along, gathering under the banner of low-ranked sergeants. In the twenty minutes it took for the duke to climb his way to the top, with Jillybean in tow, there was a force of approximately seventy valley men arrayed on either side of the Azael.

Jillybean, her fly-away hair, no longer flying, but rather plastered to her head from all the sweat, was just gazing down once again at the Estes Valley and was wondering, with some disappointment, how the fight had been so one-sided, when the soldiers counterattacked.

With the Azael congregating on one of the narrower portions of the ridge, the bullets lancing into them couldn't fail to find a target. A flash of something zipped right across Jillybean's nose and blood splashed on her arm. For a moment she thought it was her own blood it was so hot and fresh. She scurried beneath a log and curled up like a fetus, while all around her, men screamed, blood flew, and guns hammered the air.

Then there was silence. It was such an abrupt change that she could hear the drip of blood onto an old dried-up leaf. There was a dead man lying over her log. He had the glassy stare of a gutted fish and a hole in his head above his right ear. Death was so common that she didn't even blink twice at the man and the most she could think was: *Too bad it wasn't the duke.*

In the three seconds before the Azael, almost as one, returned fire. Jillybean took the time to examine herself, finding that she was decidedly fine. She amended this, seconds later as the duke's thousand men opened up, spraying every hill and rock, every pine and shrub with upwards of fifty thousand bullets. The men emptied their magazines, reloaded and then emptied them again.

Jillybean couldn't imagine that anything could have lived through that onslaught. And yet, somehow, the soldiers did, many of them, probably most if not all of them. As the Azael were reloading, the soldiers began a deadly return fire that was based on accuracy as opposed to volume of bullets expended.

The Azael huddled behind anything that seemed to give them cover and still the soldiers found their marks. For ten long minutes the Azael absorbed outrageous casualties with no one finding the courage to stick their heads up and risk being shot. Finally, the duke cried out: "Someone do something, damn it! Brad, where are you?"

"Here," Brad called from somewhere up ahead. "The duke is right! We can't just sit here. On the count of three, half of us fire and the other half advance. One, two, three!"

No one advanced. All of the Azael shot their weapons, most without bothering to aim. Under the cover of all that wasted shooting, the valley soldiers continued to fire and continued to kill. "What the fuck?" Brad cried. "If we stay here, we'll all die." No one even lifted their heads.

They weren't trained like the soldiers had been. Their fear outweighed all other considerations, including actually winning the fight. And they surely didn't trust their leaders who, apart from Brad, were cowering just as much as anyone. They were saved, for the moment, by the appearance of Duke Paulus' regiment which came hurrying down from the opposite ridgeline in four foolishly compact waves.

At first, they jogged through the flat area between the two lines of hills unopposed, but halfway across, fire from the north flank caused them to throw themselves under cover. Jillybean couldn't believe what she was seeing. Almost a thousand men had been stopped by a handful of soldiers.

Still it took the focus off the northern flank and Brad started squirming forward, hissing: "Come on! Now! Everyone move." This got a hundred men moving but they weren't moving at the same time that cover fire was being laid down, resulting in twenty of the men being shot before they had progressed thirty yards.

Brad saw the problem and implored people to shoot while others moved. He was the lone voice of reason and authority and somehow managed to corral a company of men to act in some sort of harmony—but it was too late.

Jillybean saw that the soldiers who had run off in the first heat of the battle were being led back up the ridge. Half moved straight east, obviously moving to shore up the defenses against Paulus' men and the other half were coming at a diagonal heading to fight Menis' regiment. What was worse, for the Azael, was that dozens of engines could be heard echoing along the mountain sides.

That meant reinforcements were coming. Jillybean almost cheered. She bit it back by the barest of margins though she couldn't help smiling, not that anyone noticed what the little girl in the yellow dress was doing. They had heard the engines as well. Some were foolish enough to raise their heads.

When two men had their brains spattered onto the rocks, the rest hid themselves. The log Jillybean was under sat partially on two rocks giving her a six-inch port to see through and she thought it no wonder that the Azael were afraid to move. The valley soldiers they were fighting were almost magically invisible.

They blended so well with their surroundings that all she saw of them were little twinkles of light.

The duke couldn't see anything. He was cowered behind a rock, and as extra protection, he had dragged a corpse onto his back. The only view he had was of Paulus' men crawling under fire. "Are we attacking?" he cried out. "Why aren't we attacking? Jay! Frank! Brad! Get your men up right now or I'll cut off your worthless balls myself and stuff them down your throats."

"Let's go, Azael!" Brad bellowed. "Start shooting. Start moving." He inspired a surge and fifty men started running in short bursts toward the northern flank. The men on the southern flank, who were without any leadership, refused to budge.

Jillybean didn't think things looked good for the soldiers. Yes, they had men racing to the rescue but there weren't that many of them, while the Azael were covering the ridge like ants, seemingly everywhere. And now that Azael were beginning to fight back, the twinkling lights from the soldiers were dampened, which only emboldened the Azael more.

Now, groups of four or five would leap up and rush forward and sure, one would invariably go down screaming but the rest crept closer and closer to the soldiers.

But the soldiers of the valley weren't out of it yet. They had tricks up their sleeves and more gadgets than the Azael. First grenades came flying out of the forest sending shrapnel pinging off rocks and biting into flesh. Everyone went down as smoke filled the air, and not just the black smoke one would expect, there was also blue smoke that didn't make any sense to Jillybean.

She wasn't the only one who was confused. Many of the Azael were staring at the smoke in stark puzzlement. Someone even yelled out: "It's poison!" This caused the attack to stall a second time.

The smoke wasn't poison, of course, it was a marker. Moments later there came a whistling noise followed by an explosion so loud and so violent that Jillybean thought the entire hill had been thrown into the air. She was too stunned for thought and could only grab her head in her hands and try to weasel deeper into the earth.

The whistling came again and was followed by another mind-numbing blast. Jillybean heard someone screaming, a shrill sound of horror and it too was so loud that she thought that maybe it was more than just one person, maybe it was a dozen men. Before her ears could sort out what was what, there was another explosion, followed by another, and another, and another.

Jillybean had never been so frightened. Her fear was beyond her control and was so total that even Eve could not take over the reins of her mind. She felt like a rabbit caught out in the open by a pack of ravenous wolves. Her instincts told her to stay hidden under the log where she was protected from the blasts, but then she saw the first of the men jump up and run. He was followed by a hundred others and before she knew it, Jillybean was running as well.

All around her were men racing straight down the hill. In their panic they trampled everyone and everything smaller than themselves and that included Jillybean, who was shoved hard in the back. Her feet lost the little control they had and then she was tumbling in a blur of sky and mountain.

It seemed she spun a thousand times, going faster and faster until she fetched up against a worm-ridden log with a thud that rattled her brains something good. The log was very old and so decayed that it was practically mulch, which explained why she wasn't killed when she crashed into it.

Still, she had been jarred into a semi-state of consciousness so that she could see the waves of men rushing down the mountain at her, but she couldn't understand why they were running or even who they were.

Brad suddenly appeared, standing very tall above her, his long, blond hair flying. He didn't speak, he only scooped her up and went right on running. Somewhere between the flat, open area and the start of the next ridge, her concussion caught up with her and she passed out. It was a long spell and the sun was well and truly down by the time Jillybean started blinking her eyes.

She found herself just on the edge of the heat border of a raging bonfire. Her right side, the side closest to the fire was warm while her other side was chilled and damp. Groaning, she sat up. She wanted to get closer to the fire, but she didn't feel good. Her head spun and her body ached as if she was sick with the flu. The greater part of her wanted to crawl away into the dark.

It was the king's bonfire and he raged with greater strength and anger than even the ten-foot high flames. He laid blame everywhere and on everyone though mostly it fell on his brother. "Three hundred men dead! Three hundred! And for what? For a girl? Menis, this is your fault. You brought this embarrassing defeat on us with your stupid, childish lusts and your pathetic leadership. What do you have to say for yourself?"

Menis stood, with his head hung, refusing to look up into the face of his outraged brother. "There were more of them than we anticipated and they had artillery and they..."

"Those were mortars," Brad said, "Big ones and expertly fired. Our men haven't been trained to withstand that sort of..."

"No one asked you!" the king thundered. He turned to Menis and glared. "You need to fix this. I don't care how, just do it or I'll be forced to take away your title and your lands." The king turned from his cowering brother and stomped off. The gathered court left, as well, but not before looking down their noses at Menis.

Soon it was only the duke, Brad, Jillybean and Kay who stood just at the edge of the firelight, keeping perfectly still, perhaps wishing she were invisible. With Jillybean around it was a possibility. The second the duke saw the little girl sitting up, he pointed a finger at her and hissed: "Kill her! Right now! She's a goddamned jinx. From the moment I laid eyes on her I've had nothing but bad luck."

Brad didn't make a move for his weapon. He appraised Jillybean with the firelight dancing in his sharp blue eyes. "I wouldn't kill her if I were you. She's not a jinx, she's a tool...no, better yet, she's a doubled edged sword, and a very dangerous one at that."

"I don't care, kill her."

Very calmly, Brad said: "No. I have a better idea. Listen." He cocked an ear and everyone followed suit, holding their heads perfectly still as they heard the far away sounds of gunfire. "That's our enemies fighting for their lives. They haven't used that many guns since the first day. That tells us that they're getting desperate, that maybe they are having their problems just like us."

"Yeah, so?" the duke asked.

"So, they are likely on the edge of breaking up. Maybe one man is holding them together, keeping them going. Maybe if we kill that one man their will to fight will drain right out of them."

The duke's eyes grew large. "You want to kill General Johnston."

"No, I want Jillybean to kill him."

Chapter 27

Captain Grey

He was the most accommodating of patients…on the first day, and that was mostly because he spent nearly the entire time sleeping. Although he did pretty much the same thing on the second day, he became quickly irritable. He had never been one for reclining for very long time. Even back "before" he could barely watch a full-length movie without either nodding off or getting up in order to do *something*.

By the third day of his recuperation, he had to send Deanna off to help Neil, afraid that in his state of irritation he would be a jerk to her accidentally. The C.N.A. who was as nice as a girl could be, wasn't so lucky and felt the bite of his tongue more than once, the last being when she offered him the bedpan before what she called "bed time." So far it had been "bedtime" from the moment he'd been carted into the clinic and he was heartily sick of it.

Day Four felt exactly like day Three except it seemed to have gained extra hours and each of those hours had packed on more minutes than normal and those minutes consisted of long-lasting, elongated seconds. All day long he felt like he was on the verge of a full-on, toddler-sized meltdown that was just looking for a trigger to set it off.

Once the official bedtime for day four occurred and the clinic grew quiet, Grey broke rule after rule and didn't care one whit about the consequences.

Slowly, he swung his legs out of bed and stood on his own two feet. It hurt. Even with the drugs they had pumping through his veins, he hurt in all sorts of places. During the first three days, the pain had been greatest in his burned lower right calf. That had been agony every time the sheets had whispered over his bandage. Slowly, that pain had faded into the background as his arm took center stage.

His shredded bicep throbbed with each beat of his heart and at night it got so bad that he started hating his own pulse. It was just like the clock, counting the seconds one after another, only the thrumming clock in his arm came with an ache that couldn't be totally drugged away.

But standing helped. Though his head spun and all of his aches became extra achy, it was progress. After a spell, he moved, as a decrepit old man might, with little, frightened shuffling steps, all the way to the bathroom, where he took a leak like a proper man should: standing, with his head back and his eyes squarely on the "pee spot" four feet above the rim of the toilet. A groan of pleasure escaped him.

He then made his way back to his bed and collapsed in it to sleep like the dead for the next four hours, whereupon he was afflicted, as he had been for the last two nights, by a terrible case of insomnia. He'd never had insomnia before and he thought it worse than his wounds. Normally, he was asleep within thirty seconds of his head hitting the pillow.

He chalked the insomnia up to the fact that he hadn't been doing anything but lying around and sleeping for so long that it was causing his body to rebel.

"Well, screw this," Grey said, slinging the blanket back with his good right arm. Doing nothing, even when it entailed trying to force himself back to sleep was against his nature. He stood for the second time in four days and couldn't resist the urge to stretch. It felt so good to hear his spine crack that another groan of pleasure escaped him.

All in all he felt good, or as good as he could with the pain and the constant threat of death hanging over him. Margaret Yuan warned him twice every day that if he moved his arm he would die. Deanna mentioned it six times a day, and even the C.N.A got into the act, morbidly explaining what would happen if he wasn't careful—she at least, Grey could tell to shut up.

He was under the strictest orders to keep his left arm completely still. It sat hobbled in a cocoon of bandages with a sling over it which was pinned to his hospital gown. The arm longed to stretch with the rest of his body. In fact, the unnatural confinement the arm endured was half the pain he was feeling and, although he was sure that it was mostly mental, he wanted more than anything to set his arm free.

But he did not. He knew that the warnings were well founded.

Moving the rest of his body was another story. That night he walked the length of his room, all thirteen feet of it, twenty times before he was once again overwhelmed by exhaustion. Sleep came easily after that and the fifth day dawned with him smiling as he almost always did when he woke. A quick prayer passed his lips—again, as usual—and then he was ready to get up again.

This was postponed, first by the C.N.A, who checked his vitals, frowned at his lack of urine production in the urinal and then left to get his breakfast. Then his plans were interrupted by Margaret Yuan, who clucked like a mother hen while she surveyed his chart, and then by Deanna, who didn't wait for Margaret to leave the room to kiss him full on the lips.

Deanna smelled like sweet pears which seemed impossible with a war going on. He couldn't help smiling at her and he really wanted to tell her of his progress in walking and healing in general, however he knew her: she would cluck worse than Margaret ever would and she would insist on staying with him in order to curb these fledgling attempts at freedom.

So he simply breathed her in and smiled, happy that she was happy. He was encouraged that the Azael were being frustrated in their attempt to overrun the valley and that the people were fighting back with such determination. And he was happy that Neil was doing so well as governor. Overall her visit was a blessing and yet he couldn't wait for her to go.

He abhorred the urinal and everything it represented: imprisonment, frailty, an old man's death…and he had to pee, badly. Thankfully, Deanna didn't stay nearly as long as she wanted to; Neil was keeping her so busy that she was also scheduling times in order to relieve herself.

The moment she was gone, he was up, finding himself much steadier than the day before. His head hardly spun at all, and when he stood before the toilet, he didn't need to hold onto the wall with his good arm. He then paced his room thirty times before being caught in the act by a most irate C.N.A. who could not understand anything beyond what the "doctor ordered."

Satisfied with his exercise, at least for the moment, Grey ate his breakfast, asked for seconds and ate that as well, and considered thirds—he was healing after all and he knew that a good appetite was a sign in the right direction. However, a third helping felt like too much and he ignored his ravenous belly.

Before his eleven o'clock nap, he walked twice more, knowing on an elemental level that it was the right thing for his body. He then ate and slept again.

When the Azael attacked and the gunshots began to ring out on the eastern ridgeline, it felt strangely expected to the captain, as though he had been waiting for exactly that. As the C.N.A and Margaret ran to the windows in fear, and Jillybean huddled under a log, watching the battle unfold, Grey reached over and pulled out his IV, letting it trickle onto the floor.

His clothes had been scissored into rags when he had first come in and so there was nothing he could do but walk out of his room in his hospital gown. The C.N.A, stared in amazement, while Yuan threw what could only be called a medical hissy fit. She slammed a clipboard down on the counter and then pointed a finger into his face, demanding that he get back into bed.

"Sorry, I can't do that," he said, as he pushed his way through the front door. He wasn't stupid. He knew he wasn't close to being healed and so he kept his left arm held tight to his chest and he didn't go past his depth. There was a single Humvee left in the parking lot and he helped himself to it.

The engine's roar was satisfying to his soul. One-handed, he steered the vehicle to the armory; what once had been a museum dedicated to the rather limited history of Estes Park. Since everything was more or less history now and not a single person in the valley had cared about the dull knickknacks and old timey pictures, they had been tossed into a dumpster without a qualm and now the place smelled of that particular military odor which civilians always turned their nose up at but which modern day warriors greeted with the familiarity of a son coming home for the holidays.

Grey, who hadn't hesitated a second, was one of the first men to the armory and, despite his lack of uniform; he carried the weight of authority in his voice. "The mortars!" he barked when he saw a man lumbering under the weight of a crew-serviced fifty caliber machine gun. A fifty cal wasn't the worst weapon under the circumstances, but it wasn't the best either and it was an officer's duty to make sure his men had the very best weapons and training for any given circumstances.

"Get two mortars loaded in this Humvee!" he ordered, hoping that no one else noted the frailty he was hearing in his own voice. "Who here is rated with the 252?" he asked. Of the dozen or so soldiers present, only four hands went up. Grey was a little surprised that it wasn't more since General Johnston insisted that the men were cross-trained in a variety of weapons.

Still, four was good enough. Grey pointed at two of the men. "You are my gunners. Grab four men each as your crews. We're heading up to Loveland Heights which..." A wave of dizziness almost sent him falling into an ammo crate of mortar rounds. After a breath, he steadied himself and went on: "Loveland Heights is close and there's a dirt path to the top. And...and we will be well within range. Now, let's go kick some ass." He meant for his *let's go kick some ass* statement to come out in a roar to fire the men up; however it came out quiet and phlegmy.

Regardless, the men rushed around, taking what they needed, before dashing for the Humvees parked in back. Grey trailed them, limping and fighting the pain in his body and the dizziness in his head. He was too slow to get in the lead Humvee which blasted out of the parking lot sending gravel machine gunning out the back, so he headed for the second.

Every seat was taken except the driver's spot. Grey began to ease himself into it when a PFC came up. He was a young man, as all PFCs were, with a bristle of brown hair trimmed so short a man could putt right across it. "I'm sorry, sir, but that's my seat. I'm driving."

"Not today, son," Grey answered and slowly lifted his burned right leg into the vehicle. The PFC put out a hand and easily stopped Grey. "What the hell are you doing?" Grey demanded. "Remove that hand. That's an order in case you've lost your hearing along with your mind."

The soldier didn't budge. "I'm sorry sir. We need a driver who can use both hands. Besides, you're...you're too injured to fight." Gently, but with a strength Grey was too weak to deny, the man pushed Grey back. He climbed into the vehicle but before he drove away, he added: "My name is PFC Victor Shields if you feel the need to bring me up on charges."

"Son of a bitch," Grey said, quietly to himself when he was breathing in the exhaust of the speeding Humvee. "Do I look that pathetic that a damned PFC is brazen enough to talk to me like that?" He glanced down at himself and decided that the answer was yes. Not only was he covered in bandages, his hair shot up at all angles, he had five days of growth on his face and his white ass hung out the back of his hospital gown. He looked pathetic.

Embarrassed, he glanced around for another Humvee—there were none in the parking lot, though more were speeding toward the armory.

Not wanting to be seen in such a sad state, Grey limped away down the block, with all of his wounds flaring up. Each step was a misery for him and he was just beginning to think that he could very well faint right there on the side of the road when he saw a Humvee parked in front of the Holiday Inn two blocks away.

"I can make it there," he assured himself. He almost didn't. His head was spinning and his muscles flagging by the time he staggered up to the Humvee. He was pleasantly surprised to see Neil and Michael Gates in it. What he didn't see was the pistol in Michael's hand. Nor did he see that Michael's index finger was curled around the trigger and that the hammer was back, meaning the weapon was within a flinch of going off.

Grey's stagger ended in a stumble. He thumped heavily against the passenger side window causing Michael to jump. There was a shockingly loud *bang!* from inside the Humvee followed by a *crack!*

Neil sat in the driver's seat with his mouth hanging open. Behind his head the window had a hole in it with a thousand cracks emanating from it. "Did I do that?" Grey asked, opening the back door. His words came out in a tortured whisper—his throat was scratchy dry and for the first time he was missing his IV.

"No," Neil said. "This is all my fault."

That made no sense to Grey. He had finally seen the gun in Michael's hand and it clicked in his fuzzy thinking that the *bang* had come from it. "Put away the gun, Michael before you hurt someone."

"I intend to hurt someone," Michael answered bringing the gun up so that its smoking barrel was inches from Neil's face. "Him. He killed Marybeth."

"That's...wrong," Grey told him, still whispering. "It was the Azael who shot her. You can't blame anyone but them, but...but if you were going to blame someone else you could blame me. I took all the blood that was available."

This explanation failed to budge the gun even an inch, Neil was still staring right down the barrel. He didn't seem too alarmed, in fact, he seemed relaxed, perhaps even relieved. "He's right, Grey. I killed Marybeth. I turned off her IV."

"Oh," Grey said, his head spinning so badly that the confession of murder lacked the impact he had expected.

"That's why he has to die," Michael said. He thumbed back the pistol's hammer and asked: "Any last words?"

Still, Neil appeared completely unruffled. "Yes, I guess I do have a few. In my defense, Marybeth asked me to kill her. She knew we were almost out of blood and since she wasn't going to live much longer, she wanted to give Captain Grey a chance. I didn't want to do it, even for your sake, Grey, but she made me."

"She made you?" Michael scoffed. "She was too weak to make anyone do anything. If she was so set on this, why didn't she turn the IV off herself?"

Grey knew the answer. "That would be suicide. It's something that can't be forgiven."

"That's what she said," Neil agreed. "So, she asked me to do it. She said that I was forgiven, but it doesn't feel like it. It feels like I'd deserve it if you shot me, Michael."

"Don't do it," Grey said; with every word uttered, his whisper had degraded to almost nothing. "You should thank him, Michael. He didn't kill your wife, he saved her from an eternity in hell. Now...now if you guys don't mind, I feel pretty shabby and...and I think...I think I might..."

He was suddenly too weak to finish his sentence. He stayed conscious long enough to hear Michael crying and the sound of mortars rumbling in the distance.

Chapter 28
Jillybean

Back in rags. Back to stumbling along when she should've been skipping. Back to plotting and blood and explosions and death. Back to fighting her own mind as much as she was fighting any enemy.

The only thing new was the contemplation of death. She was walking toward death in a star-filled night. Death, in dirty Keds, was making its way to this unknown and, as far as she knew, innocent general. That was sad, but what would be sadder would be the tortured deaths of thirty-two women, who were equally innocent.

While Eve was perfectly happy with the assignment, Jillybean had balked at the idea of assassination. "Please, don't make me." She had cried and begged on her knees, but it had been in vain.

"Let me help you understand," Brad said, and then he had gone among the women on the bus with a belt, whipping them into tears until they were pleading in one harsh voice for Jillybean to save them. "You can end all this suffering," Brad told the little girl, his eyes blazing, his face aglaze with sweat. "Just do as the duke told you and put the pills in the general's drink without anyone seeing, and they'll live."

She had four bright green pills sitting in a little Ziploc baggy in her pocket. She was afraid of touching them, thinking that the poison in them would leach out into her skin. Still, they were always on her mind. When she was supposed to be paying attention to the monsters around her, she was feeling the baggy through her monster clothes and wondering about death.

Death was also coming for Jillybean.

It had its long, bony fingers stretched out for her soft throat. She knew this for a fact because she wasn't going to be able to kill this general and get away with it. Everyone would know who had poisoned him and they would grab her and put her in jail, but only for a little while, only until they decided to kill her.

She'd be a murderer and everyone knew what became of murderers: they were shot with a gun or stabbed with a knife or fed to the monsters or hung like those poor people she had seen dangling from a telephone pole outside the town of the Azael.

253

Subconsciously, she touched the skin of her neck as a lump built in her throat. She didn't want to die and she especially didn't want to die by being hung on a pole.

None of the ways were particularly agreeable to the little girl though she held out hope that taking one of the pills wouldn't be so bad. The duke's strange and scary chef had handed over the pills in their baggy saying: "One should do it but give him all four, just in case." He had grinned a dark crescent that had reminded Jillybean of the entrance to a carnival fun house that she had gone into with her parents, years before. The fun house had been freaky but it was flowers and candy compared to the duke's skeletal cook who chilled the little girl to the bone.

Again, she touched the baggy, thinking that Deanna hadn't seemed to have suffered at all when she had been drugged. If the general went out just as peacefully, Jillybean decided she would then swallow one, too.

All of this was, of course, dependent on whether Eve would allow it. Jillybean could feel the other girl getting stronger and stronger the closer they came to the Estes Valley. She also seemed delighted at the prospect of killing the general.

And I won't let you kill me, neither, Eve said. *Trust me. I'll get us back home in one piece.*

Jillybean wanted to know where Eve considered home, but she couldn't ask. The monsters were squished in on her too much for her to make even the slightest sound; they would be on her in an instant with their fangs and their claws.

She'd already had a near miss a few minutes before. All of the monsters were scary and disgusting, but she found herself next to one whose intestines were hanging outside of its body in a knot that looked like a child's attempt at tying a bow. One loop of it was fatter than the rest like an overinflated inner tube, and when the beast stepped oddly on something underfoot and lurched into Jillybean, the intestine, wet and tacky to begin with, burst, releasing a torrent of hellish, black soup onto the little girl.

The smell of the putrefying juices was dizzying and she couldn't help retch. The zombie, ignoring the fact that its intestines had just ripped open and were now dragging on the ground, turned on her with its jaws wide and hungry, and its eyes blazing. It would have eaten Jillybean right there but a monster just behind it had heard the human sound from the human girl as well and had eagerly rushed forward, stepping on the hanging entrails of the first.

The two had fallen in a jumble, giving Jillybean a chance to lose herself deeper in the crowd. She had cried, beautiful clean tears that streaked her mudded face and the entire episode had turned her mind to death.

It wasn't a good topic for a girl who needed to keep her wits about her. Thankfully, she saw the steep hill that she and Brad and clambered up days before. As casually as possible, while still remaining in monster-mode, she angled for the hill. The real monsters shied away from it which meant it was, thankfully, clear of them. She went up it on a diagonal—a very difficult thing to do as she still had to lurch and use her arms only occasionally lest she look too human again and have them all after her.

Eventually, she made it up and once over the crest of the hill, she was able to stop and rest. The view below her made up for the harshness of the walk along the crowded highway. In the dark, Estes Park was a bowl of serenity snuggled among high peaks and rugged mountain ridges. It looked peaceful as if war were a million miles away instead of knocking on its front door.

There were lights in the valley, making the place seem magical to Jillybean after so much time in the dark. And there were burning bright fires that shot sparks high into the sky. Even from a distance, Jillybean thought the sparks looked like fairies escaping the earth.

Perhaps best of all, the air was clean and pure. The Azael always kept themselves surrounded by the monsters so that they lived in a perpetual stink. Jillybean filled her lungs, deeply and nearly choked; the black gunk from the exploding intestine was still on her monster rags glistening in the star light. Quickly, she pulled off her outer garment and chucked it aside.

That was better, but what would have been the very best was if she could get an entirely new set of clothes. She'd been wearing the same two outfits since she had been captured and they were both grimy and smelled sour. Looking like a raggedy urchin was something her mother would have frowned upon and so Jillybean decided that before she met anyone, she would find a change of clothes.

She crept down out of the hills, avoiding the fires where there seemed to be both crowds of people and monsters, and she kept shy of the lit homes and businesses. Her tiny feet pattered in the dark until she came up to a number of cabins by the side of a river.

They were rental properties, but she mistook them for cozy little homes. One of them had a pine needle and pollen covered Honda parked in front. Going up on tip toes, she peeked inside and saw a pair of car seats in the back: one for a tiny baby and another for a bigger kid, both were trimmed in sun-faded pink— pink, that's what meant they had been for girls. Grinning, she went to the front door of the cabin, hoping to find a little girl's room inside that she could raid.

Instead she found a sad scene of death that suggested that there had been monsters in the valley before the soldiers came. The front door had been torn down; there was glass strewn and chairs overturned. In the single bedroom there were the remains of three bodies, two of which were very small and the third was scattered in pieces, a bone here a bone there, a pile of clothes in a thatch of moldering flesh.

Jillybean sat down on the bed letting out a weary sigh. "That's too bad," she said.

That's life, Eve replied in her head. *Get used to it.*

"Well, I don't like it," Jillybean snapped, wondering why she was talking to Eve in the first place.

Because you're lonely.

"I'm not so lonely as to carry on a conversation with a murderer which is what you are, in case you forgot. Now, if you'll excuse me." Jillybean pretended that Eve wasn't hanging just over her shoulder and went to explore the place.

There wasn't much to it. Everything of value such as food or flashlights had been looted ages ago, however Jillybean found a little girl's suitcase. Across the top was written in magic marker: Amber D.

"Hi Amber," Jillybean said to the larger of the two skeletons. "I hope you don't mind me borrowing some clothes."

Eve laughed at this. *You're not borrowing them, you're stealing them. I thought you didn't like thieves and liars? That's funny because you're both. And you don't like me because I'm a murderer, but what are you going to do to the general? What did you do to poor Ernest?*

"It's not the same," Jillybean hissed. "And we're not the same. I do bad stuff because I have to. You like to be bad and evil! You like to kill."

We're more alike than you think, Eve said and then with a ghostly laugh echoing in Jillybean's head, she left.

"We're not alike at all," Jillybean snarled, yanking open the suitcase. She gazed in wonder at the vibrant colors and the neat folds and the cleanliness. Everything looked perfect...but a little small. Amber D had been six when she had died and not a very big six either. Still, Jillybean was scrawny, borderline malnourished. The purple undies fit properly and so did the pure white socks. A long sleeve shirt the color of cream didn't extend all the way down her wrist, so she hiked it up to her elbows and the longest skirt in the suitcase sat high up on her knees, making Jillybean feel extremely exposed downstairs.

She looked down at her dirty legs. "I need a bath...but in the morning." It was after midnight and she was tired. Since she was no longer afraid of the dead, she slept in the same room as the three bodies and didn't dream.

Gunshots woke her. They were far off but persistent and the constant crackle finally crept into her sleeping mind. She woke up in a fit of depression—she was going to commit murder that day. It was hard to smile once that thought entered her head.

She went about her morning in a grim mood. Her first act was to bathe. With the mountain water so cold that it stung the flesh, she built a fire and heated rounded river stones in small pans stuck directly in the flames. She then hauled water and filled the cabin's bathtub to the halfway point; once the stones were set in the water, it became pleasant enough and she washed away ten days' worth of grime.

When she was clean from head to toe, she saw that her body wasn't the pale white it had been. She was covered in splotchy bruises; some a deep purple, some black, some an ugly green. There were so many and so horrible that Jillybean was afraid to look in the mirror.

You're ugly, Eve said, twisting Jillybean's lip in disgust. Jillybean couldn't reply, except to pout, because it was true. Brushing out her hair helped—her mom used to always say she was prettier when she got the tangles out of her unruly hair—and it also helped to hide her many bruises beneath her clothes, but nothing could change the hard and nasty feeling crawling around in her guts. Eve was inside her, biding her time, knowing that she'd soon be free.

Jillybean hummed and pretended not to notice. Once she was dressed and ready, she tucked the bag of pills away and hid the paperclip she'd taken from the duke's ammo tent before heading out to kill.

The cabins were down in a little dell off the river and when she climbed out she saw that she wasn't all that far from what used to be downtown Estes Park. There was a run of brick buildings that were quaint and a little play area for children to run around in and there were restaurants, all of which were dark and forbidding.

Jillybean tried not to think about the restaurants, but too late, her empty stomach started growling and making noises as though some sort of giant salamander was talking inside her. She ignored her belly, as she had for most of the last of year, and walked through the town which seemed oddly empty. That was a good thing. She didn't want to run into any of her friends by accident.

With all her heart she wanted to see Neil and Captain Grey and Deanna and most of all, her apocalypse sister, Sadie, however she was far too ashamed at what she was planning to do to see them. And so she slunk from shadow to shadow ready to dart down this alley or into that empty store at the first sign of any of her friends.

She was halfway through the town before she came into contact with an actual person—it was a soldier barreling down the street in a truck. Right away, she saw it wasn't Captain Grey and so she stepped out into the street, waving a skinny arm. The soldier, lanky as a string bean, sporting an array of zits and a flat-topped crew-cut, stomped on the brake. He came to a halt a few feet from her and did nothing but gape at her as if he had never seen a child before.

"How old are you?" was the first thing out of his mouth.

"Seven," she answered, holding up the prerequisite number of fingers. The two stared at each other for another minute before she tilted her head and asked: "Where is General Johnston? I have to talk to him."

He blinked and then shrugged. "At the hotel, I guess, but what do you want with him?"

To kill him.

That answer would never do, so she amended it to: "I just have to talk to him is all." She could feel Eve inside her growing and laughing and trying to peer out from her eyes and attempting to use her mouth to speak and her hands to touch. Jillybean shoved her back down, angrily. "Where's this hotel? Can I ask?"

The soldier jerked his thumb at the white building that dominated the valley. It was an immense structure that stood on a northern hill overlooking all of Estes. It seemed fit for a general or a king.

"Ok, thanks," she said and smiled before starting to trudge in its direction. The soldier blinked again, what appeared to be his main form of communication and then shrugged, his secondary form, and then spun his wheels as he left the girl behind.

Jillybean promptly forgot about him. Her mind and that of Eve's was wholly taken up by her mission. She went to it with feet dragging, while Eve went with the excitement of the kill rushing through her veins. It was blood lust pure and simple and it made Jillybean shiver and her hands wouldn't stop shaking.

Keep going, killer, Eve whispered when Jillybean stopped to take a breath. The hills were sharp and the air thin and she was famished and tired from her labors and the burden of murder was like a weight pressing down on her.

Another Humvee passed her by, its driver staring hard. She tried to smile but her heart wasn't in it. All she could think about were the pills in her pocket and the black beast growing over her shoulder. She had to resist the urge to look behind her every few seconds, fearing that Eve had grown a human body.

When she did risk a look, there was never anything there and she didn't know if that was good or not. If Eve became real, Jillybean could run away from her and be her own person...a person who didn't have to kill.

Too bad but you do, Eve said.

Jillybean ignored her and leaned into the last of the hill as she came up to the hotel. It was an impressive three stories in height and reminded her, with all its fancy trimming, of her Victorian dollhouse she had left back in Philadelphia.

She went through what she thought were the front doors only to find herself in an empty ballroom. It was all very pretty with its intricate crown molding and its polished hardwood floors and the beautiful murals on the walls, and yet the splendor meant nothing to her. Her mind was in a dark place and her soul was in a darker one.

A woman in uniform strode by and, just like the other soldiers, she stopped to stare at the little girl. "Can I help you?" she asked in a soft whisper, her eyes fixed on Jillybean as if the girl might turn to smoke if she blinked.

"General Johnston, please," Jillybean asked.

The soldier turned her head slightly, confused. "The general? He's in with the governor. Can I ask who you are?"

"My name is Jillybean and I…I…have information for him. I just escaped from the Azael and there are things he should know."

"Escaped?" She had twitched at Jillybean's name, but the word 'escape' seemed foreign to her. "Sure…I guess. He's on the second floor just around…never mind. Let me show you." The soldier started to walk but she stopped and put her hand out. Jillybean was glad to take it. The hand was soft and dry, adult-sized and reassuring in its strength. Jillybean practically clung to it.

Together they went through the hotel until they were outside a door with a placard that read *Hotel Manager*. "I've got to go, but just wait here for the general. It won't be all that much longer."

The wait was a million years. Eve cackled and hissed and grew to be a black shadow hanging on Jillybean's shoulders. The prospect of murder gave her strength and Jillybean shrunk in comparison.

Jillybean tried to justify herself: "It's one life. In return I save thirty-two. Brad said that was a good deal and I think so, too."

It's one more death you mean. One more murder on your soul. But if it's too much for you, I'll do the dirty work. I'll slip the general his pills. Don't worry about that.

"And you'll never let go, either, will you?" Jillybean knew the answer to that. Eve would take over and never give up control. She would use the weight of guilt, a million pounds of it, to bury Jillybean in the black nothingness of her own soul. Eve didn't even bother to answer the question.

Jillybean longed to run out of the room right then. She wanted to just ghost out of there and forget everything, but at exactly that moment the door that was marked Hotel Manager came open and Neil Martin stood there before her.

He had changed. The old Neil would have laughed and hugged her, the new Neil narrowed his eyes at her in a way she couldn't read.

"Hi Mister Neil, Sir," she said.

His mouth came open and he started working his jaw up and down but no sound came out. The general was right behind him. He was very tall and muscular, like Captain Grey, but he was dark skinned and his eyes were older. He seemed to have a deep font of wisdom in those eyes. It was though he could see right through Jillybean and into her black soul where murder was her secret.

"You're alive," Neil finally said.

"Yes, I…I escaped." The lie wasn't easy to tell with the general staring down at her. It was an effort to spit it out.

"You escaped from the Azael?" the general asked. "That must be some story. Maybe you should step inside and tell me all about it." He indicated his plush office. Jillybean glanced inside—there was a broad-surfaced desk of dark wood and on it was a steaming cup of coffee.

The pills in her pocket were like anchors.

"I—I don't think I can," Jillybean said, and then took a step back as the walls of the little antechamber felt to be closing in on her like the walls of a jail cell. Suddenly, she fled, running back into the hall, however the walls there were still too close and so she dashed into a stairwell which was windowless and black as pitch.

Of course, you can't, Eve said. She was no longer behind Jillybean; she loomed in the dark air in front of her and seemed to have grown to great size. *Killing isn't your thing. You're too sweet to kill, that's why you should let me do it. I'll make it quick.*

Jillybean started to shake her head; however it was only a tiny movement. She could feel herself giving in to the idea of murder. It was why she was here, after all. "I—I just don't want to know," she whispered. "I don't ever want to remember what you..."

Light blared into her face, cutting off her words and before she knew it, Neil was in the staircase with her. For some reason, he shut the door behind him so that he was nothing but a shadow with a glint of white teeth. "What's wrong?" he asked.

She had a thousand answers to that question but only one left her lips. "I...I think I'm evil," she answered. "I know it." Inside her, Eve hissed like a snake. It was a warning and pictures started flashing before her eyes: the whore-bus splashed with blood, the aisle between the seats a red river, the women lying in grotesque fashion with their throats cut wide open so that it looked as though each had grown a new grinning mouth.

"Ahh, Jillybean." A hand reached out of the darkness and took her shoulder. She jumped. "What's this about being evil?"

Don't tell him anything, Eve said in a threatening tone. *He'll lock you up and then this will happen.* The images of the dead women came into her mind again; they were so real that Jillybean could smell the coppery blood. Her head began to spin.

"I—I don't know," she stammered. "I need a second...a second to be alone."

The hand on her shoulder grew tighter. "I don't think that's wise. I think it's best if you talk about what's going on."

"I can't do it," Jillybean said. She was speaking to Eve but Neil thought she was speaking to him and he started talking in that sweet fatherly way of his, however she wasn't listening.

Eve had her mind in a grip. *If you don't kill the one man, then thirty-two will die, and they'll die horribly. They'll die screaming and bleeding and cursing you, Jillybean. But you can save them, just let me kill the man.*

The darkness began to spin and if it hadn't been for Neil, she would've fallen. "But what about all the people here?" she asked, meaning the thousands of people in the valley.

"What?" Neil asked. "What people?"

Who cares? Some will die, heck, maybe all of them will but it won't really be your fault, Eve said. *They're going to die anyways, Jilly. You can't save everyone.*

"Why not," she challenged.

Neil cracked the door, blinding them both. Jillybean looked around, expecting to see Eve standing with them, a velvety black form made of pure evil. She wasn't there, she was in Jillybean's head.

Because you can't save them, Eve said. *Because you're not that smart. You walk around showing off to all these stupid people but we both know the truth. You know a few tricks and you can see some things that these blind sheep miss, but deep down you know you're nothing. Deep down, you know you're weak. And you know that when the time comes, you'll let me kill their stupid general and once I do there won't be any coming back. I'll own you for good.*

Jillybean knew she was right. About all of it. Jillybean couldn't save the thirty-two without killing the general and Eve was already so strong. She was afraid what another death on her conscience would do to her. But she had no choice.

"I think I should go see the general now," Jillybean said.

"Ok, but are you sure you don't want to talk about what just happened?" Neil asked, eyeing her closely. "You were talking to yourself."

Neil would never understand about Eve. "I know," she said and didn't explain further. Taking Neil's hand, she led him back to the general's office. "I think I should talk to him alone," she told Neil.

"Sure," Neil said. "I'll be right out here." He shut the door leaving her alone with the general and with Eve.

You should do it, Eve said. *You should put the pills in his drink. It'll make feel you better. It'll be like you were personally saving those women.*

And if I do, I'll disappear forever, Jillybean thought to herself. Eve was growing monstrous in her mind, a demon shadow with wings that struck out the light. She was the grit under Jillybean's nails and the dull pain in the deepest of her bruises. The little girl could feel Eve's black evil down into her toes.

"So, before we begin, can I get you anything?" General Johnston asked in a kind voice, not realizing that he was setting himself up, perfectly.

A tear escaped Jillybean's eye as she said: "Water, p-please."

He mistook the cause of the tear. "Sure, just relax. You're safe now. I won't let anything happen to you." She was sure that he would keep her safe. He was just as wonderful as Captain Grey had described. When he left, Jillybean broke down, the tears flowing without letup, like salted rain.

Do it! Eve hissed. *Do it now!*

Eve had her now, almost completely and Jillybean couldn't have stopped herself, though she didn't try. She kept telling herself that by killing the general she was saving thirty-two people. It was a good a trade even if in the end she wouldn't be around to see it.

Eve guided her shaking hand and, so easily it was terrifying, the three pills plopped one after another into the general's mug. The last she kept for herself.

Chapter 29
Jillybean

The general came back into the room holding a water bottle, its contents pristine and pure, quite the opposite of what lay in the mug that sat between the two of them. The coffee had been black, just as dark as night, but now there was a tiny stream of bubbles, like champagne bubbles, coming up from the depths of the mug.

Stop staring at it, you idiot! Eve seethed.

Jillybean pulled her wet eyes up to look into the general's face. He smiled easily and said, "Drink, it'll make you feel better." Obediently, she took a sip of her water; she didn't want to take too much, knowing she would need to save as much as possible to swallow her own pill with. She hated taking pills, they always got stuck in her throat and tried to choke her. Of course the lone pill tucked in her panties would do more than that.

"It's ok, they can't hurt you here," Johnston was saying and when he smiled, Jillybean almost believed it. "Neil and Captain Grey have told me a lot about you. They think you're very smart. I bet you are, too. Do you think you might be able to remember if any of the Azael talked about their numbers? Or what sort of weapons they have?"

The bubbles were beginning to collect on the surface of the mug. *Start talking*, Eve told her. *Keep his mind focused on you or he'll see and then they'll know and then they'll put you in jail. If that happens, then Kay and all the others will die.*

She knew this, of course, but it physically pained her to be in the same room with her victim. "I—I only saw men with guns, you know, army man guns, but they had these tents that had different kinds, too. I was in one and they had big machine guns and also grenades."

Johnston cocked his head at this. "You know about grenades."

"Yes," she said and didn't add: I've killed people with them, lots of times.

"What about tanks? Did they have any of them?" She nodded and his face grew grim. "How many tanks did they have?"

The Azael had two tanks which were always kept far down the road from where everyone camped. Jillybean raised two fingers and the general couldn't seem to decide if that was a good or bad thing; his face suggested both. He drummed his fingers on his desk for a moment and then reached for his coffee mug.

This is it! Eve cried. A sharp pain lanced Jillybean's insides as her guilt became almost a physical presence in her chest, growing and growing and, as it did, the other girl grew as well.

The general picked up the mug and then set it down on the side of his desk. Then, as Jillybean practically wilted with relief, he dug out a book from a drawer and opened it up.

"Is this the tank you saw?" He pointed to a picture of a green army tank that had a gun the size of a tree trunk poking out the front. The picture was titled M1A1 Abrams.

She shook her head. "The ones they have, gots wheels on them." He flipped pages in the book until he found a picture marked M1126 Infantry Carrier Vehicle. "That's it," she said.

"With this kind of gun on the top?" The picture showed a canon like the other tank had sticking out of the front of the vehicle.

"No. It had a machine gun."

The general looked sick and somewhat relieved at the same time. "They're Strykers and they can be pretty tough. But at least they don't have real tanks. That means we have a chance. Not a very good chance, but still a chance." He closed the book, composed himself and, placing a fatherly look over his anxiety, asked: "What about the number of men?"

Jillybean was quick to answer: "Five thousand."

This shocked the fatherly look right off the general's face. "Five thousand? And how many zombies are there?"

"Half a million," Jillybean answered. She'd heard the number bantered around by everyone in the camp. The Azael seemed very proud of it, though she didn't know why.

"That's...that's too many," he said in a whisper. "We'll never win." He grabbed up his mug and stood, turning from Jillybean to stare at a flag-sized map of the valley that was pinned to the wall.

He just stood there, staring as the seconds ticked by and the ache in Jillybean's stomach flared greater than ever. She wanted him to drink his coffee and get it over with. Eve did as well, knowing that when the general died the guilt would be too much for Jillybean and she would hide away inside herself and then Eve would be in charge and she would do hideous things so that Jillybean would be too ashamed to ever come out again.

Almost to spite them both, the general slowly raised the mug, his eyes and mind on the map. As much as Eve wanted to watch, Jillybean couldn't. She hopped up, heading for the door when something about the map caught her eye. It was marked up with red lines; two of which followed the highways heading into town, routes 34 and 36.

The red ink stopped as it neared the town but the roads did not. They merged and then went west into the mountains. "What are those little Xs?" she asked. Just shy of where the red lines ended were a series of small Xs on both highways.

He had been about to drink from the mug but paused and pointed at the map. "That's where the walls are," he answered. The cup came back up, however Jillybean didn't notice, her mind was suddenly too engrossed in an idea or at least the beginning of an idea. It was there, a plan, just on the verge, but she couldn't visualize it.

"Does this place have a roof, one I can get out on?"

The mug came down as he answered: "No, but there's a cupola that gives you a view of the entire..."

She remembered the cupola and guessed which set of stairs led to it. "Don't drink that," she said, tugging at his arm. "Put it down and come on."

He said something however she couldn't hear what. Eve was screaming in her mind, drowning everything else out: *What are you doing? Make him drink that coffee!*

"No," Jillybean hissed as she barreled out the door. Neil had been leaning against the far wall and now he came forward, a surprised look on his face. He, too was speaking words that went right past her. She knew what she was doing was rude and so she paused and said: "I can save them," as way of explanation.

Johnston looked doubtful, Neil hopeful, while Eve was angry. *You're not smart enough*, the evil girl said.

267

"I am, too," Jillybean replied over her shoulder. She was already running down the hall to the central stair, figuring that since the cupola was in the exact middle of the roof this was the logical way to go. With Neil and General Johnston following, she made it to the top of the building. The view was fantastic, but it wasn't jarring the half-formed idea out of her head; Eve was filling her mind with so much static, it was hard to think clearly.

Johnston came up right after the little girl and stood staring out at the million-dollar view. Neil came up much slower, panting and holding his side. "What's the plan?" he asked between gasps.

"I...I don't know," Jillybean answered. "It's right here." She touched her forehead. "But I can't get it out. Eve won't let me. Maybe...maybe if I saw the map again."

"Sure, I'll just...uh, zip down and get it."

The general stopped him. "I'll get it, Neil. You clearly haven't acclimated to the altitude at all." Johnston left, going at a quick clip, breathing easily.

"Show off," Neil said, his mangled face turning softer with his boyish smile. He looked out and said: "Wow, it sure is pretty up here. So...you've got a plan. Good...good, uh, is it coming to you yet?"

Eve began to shriek like a mandrill and Jillybean could only stuff her hands over her ears and shake her head. The worry on Neil's face over Jillybean's bizarre actions was plain to see but he tried his best to pretend like nothing was wrong. "Take your time."

She didn't think there was time to waste. Unable to sit still, she began to pace, her anxiety mounting. Time was suddenly important to her and after a few minutes of pacing she realized that the general should have been back with the map already.

Oh, I wonder what could have happened, Eve said with theatrical innocence before sending a moving picture into Jillybean's mind: *the general walking briskly down into his office, pausing to take a big slug of his coffee, downing half of it before his face squinches up. The taste is off but he doesn't think poison, not yet. He then takes down the map, gently because he is, after all, only humoring the girl. He even takes the time to fold the map and that's when his stomach rolls over unpleasantly.*

Something wrong with the coffee, he thinks and picks up the mug and gives it a sniff. It smells ok and so he takes another sip: fine but a touch sour. With a shrug, he sets it down, turns toward the door, whereupon his stomach rolls again, sharply this time, causing him to stop, one hand holding his gut. Something is definitely wrong only he doesn't consider it anything beyond a possible new case of diarrhea. He pauses there in his office doorway rubbing his stomach until he decides: better safe than sorry.

In his top drawer is a bottle of Pepto Bismol in pill form— he had never liked the liquid stuff and in this case, not having it kills him. The liquid would have coated his stomach, slowing the absorption of the cyanide; the pink pills had to dissolve first and by the time they do, he's already dead.

Two minutes before that occurrence, he swallows a couple of the pills, chucks the bottle back in the drawer, grabs the map and presses on in the army way, despite the uneasy feeling in his stomach.

He hurries back to the stairs and finds himself curiously out of breath. At the third floor, he has to stop and suck in the thin air and for the first time starts to worry that something is very wrong with him. As he makes his way to the cupola, his head begins to spin and he can't gasp hard enough to fill his lungs enough. Just outside the door, he collapses.

Just then, there was indeed a real thump from beyond the door, only it wasn't just a single soft noise as Eve envisioned. There was a series of them—the unmistakable sound of someone falling down the stairs. Jillybean jumped to the door, feeling her soul coming unglued from her body. Her hand was clumsy on the door as though her skin was too large for her bones. She fumbled twice for the knob before Neil pushed her hand away and opened it himself.

There at the bottom of the stairs sprawled General Johnston lying in a contorted jumble of arms and legs. There was pink foam coming from his mouth. As Jillybean stood there in shock, he started to twitch; first just a foot and then his entire body. He spazzed for a few seconds, his head making hollow noises as it knocked against the concrete wall, and then Neil was flying down the stairs.

Too late. The general was dead and it felt as though Jillybean was next. Her world spun into black and she found herself falling into nothingness.

Chapter 30
Sadie Walcott

The news of General Johnston's death from "unknown" causes reached every ear within forty minutes. The news that Jillybean was in the valley took much longer and yet, somehow Sadie guessed it right away.

The general had been in great shape and Sadie knew that he hadn't "just died." That was laughable and it meant that someone had killed him. Few people in the valley could have killed him and not one had a reason to. That meant he had been killed by someone from outside—one of the Azael? Not likely or the cause of death would have been revealed in order to stoke the anger of the people.

No, Neil had purposely kept the cause of death a mystery, and Sadie knew him well enough to know that it meant there was an element of shame involved.

Within a minute of her hearing the news, she was up and out of bed. A shaken and distraught Veronica Hennesy had woken her to tell her the news, though she did so in a generic, factless manner. "Neil wants to see you," she added, once Sadie's eyes had focused. This was an even greater *tell* that Jillybean was there. Jillybean had been their shared responsibility, and their shared failure; she would be the only reason Neil would want to talk to her so soon after a beloved figure had died.

"At the clinic?" Sadie asked and only got a slow nod in return from Veronica who seemed too stunned for any other response.

Sadie walked past her and left the little place she shared with Neil. The morning sun was dazzling causing Sadie to blink and squint until her eyes adjusted.

"How was guard duty?" Veronica asked, from behind her. "Scary?"

The casualties among the soldiers had been adding up and so Sadie had volunteered to stand guard on one of the lonesome hills surrounding the valley. The dark had been intense and throughout the night there had been a thousand secretive sounds coming from all around her. "Yeah, it was." Scary didn't quite cover it.

Now she was scratchy-eyed, yawning and, besides guessing that Jillybean was behind the death, she was slow witted. A run seemed like the thing to wake her up and so she politely refused Veronica's offer of a ride and took off across the valley.

It was an easy eight-minute mile for her and she was barely winded when she jogged up the steps of the clinic. The place was crowded, filled mostly with stern-faced soldiers who looked on the verge of either crying or breaking something with their bare fists.

Sadie wormed her way through them, fighting to get to Captain Grey's room where the throng was greatest and the silence heaviest. Neil was there and when the two locked eyes, Sadie's suspicions were confirmed. "Where is she?" Sadie asked, keeping her voice low and her head turned away from the men.

"In Marybeth's old room but...but it's not her. It's the other girl."

This wasn't a shocker either. Sadie gave Neil a squeeze on the arm and slipped through the men, finding Marybeth's old room curiously unguarded. She went in, closing the door quickly behind her.

Jillybean was sitting on a gurney, her left hand cuffed to the railing. The little girl looked like she had gone through hell in the past two weeks—her arms were bruised in a dozen places, her face had healing scabs in four more and both her eyes had fading green and purple half-moons beneath them.

She'd been beaten. She had volunteered to go back to detonate the bombs and she had paid the price for her courage and that included losing the last of her mind.

Two other women were in the room: Deanna was one and a steely-eyed sergeant the other. The sergeant was dressed in camo, her hair sat in a severe bun atop her head, and her hand never left the grip of her pistol. The room was as silent as a tomb.

"Can I have a few minutes alone with her?" Sadie asked. "I'd like to talk to her."

The sergeant answered: "No. The governor told me not to leave her side."

"I speak for the governor," Deanna said. "It'll be ok. Please go wait outside the door." There was so much calm authority in her voice that the sergeant only hesitated a second before obeying.

"Do you mind leaving as well?" Sadie asked Deanna. "I'd like to..."

Deanna interrupted, saying in a hard tone: "I'm staying."

"I want her to stay," Jillybean said. "I want to apologize to both of you and to everyone. The Azael made me do it. I didn't want to kill the nice general, but the duke said he would kill all the sex-women if I didn't. He beat them until they begged me to do it and he beat me, too, see?" She pointed at her battered face.

"Do you have any proof of this?" Deanna asked.

"I don't have any fingerprints or nothing like that if that's what you mean. I just have that last pill I was going to swallow. I was supposed to give the general all four but I knew I couldn't live with myself knowing I had done such a bad thing. I was going to suicide myself and that's what means I was going to eat the same poison, only I fainted and Mister Neil found the pill."

Sadie glanced at Deanna whose look was softening. "How much of that is true?" Sadie asked her.

"All of it, as far as I know. The partial remains of three pills were found in the general's coffee cup. Margaret Yuan thinks it was cyanide. She's doing an autopsy right now, but she's no expert. I think it's moot, either way. Jillybean has confessed and Neil did find the extra pill on her so really it's case-closed. The only question is what do we do with her? She says she was trying to save thirty-two women; those are some real extenuating circumstances. Coupled with her age, she would've gone free in the old world."

This statement made no sense to Sadie. "We don't live in the old world and besides, that isn't Jillybean. That's Eve."

The little girl began vehemently shaking her head. "No, I'm Jillybean. The other girl is gone. I figured out how to lock her away. You have to believe me."

"I don't," Sadie said, walking up to her bedside. She reached out a hand and the girl shied away before looking at it doubtfully. Sadie had her pinky out. Too slow, the girl realized what she was supposed to do and when she went to hook her pinky in Sadie's, the older girl withdrew her hand.

"You aren't fooling me, Eve."

Eve glanced toward Deanna in a move that was too calculated. "You're right, Sadie, that is Eve," Deanna said and then let out a mirthless bark of laughter. "You had me going there for a bit, but not anymore. You're going to pay for what you did."

"I didn't do anything," Eve replied. "It really was Jillybean. I wanted to get the hell out of this entire state, but Jillybean wouldn't listen. You see, she really believed that by killing the general she was going to save those women. Pretty stupid, huh?"

"What do you mean?" Deanna demanded.

"You of all people should know what's going to happen to those women. They're whores and they're going to stay whores until they're all used up or ravaged by disease. Then, if they're lucky, they'll be allowed to leave. They'll get the chance to wander free in a land of monsters with nothing but the rags on their backs. No, Jillybean didn't save anyone, not even herself. She's locked up in my head forever." Eve grinned, showing little kid teeth.

Sadie recoiled from the horror that the little girl had become, however Deanna, bristling with wrath, stepped forward. "I'm glad Jillybean is gone. It'll mean I won't have any qualms about prosecuting you to the fullest. The penalty for murder is death."

"It wasn't me, like I said. It was Jillybean. If I had killed the general, I wouldn't have fainted and I wouldn't have done it with a witness just outside the door and I would've had a getaway planned. You can't pin this on me. This was all Jillybean."

"And what about Eve's murder?" Sadie demanded. "That was all you." The moment the words left her mouth she wanted them back. Was she really going to help put a seven-year-old to death? A girl she had once called sister?

Eve glared, her mouth a hard line and her eyes black with hate. "*I* am Eve."

"That's not a denial," Deanna said and then turned to the door. She opened it and motioned the female sergeant back into the room. "Strip her all the way down, including her panties. Then I want this entire room emptied. Everything has to go, including what's in the drawers and cabinets. Then I want the windows nailed shut and a guard kept outside that door twenty-four/seven."

The sergeant's face held barely concealed puzzlement. "Don't you think you're going a bit overboard? She's just a little girl."

"No, she's not," Deanna shot back.

273

They had no real facility to hold Eve. The town had not been looted with the same destruction as other small towns and, curiously, the local police station was the only building that had been torched.

Sadie stayed to watch as Eve was stripped down. "Open your hands," Sadie ordered, when Eve was completely naked. Her handcuffs rattled as she showed her empty palms; she even raised her feet to flare her toes. Sadie wasn't satisfied. "And your mouth."

Eve glared and then stuck out her tongue before opening her mouth wide. Satisfied, Sadie left her and went to see Neil; however he was in another meeting and had two more following that.

Feeling glum, and with nothing to do, she walked to the little bungalow that she and Neil called home and went back to bed. Sleep was very slow in coming. She couldn't help but think that they were taking the wrong tack with regard to Jillybean. The good girl was in there somewhere and when she was good she was an angel.

Four hours of sleep was all she could steal before her mind began worrying again. She laid in bed another hour staring at the ceiling, wishing there was some way she could exorcise Eve out of Jillybean's body as if she was an evil spirit and not some sort of mental aberration.

Eventually, Sadie got up, shouldered her M4, and went for chow. The mess hall, what had been the town's only grocery store, was a quiet place for once. There was an air of defeat among the crowded tables and more than one gruff half-barbaric soldier had tears in his eyes. Sadie kept to herself, eating quickly and ducking out before anyone could even think of engaging her in conversation.

With only sullen thoughts dogging her, she decided to go on shift early and relieved a lonely buck private who was eager for news. He'd heard that General Johnston had been murdered but nothing else.

"Go ask in town," was all Sadie said. There was no way she was going to say that her sister had poisoned to death the one hope the people of the valley had. That was a harsh but true thought. Neil was too new to be seen as anyone's savior. Yes, by his and Deanna's guts alone, Red Gate 3 had been held against all odds, and yes, he had practically sacrificed his best friend and daughter in order to stop the howitzers, but these were nothing compared to Johnston's stoic calm and unrivaled leadership.

The night progressed slower than any other. Sadie lost herself in the stars. She stared upward as they gradually pin wheeled across the sky and not for the first time, she wished she knew the names of the different stars and constellations. The only one she knew for sure was the Big Dipper and for hours she checked its progress as it started off flat, looking like an actual dipper before it slowly turned on its side as if it was pouring out its celestial contents into the black of space.

At six when the sky was the color of pink pearl, she was more than ready for her replacement. When he finally showed, dragging his feet, Sadie rushed off to find Neil.

"We're going to abandon the valley," he said right off the bat. That simple statement drained the energy right out of her and she wanted to climb back in bed and yank the covers over her head. He sighed, probably thinking the same thing and then went on: "We can't win against both the zombies and the Azael and, with the general dead, no one seems to want to try anymore. But it's the wrong move, I know it. People are already starting to talk about going their separate ways. We'll be divided and weak."

"And what's going on with Jillybean?" She half expected him to say she had escaped during the night.

He took a long breath before answering: "We're having a hearing this afternoon. It's not really a judicial proceeding, it's more like a bunch of people coming together and making a decision. I want you to attend."

"In what capacity? Do you want me to be, like Jillybean's advocate? Or her…" She couldn't bring herself to say the word prosecutor.

"In whatever capacity fits you. All we're looking for is the truth and, perhaps, a solution to the problem she represents."

Jillybean was a tremendous problem, that couldn't be denied. Had she been an adult she would have been taken out back and shot long ago. But as a child, it wasn't so easy, and as a child gifted with amazing mental powers, it was even more difficult. Sadie knew that empires could hinge on her mind.

"I'll do my best. What time?"

Neil told her four and then excused himself. "Meetings and more meetings," he explained and was gone.

For the second day in a row, sleep was a difficult thing to cage. She slept intermittently as though her R.E.M. cycle was synched to someone sending out a message in Morse code: three long, two short, two short. She woke just after one in the afternoon and remained awake. By two, when the room was splashed with the afternoon sun, she'd had enough and so she got up and decided to go "shopping."

This meant she went to poke through people's houses to find clothes that didn't belong to her. She didn't want to look like some punk-kid at the hearing, she wanted to be taken seriously even though she had no idea if she had anything to say or even what side she was going to take.

By a strange coincidence, Sadie found herself walking by the same little cabin that Jillybean had spent the night in two days previously. The open front door drew her and within a minute she had on a floral print dress that undoubtedly belonged to the larger of the three corpses that were sprawled in the single bedroom. By another happy coincidence the corpse had Sadie's foot size as well.

When she looked at herself in the mirror, she felt like some suburban mom and this feeling extended beyond the looks department. Her eyes were drawn to the open suitcase with the name Amber D written across the top. Sadie picked out a dress and a pair of sparkly converse sneakers for Jillybean. The little girl had done too much for Sadie and everyone Sadie had ever counted as a friend to go into court with her life on the line in only an open-backed hospital johnny.

"Put this on," she said to the surly thing in Jillybean's body thirty minutes later. "And try to be pleasant or they'll hang you."

Eve did her best, however it was like asking a rattlesnake to embrace its sweet side. When she spoke, there was an undercurrent of oily villainy. She was evil and couldn't seem to hide it. The facts, which were piled higher than her head against her, didn't help her either; she'd been caught red-handed with one murder and had admitted to a second.

After the reading of the evidence, Neil called a number of character witnesses all of whom were arrayed against Jillybean. Joslyn Reynolds, Fred Trigg, and Veronica Hennesy, all told the truth—the damning truth. Sadie was called as well and as much as she wanted to be on Jillybean's side, every word out of her mouth felt like a nail in Jillybean's coffin. For every up there was a down. For every life saved there were two dead. Her heroics seemed to fade compared to her atrocities. The events surrounding the death of baby Eve was the clincher and couldn't be overlooked.

It was obvious that Neil wanted to speak in some capacity other than that of an official, as did Captain Grey and Deanna, however they were part of the ten-person panel and couldn't express their opinions, not that it mattered much. The little girl had been caught dead to rights and, due to their present situation, she couldn't simply be allowed to go free and neither could they afford to incarcerate her indefinitely—not only was she too dangerous to let sit in a cell, indefinitely, it was a drain of manpower that they didn't possess.

At the end of the proceedings, Eve left with Sadie to sit in her hospital room. "They're going to kill me, aren't they?" the little girl asked.

The answer was yes, however Sadie lied, saying: "You never know."

Neil came in twenty minutes later, looking sick to his stomach. "Tomorrow at sunrise," he said right off the bat.

As Sadie choked on the breath in her throat, Eve blanched. "Sunrise? Don't I get some sort of appeal or second chance or anything?"

"No," Neil said. "The verdict was unanimous on both counts, I'm sorry. Your obvious mental instability wasn't a mitigating factor, either."

Eve's lip began to jabber up and down and she looked completely bewildered as if the idea that she could really die had never entered into the realm of possibility. "W-Will it hurt?" she asked with trembling lips.

This was the Jillybean that Sadie loved so much: soft, innocent, vulnerable. Sadie looked to Neil. 'No, it'll be painless" he answered. "We'll inject you with morphine. Enough of it will put you to sleep and a little more will stop your lungs. It'll be just like falling asleep and not waking up again."

Eve was quiet a long time, her eyes fixed on some point far away beyond the walls of the clinic and perhaps beyond the mountains as well. Eventually, she broke her stare and smiled. "Painless? You were always a little bitch, weren't you, Neil?"

Chapter 31
Jillybean

She heard it all. Eve had pulled her up from the blackness to listen to the trial. The evidence was irrefutable. She had poisoned General Johnston in the hopes of saving thirty-two others...but they weren't ever going to be saved.

That was Eve's big joke. The thirty-two women weren't going to be killed, at least not in the traditional ways. There'd be no executioner's bullets to the back of their heads, and there wasn't going to be a hangman's noose around their necks and there wasn't going to be a madman's knife plunging into their bodies over and over again.

No, Jillybean had been fooled. The women were going to remain sex slaves until they died of syphilis or hepatitis, or they angered the wrong man who would crack their heads against a rock without a second thought, and then shrug out an apology to this duke or that before going on their merry way.

Jillybean had heard it all and was glad she was hidden away where no one could see her. She was so ashamed of herself that she wished Neil would speed up the execution. She was looking forward to death. Her death was going to be a good thing for the world. It would be a happier place without her in it and that went double for Eve.

"Now don't be like that," Eve said in a consoling voice. They were alone in her hospital room where it was deep, dark night. "You've done some really good things. Remember when you saved Neil from that hand grenade? That was good."

It was a hand grenade that you threw! Jillybean shot back.

"Well, sure, but you still saved him. And what about the bridge? You saved all the renegades there."

So? What's your point? Why are you suddenly acting like this? Eve was being nice and Jillybean didn't trust it one bit.

"My point is that your friends are in trouble and we should try to find a way to help them. They're going to lose the valley without you. Is that what you want? Do you want to see them driven out of here and then hounded from place to place? How many more people will die if you don't do something?"

Why do you care what happens to them? Jillybean asked, although the answer was already filtering into her mind. *Wait, you think they'll release us just because we help them? I don't think they will.*

"I do," Eve said. "All we have to do is dangle a portion of a good enough plan in front of their eyes and make it contingent upon our release. They'll fold I bet...I think, maybe. They'll postpone our execution at the very least and that'll give us a chance to escape. I know you have something cooking. What is it?"

I'm not telling. I don't want to escape, Jillybean replied.

"Not even to save those thirty-two women?" Eve asked. "For real I mean. You could do it, I know." A second before, Jillybean had been resolute in her desire to die, now she wavered. Eve pounced: "Think about it. If you save them and save the valley, your slate will be clean. You'll be one of the good guys again. People will love you and they'll say: thank God we had Jillybean to save us."

Pictures flashed in her head: cheering crowds, people waving and smiling, a parade with jugglers and acrobats going down Main Street with her sitting in the back of a convertible pink Cadillac with the top down.

She shrugged the picture away. *Those are lies. They'll never let a crazy person go free.*

"You never know. If you let me in on the secret, I can practically guarantee we'll go free."

And how many people will you kill to guarantee our freedom? I won't let...

The front door of the clinic came open with its usual squeak and Jillybean could feel a draft of night air come in from under the door. There were soft voices speaking and then the tread of boots in the hall. Someone said: "Good morning," in what was a whisper.

Eve was suddenly so afraid that she wanted to hide beneath her blankets; Jillybean was filled with such guilt that she didn't fight it. They hid, remaining perfectly still as the light was flicked on. Through the sheet they saw the silhouettes of two people; they looked like demons to Jillybean, coming to collect her soul.

"Jillybean, it's almost time." It was Neil Martin, speaking in a soothing tone. "We have breakfast. I made you French toast. I know it was your fa-favorite." He sniffled back tears and so did the person beside him, whom Jillybean knew was Sadie by the way she held her slim form.

Although Jillybean wanted to cry, Eve was immediately suspicious. "Why would you make me food if you're only going to kill me afterwards?"

"I don't know," Neil answered. "Tradition, I guess...maybe because it's a nice gesture."

"I get it. It's because you feel guilty," Eve said. She flung the sheet from her head and stared angrily at the food for a moment before she softened her features and held out her unchained hand. "I mean, thanks."

Neil brought her the tray and then stood back as she began to eat, greedily. "You know Jillybean could save you guys," she said around a mouthful. "She has a plan, a good one, too, only she won't tell me what it is. She thinks I'll be bad or something."

Sadie's eyes narrowed, however Neil practically leapt forward. "What's the plan?" he asked, eagerly.

"Like I said, I don't know. She knows it but she won't tell me." Eve said this conversationally as if it was only an interesting subject to discuss over breakfast.

"Will she tell us?" Sadie asked. Eve grinned but didn't answer. She stuffed a slab of French toast in her mouth and chewed happily. Sadie grunted before saying: "She'll tell us but you won't let her, is that it?" Eve nodded and cut off another mouthful. Neil looked confused and so Sadie explained: "She won't let Jillybean tell us as long as we're going to kill her."

"Yep," Eve said. "Hey, do you guys have any juice or anything? This is real good French toast, Mister Neil, but it would go down easier with a drink."

Neil didn't make a move for the door. "I might be able to get you a postponement, but I can't guarantee anything else."

"Then I can't guarantee anything either," Eve stated matter-of-factly. "Like I said this is real good French Toast, by the way. Too bad Jillybean isn't getting none."

"Watch her," Neil said to Sadie and then left the room. While he was gone, Eve and Sadie only stared at each other without a word spoken.

A few minutes later, Neil came back with a wan looking Captain Grey and a sharp-eyed Deanna Russell who seemed to be looking for an excuse to stick needles in Jillybean's arm and kill her.

Grey spoke first: "Neil has explained to the panel that you have a way to stop the zombies?" Eve nodded. Grey ran a hand through his short hair, looked out the window for a span where the sky in the east was on a countdown to death.

After a sigh he began as if reading from a script: "We will release you, however we have our own stipulations. To start with, I'll have to be persuaded by *Jillybean* that this is a legitimate plan. For two, the plan will have to actually work for you to gain your freedom. Number three, you will remain a prisoner and in custody the entire time you are in the valley. Number four, you will only be released once the danger is past. Number five, you will be released at a minimum distance of five hundred miles. I will escort you in any direction you please. Any questions?"

"None."

"Good. The final stipulation is that you will not surface at any point from now until you have reached that five-hundred mile border. That means we will only have dealings with Jillybean. If it is even hinted at that you are running her body, this entire agreement will be revoked and your execution will be carried out in the most expeditious manner."

He paused to take a breath and Deanna was quick to say: "By expeditious, the captain means we will kill you on the spot by any means available...gun, knife, rope, whatever."

Her blunt words caused Neil to frown. "We will be as merciful as the situation dictates. So, do we have a deal?"

"No," the little girl stated, bluntly. "I don't agree to the final stipulation. Jillybean hates me. She might even act like me in order for you to kill us both."

"You'd deserve it," Deanna snapped, glaring at her.

Without blinking, Eve glared right back. "*She* was the one who killed your general, not me. You should hate her just as much as you hate me."

Deanna started to open her mouth to retort when Neil stepped in between them. "It's a moot point. The demands are non-negotiable and since you've disagreed, we will begin the execution now." Neil came forward with a second pair of handcuffs. The moment he did, Eve went wild kicking and scratching with her free hand, however she hadn't nearly Neil's strength. He pinned her arms down while Sadie held her feet. Deanna took the cuffs and locked the little girl to the gurney with her arms pulled wide.

She kicked as they wheeled her out of the room and only calmed when Jillybean spoke into her ear: *They're really going to kill you.* It was a cold realization for both of them and an even colder dread began to filter out of their collective soul. It froze their insides.

Seconds later, they were in one of the operating rooms. It was filled with scowling strangers. Neil spoke to the assembled group. "Jillybean has been found guilty of two counts of murder and is to be executed forthwith. Do any of you wish to change your decision concerning the penalty of death?"

"I take it she didn't accept the deal?" asked one man in an army uniform. Neil shook his head, sadly. "Then, no," the man said. "I'm not going to change my mind." Each person in turn after him, only shook their heads, solemnly.

Neil was pale as a ghost when the last woman shook her head. Listlessly, he said: "It's the decision of the court that Jillybean will die. May God have mercy on her soul." He turned to an Asian lady who held three capped needles in her hand. "Do it, Margaret before I change my mind."

The lady was slow to come forward; Eve saw this as cruel and cursed her. Jillybean knew better and saw the sadness in the lady's eyes. She didn't want to have to do this and neither did any of the people on the panel. Even in death, Jillybean realized she was hurting people. She was tired of it all and wanted her life to be over with but at the last second Eve's fear of what came next proved too great.

"Stop!" she cried, with sudden wretchedness as the first needle was uncapped and its deadly point neared her flesh. "I'll do it. I'll agree to your stipulations."

Neil grabbed Margaret's arm in a grip of steel keeping the needle from advancing. "Do you agree to all of them?" he demanded.

"I just said I would," Eve said. "Here, you can have her."

Just like that, Jillybean found herself in her own body. It felt foreign and frail and sort of rickety, like an ill-made robot at a science fair. Her hands were shaking and her chest was quivering. There were tears in her eyes and on her cheeks. "It— It's me," she said to Neil who was staring hard at her.

He wasn't so quick to believe her. "Where, specifically did we first meet?"

"Atlanta, outside the CDC. You were going to give me to the Believers in exchange for Sadie." Jillybean turned to look at her apocalypse sister. "But you wouldn't let him."

Sadie choked as tears began flowing. "I couldn't do that to my sister. Is *she* still in you? Can you feel her?"

Jillybean nodded. "She's watching me and listening."

"Can you control her?" Grey asked.

Now, Jillybean shook her head. Eve had become too strong for her to control and she knew the reason but wouldn't admit it. Before it was her fear that brought Eve about; now, it was her guilt and her shame. These couldn't be fought or overcome as the fear had been. Guilt and shame were poisons rotting her strength, tearing her down, making her weak in the mind.

"I killed the general," she admitted in a tiny voice like a mouse's. "I thought I was saving the sex slave women but I know now that I wasn't. They'll never be saved. They'll never be free."

Captain Grey stepped forward; he was covered in bandages —she was sure that she had something to do with them and she tried to turn away. He stopped her with a gentle hand. "Let's not worry about that right now. That's the past and nothing can be done to change it. It's better if we deal with what we have before us. Let's hear your plan."

Doubt suddenly flooded her chest. "I don't know if I have one. I was close to thinking of one but then the general died and Eve took over and...I sort of forgot all about it."

The assembled adults glared at her and she knew that they were feeling tricked. Inside her, Eve grew perilously large, threatening like the demon she was; she hissed: *You had better think of something quick or your good buddy, Mister Neil will kill you.*

Thinking up a plan was impossible right then. With the fury of the adults emanating through the air, and Eve's monstrous presence, and the killing needles just feet away, looking sharp and oh, so deadly, and with her own guilt overshadowing everything, Jillybean couldn't think of a single thing.

Neil was the only one who hadn't glared. He stayed perfectly calm. "How about this? Let's return to the hotel. We'll go up to the cupola and see if the view and the map jog your memory. We'll go, just the two of us, oh, and Sadie, too."

He wanted her to go to the scene of her most heinous crime? How was that going to help? She was sure her guilt would over-shadow everything. "Yes, we can do that, but just us two, Mister Neil, please. I don't want Sadie to see where the bad stuff happened."

The glares and the hateful suspicion grew in the adults. They thought she was planning some sort of escape. "No," Captain Grey told her. "You'll not go alone with Neil. I will go as well and I will evaluate any plan." Even injured as he was, Grey was a deadly man and no one second guessed him and so, five minutes later, the three of them were treading slowly up the dead-quiet stairs of the hotel.

Grey moved at snail's pace. He was going so slowly that Neil looked over Jillybean's head with a questioning look. Grey said nothing though a message passed between the two men. Jillybean knew because of the way Neil tried to pretend that he didn't read anything in Grey's expression.

They're trying to give you time to think of something, Eve said. *So get thinking!*

That was a relief. Jillybean's first thought was that they were going to throw her off the roof when they got to the top and she was unable to spit out a plan in two minutes. Dying from the morphine sounded much better.

In spite of the slow speed, they eventually passed the point where General Johnston had died and made it out onto the cupola, a small dome-covered open room at the very tallest point of the roof. The view was fantastic. In the east, the sun was just broaching the horizon, casting the entire valley in a topaz hue while in the west the world was still dark, more shadow than shape.

They'll go west if I can't think of anything, Jillybean thought. She saw their fate clearly: They'd go west, into the shadows of unknown where nothing grew but scraggly pine and thin mountain grass. With their livestock slowing them down, they would be chased from place to place by the surging zombies and if they ever came to a spot where the road was destroyed by a landslide or a flood, they'd die.

"What do you think, Jillybean?" Neil asked, holding out the map of the valley.

"I think that's the prettiest sunrise I've ever seen," she answered, turning from the dark part of the world. She had no plan and couldn't remember what she had been thinking two days before when she had led Neil and the general up there.

Figuring that this was going to be her last sunrise, Jillybean made the most of it. She hooked a naked foot on the railing and leaned out, watching the light gradually eat up the darkness. It progressed in a slow fashion and Jillybean couldn't help but see that this was exactly how the zombies were going to sweep over everything: from east to west, straight across the mountains and beyond to that unknown land.

Just like the light, there was no stopping them...and did it even make sense to try? Of course not.

"That's better," she said, as the plan evolved right before her eyes.

Chapter 32
Neil Martin

After hearing the bare outlines of Jillybean's plan, Neil settled in next to her and looked out over the valley. The sunrise was beautiful but he didn't see it; his eyes were unfocused and his mind was busy filling in the details that would make her plan a success.

It really didn't take much. The plan was simplicity itself. "I can't believe I didn't think of this a long time ago."

Captain Grey came to lean on the railing on the other side of Jillybean. "Don't beat yourself up," he said. "What she's suggesting is completely counterintuitive."

"For you maybe," Neil replied. "You're a soldier, I'm not. It's a little embarrassing that I couldn't see the forest for the trees." *And it's more than a bit frustrating that I have to keep relying on a seven-year-old*, he said to himself. Aloud he added to Jillybean: "I just wish you had come sooner and under better circumstances."

The little girl hung her head and refused to look up or say anything. Awkwardly, Neil rubbed her back. "Don't blame yourself. This is my fault. I should have never let you go back to the Azael...and I should have relied more on my own wits and I should..."

"Stop it, Neil," Grey said. "Like I told Jillybean, that's in the past. Look to the future and be thankful that we have one and be thankful that Jillybean has one as well. The plan is good. We should go tell the others and get working, there's a thousand things to do."

At a much quicker pace, the three went back to the clinic, where they found the judiciary panel seated outside, waiting. Sadie looked fearful and then when Neil gave her a smile and a nod, she broke down crying, turning away. Most of the panel didn't understand that the tears were tears of joy and grew grim until Grey explained how they were going to save themselves.

"That may take care of the zombies," a woman named Teresa said, "But what about the Azael themselves. They still outnumber us three to one and the little girl's plan leaves us even more vulnerable than before."

A few of the others agreed. Jillybean, looking puzzled, said: "It doesn't leave you vulnerable. I know that's what means unsafe. All you have to do is...wait...if I tell you this part of the plan, too, can I get more of them French toasts? Eve ate it all and I didn't get to have any."

"You don't have to explain anymore," Neil answered. "The follow-up aspects of the plan are fairly obvious. I think we got it from here. And yes, I'll make more French toast for you." Actually Neil had the same fears as Theresa but he vowed he would figure things out on his own...either that, or he would see what Captain Grey was thinking on the subject. The soldier had been very quiet on the way back; it was obvious that he was musing over the plan and its details.

"Maybe you shouldn't be making *her* another meal," Theresa said, looking down her nose at Jillybean. "Plan or not, she is a killer."

Neil bristled: "I will make French Toast for anyone I please. Your job is done, Theresa. The panel has fulfilled its purpose. Justice, as unanimously voted upon, has been rendered. Everyone report to your supervisors and prepare for a very long day and an even longer night."

The panel broke up until only Grey, Deanna, Sadie and Jillybean were left behind. "Jillybean still needs to be locked up," Deanna said. "I'm glad that you are cooperating but we all know the danger."

"I'll do it," Sadie said. "And I'll make her another breakfast. I know you're going to be busy, Neil."

Busy was an understatement. First came a long meeting in which all of the army officers and all the civilian supervisors were present, sitting on fancy white-backed chairs in the ballroom of the Stanley Hotel. Just like the judiciary panel they were cautiously optimistic when Neil explained the first part of the plan; however, they cheered when Captain Grey explained the second part.

Only one man didn't: Fred Trigg. "To go back to the earlier part, you're making it sound like it will be a piece of cake but you're talking about constructing, like a four-mile wall. That's impossible."

"Actually, it's closer to nine miles," Neil said, "And no, it's not impossible, just very difficult. The good news is that some of the walls are naturally occurring. Where the hills are steep enough we'll count those as walls. Now, I don't want to hear the word impossible again and I don't want to hear how something can't be done, I want to know how it can be done."

"May I interject?" Deanna asked. "I'm not being unrealistic or pessimistic, I just want to state a fact. Building these new walls will, by necessity, take away from our efforts at building the walls across the highways. You can't do both at once since they use the same man power and materials."

"How long will the current walls hold?" Neil asked.

Deanna shrugged and it was an army major who answered: "Thirty-six to forty-eight hours, give or take. With the bonfires going at night it takes the pressure off, however it sounds like you want to reassign the wood crews. If that's the case, then I'd say twenty-four hours."

Neil smiled despite feeling the sweat building up in his armpits. His choices were impossible: maintain a slowly eroding defense that had been sapping the strength and life from his men, knowing that the end result would be a coordinated retreat to a destination that was still unknown, or he could risk it all on a *chance* at victory.

"Then we had better work like fiends in the next twenty-four hours," Neil said, making the split second decision to hang their fate on Jillybean's plan. "From this moment on, there will be no breaks. We will not sleep and we will not rest until the walls are complete. I want the night crews woken and if I see a single man sitting on his ass or taking a smoke break, he will be arrested."

He then began assigning duties. Most were the same: "Take your team and find me cars. I need at least two thousand of them." When he said it like that, it did indeed sound impossible, still he kept a confident smile on his face until he came to Deanna. "Get about a dozen of your most trusted people," he said in a whisper. "I need to know exactly how many linear feet of wall we need."

In other words, he needed to know how screwed they were.

He would have to wait five hours for the exact length to be compiled. The walls were going to be very long since both I-34 and I-36 had to be lined with walls of one sort or another. Cars were the obvious choice to use as a medium. They were more or less portable in that they could be pushed, towed or fed enough gas to be jumped and driven on flats to where the *flipping crew*, a group of twelve men, waited to dump the remaining gas before they worked the car into position and then heaved it, by muscle alone, onto its side.

Each car was an individual link in the wall.

Neil tried to be everywhere and tried to oversee everything which of course was impossible since the walls were being built along two separate highways. Deanna caught up with him just after 2p.m. Her look was so intentionally neutral that Neil was afraid to ask.

"It's longer than we thought," she said as soon as she was close enough to whisper. "We have six miles to cover and if we average cars at eleven feet long, we'll need about three thousand of them." Neil choked and his heart skipped in his chest. "Yeah, that was my feeling as well," she murmured. As he struggled to grasp the number, she went on: "In light of that, I sent my team to make a survey of the number of cars available in the valley and the surrounding towns."

His mind was whirling and the number three thousand ran in circles. That was just too many cars. He figured that they had already used over a thousand on all the different Red and Blue walls. There couldn't be that many more left, certainly not three thousand. "Recall your team," Neil said. "I can tell you already we don't have enough. What we need are ideas."

The two stood there for a minute in silence both pondering options. Finally, Deanna shrugged. "We can look at pulling up some fencing. There were some rolls of it at the Department of Transportation."

Five miles worth? Neil wondered, not bloody likely. He kept his skepticism hidden. "Good, start there, but don't end there. We need out of the box thinking. Talk to your crew. Brainstorm and report back to me as soon as possible. Oh, and include Grey in this. He was hobbling around earlier trying to help, but only getting in the way."

"He was out of bed!" She turned on her heel and stalked away in a fury.

"Don't forget the wall," he said. She didn't turn, she just waved a hand. Neil watched her hurry off to the hospital and silently wished Captain Grey good luck. He then went back to the Stanley Hotel. The place was morgue quiet and a little unsettling being so deserted. Neil had sent all of his staff, except one radio operator, off to work like everyone else. The sound of his footsteps echoed and he took more care to walk softly as he made his way to his office and stared at his useless desk.

After a few seconds, he tiptoed to the map room where he traced the outlines of the two highways as they merged in the center of Estes. He whispered: "Three thousand cars." They would never find half as many. He then went to the cupola and looked out at the valley, hoping an idea would come to him as it had Jillybean. The afternoon faded around him and yes, it was true that he was ignoring his own dictate about working continuously, however he hadn't really been helping. He had been out there just so that he could be seen "working," for the sake of appearances.

At six, when the sun was hanging pendulously over the mountains and sinking fast, Deanna found him. "I knew you'd be up here," she said. "When you weren't with Jillybean, this was the first place I looked."

"And?"

A pained expression washed over her face. "Our wall is going to come up short...alot short."

Neil grew irate. "How short?" he snapped.

"Two miles, maybe more. Fences aren't big in Estes; most people use those split wood fences, you know, those log deals?" He knew what she was talking about: a single log held up at either end by two smaller crisscrossing logs which were embedded in the earth. They wouldn't stop even a single zombie.

"Did anyone come up with any better ideas?"

She sort of half nodded and half shook her head. "Kinda. We're going to use barbed wire. There's tons of it when you get out of town a little ways."

"But...." He read the "but" easily in her eyes.

"But, it's all old and rusty and snaps easily if you apply too much pressure, which means we will need more than three strands per fence." She wasn't done with the bad news, that much was obvious, and so he gestured for her to keep going. "Yeah, ok we also have a post problem. We can't string the barbed wire on nothing so posts will have to be dug and, if we have any hope of them staying in place they'll also have to be cemented in place."

Neil felt panic coming on. "Cemented! It'll never dry in time. And do we even have that much cement?" She shook her head. "What about trees? We can run the barbed wire around trees."

"We've already thought about that. Even using trees, we still came up with the two mile figure. The bottom line: we won't be finished when Blue Gate 6 falls. I was just out there. The wall is half-stacked with zombies already. It'll be a miracle if it lasts until morning."

"And Red Gate 4?" Neil asked.

"Because of the steep slope we built it on, it's holding steady. And so are the smaller overflow areas. For reasons we don't know, these have been trickles compared to the last week." She paused and a pained expression swept her. "Neil, we have to abandon this idea. It's not going to work."

Abandoning the plan really wasn't an option anymore. The valley had been scoured for cars and trucks and busses and even mobile homes. There had been hundreds left, not thousands, which meant their ability to build ever more walls across the highways was very limited, which meant they were doomed one way or the other.

Neil turned from Deanna and ran for the stairs. "I've got to talk to Jillybean," he cried.

It was not far to the clinic where the little girl was being held prisoner and yet he was completely out of breath by the time he arrived. It wasn't just the altitude or the fact he rarely did much in the way of exercise; it was also the panic over the idea that he had just screwed every person in the valley.

Because of the emergency they were in, Margaret Yuan had lost her C.N.A. and it was a white bandaged Captain Grey who sat at the front desk. He looked sour at having to be cooped up and as Neil fought for air, the soldier gave him a hard look and accused: "You told on me, and now Deanna is having people checking on me every five minutes."

"It was...for...your own good," Neil replied, gulping air. "Is Jillybean still here?"

"Where else would she be?" Grey asked. "I check on her every ten minutes, she's not going to escape if that's what you're thinking."

Even though Neil had personally checked every weld on the gurney, he didn't put it past her. "Just checking. I need her help; the wall isn't progressing as well as I had hoped."

Grey grunted out a mopish: "Yeah, I heard. I've been racking my brains but every item that might work requires time we don't have or other materials that are more scarce than cars."

"Yeah. Well, wish us luck," Neil said and then superstitiously rapped his knuckles three times on the fake wood paneling. He left the captain and proceeded down the hall passed two rooms occupied by people who had been injured that day: one had a car fall on him and wasn't expected to make it, and the other had his leg torn open falling off Red Gate 4.

Neil nodded to the man with the leg wound and then went to the next room down. Other than Captain Grey watching from the front desk, it was unguarded. Still there were precautions: the handcuffs, the windows nailed shut, and the alarm built in on the only other exit from the building.

Regardless, Neil looked in on Jillybean, half-expecting her to be long gone. She was still there, looking even more mopish than Captain Grey. And she looked pitifully lonely. "How are you doing?" Neil asked from the doorway.

"K," she answered with a little shrug.

"Good...that's good. Hey, uh, Jillybean? I have a question."

She displayed no surprise at all. "What part of the plan are you stuck on?"

"The wall. We don't have near enough materials."

She nodded as if she had expected exactly this. "Do you remember the lights at New Eden?"

Neil closed his eyes for a full five seconds, remembering the lights and cursing himself for not having thought of them himself. "So easy," he said. "So darned easy. Thanks, Jillybean. I'm sorry that I can't stay but…" He really had to go; however, the little girl with the fly away hair looked so pathetic that he hesitated.

"You shouldn't stay," Jillybean said. "The sun will be down soon and the lights only work at night."

"I'll be back," Neil promised and then ran out of the room. As he ran by Grey, he said: "Remember the lights at New Eden?"

Grey answered: "Son of a bitch!"

Neil grinned as he ran out into the evening. Once again, the depot at the Department of Transportation was going to come in handy. They had hundreds of cones with blinking lights.

For the next five hours, Neil put the finishing touches on walls that were so altogether flimsy that in spots they consisted of little more than beams of light.

By eleven that night, the walls were finished and the lights strung. The people were sent into hiding and the soldiers were re-dressed and drilled on their roles in the coming fight. And in all this, Neil didn't forget his promise to Jillybean.

Thirty minutes before the first detonation was scheduled, he slipped away, driving his Humvee into the deserted main part of the town. Many of the shops were still intact—they were filled with touristy knickknacks and thus of little value to anyone in an apocalypse.

He was sure he would find what he was looking for and in the second shop he visited, he found the doll. It was a foot and a half tall with porcelain blue eyes and perfectly styled hair. Its dress was white and flowing and the shoes on its feet were glass. The doll was perfect and he hoped to God it would work. He had an idea of his own that couldn't be spoken aloud, that couldn't even be hinted at.

He brought Jillybean the doll and presented it to her, saying, "This may be the most beautiful doll left in America."

She stared at it in amazement and then began to slowly nod in agreement. "It is. Thanks, Mister Neil, it's very nice. It's… wait, take it back, I don't deserve it."

"No," Neil said, sternly. "You do deserve this. Besides, it's a gift. You can't deny a gift. Just don't let *her* have it. *She* doesn't deserve it."

"I can't control her," she answered, tears growing in her eyes.

"Try," Neil said. "This is for you only." When the little girl nodded, Neil left and for the first time in a week he smiled a genuine smile. Jillybean wasn't the only person who could scheme.

Chapter 33

Captain Grey

At eleven sharp, the power plant feeding electricity to the valley was shut down, the civilians were safely hidden and the soldiers were scattered across the valley in strategic locations. They were dressed in rags and their weapons were stowed in the tall grass or set, ready to go, behind rocks or trees.

Neil gave the word. "Go," he said, simply and, moments later all of the remaining explosives in their arsenal went off in a muffled chain of thumping bangs. There was some light and fire, a few sparks and some smoke that couldn't be seen in the dark; the explosions were dull and that was planned. They were supposed to be as understated as possible. There was no need to arouse suspicion that a trap had just been sprung, after all.

Grey smiled. "Congratulations," he said to Neil. The two shook hands as a tremendous flood of zombies swept over the remains of the walls. They were positioned on a hill a quarter mile from the now ruined Red Gate 4. With them were Sadie who would never leave Neil's side when there was a fight brewing, and Deanna Russell who was equally fierce when it came to protecting Captain Grey.

Michael Gates was also on the hill; he was quiet with simmering anger, hoping to see that his wife's sacrifice had been worth it. The three battalion commanders were also there along with their radio operators. The commanders were the most pensive. They didn't know Jillybean or her ability to plan and destroy.

The three colonels took their orders directly from Neil who had yet to appoint a successor to General Johnston, something that had caused no small amount of consternation among them, which Grey fully understood. No military man really wanted to take orders from a civilian.

It galled them and yet they spent an inordinate time casting glances Neil's way, wondering if he was seeing them doing their jobs in a professional manner. They each coveted the spot as commanding officer of the valley.

The only person who wasn't there and who really belonged was Jillybean. Yes, she was a murderer but she was a hapless one who was victim of her own soft heart and the terrible pressures that had been exerted on her by both friend and foe alike. Grey had agreed with her death sentence, though he'd had to drag himself to the decision.

He had viewed her as collateral damage. She had been caught in the crossfire of her own mind. It was unfortunate and heartbreaking but the death of innocents occurred in every war.

"Oh, jeeze," Sadie said. "Here they come."

The zombies, finally unleashed, were pouring over the tremendous mound of dead by the thousands; it was a terrifying flood and yet, because of the dark they were heard rather than seen. Grey, who had been temporarily relieved of his command due to his injuries, put a rifle to his shoulder and his eye to the Starlight scope. The beasts suddenly sprang into "focus." They were a light green mass of crooked arms and seemingly bald heads against a much darker background.

"They're over the wall," he said. Now came the moment of truth. They had no way of really knowing what the zombies would do when they were set free after a week of fighting to get into the valley.

The hill was silent, waiting on Grey to update them. The lead zombies didn't follow the course set for them, nor did they deviate from it, exactly. They stood staring around, wondering why there weren't people around to eat. They had expected some sort of treat for all their hard work, but there was nothing. The walls across the highway had been deserted and all that greeted them was a canyon— natural mountain walls on one side and on the other there was a row of cars that had been heaved onto their sides —nowhere was there food.

The lead zombies stood there in confusion and, seconds later, they were trampled by those coming from behind. Pressed onward from the rear, the horde mindlessly followed the highway. Miles back, the Azael on their horses were pushing them on; unwittingly helping their enemies.

"It's working," Grey said, when there was no doubt.

There had been a great fear that the zombies would test the flimsy walls of cars running along the highway; these couldn't stand up to any serious test, however the zombies came on stupid as always, following the path of least resistance.

"Let me see," Neil said, holding his hands out for the rifle. He looked down the scope for a few minutes before a grin broke out on his face. "Just in case, let's deploy the pace car."

One of the colonels spoke into a radio and a jeep flicked on its lights and revved its engine. As expected, the zombie hoard picked up speed and charged at it. The driver of the jeep waited until they were twenty feet away and only then did he drive forward keeping just ahead of the flood.

"The plan is a success," Neil declared.

"It's a little too early to say that," Grey said. "Not one of the walls has been tested and they haven't reached the lights yet." The question was; would they follow the lights and the jeep or would they stray, flooding the valley at the worst possible time?

They waited for what felt like an agonizing amount of time before the first check point on the road called in: "Pelican 1 is green, say again, Pelican 1 is green." There were sighs from everyone on the hill. Pelican1 was the call sign of the watcher above highway 36. She was the first of eight spotters lined along the highway. Green meant that the surge of zombies was moving along the road and not attempting to scale the walls or push them over.

A minute later: "Taco 1 is in the green. Repeat: Taco 1 is in the green."

An hour went by before the slow moving zombies had progressed to "Pelican Point" which was where the wall of overturned cars ran out and there was no longer anything keeping the zombies from simply walking off the road except a long row of lights on timers.

The lights, spaced fifty yards apart, flickered every thirty seconds, each set at one second intervals so that light looked to be zipping up the highway. This same set up had insulated New Eden—the zombies had been mesmerized by the lights and went round and round the compound chasing them in an infinite loop. This was the same idea except Neil was trying to send the zombies straight through their town and out the other side and into the mountains beyond.

Where they went after that was going to have to be someone else's problem.

Grey had chosen Veronica to sit atop the hill overlooking Pelican Point. He trusted her judgment. "This is Pelican Point, we are green! Say again, this is Pelican Point, we are green!" In her excitement, she was almost shouting into the radio.

Neil thumbed his mike as soon as she finished. "Pelican Point, this is Noodle. We are reading you five by five. In fact, it may be ten by ten so you may want to keep it down. Is the pace car out of sight?"

Veronica was much quieter as she answered: "I waited to radio you until they were, just like you asked."

"Thanks," Neil replied and then looked around at the figures sitting around him. They were mere squatting lumps, shrouded by the dark. "Now I can say it: the plan worked!" Jillybean's plan had been the very definition of simplicity: *You can't win by fighting,* she had said, *so your first step is to stop fighting. Treat the monsters like a river, control them, direct them, give them something to chase and send them on over the mountains.*

One of the colonels said: "I can't believe it."

"Why not? It's simply a judo move," Grey said, "using your enemy's strength against him. I just wish one of us would have thought of it sooner."

"Are we sure we want to let the little girl go?" the same colonel asked. "For one, this girl is clearly troubled and for two, she would be a valuable asset."

At the term "asset," Neil ground his teeth. "She is not an 'asset,' she's a little girl who needs to get away from situations like this for her own good. Besides, she is more dangerous than you know. She will get away sooner or later, that is a guarantee and when she does, you'll see that the poisoning of one man was just the beginning."

This shut the colonel up and no one spoke for a long time. They took turns looking through Grey's Starlight scope as the masses of zombies moaned down the highway, pushed from behind by the eager Azael and drawn forward by the Jeep and the miles of blinking lights.

They received periodic reports as the night drew on, most of which were simple statements: *They're still going* or *Taco 3 is still green*. Only one held trouble: "This is Taco 6 we have a leak."

"How bad?" Neil asked. Grey could hear him trying not to let his anxiety come out in his voice—he was failing.

"Not bad," came the reply. "An old Cadillac fell over. It's still partially blocking things but we are getting leakers. It's too dark to see how many, however."

Silence again on the hilltop. This was one of their greatest fears. The Azael would follow quick on the footsteps of the zombies and it was going to be a tough enough fight without having zombies roaming the valley.

"What do we do?" Neil asked.

"We don't do anything," Grey answered, "At least not yet. The valley has to remain completely quiet and dead for as long as possible. Any screams or gunshots will have the entire zombie army turning around."

Doing nothing was nearly impossible for the others: they tapped their toes, or paced or checked their weapons, repeatedly. It was easy for Grey. He was tired and stiff from the night air. His many wounds ached and so he popped painkillers that he knew would make him drowsy. Sleeping was a fine idea. There would be nothing to do while the zombies tromped by beneath their hill by the hundreds of thousands and it would take hours before they had all passed safely through.

Grey zipped his coat tight, leaned into Deanna and was soon asleep as only a soldier could. At dawn, he woke to see only Neil and Sadie keeping watch; everyone else had nodded off at some point during the long night and were fast asleep. Grey stood and stretched as best as he was able to with sixty stitches in various parts of his body and then rubbed himself, working the night cold out of his bones.

When he had his blood flowing, he went to the lip of the hill where he found that the binoculars he had brought with him weren't needed. The zombies were still pouring over the remains of the walls and were still marching on into the valley and through the town. The entire mess of them seemed very close. In daylight it was a sight that made even a veteran like Grey shiver.

"It's not going to be long," Neil told him. "Sadie and I heard the sound of hooves clocking on cement a few minutes ago. Should I cue our horsemen?" Eighteen volunteers who were experienced in handling horses had been specifically outfitted in 'Angel' costumes; they and the only horses the valley possessed were hidden in the forest just off the road, ready to keep driving the zombies on when the Azael broke away.

It was just a guess but Grey figured that the Azael wouldn't rush into the valley right after the zombies came through. "They're cowards. They will let the zombies do their dirty work for them," Grey had said to the volunteers. "Your job is to get those stiffs as far into the mountains as possible."

"Not yet," Grey said to Neil. "There's still too many of them...wait. I was wrong, look!" He pointed down the road where a single glint of metal shone. It was the horsemen of the Azael pushing the last of the zombies forward. The horsemen stopped just shy of the tremendous mound of dead that sat in front of the remains of Red Gate 1.

The mound, comprised of rotting corpses, was too treacherous for their horses and so, after gazing down at the series of destroyed walls and the tens of thousands of dead and mostly dead zombies littering the roadway for what looked like miles, they turned their horses around and disappeared on the other side of the hill.

"Now cue the horsemen," Grey commanded. With three ranking men standing right there, it really wasn't his place, yet no one even blinked and the order was given. Far down below them, the horsemen split into two groups, one heading to the last of the Red Gates and the other half to the Blue.

The group on the hill had a good view of the horsemen at the Red Gate. Even from a distance, they looked pathetic compared to the Azael. Their "wings" were made of cardboard that had been wrapped in aluminum foil and their "Armor" was nothing more than more foil banded around their arms and legs. The group made a ragged line and took over the process of driving the zombies before them.

"Now for the hard part," Grey said. He took the radio from Neil and spoke into it: "All teams make ready. Maintain Emcon blackout and don't shoot until you see the whites of their eyes. Good luck and God bless."

Now, there was movement in the valley. Men came out of hiding. Most walked for a few hundred feet in strange directions and then pitched onto the ground. From above, with their shredded clothes and mudded faces, they looked like dead zombies scattered everywhere—it was what the Azael were expecting to see.

Other groups weren't nearly so visible. The hills along both roads were studded with men, dug in and camouflaged, only waiting on the word to unleash a much-needed vengeance. They waited well over an hour for their chance. An Azael truck crested the far hill. It was a five-ton, bristling with men and guns.

"We got bogeys at Red," Grey said into the radio. "Anything at Blue?"

A one word reply came: "Negative."

"Looks like Jillybean was right about this, too," Grey said. "This is where the fight's going to be."

No one said anything to that, they were watching as the truck took on the great mound of corpses. With all wheels turning, it plowed into the mound and promptly got stuck as it became embed up to its axles in the muck of flesh and blood. A second truck tried with equally disastrous results. The rest pulled over and their men piled out, but they did not advance.

"What are they waiting for?" Deanna asked. She was nervous, frequently wiping her hands on her camouflage pants. Like all raw recruits, she clearly wanted the fighting to start, perhaps afraid that her courage would fail her.

"I hope they're not waiting for the Strykers," Grey said. Everyone had agreed that it was likely that men on foot would precede the vehicles and thus the one anti-tank crew was stationed closer to the front of the valley, hoping to knock out the vehicles after the men were engaged.

But that wasn't the case. A Stryker appeared next. It paused with its sharp angled nose pointing downward; it gunned its engine and went at the mound with its eight wheels digging in and churning. With ease, it went right up the mound and then it went at the next ugly hill without slowing.

"Do I give the order to fire?" Neil asked in a wavering voice; it was clear that he knew in his gut that it was too soon, however one of the Strykers was right beneath the single anti-tank crew—they wouldn't get a better chance to destroy it than this. One colonel nodded, another shook his head, tentatively and the third was studying his map as if it contained the answer; after a moment he slowly nodded, but it was far from convincing. Neil turned to Grey: "Do I do it?"

"No," Grey answered without hesitation. To shoot too soon would turn the fight into a slugging match. He was certain that his men would give the Azael a sharp whipping; however he also guessed that the Azael would be able to retire in good order; they would live to fight another day, perhaps a day in the near future and perhaps they would come back with stronger weapons and better tactics.

However, by holding their fire and allowing the Strykers access to the valley it would give the main host of their enemies precious minutes to march themselves into the trap that had been set for them. They would walk into a *kill zone* and it was unlikely many would walk back out again. Of course, having the Strykers able to roam at will would put the defenseless soldiers lying in the fields at the entrance to the valley in grave danger. Their casualties would be horrific.

Neil stared at the Stryker, his hand holding the radio shaking. He watched as it bypassed the hill they were on and seconds later it rumbled out of range of the carefully emplaced anti-tank missile crew. They were now committed to a costly battle.

The next Stryker came on in an equally simple manner and behind it came thousands of the Azael on foot. They were dressed in their swirl of scarves that made it seem as though a strange, morbidly happy parade was marching over the remains of the undead. There were thousands of them coming on, rank after rank. They walked with mincing steps and many tripped over the uneven ground. Up and down the hills they came, but Grey had already turned from them.

He had to get to the Strykers.

"Where do you think you're going?" Deanna demanded in a hiss.

"Where I'm needed," he answered. "Here, use this." He handed her the scoped rifle; she shoved it back at him.

"You're not going anywhere," she seethed. "If you're not well enough to lead your company, then you're not well enough to fight!"

Neil took her arm and pulled her back. "I'm afraid you've fallen in love with the wrong man. This is who he is. Don't interfere. Don't come between a man and his destiny."

She glared at Neil as if looking at a cockroach. "You'd sacrifice your best friend, wouldn't you?"

"Yes," Neil answered without hesitation. "I'd sacrifice him, you, me and everyone on this hill to free us from this menace. Your choice, Deanna is to let him go or take the rifle and go with him and guard his back."

"Neil!" Grey growled. "Shut your mouth."

Neil didn't blink. "Go with him, Deanna and take Michael. Stop those Strykers. It's your one mission." He paused and then glanced at Sadie. "I want you to go as well. I'll be safe here."

Sadie stepped forward, her thin face set in rocklike courage. Deanna looked like she was going to spit out something angry however at the last moment she pursed her lips tight and said nothing. Michael only shrugged and shouldered his rifle. Grey ground his teeth and glared fiercely, but he knew he couldn't disobey a direct order, nor did he have time to argue. The Strykers had paused just on the verge of the valley, perhaps waiting for their infantry to catch up, but they wouldn't wait too much longer.

Grey led the way, trying his best to ignore the pain and the awful thump of his pulse in his left bicep—he could almost hear his own heart tearing out the stitches keeping his artery held together. There was a quarter of a mile between them and the Humvee that was safely hidden on the far side of the long, rocky hill. He began jogging at his best pace.

Very soon he was winded and his strength began to flag.

As Sadie had run ahead, Deanna took the long rifle from him while Michael, who was a buffalo of a man, came up under his right arm and practically carried Grey along. Still, with the steepness of the hill, it was slow going. They had just caught sight of the Humvees nestled in the woods when there came a smattering of gunshots which was returned with fantastic vigor as if all five thousand of the Azael had opened up at once.

"No!" Grey cried. Someone had fired too early and now the soldiers were in deep trouble. Not only were the Strykers loose in the valley with nothing to stop them, the trap that had been set up had been sprung too soon— the army of the Azael had yet to fully enter the kill zone.

Ignoring the pain and his spinning head, Grey raced to the closest Humvee. He could hear Neil screaming over the radio: "Everyone fire for God's sake!"

303

Chapter 34
Jillybean

At eleven, the power was cut as she knew it would be; Neil
would never take a chance that someone might accidentally flick
on a light switch at a crucial moment. This was what Jillybean
was waiting for in order to begin her plan of escape but she
didn't jump up right away. Instead she lay there for a few
moments, sighing deeply.

She was leaving and even if she somehow managed to not
die, she would be alone without her friends. They'd become only
memories to her, just like Ipes was a memory and her daddy an
even more distant one. Right then, she missed them both terribly,
especially the zebra. When he had left, he had taken a part of her
with him. He had taken the part of her which knew what it meant
to be happy—she hadn't had a real laugh since he left.

"Doctor Mrs. Yuan?" she called out, not wanting to dwell on
that any longer.

Margaret was there in a second. "Don't be afraid, dear. The
power will be back on in the morning."

"I'm not afraid. It's been dark plenty since the monsters
came. I just gotta go baffroom before bed."

As always, Margaret broke protocol and uncuffed Jillybean
and escorted her to the toilet. She was still careful, however,
keeping a beam of light on her at all times. The little girl did her
business, making a point of yawning heavily. Margaret then
walked her back to her room where she cuffed Jillybean to the
metal frame.

"Goodnight and sweet dreams," Margaret said and shut the
door. Jillybean knew that she wouldn't come back to check on
her; Margaret didn't really understand about her at all.

The second she had left, Jillybean, who was wearing only a
hospital johnny that had been cut to fit her, reached to the back
of her neck and dug through the mass of brown curls to where
she kept a paperclip tied to a strand of hair. She had known
before she had poisoned General Johnston that she was going to
be captured and searched. She had also guessed that the search
would be cursory.

In seconds, the clip was free and she began to work it into the keyhole of the handcuffs. It was then that Eve reared up inside of her. "No," Jillybean hissed. "If you want to escape, you will have to stay inside. I have a plan and you'll only screw it up."

Eve was quiet, taken aback by the force of Jillybean's wrath. She then sneered: *A plan? Who are you going to kill?*

"The king of the Azael, if I can, and maybe a lot more of them, but you have to remain inside until I'm done and only then can you come out."

Will there be a bomb? Eve asked, gleefully.

"I hope so. Now hush so I can concentrate." She really didn't need to do much concentrating, the plan was fully developed in her mind. There had been nothing else to do during the last day. She even had twenty-two separate contingency plans just in case something went wrong at any given point. One of those contingency plans included a separate way to release herself from her cuffs if she couldn't do it with the pin.

Thankfully, they snapped open with ease. The clip went back in her hair and the cuffs she tied to her Johnny. The only other thing she took from the room was the doll that Neil had given her. She really didn't understand it as a gift...well, the doll was a doll and a pretty one and that was thoughtful, however the cryptic message that came with it—*Just don't let her have it. She doesn't deserve it*—didn't make any sense.

Eve was too strong to be denied anything. The only reason why Jillybean was still in charge was that Eve needed her mind.

Cryptic message or not, Jillybean liked the doll and wasn't going to part with it unnecessarily. She tucked it under her arm and slipped to the door. She almost didn't need to creep. The dark was so thick that she could have skipped down the hall and no one would've seen.

Still, she was careful. Her steps were light as air as she made her way to the back door where the sign that read: *Alarm Will Sound!* was barely readable at five inches. Without electricity, the alarm of course did not sound, though she had a contingency just case it did: running.

It didn't blare and she didn't run. She made her way quickly and stealthily out the door and across the valley to the Big Thompson River and followed it until she came to the cabins where Amber D and her family rotted eternally away.

Jillybean needed shoes, even if they were too small and she needed proper clothes and she needed more of everything. Her plans and their contingencies included a need for string, tape, a kitchen knife, a lighter or matches, a backpack, needle-nose pliers, wire and something heavy that she could use as a weapon —the tire iron from the Honda parked out front would work just fine she figured, and lastly a set of keys which, unfortunately, she found in the pocket of one of the corpses.

They were wet and smelled of something vile. She took them down to the river and dunked them in the cold water until they glittered up at her defying the night.

What do you need keys for? Eve asked. *The Honda can't have any gas. Are you just stalling? I'll take over if you are.*

"They're part of the plan," Jillybean said. "And no, I won't tell you what part, so don't even ask."

She didn't find everything on her list at Amber D's little cottage. It took her a number of tries at different places but she ended up with everything she needed plus some things that were strictly luxuries such as a blanket and pillow. The frilly white dress that hung to her knees, which was the hardest item to find, was both a necessity and a luxury—luxury only because it was so cute.

The dress wasn't practical for battle and so she stowed it in the backpack. Wearing borrowed blue jeans and a white long-sleeved shirt with a Power Puff girl emblazoned on the front, she went back to the river. It was getting close to one in the morning at this point but Jillybean had plenty of time; she knew the walking speed of a zombie and she knew the distance they had to travel. She used her new found math skills to calculate a 7 a.m. end time for the march of the zombies.

Plenty of time.

She traveled up the river, just a little ghost in a world of shadows. As she neared the entrance to the valley, she started to come across little knots of soldiers hidden in ravines or in little holes in the ground like those a woodchuck might make. It was easy to avoid them since the men spoke quietly to each other. Their whispers carried further than they realized and she was able to slip around each group.

And then she was climbing the first of the hills and her breath was quick. As she crested the first, she saw down and to her right the highway she had used twice already to get to Estes. It was covered in the dead, but instead of standing around as they had been, they were pushing expectantly forward.

Jillybean smiled, briefly. The smile was pulled into a gaping "O" as she was overcome by a yawn. It was a signal to get moving again. She climbed out of the valley and came to the first ridge and looking back she had a great view—it would be from here that King Augustus would direct his battle.

He would want to be close enough to watch the progress but not close enough to be hurt.

The little girl walked all around the ridge; her eyes were now well accustomed to the night and she was able to take in every nuance of the land. It did not hold much promise of escape which was too bad, she would have liked to get away if she could.

The one contingency she couldn't plan for was her ending. Eve was unstoppable. She was quiet only because she wanted to see an explosion and she wanted the king dead. *And Menis, that slimy bastard*, Eve said. She was always listening unless Jillybean was especially guarded. *And Brad, too. He has to pay for hitting us.*

Jillybean knew that in the end, *she* would take over. It was a foregone conclusion, and that was ok with Jillybean. She was tired of living with so much pain and guilt. Eve would bury her in the blackest part of her soul and Jillybean wouldn't fight it. She would go and never come out.

"But, first things first," she whispered and then began walking along the hills that stretched seemingly forever eastward. She only went a little over a quarter of a mile, to a point overlooking the highway. The dead were still flowing, but in the morning, she figured this was where the bus, filled with the thirty-two sex slaves, would end up. They would be in the back of the line of vehicles just like always.

"Now for bed," she announced to the surrounding night and then went back further into the hills and found a little rut in the earth that had collected leaves. Wrapping herself in the blanket and then covering her entire body with the leaves she settled down to sleep and, like any veteran, was out in seconds.

Five hours later, the sun woke her though she didn't immediately jump up. Her eyes cracked and her ears perked up, hearing the clop-clop-clop of horses; the sound was going right-to-left, meaning the horses were heading east. The horsemen of the Azael had done their part; the zombies were in the valley and the army would be coming next.

Jillybean crept forward until she could see the now mostly empty road. There was a crow-picked body below her that was long dead and a little ways down was a fresher corpse, the flesh of which squirmed unpleasantly from a fever of maggots feasting away.

There were also a number of zombies crawling or scraping along. These were purposely run over by three big army trucks that snorted up the incline. The two strange looking tanks came next and after them came six Humvees. In the lead vehicle, Jillybean saw the king and two of his brothers—Eve flared up in hatred and Jillybean had to turn away to control her.

After the Humvees came the thousands of soldiers. They marched up in their silly scarf outfits. They thought that they were only going to have to deal with zombies, something Jillybean found amusing. After the soldiers came more trucks filled with all the supplies that had been needed for the siege.

Each duke had their own set of vehicles and Menis, because he was out of favor with the king, had his bringing up the end of the convoy. The only vehicle behind his was the whore-bus. It was always last, as though the Azael were embarrassed by it.

The bus stopped seventy feet down the road from where Jillybean had guessed that it would. She was just starting to shift laterally when there came a great blat from an engine. This was followed by a revving noise that echoed in the hills.

"I'd better hurry," Jillybean said to herself. She paused to pull from her backpack the three items that would free the women: handcuffs, the tire iron and the set of house keys she had taken from Amber D's mother. The cuffs went loosely around her wrists; the tire iron went down the side of her pants where it bulged, obviously if one were observant; the keys were kept hidden in her hand.

As she made her way down the hill with her backpack bouncing, she saw the mean woman who guarded the bus, step out to stare up the road. She stared in the direction where the five tons were trying their luck getting over the mound of dead before Red Gate 1. The old guard had a bent cigarette in the corner of her dry, gash of a mouth.

Her eyes widened as Jillybean came down the hill right at her, the sun glinting from the handcuffs. "Where the hell did you come from?" the woman demanded with one glance at the cuffs and a second up the hill.

"The king sent me," Jillybean lied. "But I had to use the baffroom real bad."

The woman grunted and smirked. It was obvious what she was thinking: *Idiot, you should've run away*. "Well get up there." She pointed nicotine stained fingers up at the bus.

Jillybean mounted the first step which was very high for such a little girl and, as she did, she simultaneously slid a hand out of the loose cuffs and dropped the house keys she'd been carrying in her closed fist. They *clinked* loudly and lay twinkling in the morning light, sending out brilliant silver shards. This was part one of her plan.

"What the hell!" exclaimed the guard in anger and then reacted exactly as Jillybean predicted: she bent for the keys which she undoubtedly saw as evidence of a crime. This was part two.

To overcome a full grown adult is not an easy thing to accomplish for a skinny, little seven-year-old. One must first have the element of surprise on their side. Secondly, they must be able to strike from a position that will allow the full use of their limited strength, and thirdly they must strike without even a wisp of mercy weakening their blow.

"Go ahead, Eve," Jillybean said, unleashing the monster within her. Inside the little girl there was a roar of happy excitement and a hot lust. Her arms went numb and her hands felt ghost-like, but still the tire iron slid out of her pants without a problem and went high in the air.

Eve, wearing a crazed grin, waited to strike until the guard heaved herself up, keys in hand. The woman only had time to squawk like a chicken before Eve smashed the iron into the top of her head.

"Uhgi," the woman blurted, her eyes losing their focus. Her hands fluttered like wandering ghosts in front of her bosom until Eve hit her again in exactly the same spot. This still didn't knock the woman unconscious. She fell forward, knocking Eve backwards onto the next step up. Eve was in an awkward position, and unable to use either her height advantage or really much of her strength.

She began whapping the woman on the back of the head with the tire iron using only the power in her stick-like wrist. The woman twitched, sporadically with each strike; it was more than a bit disgusting.

"Stop!" Jillybean ordered Eve. Perhaps because the subsequent attacks had been so unsatisfyingly feeble, Eve relinquished control and did so without much of a fuss. When Jillybean had her body back, she squirmed out from beneath the woman who was making a pitiful moaning sound deep in her throat. The little girl then poked through the guard's pockets, finding the keys to the bus as well as the keys to the chains that the thirty-two sex slaves wore.

"What did you do?" one of the women asked in an accusation. No one had moved or cheered Jillybean on. They were mentally whipped.

"I'm freeing you," Jillybean answered, holding up the key to their chains. Except for the continued moans from the guard, there was only stunned silence on the bus. "You're being freed whether you like it or not," Jillybean groused. She went to Kay first and was happily surprised when Kay lifted her hands.

"I thought we were losing," Kay said.

"No, we're winning, the Azael just don't know it yet." The lock clicked open and Jillybean helped the woman out of her chains. "Come on. We can't let anyone see the guard."

The guard was sitting on the steps of the bus as blood rivered out of her hair; she seemed uncertain as to where she was and even who she was. Kay put out a hand and the guard took it no questions asked and let herself be led back onto the bus where Jillybean chained her to Kay's cringing seatmate.

"What the...what the fuck?" the guard said, slurring her words.

Jillybean ignored her. She turned to Kay and pushed the bus keys into her hands. "Here, get the other ladies free but, whatever you do, don't try to leave until the explosion."

Kay had haunted eyes. They were dark like the circles beneath them and they jumped all over the place. "There's going to be an explosion?"

"I hope so." Jillybean's contingencies were falling apart. The big army deuce and a half that was carting around Duke Menis' munitions wasn't the next truck in line as it had been all week. The one in front of the bus was loaded with boxes of MREs and shiny kegs that held beer. She could only hope that the munitions truck wasn't too far ahead. It was daylight out, and she had only one way to get into the back of the truck: climbing up the rear gate…something that was sure to be challenged by anyone who saw her.

"Just keep in line with the rest until it happens," Jillybean ordered, feeling as though she was the adult. The feeling left her as she turned and had to take overly large steps to get off the bus. It made her feel small.

The line of trucks had been moving forward in little spurts as the soldiers advanced into the valley and now the bus was fifty yards back. Jillybean jogged with her backpack swinging until she was just behind the last truck. On a whim she climbed up the tailgate and peeked into the back.

Only food and beer.

"Shoot," she murmured, under her breath, and then jumped down. "Time for Plan B…or is it Plan C?"

It didn't matter. What did matter was getting to the munitions truck as fast as she could. Walking along in the shadow of the truck, she dug in her backpack, gently pushing aside the doll and finding her steak knife. It cast only a dull gleam. Still, the blade was sharp enough for what Jillybean needed. She ducked under the truck and scurried forward until she was between the twin fuel tanks. Then it was just a matter of cutting the fuel lines.

Very quickly, the engine sputtered and died.

Nervously grinning, she waited at the front of the truck until the men climbed out to investigate. They checked under the hood first and then, thankfully, one said: "We should check the back." His words came out slow and a little uncertain. Although it only took one man to "check the back," both of them walked back to look in the beer-filled bed.

Jillybean ducked out from underneath the truck just as a storm of gunshots erupted in the valley. The fight was on; she had to hurry.

Without looking back, she made her way to the next truck which contained Duke Menis' personal items, including a king-sized bed and a portable bathtub the size of a Volkswagen bug. Jillybean ducked under it. She realized that she had been lucky with the fuel lines and so she attacked the brake line this time.

Seconds later, the truck revved and started forward. As it neared the truck in front of it, there was a curse, a grinding of gears and then, as the emergency break was pulled, the entire thing shuddered to a halt.

Again, Jillybean huddled near the front as a pair of men got out, however intuition struck her and she crawled out from beneath the vehicle to hide behind the front tire just as one of the men ducked down to look under it. "I don't see anything," he said after a cursory glance.

"So, what do we do?" the other asked.

"I don't know," the first answered. "We ain't mechanics. I say we leave it here, I guess. Come on, we aren't going to get jack sitting back here doing nothing." There was a creak of doors, a scrape of metal and leather, and then the two men jogged off with packs on their backs and guns in their hands. So far, so good.

Jillybean hurried to the next truck in line, twenty yards ahead. Thankfully, this was her truck. This was the munitions truck where she would find what she needed to kill the king.

She wasted no time as she climbed in the back.

Chapter 35
Sadie Walcott

The gunfire in the valley was at a fever pitch by the time they got to the Humvees. Grey was hobbling nearly as fast as most people could run; his face set and so determined that it would have been useless for someone to tell him to slow down and think about his sutures. Not that Deanna didn't try.

"Grey! What are you doing? Slow down. You could die right here." She was beside herself with fear for him and was practically begging.

Sadie thought it was sweet how concerned she was. Sweet, but foolish. Deanna was a woman in love with a dangerous man and one thing was certain, he wasn't going to change, especially when there were enemies threatening the people he cared about. He was going to risk everything for her, even if, later, the guilt killed her.

In truth, Sadie was envious. She had never had much luck with boyfriends, but since the apocalypse her luck was utter crap. Her first beau, John Crider had been an immoral criminal; her next was Mark Wilson who turned out to be a sniveling coward. After that was Nico, the Russian soldier. She had only known him for a month and she had been literally delirious for most of that time. She had thought she was in love, but now she could barely remember his face.

Then there was Morganstern who hadn't been a boyfriend at all, but could have been if he had lived. He had been brave, handsome and gallant, but he died like most brave, handsome, gallant young men did. He could have been like Captain Grey and it could have been her instead of Deanna acting the part of the fool in trying to tame a beast of a man.

"I'm ok," Grey said to Deanna. It was clear he wasn't. Sadie had never heard him rasp like that with every breath and nor had she ever seen him hold on to every trunk and branch they passed. He was sweating even though the pace was child's play to Sadie.

313

He was almost careening from tree to tree by the time they reached the Humvees and still he was first into a vehicle which had a little four foot by four foot uncovered bed. Sadie allowed Michael to get in the passenger seat; she and Deanna took the back seats. The second the back doors were closed, Grey stomped the vehicle forward.

Next to her, Deanna sat stewing in an air of worry. Sadie knew that it was the wrong attitude when going into battle. Deanna should have known better, however the protective force of love wasn't going to be denied, it was too strong. As they drove through the thin forest of pines and the heavy monuments of million-year-old rock, Grey shot a look back—first at Deanna and then at Sadie.

His eyes spoke to her and the girl in black nodded to the unspoken request. She knew the issue and she knew the remedy.

A minute later, as the two Strykers raced into the mouth of the valley blasting everything in sight, Grey kept the Humvee hidden by driving among the trees before he pulled up behind a string of low hills where the three-man FGM-148 Javelin team was sitting uselessly, pointing their weapon down at the highway. "Get in!" Grey cried. He then glanced back at Sadie and Deanna: "Help them," he said and again caught Sadie's eye.

The pair of women hopped out and ran around the vehicle but the men didn't look as though they needed any help. One man hauled a mottled green tube in one hand, another carried a missile on his back and one in his arms as though it were a very big baby, and the third carried a rifle.

The two men with the Javelin parts jumped into the bed and the rifleman climbed into Sadie's seat. Deanna headed for the empty seat and that was when Sadie leapt on her back, pinning her arms to her sides.

"What the...what are you doing?" Deanna cried.

"I have my orders," Sadie explained, speaking into her ear. They were legitimate and sensible orders. The fight was going to be a sharp one and Grey needed to be free to engage the enemy without Deanna there second guessing him or worrying over him. He wouldn't be able to fight under those conditions.

The captain fed the Humvee gas and he began to steer it around the hill and that was when Deanna dumped Sadie on her butt. The older woman was taller and much stronger; she was practically a Valkyrie. All it took was for her to plant her feet, torque her body violently and give her shoulders a tremendous buck, and Sadie was down.

Deanna took off for the Humvee yelling something that was drowned out by the thunder of the machine guns from the Strykers. They were close, way too close for a girl who had left her M4 in the Humvee! Regardless, Sadie jumped up as if she had landed on a spring. She did not follow after Deanna and the Humvee; even she wasn't fast enough to catch the vehicle. Instead she cut across the low hill, guessing that Grey would wind through the trees in the same direction from which he had come.

Which he did not. As Sadie topped the hill, she saw the Humvee skirting the edge of the valley where the cover was good. They looked to be searching for one of the Strykers to take a shot at; however the Humvee was behind a rise and didn't see that the Strykers had turned back toward the mouth of the valley.

Sadie's vantage was almost perfect. She could see all of the action from where she stood. The valley began as a slightly curving U shape opening into a natural bowl a mile wide that was covered in waist-high summer wheat. The bowl was supposed to be where the kill zone was, however the only people dying in it were the soldiers.

The premature attack had left more than half of the Azael at the top of the U where they spread out using the natural advantages of height and their greater numbers to split the soldiers of the valley into three separate fighting groups, none able to support the other. Those getting the worst of it were the soldiers in the bowl who had been playing dead, waiting to spring their trap.

These soldiers were without a hint of cover and even as she watched, one of the Strykers came roaring up and machine-gunned two men and then turned hard to the right to run over a third. The Strykers were twin dragons, spitting fiery lead. They roamed the wheat field at will and were impervious to everything the soldiers had left in their arsenal.

It seemed to Sadie that their moves were synchronized. When one banked all the way around and started racing toward where Captain Grey had broken out from the safety of the forest, the second Stryker turned at the same instant.

"They're being directed," Sadie whispered. Of course, they were; it would be stupid if they weren't. The only questions were: by whom and from where? Across the valley was a ridge with an even better view than Sadie's. Without hesitation, and still unarmed, the Goth girl raced down the hill and out into the valley.

In a second, she regretted leaving the safety of the hill. Bullets whipped across her face, sometimes invisibly, sounding like sizzling bees, and sometimes they flashed by in a glow of yellow. Undeterred, she charged on through the tawny grass until she tripped over a severed leg. Then it seemed as though it was raining lead. Holes erupted in the dirt all around her and the air was filled with golden slivers of wheat that had been mowed by 5.56MM bullets.

As fast as she could, Sadie crawled from what had become her own personal kill zone. She crawled just ten feet before she found a blood trail and for some reason, she followed it until she found the soldier who had lost his leg. He was a miserable thing: covered in dry, brown mud that was iced by bright, almost merry looking red blood. With shaking hands, he was trying to tie his belt around his stump.

"Oh, Sadie," he said with weak relief. "What are you doing here?"

She was surprised that he knew her name. She didn't recognize him; not his face, or his voice or the mostly obscured name stitched on his shredded uniform. "I'm...I'm trying to get to that hill," she answered as she crawled to him and shoved his hands away. Blood was jetting from the leg at regular intervals making the belt slick; quickly her hands were filthy with blood.

"I was too," the soldier said in a drifting whisper. "I—I think a lot of us were, but—but the only way to get to it is to run west first, like you're running away. But we have to—to hurry. They're shifting..." His words fell away and he suddenly looked as though he couldn't care less about the battle. "Ol' Morg liked you, you know."

Sadie heaved the belt tight with all her strength and then looked again at the man, closer now, realizing it was the gruff staff sergeant she had met at the top of Red Gate 1 when the zombies first attacked. "I liked him, too," she told him. "He was very brave, just like you, sergeant."

Even dying, and Sadie was sure that he was a minute or so from dying regardless of the belt, the sergeant wasn't soft. He grunted a quiet laugh and changed the subject back to Morganstern: "He said he was going to marry you. Right there when we were fighting the stiffs...hey, where's your weapon?"

It was sitting uselessly in Captain Grey's Humvee. "I lost it."

He gave her the hardest look left in his barren arsenal; it was more of a fatherly frown, like one given out when a child brought home a report card with C+ in English. "Take mine," he said. The sergeant might have lost his leg, but his M16A2 was sitting in the wheat, inches from his hand. "And this, too." He hauled off his chest rig and then sat back with his breath laboring in and out.

Sadie gladly took both. "I'll be back for you," she said, rising to a crouch.

"No, you won't," he answered. "I'll be dead soon." There it was, the truth spat out like a lump of rock. "Now, go on, soldier."

She didn't hesitate. Time was not on their side. Taking the sergeant's advice, she booked it straight west and this time fewer bullets streaked after her. Eight other men were running as well and she quickly caught up with them. The lead man was an officer; he glanced over at Sadie and then past her with eyes that bugged.

As she ran, Sadie turned to see Captain Grey's Humvee darting through the trees. It was being hemmed in by the two Strykers and being peppered by bullets. The Javelin crew in the back got off a shot; however the missile struck a tree branch, and spiraled into the ground in front of its target sending up a torrent of dirt.

Grey spun the wheel to the left, using an outcropping of rocks to cheat the machinegun bullets that had been coming closer and closer to the mark. He should have come shooting out from behind the rocks a second later, but he had doubled back and was now behind the Strykers! He slammed on the brakes, yanking the wheel hard to the left to give his team a better shot.

The Strykers stopped at the same time, spinning hard to bring their guns to bear. They weren't in time.

There was a gout of sparks from behind the missile tube and something silvery leapt out of it and raced at one of the Strykers, trailing flame and smoke. A second later, the Stryker disappeared in a flash of orange light and a pall of smoke. Grey was already moving but too late—the other Stryker had him dead to rights and opened up with its .50 caliber machine gun.

Sadie watched in horror as first the Humvee's glass blew out, then its crew cab was filled with hot chunks of metal; blood and flesh flew. The heavy rounds turned the Humvee into Swiss cheese and the Javelin crew in back was literally torn apart. The Stryker fired for half a minute.

Sadie staggered, her legs going to jelly, her head torqueing further and further around, her eyes sprung with sudden tears, and her soul hoping, praying to see Captain Grey emerge from the wreckage—he did not.

A hand grabbed Sadie. "Don't look," the officer said. "Stow it. Cram your feeling down and carry on with the mission." He pulled her along until her legs forgot Grey's death and she was able to run on her own. She did her best to *cram her feelings deep*, but they came right back up as hot angry bile. Grey was dead and she was suddenly furious...it was what kept her going.

A minute later, the officer said: "This way." He was pointing to the right, toward the ridge.

"Not yet," Sadie said. They were still too close. The officer didn't listen; he turned up the hill followed by all of his men but one. The soldier ran on with Sadie. After thirty seconds, they were beyond the battle and now Sadie turned. The soldier didn't turn with her. He kept running; he was the one soldier to run away from the bloodbath.

After seeing Captain Grey's sacrifice, she wanted to pronounce the fleeing soldier guilty of desertion and shoot him in the back, not to kill him, but to maim him so that he would still be alive when the Azael took over everything, so he would have to live with what his cowardice caused.

These were harsh thoughts and she regretted them as soon as they popped into her head, but she had no time to dwell. New shooting broke out not seventy yards to her right where the seven soldiers had tried to mount the ridge. A spur of hill was between them and all Sadie knew was that there seemed to be a huge amount of firing from the top of the ridge and only sporadic shots coming from the bottom.

The disparity did nothing to stop her and she charged over the spur without fear, almost running right into three of the scarf-clad Azael. They had clearly been looking to flank the soldiers and were shocked to find Sadie right there, ten feet away.

Sadie was hot and fired first, raking them with her M16 held at hip level. They went down but not before two of them fired back—one shot three times into the dirt at Sadie's feet as he fell forward, his face contorted in agony, and the other laced the air right above Sadie's head until she put a second three-round burst into him, knocking him back.

She didn't stop to check whether any of them were still alive, she ran on, down one slope and up another. Before her the battle was playing out as a microcosm of the larger fight: the Azael were more numerous and better positioned while the soldiers had superior training and were lethally accurate.

A dozen of the Azael were already dead, but so, too were four of the soldiers and the rest were pinned and were being riddled even as Sadie watched. Without consciously thinking about it, she dropped her used magazine and slapped home a new one. She found a downed tree, set the barrel on it and began a flanking fire that the Azael were slow to realize was being directed their way.

In their multicolored scarves, the Azael were prime targets, and, with greater accuracy than she knew she was capable of, Sadie killed four of them before bullets started heading her way. She had no real training in battle, though she had been around Captain Grey long enough to have picked things up. She ducked down as bullets started cracking into the downed tree and instead of popping up and firing again, she squirmed to her right where the branches of the tree offered concealment but no cover.

She was practically invisible and two more men died before her muzzle flash gave her away. Next, using the hill as cover, she shifted thirty yards to her right as the tree and branches she had left behind were rippled with bullets. A narrow creek bed was her next fire point. She was low, mostly hidden from view.

319

Two Azael suddenly broke from cover and began sprinting higher up the slope, thinking to flank her. Just before she fired, they ducked down behind a rock.

"If they come out," she whispered, leaning into the M16 and aiming to the left of the rock. Someone diagonal from her fired at her, kicking up clods of dirt—she didn't budge and was rewarded when the two men started sprinting again. She sprayed them with bullets and they both went down.

Only then did she move, slipping back toward the tree trunk. As she moved, she dropped the second magazine and reloaded. This time she only edged her head up enough to see; someone fired at her from beneath a bush missing high.

Sadie slunk down and scrambled around in the leaves until she found a good-sized rock which she threw down the slope where it made a loud *clack* noise as it banged against another rock. The remaining Azael fired in that direction and that was when Sadie popped up, firing into the bush. There was a scream and then silence. She held her position, listening. There was at least one more of them. If he moved, she would fire, if he didn't then she would move.

That was her plan at least but then she heard thumping and the crash of branches—the man was running away!

She couldn't allow it. She had to kill whoever was on the ridge directing the Azael army; it was probably their only chance to win the battle—they couldn't be warned of her coming. In a flash, she was up and chasing the man. He had ditched his rifle and she did as well, gaining speed, but losing lethality. In seconds, she was among the dead; men who had died by her hands.

Only one was splayed out in the open, the rest were strange colorful humps, slumped among the greenery. She leapt the one who was lying in her path. He looked strangely dead. There wasn't a mark on him as though he were only a plastic manikin or a realistic cyborg with all its inner clockwork rundown. He looked like he should've been breathing still.

Then she left him behind as she raced forward like a leopard after a wounded gazelle. The fleeing man was panicked and slow. He kept looking over his shoulder with eyes as big as fists and his mouth contorted in a soundless scream. She caught up with him so quickly that she hadn't yet figured out how she was going to kill him or even if she could. Using her momentum she drove him off the path. His legs were going in such spastic circles that it didn't take much effort to send him careening into a tree.

He hit hard, rebounded and fell at her feet as though he was going to kiss her shoe. She kicked him in the face and then repeatedly stomped on his temple until he stopped moving.

She then spat on the back of his bloody head. "That was for Grey," she hissed.

Breathing hard, she stood straight and true, feeling flush and alive. It was an effort for Sadie to quell the fantastic desire to throw her head back and let out a bloodcurdling scream of victory. She couldn't. Her work was not done and she left the dead man to run back for a weapon.

There were many to choose from, however she went after the M16A2 she had been given by the no-named sergeant; she trusted it. The gun was clean and meticulously cared for; it was the weapon of a true warrior. She checked the load and went to finish her battle.

A few minutes later, she saw that her battle would be thirty to one against the toughest of the Azael. Sadie didn't blink.

Chapter 36
Deanna Russell

The air that she strained through her lungs felt to be comprised of styrofoam for all the oxygen it seemed to contain. Each breath was a trial, while her tired legs were altogether numb which made up for the fact that there seemed to be a railroad spike lodged beneath her ribs. And still she ran on, chasing after the Humvee although it had disappeared five minutes before, lost among the hills and trees.

She kept running, drawn on by the distinctive roar of the Humvee's engine. It had the growl of a jungle cat, while the two Strykers that were trying to corner it with their big Caterpillar C7 engines, sounded like unstoppable mechanical nightmares. Their .50 caliber machineguns hammered the air repeatedly and she had to tell herself that they were missing their mark, because why else would they keep firing?

But what if *he* were wounded?

Although there were five men in the vehicle she could only picture Captain Grey. He was the only one with a name and a face. He was the only one that meant the world to her. He was the only reason she ran on against all hope.

An explosion stopped her, momentarily. With her breast heaving, she paused to listen hoping to hear only a single big Caterpillar running...but no, they were both going as strong as ever and so too was the trusty Humvee.

She forced herself to get moving again, working her leaden legs on and on, until she heard the second explosion. This was a more substantial blast. There was the sound of metal on metal. A great *Krannng!* split the air and then there came the long, sustained firing of a single .50 caliber. It went on and on.

For thirty seconds, Deanna stood listening to the sound, knowing full well what it meant. Then there came the mechanical hum of but a single engine. A lone Stryker pulled out of the woods on the edge of the valley, heading back to the battle, unopposed.

A whimper escaped her as she began running again. In truth it was more of a slow jog, and even that was an effort. She was exhausted, but her slow speed had more to do with the dread certainty of what she was going to find when she came to the spot where heavy black smoke roiled into the air. She had a picture in her mind of what she would see there—it was a child's paint by numbers compared to the reality.

Through a screen of pine, she saw the Stryker. It was canted against a tree with its wheels toward the eastern mountains and a gaping hole in its side from which a noxious smoke poured. It, the mechanical beast, was as dead as anything she had ever seen.

She came further down the incline going even slower until she was slightly above the Humvee and then she stopped, unable to go on. It was torn apart. It looked as though it had been chewed up and partially digested. Both of the passenger side doors were hanging by a single hasp each; every window was blown out and the tires sagged. There were fist-sized holes everywhere along its body and yet, somehow it was still running, the engine hiccupping and choppy, but still running.

Though that hardly mattered. There was no one to drive it. The Javelin crew was in pieces. She could see the lower part of a leg off to the side and a hand sitting neatly on a rock. The small bed in back was a stew of blood and flesh and chunks of things that belonged only in nightmares. The interior wasn't any better.

Michael Gates had been in the passenger seat, so it was only a guess that the bloody thing sitting there was him. He had been struck thirty or forty times and it looked as though an axe had been used to hack him into pieces. What was left of the man behind him was only slightly less vomit worthy, but only by a hair. He had no face. There was a hole where his face should have been, a hole she could put her entire hand in.

She forced her eyes away.

Grey had been driving and the high angle at which she stood didn't allow her to see what had become of him. She should have turned away right then. She should have said a prayer and gone back to Neil to tell him that his best friend—the best man in the valley—was dead. Instead, she came down the slope, sniveling like a child, needing to see for herself that he was really dead.

Slowly, certain that she would find him as mutilated as the others, with his handsome face a gaping maw of blood and splintered bone like that of the man in the back seat. So very slowly she came around the rear of the Humvee, trying to give herself a few extra seconds to prepare for what she was about to see.

Nothing however could have prepared her to find Grey completely gone. The driver's door was open, but he wasn't in the seat or on the ground in a pool of blood. She looked around at the thin forest in amazement. "Grey?" she called out.

He answered in a voice worn down to nothing. "Yes?"

She ran around to the front of the vehicle to find Grey sitting with his legs jutting out, leaning against the grill. He was half turned towards it and was fumbling with a hunk of something that was half shiny metal, half smeared with blood.

At first, she was thrilled to see that he was still alive and then she saw the hole in the back of his shirt. The blood there was bright and fresh and growing fresher by the second. "Oh God!" she cried coming down to his side and seeing that he had a wound in the front of his chest that corresponded to the one in back.

"It's ok...it's ok," she said in a wavering voice. "Oh God, please let it be ok. Can you talk? Does it hurt?"

He let the metal thing drop and he sat staring at her, breathing like he had a lung full of clam chowder. "No...not much. Help me."

"Of course." She started fumbling at his collar, trying to unbutton his shirt so that she could inspect his wound.

With a surprisingly soft hand, he pushed hers down. "No. The missile. Help me...attach it...to the..." A weak cough stopped him in mid-sentence.

She set her jaw and told him, "No. No more bombs. We have to get you to the clinic." She hopped up and looked at the Humvee. It was in such a disgusting gore-filled state that her stomach rolled as though she had swallowed a quart of lard. Trying to keep from puking, she went to the door behind the driver's seat and opened it. The seat was amazingly clean, barely any blood at all. It was, however, holed in five places and she thought: *This was supposed to be my seat.*

Deanna suddenly realized that if Sadie hadn't stopped her from getting in, she would be dead right then, very, very dead. It sent a shiver right down her back.

"I'm not going to the clinic," Grey rasped. "I have to stop that last Stryker. Help me...if you love me you'll help me."

"That's not fair," she said, turning from the bullet ridden chair; from one horror to a worse one.

A shallow grin crossed his pale features. "All is fair in love and war. I know you hate what's happened to me. I need..." Another soupy cough stopped him for a few seconds. "I need you to hate for it to happen to them." He raised his good arm and pointed out into the wheat field where the Stryker was gunning everything that moved.

There had been four hundred men in that field. Deanna guessed that at least a hundred of them were dead and the rest were hiding in the grass instead of helping their friends pinned down in the hills.

"I-I do hate it," she said, feeling that by uttering those words she was going to lose the man she loved. "What are you going to do?"

He tapped the metal object which was nearly as long and thick as his leg. "The tube is shot up. I'm going to attach this to the front of..." More coughs, weaker now, stopped him.

Deanna didn't need him to continue. What he was suggesting was as obvious as it was insane. "You're going to attach that...that thing to the front of the Humvee and ram the Stryker? Will that even work?"

He shrugged and it wasn't much of a shrug; he lacked the strength. "If it doesn't, I have those." He jutted his chin at a pair of hand grenades. Compared to the missile, they looked tiny and no more effective than if he threw mothballs at the heavily armored Stryker.

"That's suicide," she said as breathless as he was.

"No greater love," he answered. "John fifteen...fifteen something."

It was a second before she realized that he was quoting the bible. She knew it went something like: *No greater love, than a man who lays down his life for his brothers*. New tears came to her eyes, they were bitterly hot. He was going to kill himself and there was nothing she could say to stop him unless she wanted to look like a complete selfish bitch in his eyes. She never wanted him to look on her like that and at same time she couldn't let him kill himself.

"Let me help," she said and knelt down in front of the rocket. Like any real man, he had a roll of duct tape to do the job with. It wasn't easy and time was against them. It took her a minute and the job was ugly, still the missile was strapped in place. She then grabbed the grenades and placed them on the radio which was covered in Michael's blood and shot to shit. She could tell it alone had saved Grey, absorbing who knew how many of the .50 caliber rounds.

She turned to find Grey trying to kick himself over to the driver's door. "I'll just need a little help to get in."

"I don't think so," she said, squatting down in front of him. "I'm going to do this."

He seemed to lack the strength for emotion. His face was slack and all he could say was. "But you'll die...I don't want you to die."

"No greater love," she answered and then kissed him. He tried to hold her back but he was too weak.

"Please, don't," he whispered. "Let me...I'm dying anyways. Margaret can't help me, we both know...we both...know that."

She rubbed away his tears but let her own fall. "You're too tough to die, but you're too weak to drive. Just tell me you love me so I can go."

"I do love you."

"And I love you." There, it was out. She loved him. It was a terrible and ridiculous thing to say it right there. And a wonderful thing.

She was leaving the first man she had ever loved to go die alone and probably in vain and, strangely, it felt ok; it felt right. Part of that feeling was based on the fact that she couldn't live without him. She was going to die but it would be a brave death, one worthy of this man.

Deanna kissed him one last time and then leapt into the Humvee. With a final wave, she gunned the engine and the beat-up machine jumped forward, faster than she expected. In seconds, Grey was lost in the trees and she was running out across the field—it was a field of gold. The morning sun was hitting it at just the right angle burnishing the land in beauty.

She had to force herself to ignore it. The Humvee, though surprisingly spunky, was running on two partial flats on the right side, giving it a list to starboard that she had to fight in order to keep it on course. The ride was a rough one as well, the roughest she had ever been on. It would be charitable to call it turbulent. The vehicle shuddered along the rough ground, losing the two passenger doors, and most of the remains of Michael Gates, when she hit a small gully.

Somehow, he actually left his head behind where it bounced around the footwell like a lotto ball hoping to be drawn. That too had to be ignored; though it was straight up impossible for Deanna to do so because, as she drove it, would leap around in her periphery. She kept hoping that it would hop out of the Humvee on its own, but it did not and she drove with half her mind on it, fearing that it would eventually bounce into her lap.

The Stryker, dead ahead, focused her.

It was gunning around in odd shaped ovals and it was a moment before she figured out that it was trying to run someone over. She could see a soldier sprinting like a rabbit, darting here and there, making quick turns. His face was pulled back in a grimace of terror.

He did not get away.

The Stryker caught him and ground him under four of its tires. It hurt to watch the spectacle and yet the soldier's death gave Deanna two advantages: first, she cast off the last remaining fear she had over dying and second, the men in the Stryker had been so preoccupied with the soldier that they didn't notice the Humvee closing fast.

Had she a choice, Deanna would have chosen a head on collision since it offered the surest destruction of the Stryker. A side blow would have been good as well but only because the missile was pointed up and to the side.

Unfortunately, she was stuck with a straight blow to the rear and worse, she had been finally spotted. At fifty yards the Stryker suddenly sped up and its .50 caliber began to swivel in her direction. Her only option was to stomp the gas pedal and strike before the gun fired.

At fifteen yards, the gun began blazing, looking as if it breathed fire instead of lead. She was going too fast now and the guns couldn't track her in time. The fat bullets went over her head, the sound of them striking the roof added to the din of the racing engine and Deanna's own scream. It was her death roar, it was her time to die.

And then she struck with a great crash. The missile erupted in flames and brilliant sparks, which covered the hood of the Humvee and sent a wash of blinding heat over Deanna. There was flame but no great detonation that would spell the end of the Stryker. The missile had built in safety features that kept it from exploding until it reached a certain speed.

Deanna found herself disappointingly alive and still stuck with the job of defeating the Stryker which, other than a dented in rear door and a scorch mark on its bumper, looked completely unharmed. It had been turned slightly by the force of the blow and as she watched, its gun began to turn in her direction.

Forgetting everything, she jumped out of the Humvee just as bullets started *thocking* into the hood. She ran left at a diagonal, knowing there was only one way to be safe from the machine gun and that was to get as close to the Stryker as possible. The gun tried to track her but was a second too slow and she was able to run up to the vehicle and crouch in its shadow.

The Azael weren't fooled; the Stryker jumped forward and Deanna had to run to catch up, grabbing onto the dented-in door so as not to be left behind where the gun could blast her into goo. The gap between the door and the armor plate was plenty big enough for her fingers...in fact, she suddenly realized, it was plenty big enough for a hand grenade!

If only she had one.

She had left the grenades sitting on the radio and there would be no going back for them, or so she thought. "He's on the back!" someone inside the Stryker yelled. "I can see his hands!"

The driver stomped the brake and then dug the vehicle into reverse and charged backwards right at the Humvee. He was going to squish her. She barely had a handhold and only a little lip of metal for her right foot—there was no way she could leap to safety. To drop meant to be run over and so she climbed in order to escape death.

Unfortunately, climbing takes strength, skill and time; she had none of these. The best she could manage was to swing one leg up and hook her heel on the door, and then the Stryker struck the Humvee with a squealing of metal on metal. Her grip was jarred loose and she was flung onto the roof of the Humvee to land with a bone-cracking thump.

She saw stars, and her lungs fought to take even the tiniest sip of air, but she was alive and she knew if she wanted to stay that way, she had to move.

Groaning, Deanna rolled to her side and promptly fell off the vehicle. Though it hurt all the more, the fall suited her needs, she was right there at the driver's side. She climbed in ready to grab the grenades and end this; however the grenades were no longer on the radio.

"Oh no!" she cried, staring around at the bloody and ruined carcass of the Humvee. The grenades were nowhere to be seen. It had been a mistake leaving them sitting out. They could've bounced out of the Humvee at any time during the rough ride across the wheat field or, more likely, they had gone flying when she had crashed into the Stryker. Either way they were gone and the only weapon in sight was Sadie's M4 which might as well have been a pea-shooter compared to the hulking Stryker.

Deanna grabbed it, regardless, just as the Stryker lurched forward. She was thrown across the seat where she banged up hard against the radio mount. Once again she knew she had to get out before the Stryker got too much separation and was able to gun her down, but as she struggled up, she saw that the Humvee was being dragged by the Stryker. They were caught up together by shards of sprung metal.

This was her chance, perhaps her only chance. She crawled through the broken windshield and out onto the hood just as the Stryker hit the brake, sending her rolling right up against the bent-in door.

The gap in the door was so close that she didn't have to jump. She stood and hooked one arm in the gap while she slung the rifle with the other. Now the Stryker lurched forward and turned hard to the right, losing the Humvee after a couple of seconds. Deanna needed those seconds to get a better grip. She had both hands on the door now and was able to hook her foot again.

One of the Azael was yelling once more, but she didn't care. She had her face pressed to the crack and she saw a door release right next to her hand. Without hesitation, she grabbed it and the rear door fell open like a gaping mouth. Of course, she fell as well, rolling in the wheat, the gun digging into her back. There was no time for pain. There was no time for worry or fear. There was no time for anything other than getting the M4 off her back.

She yanked it across her body as her eyes settled in on her target: the Stryker's gunner, who had been caught unprepared as the door fell open. He was out of his seat where he might have been protected. Unbelievably, he raised his hands in surrender as she swung the rifle up.

Deanna's blood was up and she couldn't have stopped herself even if she had wanted to—she fired, hitting the evil beast who had been gunning down defenseless men. It felt surprisingly good to see him fall back, screaming. Next, she took aim at the driver who tried to turn the Stryker before she could draw a bead on the back of his head.

Too late. Blood exploded from his face, coating the instrument panel.

"I did it," she whispered as the Stryker rolled through the wheat for a few feet and finally stopped. "It's done."

But it wasn't. Not yet. That realization struck her just as the unused adrenaline coursing through her veins started her hands shaking. She looked back over her shoulder to where she had come from, past the corpse of the Humvee and the dead soldier who'd been run over. Her eyes went to the trail of smoke rising up out of the forest a mile away.

Grey was there, dying.

With all her heart she wanted to go back to him, however she knew her fight wasn't over, not yet. Good men were still being killed and there was an enemy to destroy once and for all. She stood, swaying for a moment as pain rushed across her body. Like the pain in her heart, she ignored her many injuries and trudged into the low Stryker.

The two Azael were dead.

That was good, except the driver was a bitch to move. It took all of her remaining strength to pull him out of the chair. Once he was flopped in the back, she climbed onto the seat that was bloody and still warm. She started the engine and rode to battle with tears in her eyes, blaring her horn just as Captain Grey would have wanted her to do. All around her the soldiers who had been pinned down, unable to truly fight, saw what she had done and leapt to their feet, and charged, screaming a battle cry that shook the valley.

Chapter 37
Jillybean

She was down to it now. The battle raged outside the canvas walls of the truck like it was heaven and hell finally coming to terms in a great fight. Inside the truck there was a zone of tranquility. It was a place of thought and of prayer. When Jillybean left the truck, she knew she wouldn't have long for the world. She might die, that was true, in fact she was more than likely going to die.

But even if she didn't die, she couldn't live with the guilt of all the bad things she had done. She'd leave that guilt for Eve to bother with. Jillybean would just check out and be done. And so she prayed in the clumsy, sweet manner of children who simply wished the world was a nicer place.

When she finished her prayer with: "And I'm really sorry for everything, too," she then stared around at the boxes, letting her unencumbered mind flow. She was going to kill a king, which meant that she had only one chance. Poison wouldn't work, not in this situation. She was too weak to use a knife or a tire iron against such a big man. A gun would be good however there wasn't one in the truck that was small enough for her to wield.

This left a bomb of some sort—but how to get one close enough to Augustus to kill him for certain. He was surely armed and so too would be his brothers. She had a history of bombs and explosions and those such things and so they wouldn't let her come walking up with a strange box in her hands.

"Hmm," she murmured, her eyes going over the assembled crates: claymore anti-personnel mines and grenades by the bushels and stacks and stacks of bullets, and more of the napalm which filled the truck with a heavy chemical smell. She also saw the C4, the blasting caps and the detonators, but what good would they be if she couldn't get close?

These were the same questions she had been wrestling with all the day before and she hadn't come up with a good answer then and one didn't come to her now.

"It's plan G then," she said. The plan was weak, she knew it. Everything else up to this point had been borderline genius and that included all the dozens of contingency plans she had come up with. However, the final act came down to a threat and a hope, and death of course. Maybe the king's death, if she were lucky, but her own death was the plan's most likely conclusion —this she kept from Eve.

It wasn't difficult; Eve didn't care about details. All she wanted was to kill and to see an explosion and to be in charge of their body once and for all. Jillybean was going to give her everything she could ask for and so she didn't interfere, she only lurked in the shadows like some sort of great hairy-backed monster.

Though she did come out when Jillybean put on the dress. *I like it. I will be a princess, finally. You were never a princess, Jillybean. You were always the toad.*

With all the evil that had built up in her soul, she felt like a toad, but she didn't say anything. She ignored Eve and went down her mental checklist: ensure that the detonator is in the "off" position, remove batteries as a secondary precaution, insert blasting cap into one block of C4 and add receiver, ensure that the frequencies on the radio and receiver match, add batteries to detonator, and then turn the radio on. The bomb was ready to go.

Next came the string: two lengths went tight around her waist with the ends dangling against the back of her legs. A hand grenade was attached to each.

After a glance in the backpack, Jillybean picked out the doll and looked into its china blue eyes. It was so pretty that despite the urgency she hesitated as an idea came to her: "Maybe I can live in the doll when this is all over." She thought about Ipes and how the toy zebra had been just that, a toy before Ipes came to live in it. So maybe...

That's not going to happen, Eve said. *I'm not going to keep you around running your gums all the live long day. Besides, I like the doll. I'm going to keep it for myself.*

Jillybean grew suddenly angry: "No! The doll is special. Neil said never to give it to you."

Neil isn't here, is he? And soon you won't be either.

333

This took the wind out of her sails because it was completely true. Eve chuckled, happy to have caused such misery and Jillybean was tempted to set aside the doll and let it get blown up with the truck, but it really was too pretty to be destroyed and Neil had told her to keep it.

Taking the doll and the detonator, Jillybean climbed out of the back of the truck and, with a final sigh, began walking toward the front of the line of trucks, her face a reflection of the despair in her heart. After a minute there was an explosion in the valley as the Javelin team blew up one of the Strykers. Jillybean didn't know what the sound portended; however, the man in the truck she was walking next to looked nervous which seemed about right. They had expected the valley to be filled with zombies, not soldiers.

No one said anything to the little girl in the white dress; they only stared. She didn't look around or say anything either. She was on a mission. Feeling like a church bell with the hand grenades clapping against the back of her legs, she marched up the steep hill just as a new firefight broke out to the northwest along the ridgeline to add to the huge din of battle.

She couldn't imagine that it was her apocalypse sister fighting a desperate one-sided battle against odds. In fact, Jillybean would've been amazed that the fight was going so poorly for the soldiers. She marched up the hill fully expecting King Augustus to be out of his mind at seeing his army being destroyed.

The view at the top told her an entirely different story and made her mission a hundred times more urgent. She was practically running when someone shouted: "Stop that girl!"

There were thirty men and one woman, the king's personal attendant, standing near the sharp-faced cliff overlooking the valley. Seven were the king and his brothers while the others were high-ranking officials. Brad Crane was among them and he was quick to aim his rifle at Jillybean. She stopped and raised a single hand in the air, hoping that the detonator could be seen.

"She came back," Duke Baldwin said, with a laugh. He was a perfect rainbow of scarves and, to Jillybean, he looked absurd. "What a moron! Menis, I thought you said she was smart." The others laughed, all but the king.

"What's in her hand?" Augustus asked.

Brad had been eyeing the black device as well. He edged forward, warily until he saw it clearly and then he turned back to his king. "It's a remote detonating device. For a bomb is my guess, knowing her." This stopped the laughter and the smirks dried up.

"Menis!" the king thundered. "Fix this. She is your problem child."

"No," Jillybean said in a clear voice. "I've come to deal with you, Mister, King, sir. Stop this fight right now or I'll blow up all of your ammunition." This was the "dream" plan: he would realize he couldn't fight without ammunition and he would give up and go away. The problem was he was so obstinate that she thought it farfetched that he would agree. Still she thought it worth a try.

Augustus strode forward and looked at the girl from twenty feet away; he seemed nervous about getting too close, which is exactly what she needed him to do in order to kill him. The grenades were heavy as bricks and she could only throw them so far. "You're threatening my ammo? Huh. I would've thought that you would've threatened me. That would've made more sense. Go ahead, blow up the ammo. My men have enough to finish this fight. But know this, if you do blow it up, I'll carve you into pieces and all them stupid whores as well."

He snorted at her and then backed away to see what she would do. What could she do? If she detonated the bomb, they would hurt her real bad, but they probably would anyway and, if she didn't blow it up, then Kay and the sex-slaves wouldn't know better to run away and would probably get caught. Blowing up the truck was her only real option, besides, Eve was clamoring to get out and clamoring for some fireworks. Eve became so excited that Jillybean's hands started to go numb as the other girl strove to take over.

"Hold your horses," Jillybean said in a soft tone, speaking to Eve. She couldn't blow up the truck willy-nilly; the plan had to be followed. Since Eve was just as weak as Jillybean was, Jillybean still had to get closer. She stepped forward until Brad raised his rifle.

"That's far enough," he said, "unless you plan on giving me that detonator which I would if I were you."

"No, it's important." Jillybean was suddenly filled with peace. This was as far as she needed to go; Eve would do the rest: she'd blow the bomb and under the cover of the confusion she would get closer to the king and use the grenades, something Eve was dying to do. "You may want to cover your ears, Mister Brad, sir. Go ahead, Eve."

Jillybean released the grasp she had on her own flesh and let the evil thing inside of her loose. *She* came rushing up, greedy for air and for a vision of the world and to live. Eve was hungry for life, but also for death. She was a primal force, a natural force. She was a mixture of all the hate and anger and jealousy and gluttonous self-indulgence in Jillybean's soul.

Her desires could not be controlled or denied.

Eve grinned like a crazy person and thumbed the switch, hoping to see the world go up in one great explosion—the effect was immediate and the noise awful. It rang in their ears and Jillybean shuddered. She had not yet been drowned in the depths of her own soul; Eve was too focused on other things such as setting the world on fire, to worry about one little, useless girl.

The ammunition truck seemed to leap into the air as it exploded in a tremendous fireball. A secondary explosion, one that was made of pure white light followed close behind, blinding everyone.

"Yes!" Eve cried.

Augustus strode forward and Eve, still grinning like a hatter, started fumbling at the back of her dress for one of the grenades. Before she could get one loose, he smacked her across the face hard enough to send her sprawling. The world tilted all around and her eyes went in and out of focus.

"You bitch!" he seethed, kicking her in the side and stomping her thigh. The pain was so sharp that Eve couldn't breathe for half a minute.

Breathing like a bull, Augustus stood over her; however, she was forgotten for the moment. He was staring down at the long line of trucks and seeing only the one on fire. This seemed to confuse him until he declared: "You're a liar as well, aren't you? You only had the one bomb."

When she could talk, Eve said: "I am a princess. I am beautiful and powerful. You should be bowing to me!" As she spoke she worked herself into a squat and was again fumbling for the hand grenade but couldn't manage to get it off the string. Jillybean was still near the surface of their collective mind and watched, in a bemused way, Eve's fumblings. In a detached manner, Jillybean was interested as to what was about to happen because a part of her really thought that Eve was going to blow herself up, and Jillybean wasn't going to stop her, especially since an explosion would kill the king as well and end this entire war at a stroke.

"You, a princess?" Augustus asked around a sneer. "And beautiful? Alice, get me my mirror." Alice, the king's assistant came mincing forward. She looked utterly ridiculous there on the side of a mountain in a skin-tight miniskirt and five-inch stilettos. She held out a gilded mirror to the king who faced it Eve's way.

Jillybean didn't recognize the girl in the mirror. It was a stranger and an ugly one at that. Her skin was yellow and green from old bruises while under her eyes were blue-black circles. She was scabbed and scarred, and one side of her face was swollen from where Augustus had struck her.

In a word, the girl in the looking glass was grotesque.

Eve pushed the mirror away, hissing: "What did you do to us?"

She was talking to Jillybean; however, Augustus answered: "Nothing you didn't deserve, *Princess* and nothing compared to what's coming to you." He stooped and picked Eve up by the front of her dress and glared into her face. "No one fucks with me, Princess. No one blows up one of my trucks and gets away with it."

He threw her to the ground and turned to his brother. "Menis, get over here. This bitch is your doing. Cut off her nose. It'll be a warning to anyone even thinking they can fuck with me. And cut off her right hand as well to keep her out of trouble."

Eve was so stunned that she only laid there as Menis hobbled up with a gleaming Bowie knife in his hand. In vain, Jillybean began screaming in their mind: *The grenade! The grenade!* But Eve was too overcome by sheer terror to think about anything but the knife.

Brad Crane held up a hand to his king and asked: "Why don't we just kill her? You don't want to be known as someone who is cruel to children, do you?"

Augustus glared so hard that Brad dropped his gaze. "Yes, in fact I do. You have to realize that I don't care if the people hate me, as long as they fear me. They'll fear me for certain after today." He nodded to his brother and Menis swept forward, bent to one knee and grabbed Eve's flyaway brown hair at the back of her head, accidentally pricking the ball of his thumb on the bent paperclip hidden there. He pulled his hand away, giving Eve yet another chance to grab the grenade which was tied by the pin.

All you have to do is yank the grenade! Jillybean cried.

Eve, that primal creature, was the living embodiment of *fight or flight*. When she had the upper hand, she was full of fight—at that moment, she was so stricken by the horror of having her face carved open that she fled and Jillybean found herself completely alone in her body for the first time in many months.

The feeling was disorienting. She was more aware of every sensation. Her skin tingled, enjoyably where the warm morning sun struck her...but it also vibrated angrily where she had been hit. Her eyes were sharper than before and her hearing could pick out the screams coming from the valley as if they were coming from the people around her.

She felt everything except for Eve—the other girl was simply gone.

No, I'm not, the doll in her hand said, turning its head around so it sat backwards on its shoulders. *I'm right here*, it said and then winked one of its beautiful china-blue eyes at Jillybean.

"That's not possible," Jillybean whispered. "You can't be in there."

Yes, I can. If Ipes could do it, why can't I? It's safe in here. They can't hurt me in here, but the duke is going to hurt you. He's going to slice you up until you won't be any good except as a freak in a freak show. People will puke when they see you. They will point and laugh and...

The duke interrupted them. After putting his thumb in his mouth and sucking the drop of blood away, he grabbed Jillybean again and brought up the knife. It was frightfully sharp but it no longer scared Jillybean; she had her own weapon. She reached back, found a grenade hanging on its short leash and pulled.

Just as the blade came up to her face, she showed Menis the grenade. The pin was out, it was all ready to go with just her small fingers keeping it from exploding. "I wouldn't if I were you," she warned.

"Where did you..." he said in a breathy little voice. His hand went slack in her hair and he tried to back away, but she dropped the doll and grabbed a handful of his scarves, keeping him close.

"What are you waiting for?" Augustus demanded. "Cut off her fucking nose!"

Menis was stuck, half bent over the little girl, his blade up and, although it looked threatening, it might as well have been a butter knife. Only Brad was close enough to see the grenade. Very slowly he raised his rifle to point at Jillybean. "She's got a grenade," Brad explained. "And the pin's out."

The king began backing up but he hadn't taken two steps when a gun shot rang out and Duke Menis made a retching noise like a cat about to get sick. He dropped to his knees so that he was basically looking Jillybean right in the eye. For a moment Jillybean thought that one of his brothers had shot him, but then she saw them all scrambling for cover of which there was very little on the barren ridge.

A few rocks, like the half-buried heads of giants, was all the cover available. The king and two of his brothers were behind one and they didn't see Jillybean hidden behind Menis wind her arm and throw her grenade. Desperation gave her strength and the bomb landed a few yards in front of the three and rolled almost to their feet.

Paulus saw it and screamed: "Grenade!" as he dove away. Augustus was slow to react however Baldwin was even slower. He looked stupidly surprised when Augustus grabbed him in an awkward hug and fell back, using his brother as a shield. The explosion was a gigantic wave of white noise that blotted out all sound and left everyone stunned.

Baldwin died wordlessly slumped over his brother. Paulus died seconds later as the shooter further up the ridge targeted him as he tried to get back to cover going on his hands and knees. The shooter was picking out targets left and right with deadly precision.

"Someone kill her!" Augustus yelled. He was pointing at Jillybean who was down on one knee, still using the dying Duke Menis as cover but no one seemed to be paying attention to the king. Half of the people were cowering behind the rocks while the others were shooting blindly up the ridge at a dark figure that flitted from cover to cover.

It was Sadie, Jillybean knew this as a fact. No one else was so fast and no one else would risk a fingernail for Jillybean because…because…because…

In all the mayhem and screams and smoke, Jillybean paused, realizing that she didn't know why people wouldn't help her. Yes, she had killed General Johnston, but she had been coerced. And she had helped their enemy, but for the same reason. And she had killed poor baby Eve, however she had been literally out of her mind when that happened. These were bad things but in each case there were "extenuating" circumstances. Extenuating wasn't a word in her vocabulary, but it was the concept that counted.

And more importantly than these legal ideas, was the fact that she was suddenly and completely guilt-free. The weight she'd been carrying around like an anchor slung across her shoulders was gone, utterly, utterly and foreverly gone. Eve had used that guilt to worm her way into her body— and now the guilt was all Eve's, and what was even better, Eve was no longer in Jillybean.

Euphoria, greater than any drug swept across every nerve in her body, making her want to cry and shout in joy simultaneously. Unmindful of any danger, uncaring that a dozen guns could be pointed right at her, she glanced down at the beautiful doll which Neil had given her.

You're gonna die, it said, trying to form its plastic features into an evil grin.

The words washed right over Jillybean as though she were greased. The words were powerless as was the doll itself. "Remember what happened to Ipes?" Ipes had been thrown in a river and the moment he had, his mind had lost its hold on Jillybean.

"That's what's happening to you," Jillybean said, dismissing the doll from her mind, just like that.

Jillybean turned to the real world and the real danger.

In spite of his order to kill her, no one seemed to pay her much attention. Perhaps they deemed her harmless compared to the shooter who was ripping bullets into everything that dared to show an inch of flesh.

Augustus seemed to know that Jillybean was the true danger, at least to himself. He was desperately trying to free a pistol from his dead brother's waistband, however the proliferation of scarves had caught up the barrel and was refusing to let go. He yanked and he yanked, all the time with his savage eyes on Jillybean—he was bent on killing her. He was single minded.

A foolish mindset, Jillybean thought as she reached behind her for the second grenade. It came free with a simple yank. She held it up for the king and all his subjects to see. They blanched knowing that it could snuff out their lives in a blink.

Jillybean and the king locked eyes and a change occurred. He was no longer the king. He was no longer the one with power. He was no longer the one people feared—she was.

She threw the grenade at Augustus, who was now without a brother to sacrifice. With huge eyes he stared at the grenade as it bounced closer and closer. His choices were to eat the grenade blast and die, run around the rock and die by Sadie's hand or...

He chose to leap off the cliff. It wasn't a thousand-foot drop by any stretch. It was twenty-five, maybe thirty feet at the most. He leapt, yelling: "Son of a bi..." The remains of the word were swept away as the grenade exploded, sending shrapnel flying.

There was a pause in the fighting as everyone waited to hear whether their king lived or died. Jillybean was the only one who didn't wait. Menis had died on his knees and had pitched over sometime in the previous few seconds, his knife skittering away like a child's precious marble. It was the only weapon left to her and she jumped after it. Not a second too soon her hand found the handle and she turned, brandishing the blade as though it were Excalibur.

The Azael were running at her. No longer were they thirty strong and no longer were they haughty and sneering. They ran as though an army was after them instead of two young girls.

This fact didn't register on Jillybean at first. She thought they were charging her. She thought they were coming to exact their revenge and she was determined to sell her new found life with everything she had in her forty six pounds.

The blade was a line of silver between her and them; however they ran past without seeming to notice her or her knife. It was confusing and a moment slipped by before she realized they were running away.

"Huh," she said, as the remains of the royal house of the Azael pelted down the hill toward the long line of convoy of trucks. A grin stretched across her face as one of the remaining brothers tripped and bounced like a beach ball down the hill.

She turned to share her joy with Sadie who was even then emerging from cover at the top of the ridge. She raised a hand and Sadie raised one in return. Her hand pivoted on her wrist side to side, each minor flick of her muscles becoming huge, each occurring in slow motion. Time stretched and the next second was the longest in Jillybean's life.

Brad Crane had not run with the rest. He had, literally lain in wait, lying prone in a defile that was just big enough to conceal his body, holding his fire, perhaps knowing that Sadie would show herself eventually. Jillybean could see him settle in behind his rifle in much the same way that Captain Grey would, his finger slipping down to caress the trigger.

A scream erupted from Jillybean's lips as she launched herself through the air. Brad was a beast of a man, every inch the size of Captain Grey and a hundred times more ruthless. She had no chance against him unless, that is, he chose Sadie's death above his own life.

He had a choice, Jillybean did not. The little girl had to turn her silver blade to crimson before...

His gun barked and flashed a quarter second before she could get to him.

Epilogue
Sadie Walcott

The girl in black sat in the shadows, watching and waiting. She'd been there two days already, eating little, drinking just enough, moving, but only at night when she was swallowed by shadow. She had a gun, the same gun that she had used to such devastating effect high on the last ridge overlooking the Estes Valley.

The gun was locked and loaded, ready to kill again, but she didn't think she would need it. It all depended on who showed up.

While she waited, she absently stroked the underside of her chin where a bullet had passed so close that it left a little burn mark the size and shape of a hairy caterpillar. That had been two weeks before and still the mark was there, a reminder of how close she had come to death.

She'd been cocky. After the fight of her life where she couldn't seem to miss and bullets passed around her as though she had angels sitting on her shoulders, Sadie had nearly thrown her victory away by being sloppy.

The bullet should have killed her. Brad Crane was an expert shot and at seventy meters he couldn't miss, but he had flinched. While Sadie had been standing with angels, Brad had the devil in his midst taking the form of a seven-year-old girl.

Sadie hadn't seen his death. She had thrown herself back behind the boulder she had been firing from and from there she scrambled to her right only to emerge a minute later as a pair of dark eyes beneath a pine sapling.

She had the entire ridge in view. Nothing moved. The only Azael in sight were sprawled in various death poses and each gave evidence of their mortality by their spilt blood or the holes that Sadie had put in them. Eventually, Sadie stood with her rifle at the ready. She crept down to the open area where there was nothing but corpses. There were fifteen dead men on the ridge—ten gunned down by Sadie and the rest killed by Jillybean and her wholly unexpected hand grenades.

Brad was the only one who had not died by gun or bomb.

343

Sadie found him with a Bowie knife in his back; it was buried up to its hilt. The bloody prints on it were tiny, so very tiny. They gave Sadie the creeps and she stood, warily, pointing her gun all around, half expecting Jillybean to come for her next.

But there was no Jillybean. The little girl had disappeared as neat as you please, leaving behind only a doll lying in the dirt. Sadie picked it up, stared into its china blue eyes for a second before she tucked it under her arm. "Jillybean will want this back," she said as she walked to the cliff face and picked up a pair of discarded binoculars.

From there she watched the end of the battle. She watched the Stryker driven by Deanna charge the Azael. It was followed by hundreds of soldiers screaming bloody murder. She saw Neil and a group of thirty officers, medics, and radio operators leap down from the hill they had been fighting on and attack against terrific odds. Neil fought as though he thought he was as immune to bullets as he was to the zombie virus.

His reckless courage was contagious and soon every soldier was up and pressing forward.

The Azael had panicked at this sudden reversal. They had come into the fight overly confident expecting only to find zombies in the valley. The stiff resistance and the unholy accuracy of the soldiers had come as a shock. Still they fought with bravery but, once they heard the tremendous explosions behind them and heard what sounded like a new attack on their flank and saw their king die and his brothers killed, they were on the verge of panic. The final straw came when they saw one of their Strykers destroyed and had the second turn on them.

They collapsed as a fighting force, fleeing or giving up.

Sadie should've cheered; however, she couldn't find the energy to. Exhaustion swamped her and she sat among the dead on the ridgeline until her legs no longer shook. Only then did she climb down.

She steered clear of the mop-up operations. She didn't have the heart to look the prisoners in the eye and the number of wounded was horrifying. An hour after the last gunshots had died away, she found herself looking for the gruff sergeant she had met in the field.

He was dead, lying in the golden wheat and staring up at the sky.

"I came back," she told him and then cried over nothing and everything, and especially she cried over this man she hardly knew. In spite of their great victory, she was in a funk and knew one of the reasons why: she had been able to kill with such ease that it scared her. She'd been so fast and so nimble—a snippet of a bible verse came to her: *Who shall judge the quick and the dead?* There had been times in the fight that she had felt more like an executioner than a warrior. It was unsettling.

She knelt with the no-name sergeant for hours until the sun started leaning over to the west and in all that time she didn't touch his eyes. She knew that some people closed the eyes of the dead; Sadie tilted his head so that he would have a better view of the valley.

Finally, she stood up and gazed around her with a blank look on her face. She considered searching for Jillybean—the little girl had run away and, unlike the Azael who had hightailed it and who would later find themselves starving or hunted by zombies, Sadie knew that Jillybean would be perfectly safe. The rest of the world was in danger with her out there, but she would be safe and, for the moment, that was what counted.

A billowing smoke had caught her eye then and she went to it drawn like a moth to a flame.

She found Neil directing the building of an immense funeral pyre. There was a great clot of dried blood in his hair and one arm was in a sling. "You should be at the clinic," Sadie had said to him.

He lifted his arm like a chicken might lift its wing. "This? It's nothing. I'm not going to bother the surgeon over something like this." At the time she had let the word 'surgeon' flow right over her, thinking that he meant Margaret Yuan.

Prisoners in the scarves of the Azael were hauling the dead to the fire and heaving their limp bodies in. The smell turned Sadie's stomach. She wanted to leave, but first she handed Neil the doll. "Jillybean left this on the ridge. I thought you should hold onto it just in case she comes back."

Neil looked at it in the same way Sadie had been looking at the bodies. He took it, holding it as though he was handling a soiled diaper, and went to the fire. He threw it into the middle where the flames were blue and hot enough to melt metal. "I think she might be ok, now," he said. "She just needs to know that she's been forgiven. I want you to find her, Sadie. Find Jillybean and forgive her."

That's what she'd been doing for two straight weeks. She'd started her search in the hills around the valley, going in ever widening circles. Two days later she was investigating the eastern slope of the Rockies from Loveland to Colorado Springs. This was dangerous as there were roaming bands of Azael everywhere.

They were leaderless and in many cases hungry and growing hungrier. Sadie adopted a shoot first and ask questions later approach that kept her alive. When she felt it was safe, usually when she was able to corner one alone, she talked to them and found rumors of Jillybean's passing.

The little girl moved like a ghost among them, stealing whatever she wanted and frequently sabotaging cars or equipment. Some talked about her as if she were an evil spirit that was bent on revenge. Sadie let them believe it.

The "spirit" moved gradually south east onto the plains. Sadie tried to leap ahead of her quarry. She found a car and zipped to the dusty town of Flagler, Colorado which, as seen from a distant hill, looked like nothing more than trash strewn along the highway. The closer she got, the more the description fit.

Sometime in the last month, a tornado had rendered much of the town into nothing but rubble. One of the few remaining buildings on the eastern side of town was a monumental silo that stank of rot and was home to a thousand bats. It overlooked four hundred square miles of Colorado and Sadie should have been able to see a mouse try to creep by. She wasted two days in the tower.

She tried only once more to lie in wait for Jillybean in Pratt, Kansas another prairie town that was depressingly flat and brown. Jillybean hadn't come that way either. Undeterred, Sadie headed to Missouri, where she went in search of *the river*.

Her pace slowed as she traveled with much more caution. She was a wanted woman in five states, six if she counted Gunner in Alabama, and more than once she had to evade gangs of dangerous looking men. Luck was on her side and she made it to the exact little river and the exact little bridge.

One way or the other, Jillybean was coming to this spot. Sadie knew it as fact. She picked out the perfect place to set up camp. She was far enough away where she could see the bridge and under enough cover that she could remain practically invisible. She had started with enough food for four days, mostly cornmeal she had ground herself.

Now she was down to two days' supply and still no sign of Jillybean. When the sun went down, Sadie threw her mosquito net over herself and, since lighting a fire was out of the question, ate a mixture of cold soup and corn mush. After her dull meal, she watched the stars and then slept.

As she had for the last couple of weeks, she slept soundly, deeper than she had ever in her life, perhaps even too deep. She woke when dawn was new and the forest was still hung in the gloom of night. Regardless, she knew she wasn't alone. She'd been alone for so long that she had gotten a feel for it and she knew right away that someone was near. Slowly, she reached out her hand for the M16A2.

"Don't," a little voice said, it was a little voice and yet full of danger.

Sadie's hand stopped. "Jillybean?" she asked turning her head slowly. There was a shape in the dark that hadn't been there when the sun had gone down. And there was a glint of shiny metal—a knife.

"Yes," Jillybean replied, simply.

"It's me, Sadie."

"I know. What do you want?"

She had come to forgive Jillybean, but for some reason that answer seemed wrong somehow. "I came because I care about you. How'd you find me, anyway? This is the perfect hiding spot."

"I found you *because* it's the perfect hiding spot. It's where anyone with any sense would come if they were looking to capture me. So..." she paused and Sadie just caught sight of Jillybean's pink tongue licking her lips, nervously. "So, how is everyone? How's Captain Grey?"

Sadie found it strange that she would ask about him first. Did she know and was just testing Sadie? "He was alive when I left." That in itself was a miracle. An hour after the battle, Margaret Yuan had taken one look at Grey and had shaken her head.

"He's beyond me," she had said.

Deanna had flown at her and pinned the smaller woman to the wall. "You're going to try and save him and you're going to hope to God you succeed," she'd growled.

Neil had put a hand out and, as if his touch was magic, Deanna had broken down sobbing and that was when the surgeon had walked in. He had been King Augustus' personal doctor, and had fled with the rest, but was quickly captured along with an entire truck filled with medical supplies.

Sadie had been told all of this later, but when she had walked into the clinic to inspect Jillybean's old room for clues to her whereabouts, she was shocked to see the place crawling with the Azael. Outside the clinic had been hundreds of wounded soldiers, but inside there were Azael?

Her gun came up and she had loudly demanded to know what was going on. Deanna, her blonde mane flowing over her fatigues glared her into silence. "These are my *volunteer* blood donors." She had her own gun out and Sadie could tell by the look in her eyes they were going to volunteer their blood or she was going to take it by force.

"Grey's going to be ok," Sadie said to Jillybean. "And we have Kay to thank for that. She was in such a hurry to get away that she took a hairpin turn too sharp and crashed the bus she was driving. It blocked the highway and trapped all the trucks the Azael had brought with them. We captured everything they had as well as a bunch of prisoners, including a real surgeon."

Jillybean flashed a smile like a Cheshire cat but it faded quickly. "And Mister Neil? How is he?"

"Nicked up some, but you know him, nothing slows him down. He's, uh, really the reason I'm here. He wanted me to say that you're forgiven." It sounded lame and Jillybean's ghostly smile in the new light suggested she thought it was, too.

"He can't forgive me except for what I did to Eve and, in truth, I don't need to be forgiven for that. I didn't hurt Eve. I would never hurt Eve or you, Sadie. I only have the knife because I didn't know your motives."

It felt strange sitting in the half-dark with the girl. For some reason, she felt like she was the child and Jillybean was the adult. "You seem to have your head on straight again. Oh, you'll be glad to know Neil burned your doll."

"I knew he would," Jillybean said. "Neil is frequently so much smarter than I give him credit for. Tell him, thank you for me will you?"

"You aren't coming back with me?" Sadie asked. "I could help you find Ipes. I know that's why you're here. You have a hole in your heart and you're looking to fill it. We can help with that. Me and Neil and Captain Grey and Deanna, we all love you."

Finally, true sunlight spilled over the horizon and Sadie saw a much changed Jillybean. Gone were the dark shadows beneath her eyes and the bruises and the cuts and scrapes. She was smaller than Sadie expected as well. The dark and her mature voice had made her seem older and bigger.

She was tiny and still so vulnerable that it hurt Sadie's heart to know she was all alone. It seemed impossible that this girl had slain kings and had torn down kingdoms.

"I love you, too, Sadie, but I can't be with people yet. I don't have a hole in my heart; I have a hole in my mind. I'm not complete like a normal seven-year-old. I can feel it. I'm missing something and I think it's something I have to find on my own."

This struck Sadie hard. All her life she had felt incomplete and had looked to be completed by those around her. That had been ok when the people around her were good, like Neil and Captain Grey. However, when the people had been bad, it had been disastrous.

But she had been alone for two weeks now and they had been a good two weeks. She felt strong and revived from the ordeal of the war. She smiled at Jillybean, feeling suddenly light-hearted. "Maybe you should find what you're looking for on your own. But will you come back when you find it?"

Jillybean hesitated until Sadie stuck out her pinky. Then the girl grinned, showing her rows of baby teeth, becoming once more simply a child, once more her little sister. "I will and I'll tell you all about my adventures. I just hope Ipes doesn't get me into too much trouble on the way home."

The End

Did that say The End? Well, that's a lie! The adventure continues! Not only is there a must read collection of novellas concerning what happens to Jillybean in The Apocalypse Origin, The Apocalypse Executioner #8 is now finished. Whatever you do don't read it until you find out what happens to Jilly in the origin book:

Only once you have finished The Apocalypse Origin will you be ready for The Apocalypse Executioner:

The war with the Azael has left the people of Estes Valley weakened and isolated in their mountain retreat. Supplies of fuel and ammo are dangerously low and yet Neil bets most of what he has left on a gamble to find Jillybean, who was last seen in the forests of Missouri.

Neil is the only one who sees in the little girl a chance at a new beginning. He hopes to harness her genius for the benefit of the valley, but when the gamble fails, he must send the only two people he can trust out into a dangerous world to gather more supplies.

Sadie and Captain Grey set off with a squad of soldiers… and are not heard from again.

For Jillybean, months alone without the endless danger, the mind-shaking explosions, and the screams that haunt her day and night have left the wounds on her psyche, tenuously scarred over. She can function and her mind is as razor sharp as it has ever been, but now she is cold and grim.

She's also as desperate for love as always, and on her own, she finds her way back to the valley, only to discover that the rumors of her murderous past have grown and the people of the valley have been turned against her.

With nothing to lose and her family in desperate trouble, some missing, some on the edge of banishment, she agrees to go on one more adventure. It's an all or nothing gamble with her life and the lives of anyone foolish enough to get in her way, on the line.

And as always, I hoped you enjoyed the book and as always I beg for an Amazon review and a quick mention on Facebook so that I can continue to write what I think are pretty good stories(Most people agree, except for those whose chests seize up over the occasional errant comma.)

PS If you are interested in autographed copies of my books, souvenir posters of the covers, Apocalypse T-shirts and other awesome Swag, please visit my website at https://www.petemeredith1.com

PPS If you would like to read my work as I write it, chapter by chapter, before anyone else, all you have to do is go to my Patreon page (Here) and support my writing. The tier levels are exceedingly generous, with freebies running from autographed books, video podcasts, free Audible books, signed T-shirts, and swag of all sorts. At a high enough tier, you will even get to meet me in person as I take you and three friends out to dinner.

Patreon is a great way to help support me so I don't have to go back into the coal mines…back into the dark.

Fictional works by Peter Meredith:

www.ingramcontent.com/pod-product-compliance
Lightning Source LLC
Chambersburg PA
CBHW050031030726
47506CB00001B/221